A BODY BY THE HENHOUSE

KATE WELLS

B

Boldwood

First published in Great Britain in 2024 by Boldwood Books Ltd.

Cover Design by Head Design Ltd

Cover Photography: Shutterstock and iStock

A CIP catalogue record for this book is available from the British Library.

Paperback ISBN 978-1-78513-439-5

Large Print ISBN 978-1-78513-440-1

Hardback ISBN 978-1-78513-438-8

Ebook ISBN 978-1-78513-441-8

Kindle ISBN 978-1-78513-442-5

Audio CD ISBN 978-1-78513-433-3

MP3 CD ISBN 978-1-78513-434-0

Digital audio download ISBN 978-1-78513-436-4

Boldwood Books Ltd
23 Bowerdean Street
London SW6 3TN
www.boldwoodbooks.com

For Mum and Dad, who never miss a chapter.

1

Jude Gray gazed around the arena, packed with farmers waiting for the auction to begin. She'd always enjoyed market day, not just as a business event where she could sell her livestock and bid on new animals, but as a social occasion too. It was an opportunity for her to meet up with other farmers from across the three counties and swap stories.

The place was full of the familiar faces who'd known her husband, Adam, since his childhood days. Some had embraced her as the head of Malvern Farm when Adam had died. Others, though, had needed a little more persuading and it was testament to everything she'd achieved that even the doubters had to admit Jude Gray was forged from robust stuff and had made a success of her farm despite the odds.

'You'll be glad to see the sunshine, I shouldn't wonder, Jude?' said a man of her father's age, a mixed sheep and arable farmer, who was sitting next to her as they waited for the first sheep to be brought into the ring.

'You're not wrong there, Gordon,' Jude agreed. 'When the snow came in March, I thought we were in trouble enough, but the rain since then has been relentless.'

'You lambed early again this year, I heard.'

'It suits the farm but I have to say we were regretting it when we couldn't let them out to pasture because of the weather. The amount we had to spend on extra cake to keep them fed in the sheds still makes my eyes water.'

Gordon puffed out his cheeks and let the air out slowly. Every farmer there was living with ever-increasing costs and finding it harder to make ends meet.

The auctioneer took to the stand and the first lot was announced. Jude loved the chatter and buzz of the mart and watched with interest as sheep were brought into the ring, to the rapid fire of the auctioneer's bid calling. It had taken Jude a few trips to tune into what was going on, but she'd come to master the art and was happy to place her own bids, although this was the first time she'd come without Noah, Malvern Farm's shepherd.

The auction progressed and nervously she watched her own hoggets, the previous year's lambs, go under the hammer.

'You did well there, Jude,' said Gordon when the first batch sold and Jude felt a little glow of pride.

The others did just as well and soon they were all done, which was a wonderful boost to both the nerves and the purse. Jude's heart pounded as she put her own bids in to increase the farm's breeding flock, encouraged by Gordon's experienced eye and the subsequent approvals of each choice she made.

'It's like you've been doing this your whole life,' he said at the end of the auction when the deals had all been made and it was time to exchange money.

Jude smiled warmly as she shook his hand. There were plenty of times when it felt as though the farming life she'd fallen into would be the ending of her, but on days like this, there was nothing she'd rather be doing.

* * *

Jude always drove carefully but especially so when she had animals in transit. Driving a large lorry around narrow country roads was just one of the skills she'd had to master when she'd started to take over the general running of Malvern Farm. She'd become adept at squeezing the lorry into laybys and passing spots, even reversing it if needed. More importantly, she'd learnt to block out the honking of an occasional angry driver who seemed to think if he hammered his horn loudly enough, somehow she'd gain the power to shrink the vehicle to the size of a Tonka toy to allow them to overtake.

At the bottom of her drive, she stopped the lorry and jumped out of the cab to check the honesty box which sat next to an old milk churn and a sign that marked the entrance to Malvern Farm. There were no eggs left but the money box was full, so Jude picked it up, along with a few empty egg boxes her regular customers had returned for her to refill.

Just as she was about to climb back into the cab, a shout halted her.

'Jude!' A man with a red face, yellowed grey hair combed back into a quiff and a large gut puffed as he caught up with her.

'Mike,' Jude replied, thinking there were few people she'd like to see less at that moment.

Mike Trout was a retired headteacher who'd chosen to move to a cottage that backed onto farmland and then spend his life complaining about the smell of the farm, the noise from the farm, the farm vehicles cluttering the roads and the dust from the combine harvester. When Adam was ill, instead of laying off them for a bit, Mike Trout had called the RSPCA to report neglect of the sheep in the field behind his house. The sheep were, of course, absolutely fine – the Cheviot breed being a hardy one originally from Scotland and more than suitable for outside living even in the coldest conditions Herefordshire could throw at them. The stress of a visit from Animal Welfare, however, had been hard to take. Not just because of the scrutiny of the animals and the suggestion that they might not be well cared for, but because their neighbour had chosen not to speak to them directly about his concerns.

'I'm sorry, Mike,' she said. 'I can't stop now, I have to get these sheep out to field. You know how important the welfare of our animals is to me.'

The jibe either went beyond Mike Trout's radar or he chose not to pick up on it. 'This can't wait. It's about the campsite.'

Of course it was about the campsite. Ever since she'd first mentioned the idea of turning one of the fields into a campsite to try and bring in a bit of much-needed extra income to the farm, Mike had had plenty to say on the matter.

'What is it now?' she said, trying to keep the irritated edge from her voice. 'The noise is minimal, the smell from the drainage system has been dealt with, the hedge between your garden and the camp is growing as quickly as Mother Nature will let it, so which of your senses is so offended that you are still so keen to see the venture fail?'

'There's no need to be like that.'

'Of course not,' said Jude, checking herself quickly. However difficult the man was, her provocation would only serve to make him worse. 'What's bothering you?'

'There's a new group of women who've just arrived.'

'Yes. I'm expecting them, they booked a while ago.'

'Did they tell you they were coming here on a hen do?'

Jude looked at his puce face, a vivid purple vein throbbing at his temple as though it were some kind of worm with independent life, trapped below his skin.

'Yes, I am aware. Sorry, has there been some sort of an issue?'

'Just the thought of a crowd of loud women, almost certainly out of control with their music and overindulgent partying, is enough to set my teeth on edge. And you think that's the sort of clientele you're hoping to attract to our peaceful neck of the countryside?'

'I can't see any harm in the situation. They were informed of the camp rules before they booked and reminded again when I confirmed via email. No loud music at any point, quiet hours between 10 p.m. and 7 a.m., no smoking near your hedge, etc., etc.'

Jude found it increasingly difficult to keep the weariness from her voice.

'I'll be holding you responsible if there's any kind of problem,' said Mr Trout.

'I've no doubt at all that you will. Now, if you'll excuse me, I really do need to get on.' She climbed up into the cab of the lorry and, as she set off up the drive, muttered some choice phrases under her breath.

Noah, the shepherd who was as much a part of Malvern Farm as the land itself, must have heard the noise of the lorry approaching because he was in the yard waiting for her as she drew up. Four border collies were with him, three of them sitting at his feet watching intently with their ears pricked and backs straight. The fourth, a puppy bought as a playmate for Jude's young nephew, was running around near them, as excited as he always was to be outside in the sun.

'Hello, Alfie!' Jude smiled as the puppy, now ten months old and pretty much fully grown, ran over to greet her. Pip, Jude's own dog, was second to welcome her human home and Jude savoured the feeling of the unconditional love the two animals constantly bestowed on her.

'How did it go at market?' Noah asked.

'All our hoggets sold and I bought some handsome rams and thirty-four yearlings.'

Jude felt a ripple of pride as she said this. She knew she'd got a good price for last year's lambs, and she was confident that the rams she'd bartered for would be a great addition to the breeding team come the autumn, as would most of the two-year-old yearlings. Four of them, though, were a breed they'd not had on the farm before and Jude was excited to show Noah.

She opened the door of the lorry and he went over to peer inside. His two dogs, Floss and Ned, got up to follow but one word from Noah and they sat back down, heads cocked ready for the next instruction.

'You got them then,' Noah said.

'Four Kerry Hills,' Jude confirmed proudly. 'Perfect for attracting more visitors to the campsite. You saw how well the lambs went down with the children who stayed for the Easter holidays. Just imagine next year when these girls have babies.'

She really had her heart set on getting some Valais Blacknose sheep which, with their curly white fleeces, black faces and knee pads, really were the perfect breed for a petting farm. They were known for their placid nature and were easy to tame but they were a rare breed with a price tag to match so Jude had opted to go for the Kerry Hills; their distinctive panda face markings made for very pretty lambs.

'I imagine so,' said Noah. 'Well done, Jude.'

A sharp bark from Alfie alerted Jude that someone was coming and she turned to see three women walking across the yard, all wearing denim shorts, trainers and cowboy hats, looking as though they were kitted out more for a weekend at Glastonbury music festival than a camping trip on the farm. Either that or they'd been carefully styled for the cover of a trendy magazine.

'You must be the hen do. Welcome to Malvern Farm.' Jude wiped her palms self-consciously on the leg of her dungarees. 'Which of you is the bride-to-be?'

'That's me,' said the woman in the middle, a particularly modelesque woman with long legs, dark skin that almost shimmered in the sunlight and not a single hint of cellulite anywhere. 'Shaznay Nolan. This is my little sister, Tanisha, and this is Khadija, one of my bridesmaids.'

'It's nice to meet you all,' said Jude. 'I'm sorry I wasn't here when you arrived. Did you find us okay?'

'No problem at all,' said Shaznay. 'The directions you sent were really helpful.'

'That's good. Let me know if there's anything I can help you with. I put some milk in the fridge of one of the shepherd's huts and the eggs I left out are from our own hens.'

'Cool,' said Tanisha, who looked very much like her sister except that instead of the long curls Shaznay had swept into a loose, low ponytail, Tanisha had opted for a crop so short that it couldn't be seen beneath the brim of her hat. 'Thanks for the fizz too, that was nice of you.'

'It's a special occasion,' said Jude.

She'd decided that spending a few pounds to make sure her visitors had essentials such as tea, coffee and milk, as well as little treats like chocolate eggs for Easter visitors or a bottle of Prosecco for a hen party was money well spent. It had worked for her so far, with lots of people mentioning these extra touches in the glowing feedback they left.

'I don't know if you're planning on using the barbecue or cooking in the huts, but I would definitely recommend the village shop for supplies, or you can go a bit further to the farm shop over in Storridge.'

'Look, I don't want to start with a grumble but we're having a bit of a problem with smoke,' said Khadija, the bridesmaid with a rather haughty look on her beautiful face. 'It's like bonfire night down by the huts and it's making everything stink.'

'Oh, blimey, I'm so sorry. Let me come down and see what's going on.' Jude looked at Noah. 'Can I leave the sheep with you?'

'Go on.' Noah nodded.

Jude threw him the keys to the lorry and turned back to the hen and her entourage.

'Are you all right with dogs?' she asked when she saw Alfie was making his presence very much known, demanding attention by jamming his nose against Khadija's bare leg.

Khadija took an inhaler from her pocket and put it in her mouth, breathing deeply as she pressed down to release the medicine.

'Oh, I'm so sorry.'

Jude called Alfie to heel and was pleased to see that he did so instantly.

'It's fine,' said Khadija, putting the inhaler back in her pocket and walking over to rub Alfie between the ears. 'I'm a vet so I'm used to this.'

'It's a dangerous thing letting a farmer know you're a vet,' Jude joked. 'I might be knocking on your tent in the middle of the night if there's a problem with one of the sheep.'

Khadija held up her hands. 'I'm a city vet, I'm afraid, mainly cats, dogs and guinea pigs. Although I've been working a lot with racehorses recently. You'll want Ellie when she arrives. She mainly works on farms, always got her hand stuck up the arse of some poor animal.'

'I'm looking forward to meeting her. Usually, two vets on the farm at the same time means we've hit trouble.' Khadija looked rather scornfully at Jude's attempt at a joke, but the others grinned.

'Four, actually,' said Shaznay. She held her elegant arm aloft. 'Yours truly and then there's Seren, who's setting herself up in one of the tents. We met at vet school years ago and have been friends ever since.'

Jude began to lead the three women away from the yard and towards the pond, Alfie and Pip eager to join the fun.

'And now you're ditching us for a life of matrimony,' said Khadija, nudging Shaznay with her hip. Jude thought she noticed something harsh in the way the bridesmaid spoke.

'Nah. Not ditching you, just shifting things round a little,' said Shaznay.

They walked around the pond to a gate on the other side that led into the camping field. It was less than a year since Jude first had the idea of opening a campsite on Malvern Farm and she'd worked tirelessly to get it off the ground. With grants, loans and a lot of help, the site was now something to be proud of. They went past a horsebox she'd repurposed as a shower block with two small, but very useable, shower cubicles. Next to that was a shed containing two compost toilets which she'd been a little worried about but nobody had yet complained and many had even congratulated her on her eco choice.

From there she could see the length of the field, past the cluster of various-sized canvas tents she'd set up on little platforms, down to the two jewels in her camping crown: the beautifully renovated shepherd's huts.

Or that's what she would have been able to see if the lower half of the field hadn't been completely swamped in a cloud of grey smoke.

'Looks like a bonfire or something coming from the other side of the hedge,' said Tanisha as they carried on walking towards the smoke.

'Mike bloody Trout,' Jude muttered under her breath, then to the hens, she added, 'My neighbour isn't always the most thoughtful of folk. I'll go and have a word with him.'

* * *

Jude tried careful negotiation to persuade Mike Trout to put out his bonfire but the man refused to budge. He claimed he was just burning garden rubbish but it was clear to Jude that his aim was more to smoke out the hens than to get rid of some overgrowth. It took all her powers of self-control to reason with the unreasonable man who refused to back down, until his wife appeared round the side of the house with two heavy-looking shopping bags in her hands.

'What in heaven's name is going on here?' Val Trout said as she dumped the bags on the garden table.

'Just doing a bit of garden clearance.' Mike looked suddenly very sheepish when confronted by his angry wife.

'You've filled the whole road with your filthy smoke, no doubt the village too.' Val marched over to the hosepipe that was rolled onto a metal reel. She pulled the end free and shoved it roughly into Mike's hands before turning the tap on.

'Sorry, Jude,' said Val as her husband directed the jet at the pile of smoky garden refuse. 'I take it you're here because the campsite is full of smoke?'

Jude rubbed at her eyes, which were beginning to prick from irritation. 'It's not very pleasant for my guests, that's for sure.'

'I'll make sure there are no more bonfires.' Val looked over at her husband, who had already succeeded in quelling the flames and was now damping down the smouldering pile to stop the smoke.

'I'd appreciate that. Thanks, Val.'

'How are things going at the campsite? You seem very busy.' Val folded her arms in front of her. 'Not that I am complaining. So far we've had no trouble from any of your guests.'

'That's good.' Jude wondered if she could suggest Val mentioned this to her husband. 'It seems to be popular and it's definitely starting to help keep the bank happy.'

'I'm not surprised, you and that lovely Marco did such a good job putting it all together.'

At the mention of Marco Ricci, Jude sighed inwardly. The artist who had stayed in one of the shepherd's huts for free in return for helping renovate them had left his mark in more than one way. Jude had two beautiful huts to rent out, and she also had a bruised heart from the only taste of romance she'd allowed into her life since her husband had died. Marco had asked for more and she hadn't been ready to give it. But since he'd left Malvern Farm, Jude had often wondered if perhaps she should have taken a risk. It could have all gone wrong, that was true. But just maybe, it could have gone all right.

'He certainly did a fabulous job on the huts,' Jude said.

'You know, there were a few of us in the village who wondered if you and he might get together. Do you still hear from him?'

'I've had the odd message. The exhibition that he was working on whilst he was here did really well.' Jude kept the more personal notes of his messages to herself. Particularly the invitation to go and visit him down in Cornwall and see the exhibition for herself, which had come with a gentle note about how much he missed her. She'd made the excuse that the farm couldn't do without her but really she hadn't wanted to open herself up to more heartache. She'd made her decision and she needed to get on with things.

'In fact, it went so well that he's been invited to be an artist in residence at the Eden Project.'

'Well, that's something, isn't it?' Val smiled warmly before turning her attention to Mike. 'I'd say that's enough now. You'd better turn the hose off before you ruin the entire garden.'

Jude decided to pack up a dozen eggs and a bunch of lavender from the garden to drop round later. It was always good to have Mike's wife on her side.

'Are those sheep Noah's putting in the field?' Val asked, looking towards the back of the garden and the field beyond where Noah was driving the quad bike, dragging a trailer containing the four Kerry Hills.

'Only a few,' said Jude. 'They're a new breed for us, I picked them up today.'

'How lovely! It'll be nice to have some animals behind the house for us to watch again. It's been a few years since the last ones.'

Jude smiled at the rosy-cheeked woman, wondering what on earth had made her want to marry that objectionable husband of hers.

'There'll be more soon. I'm slowly putting together a petting corner for visitors. Nothing too noisy or smelly, though, I promise.'

'What's this?' Mike had finished damping out the fire and had come to add his undesired tuppenny-worth to the conversation.

'Jude was just telling me about the petting zoo she's setting up.'

Jude cringed. Put like that, it sounded as though she was turning Malvern Farm into a tourist attraction and she knew exactly how Mike Trout would respond to that.

'A what?' he said, that old pulsating forehead worm already putting in a reappearance.

'I'd better go,' Jude said. 'Loads to do, I'm afraid, but thank you again for putting the fire out, it's very much appreciated.'

As she walked the short section of road that linked the Trouts' house to the gate at the bottom of the campsite, she could hear Mike's angry rants about the petting corner and Val's calmer tones as she told him to stop being such a grumpy bugger.

The two sisters, Shaznay and Tanisha, were sitting on the steps of one of the huts with glasses in their hands and a bowl of crisps between them.

'All sorted,' Jude said. 'Do let me know if you have any other problems.'

'Thanks, Jude,' said Shaznay. 'Come and have some bubbles with us? Although I'd avoid these crisps, they're nasty!' She picked up the packet of own-brand crisps from a discount supermarket and examined it with a look of disgust on her face.

'Okay, point taken.' Tanisha grabbed the bag from her sister and stuffed it through the open hut door behind her. 'Although I think they're fine, actually. Not all of us can afford to shop at the posh supermarkets. I haven't got your wage coming in and I've got a baby to fund too.'

She poked Shaznay in the ribs and Jude recognised the sibling banter that she and Lucy shared.

'You have a baby, Tanisha?' Jude asked.

'Just Neesh is fine.' She flicked open her phone and Jude could see her scrolling through photos. 'He's eighteen months so not really a baby these days.'

'Oh, man, you've done it now,' said Shaznay as a glowing Neesh pulled up a photo of a little boy wearing a furry brown coat with pompom ears on the hood that made him look like a teddy bear. He was standing in a garden with his mittened hands held out in excitement.

'I know, I've turned into Mum-zilla, but I won't be sorry for it. I'd do anything for this little boy.' For a second, Jude felt a tiny pang, the same one she often felt when seeing the maternal pride of a new mum.

'He's gorgeous,' she said, pushing away the unwelcome envy.

'Gorgeous until I fancy a bit of time just for me.' Neesh pursed her lips but Jude could tell from the total joy in her eyes that it was a small cost to pay.

'What's his name?'

'We called him Reggie, after his grandad. Look, here's a picture his daddy sent this morning.'

Jude took the phone and gazed at the photo of little Reggie tucked up in bed with a man that she supposed was Neesh's partner. It felt as though she was spying on an intimate family moment and she was happy to give the phone back.

'It was hard to leave him though,' said Neesh. 'But I'd do anything for my big sister.'

'This week is not just about me. It's about all of us having a proper break.' Shaznay turned to Jude. 'There's plenty of fizz to go round if you could be tempted.' She wiggled her glass.

'That's really kind of you but I'd better get on.' Jude looked up towards the tents where she could hear the low beat of music coming from somewhere indicating that there were other people around. 'Are you all here now? There were six on the booking.'

'You met Khadija. Her girlfriend Ash is here, they're in one of the tents.' Jude noticed Neesh rolling her eyes when her sister mentioned Khadija's girlfriend but Shaznay didn't pick up on it. 'I'm not sure where Seren went but she's here somewhere so we're just waiting for one, Ellie. She's the other vet, coming straight from work at the end of the day.'

'Fantastic. Well, if you've got everything you need, I'll leave you to it, then.'

'Actually, I don't suppose you've got any more toilet paper, do you?' Neesh asked. 'I couldn't find any in my hut so I've taken some of Shaz's for now.'

Jude rapped herself on the forehead. There was so much to remember when new guests were arriving and she usually forgot something. 'I'm so sorry. I'll bring some down to you.'

She waved as she walked away. There were no further bookings in the diary until the weekend so the hens would have the place to themselves for the three nights they were booked in. The weather looked good too, all set for a sunny week, which was perfect when staying under canvas, although when Jude walked past one of the bell tents, it sounded as though not everyone was anticipating a good time ahead. There was clearly a row happening between the two women within and it sounded more than a little heated.

'Calm down, Khad,' said a voice Jude didn't recognise.

'Was it you? Did you tell them?' Khadija sounded confrontational and Jude could picture the hostile look on her flawless face.

'Of course I didn't. Why would I?'

'Well, someone must have and now they've cut me off completely. I tried calling them both but they've blocked my number.'

'Oh, Khad, that's really shitty,' said the woman Jude assumed was Ash. 'But we can't let it make any difference to our plans.'

There was a cry of incredulity before Khadija replied. 'You really have no idea, do you? My parents are so prehistoric, they make the dinosaurs look like modern thinkers. They see what we've done as betrayal.'

'Why can't we just forget about them now?'

'That's my business,' Khadija growled.

'No. If we are in a relationship then it's *our* business.' Ash now sounded equally as angry and Jude, who'd been walking perhaps a little too slowly so that she could eavesdrop, realised that she was in danger of becoming as bad as one of the village busybodies. She left them to it and hoped that they would be able to push their differences to one side – for the weekend, at least – so that the hen and her party could enjoy themselves.

2

By the time Jude made it back to the yard, Noah had released the sheep into their various new homes and was parking the lorry back in its space round the side of the house. Jude went to meet him.

'What do you think of the new additions?' she asked.

'Very nice. You've got a good eye, Jude.'

'Val seems pleased to have the Kerries in the field behind her.'

'I wonder if her mardy husband will be as keen.' Noah was clearly thinking back to the last time there had been sheep in there and the subsequent visit from Animal Welfare. 'We'd better make sure everything is spot on.'

'I let slip that I'm planning on adding more animals which I don't think went down well.'

'Still saving up for those Valais, then?'

'Of course.' Jude smiled. 'But not just sheep. I'm thinking more along the lines of turning the paddock into a little petting corner for our campers. When I get the time, I can clear the stables out down there and maybe dig a pond too. I thought we could get a couple of pygmy goats and some Runner ducks, perhaps a Shetland pony as well.'

'Bloody hell, Jude,' said Noah. 'Do you think there's a chance you might be taking this whole thing a bit too far?'

'No, as it happens I don't. We've got the perfect spot here and we could really do something exciting with it. You know how hard we have to fight for every penny we make on the farm. Diversifying is the best way to move forward.'

'I thought that was the whole point of the campsite.'

'Yes, and look how well that's been going. We've had a steady stream of visitors since we opened and so many people asked about Easter that we could have booked out three times over.'

'Then why the need for a petting zoo?' Noah asked. 'Sounds like you'll be turning this place into a theme park before long.'

Jude knew Noah well enough to know that he liked a quiet life. It had been a huge act of friendship and understanding that he'd got on board with the campsite and inviting strangers onto the farm when he'd far rather just stick to what he was good at – farming. Although Jude owned the farm, she felt Noah had as much say as she did when it came to the running of the place. She certainly couldn't do it without him.

'That won't happen,' she said reassuringly. 'This is a small-scale thing but I think the farm is a good selling point for the campsite. Some people choose to visit for the hill walks or mountain biking but we saw at Easter that lots come because they want to get a taste of the farming life. They like the fresh eggs from the bantams and they love watching the lambs. The better experience we give them, the more likely they are to pass our details on to other families and then we start earning a decent return from the campsite.'

Noah nodded. 'Fair enough. On that note, I was thinking. The old Fergie lurking at the back of the tractor shed. How about we give it a lick of red paint and pull it into the camping field? Folk like an old-fashioned tractor.'

Jude gave him a hug. He was right; the old Ferguson tractor had no purpose as a farm vehicle these days but was exactly the sort of tractor children find in their story books. Small, sturdy with an upright chimney-like exhaust and no cab, just a metal seat on springs. She could already imagine children climbing up and pretending to drive it around the farm.

'You'll see,' said Jude. 'You'll grow to love the campsite and the petting farm.'

Noah raised his eyebrows.

'Well then, think how much Sebbie will love it. He's so good with Pancake and Gertie, imagine what he'd be like with a pony and some ducks.'

Jude had played her ace card. Pancake was a Cheviot hogget Jude had rescued as a new-born lamb who'd been flattened by her mother, and Gertie was the Golden Guernsey goat Noah had bought to keep her company. Jude's young nephew, Sebbie, loved the two animals deeply and Noah loved Sebbie. His soft spot for the small boy had started the day Sebbie moved in and had grown into something more akin to parental love since he'd started officially dating Jude's sister, Lucy.

'It's his birthday next week. Do Runner ducks make good presents for a four-year-old?' Noah asked with a smile.

'For this particular four-year-old, I'd say they'd make the perfect gift.'

'Right, well, I'd better go and do some research then, hadn't I?'

Noah started to walk off to the pink stone cottage that sat just at the top of the driveway. Built at the same time as the main black and white farmhouse, it had been Noah's home since he'd become the Grays' head shepherd.

'Don't forget Binnie's barbecue tonight,' Jude called after him. 'Lucy's making enough food to feed an army.'

He didn't turn to answer her but gave a quick salute and carried on his way.

* * *

Jude almost forgot the loo paper for a second time but thankfully, when Sebbie came hobbling into the kitchen when she was making burgers for the barbecue, his pants around his ankles and the news that there was no paper in the downstairs loo, she remembered.

'Sebbie Berban, get your bottom back in there.' Lucy whisked him back towards the loo. 'There are new rolls in the cupboard under the basin as you well know.'

'Oh, yes!' Sebbie exclaimed as he scurried back to sort himself out.

'He has no shame,' Lucy said, straining the pasta she'd cooked to go in a salad.

'Not always a bad thing,' said Jude, who adored her young nephew and was on his side more often than not.

'I'll quote you when he's eighteen and still flashing his bottom to people at the young farmers' parties.'

Jude chuckled at the thought, remembering some of the stories Adam and Noah had told her about the young farmers' social events.

'That's all the burgers done.' She put a clean tea towel over the tray and pushed it to the back of the kitchen unit. 'I think we're almost ready. I just need to pop some loo paper down to the campsite. Are you okay to finish off here?'

'Don't be long, the guests should start arriving in half an hour or so.'

Jude grabbed several rolls from the supply and set off towards the campsite.

There was a car Jude didn't recognise parked next to the pond and she found a man with long hair tied back in a low ponytail and skinny legs made even more so due to the skintight denim they were clad in, milling around.

'Can I help you?' Jude asked, not at all comfortable with the stranger on her land.

'Just having a look.' It seemed as though that was all the explanation he was going to give as he opened the gate and carried on walking down into the campsite.

'I'm sorry but this is private land.' Jude followed him as far as the horse boxes.

'Looks like a campsite to me,' the man replied, a rather condescending sneer on his face.

At that moment, the door of the shower block opened and Khadija came out, dressed in loose-fitting tracksuit bottoms and a baggy T-shirt which clearly had no underwear beneath it. Her dark hair was shiny and wet and she was teasing the tangles out with a comb.

The trespasser leered at Khadija. 'Nice-looking place you've got. I'll book a tent for the night.'

Khadija looked appalled at the unwanted attention and she pulled the towel she was carrying across her chest, staring at the man in first horror and then pure detestation.

'Just piss off, will you?' Khadija spat. Despite the bravado, Jude could see that she was shaking, whether from anger or discomfort, Jude could only guess.

'I'm afraid we're fully booked.' Jude side-stepped to put herself in between Khadija and the man who craned his neck to give her another lecherous sneer.

'I'll have to come back another time, then.' He pushed his hands into his pockets and walked back to his car.

Before Jude had a chance to apologise, Khadija rounded on her.

'You'd better make sure that he does *not* come back whilst I'm here.' She was still shaking and Jude now saw that it was pure anger.

Khadija didn't wait for Jude to reply before she stormed off back towards her tent.

Jude went down to drop the loo paper off at Neesh's hut and hoped fervently that nothing else would go wrong whilst the hens were on the farm.

* * *

Jude had known Binita Khatri for a little more than a year and yet it sometimes felt as though they'd been friends for their entire adult lives. This was almost certainly down to the intensity with which their friendship had begun as Binnie had been the first detective on the scene of the death of Jude's good friend, Sarah, and had been there as support, guide and advocate ever since. They'd been through such a lot together and Jude sometimes reflected on how different her life would have been without Binnie in it. Lucy had just as much cause to be thankful for the detective's friendship so when Binnie had told them about her promotion to the lofty heights of detective inspector, the two sisters had decided to throw her a celebratory barbecue.

Noah and Jude constructed a big table outside using two scaffolding planks and some old oil drums which, once covered in a sheet and loaded with food, looked wonderful. The weather was hot for May, the drinks were flowing and the barbecue was sending clouds of delicious-smelling smoke into the sky above the garden.

Binnie came up behind Jude and put her arm around her. 'Thank you for doing this. It must have taken you ages to put everything together.'

'We can't let this moment of history get away unmarked,' said Jude, turning to give her a hug. 'Detective Inspector Binita Khatri. It makes me feel as though I need to watch what I say around you now, or at least brush my hair and scrub my fingernails if I know you're coming.'

'Don't be daft.' Binnie nudged her in the ribs. 'Just a little curtsy now and again perhaps.'

Jude flipped a row of homemade burgers and turned the vegetable skewers over. 'Food's almost ready,' she called to the assembled guests. 'Grab a seat and help yourself to the salads and things on the table. I'll bring the barbecue stuff over in a minute.'

'What can I do?' Binnie asked.

'You can go and sit next to Granny Margot. She's dying for a chat with the great and wondrous detective inspector.' Jude dropped into a low curtsy and then ducked, laughing as Binnie scooped an ice cube from her glass of Pimm's and threw it at her.

Once the barbecued food was cooked through, Jude filled two platters and carried them over to the eager diners. After the tough beginning of the year thanks to the terrible weather, Jude enjoyed the feeling of the warm sun on her back and the sense that things were beginning to right themselves at long last. She took her place at the table in between Lucy and Gerwain, who worked with Lucy at Perrins House Care Home where Granny Margot was resident.

Since Granny Margot's own granddaughter had died, leaving her without any family of her own, the relationship that Jude had already cherished with the old woman had grown into something as strong as any blood connection could be and it was lovely to see her at the farm. She was clearly happy to be there too, having known the place her whole life and seen the many changes that had shaped it over the decades.

Granny Margot grinned widely at Jude, little red threads lacing her cheeks as the sun glinted off the varnished cherries on her wide-brimmed straw hat.

'You've really gone all out,' said Gerwain. 'What a fantastic party.'

'Our girls certainly know how to do things,' Granny Margot added. She reached across Gerwain and took Jude's hand. 'I'm proud of you both and I hope there are plenty more sunny days ahead for you.'

Jude squeezed the old woman's hand, silently echoing her wish. To say the past few years had been tricky was an understatement of colossal proportions and what Jude craved now was a period of calm when she could focus on her farm and her family. Not that she'd ever be in danger of becoming idle. The early summer was always busy with rapidly growing crops to tend, lambs to rear and shearing not too far away but those were the things that fired Jude's passion and made her feel alive.

When everyone had eaten as much pasta salad and as many sausages as they could manage, Noah and Lucy cleared the table whilst Jude brought out a huge lime cheesecake, courtesy of Noah, and a large batch of perfectly gooey chocolate brownies that Sebbie and Lucy had made. Jude set them down on the table in front of Granny Margot, who had a pile of bowls ready in front of her to serve the puddings into, and then her heart sank as she noticed Khadija trying to release the temperamental latch of the side gate into the garden. Jude passed Granny Margot a knife for the cheesecake and went over to see what she wanted.

'Hi,' said Jude, plastering on a smile whilst hoping that Mike Trout hadn't been up to his old tricks again and there had been no more insalubrious visitors to the campsite. 'I hope everything's okay. Is there something I can help you with?'

'Oh, hi. Yeah, I'm going to need another tent setting up?'

Jude tried not to bristle at her rudeness, especially as Khadija could clearly see she was in the middle of hosting a party.

'Have you got another guest joining you?'

'No,' said Khadija. 'Actually, it's for me. I'm supposed to be sharing one of the bell tents but Ash's a massive snorer and I don't think I can take it for the next three nights.'

Jude thought back to the row she'd heard coming from Khadija's tent earlier and wondered if that was a more likely reason for the sudden desire to change the sleeping arrangements. Either way, she'd be treating this as another booking and that meant more money coming in.

'Of course.' Jude unlatched the gate and walked through. 'I can offer you another double bell tent or, if you'd rather, there's a single A-frame tent which is cheaper. Neither have been made up but if you let me know which you'd like to go for, I'll fetch bedding and towels for you and have it ready in no time.'

'Oh, there's a charge?' Khadija looked surprised at the thought and Jude tried not to bridle. 'But I thought you weren't expecting other guests whilst we were here.'

'I'm afraid bookings are always taken per tent unless a group pays for sole occupancy. The tent will need to be set up and then cleaned again afterwards, and who knows, we may have a sudden rush of walkers wanting shelter for the night.'

Jude smiled, trying to make light of the somewhat awkward situation.

'You'd better not let that revolting man from earlier hire a tent.' Khadija stuck her hands on her hips in an unnecessarily confrontational pose.

'Of course not,' Jude said. 'Now if you let me know which tent you'd like, I'll go and fetch the bedding for you.'

'You're not expecting me to make the bed myself, are you?'

'Not at all,' replied Jude, thinking that actually that's exactly what she'd like to do so she could get back to enjoying the first party she'd been to in ages.

She walked back to the farmhouse to retrieve sheets, pillows, a duvet and towels from the huge linen cupboard but it wasn't until she was there that she realised she'd been so keen to leave Khadija behind that she hadn't got as far as establishing whether she wanted the tent with a single or double bed. She had no choice but to take a set of each which she loaded into two zipped laundry bags and took downstairs to put in the back of the Land Rover. Finally, she fetched the cordless vacuum cleaner from its docking station and the tub of cleaning equipment and drove the short way from the house to the campsite.

Shaznay and Neesh, along with three other women Jude hadn't met, were enjoying a party of their own, sitting around the brick barbecue that Noah had built which was heaving with meat and vegetables. Khadija was nowhere to be seen and Jude wondered how long she'd have to wait before being told which tent she wanted her to make up. She pulled up a little way away so as not to throw engine fumes across their al fresco dining, and jumped out of the car.

'That smells amazing,' she said, pointing to the barbecue.

'It's all from the farm shop you told us about,' said Shaznay. 'You were right, they do wonderful stuff there.'

'I'm glad to hear it. Good to see you all made it safely.' Jude smiled at the new faces as Khadija returned, already complaining about the compost toilet before she'd reached them.

'I didn't know I'd be expected to shit in a pit,' she said, with a scowl on her face. 'Has anyone got any hand sanitiser?'

Jude bristled at the insinuation that her spotlessly clean toilets and basins supplied with plenty of luxury handwash were somehow not good enough for her guests.

Shaznay was quick to intervene. 'Next time, just use my hut. Now come and sit down for something to eat.'

Jude slapped on an extra-obliging smile before she spoke to Khadija. 'I've got the extra bedding in the car so pick which tent you want and I'll make it up for you.'

'Thanks,' said Khadija, not getting up from her seat. 'I don't really mind which one.'

A woman with cropped hair and an elfin face looked at Khadija. 'You're not serious, Khad?' Jude assumed this must be Ash, the other half of the argument she'd heard.

'I just think we could do with a bit of space this week,' Khadija replied, somewhat dismissively as she turned her attention to her food. 'Ellie, this chicken is gorgeous.'

One of the other newcomers, a short woman with dark, bouncy curls and a wide grin, raised the cooking tongs in recognition of the praise. 'I am the queen of the barbecue,' she said. 'Ash, would you like to sample the chicken or can I pass you a spicy sausage?'

'I'm not hungry,' Ash replied sharply with a scowl Sebbie would have been proud of. 'I think I might just go and read my book for a while.' She stood up and walked away from the rest of the hens, leaving an awkward silence behind her broken by Khadija.

'Perhaps a tent as far away from hers as you can.'

At that moment, there was a bang like gunfire from the field across the drive from the campsite and Khadija looked up angrily.

'Bloody hell,' she cursed. 'What is that? It's been going off every few hours or so.'

Jude clenched her teeth and breathed deeply before answering. 'That is the bird scarer. We've planted a field of sunflowers for the first time this year and if we don't keep the birds off then we won't have much of a crop.'

'So that's going to go off for our entire stay here, is it?' Khadija huffed.

'Come on, Khad,' said Shaznay. 'It's not exactly loud from here and we all knew that we were coming to a working farm.'

Jude smiled gratefully at Shaznay. 'I will get someone to look at the settings and make sure it doesn't disturb you more than is really essential.'

'Thank you.' Neesh threw Jude an apologetic look.

'Now let me get that tent set up,' said Jude, very keen to get back to Binnie's party whilst her guests were still there.

'Fine,' said Khadija. 'I suppose I'll take that one as it'll be the cheapest.' She pointed at a single A-frame tent on the other side of the campsite. 'Seren, you wouldn't mind going down to fetch my case, would you? I didn't unpack much but you'll need to get my hairbrush and make-up bag from the table. Make sure you pick up my sleeping tablets too, the prescription ones I got from the doctor, they're in a white box by the side of my bed. I'm going to need those if I'm going to get any sleep in a tent.'

Jude watched as a quiet woman with thin blonde hair and round glasses got up without questioning the order. She set her plate down on the table and pushed her hair behind her ears, careful not to make eye contact with anyone as she left the group without a word.

'I'll take you down to the bottom of the field if you like,' said Jude, who felt an instant sympathy and warmth for Seren. 'Jump in.'

She held the passenger door of the Land Rover open. The woman looked unsure at first, like a small child who'd been asked to get in a car with a stranger, but eventually she gave a tiny smile and climbed in.

'It won't take me long,' Jude said to Khadija. 'I'll put your things in there ready for you.'

Jude got into the driver's seat and turned the key in the ignition.

'I'm Jude,' she said, giving her passenger a warm smile that she hoped radiated camaraderie.

'Seren,' the woman said in a soft Welsh valley lilt. 'Thanks for the lift.'

'You're one of the vets, aren't you?'

The woman nodded.

'What's your speciality? Any good with sheep?' Jude asked.

'My parents were sheep farmers so I grew up with them,' said Seren. 'I'd have loved to have ended up as a farm vet but now I mainly deal with pets. I find animals far easier to understand than people.'

Jude noticed how Seren changed instantly when talking about her job, suddenly more animated and eager to chat.

'We have plenty of animals on the farm. You're more than welcome to come and meet them whilst you're here.'

'Thanks,' Seren said, showing Jude a fuller smile which crept across her whole face.

* * *

The next morning Jude woke up with a feeling of bonhomie as the sun backlit her bedroom curtains. There was no sign of Lucy when she went into the kitchen to make herself a cup of strong coffee so she sat at the kitchen table, embracing the peace of the early morning as she flicked through the latest copy of the *Farmers Weekly*.

Pip and Alfie nudged their food bowls around the flagstoned floor, pushing their tongues into the edges until they had to come to the sad conclusion that breakfast was over. They went to see if Jude had dropped any toast crumbs and, once they'd snaffled those up, they lay down at her feet and rested their heads on their front paws.

Jude finished reading an article about the latest trick supermarkets were using to make customers think they were buying British lamb by choosing carefully which part of the New Zealand flag they highlighted on their packaging, simultaneously screwing the consumers, the farmers and the environment.

'When will they learn that if they don't look after us, they're going to lose even more farmers and then how will there be enough food produced to go round?' she lamented.

Alfie looked up at the sound of her voice and his tail started to beat an expectant rhythm on the flagstones.

'You don't care, do you?' Jude laughed as she rubbed the soft patch between his ears. 'As long as you get fed and have a good run every day.'

At the mention of the word *run*, Pip was up on her feet and nudging Jude's knee with her nose.

'Come on then, you two. Let's go and see how those new sheep of ours are getting on.'

Jude rinsed her coffee cup out in the sink and left it to dry on the draining board before shoving her feet into her trainers. She slipped Alfie's new green halter rope around his neck and made a loop for his nose so that she could keep him under control. He was pretty good with the livestock these days but he was still young and she didn't trust him enough to let him loose with them yet.

'Morning,' Noah called across the yard when Jude stepped outside. He was on his way to the shed where they kept the quad and Jude knew that meant he was about to head out into the pasture fields to check on the main flock.

Jude waved at him before heading in the opposite direction, to the paddock next to the campsite. Malvern Farm hadn't had horses since Adam had learnt to ride as a child and the double stables were now full of old jump poles and empty oil drums that had been used to set up courses. The tack room still held a jumbled assortment of saddles, bridles, grooming kits and hoof oil. Adam had insisted on keeping it as they'd both imagined having children of their own who might like the chance to learn to ride.

Although the hand of fate had had other ideas, Jude wondered if perhaps one day they'd get a pony for Sebbie instead. For now, though, the paddock was the perfect place to house her petting farm. The horse jumps could be stored elsewhere easily enough and a quick clean-up of the stables would make them the perfect shelter for the animals she planned on moving in with the Kerry Hill sheep.

As soon as Jude stepped into the paddock, she knew something was wrong. All four of the Kerries were lying down on their sides near the water trough, just beyond the stables, which sent alarm bells ringing with grave urgency.

Jude closed the gate and ran forwards across the dew-damp grass to the cobbles outside the stable.

'Lie down,' she commanded and Pip, who sensed her fear, dropped to the floor, ears pricked in attention. Even Alfie became rigid at the end of his lead, which she secured to one of the thick metal rings on the stable wall before rushing over to the closest sheep. She found her alive but weak and unable to stand.

'What's wrong, hey, girl?' Jude asked. She rubbed at the ewe's head but there was very little response.

With her heart racing, she moved to the next sheep and found her in the same state. When Alfie got bored of waiting for Jude and gave a shrill yap, the sheep did little more than look vaguely in the dog's direction.

Jude pulled her phone from her pocket and dialled Noah's number.

'There's something wrong with the Kerries,' she said as soon as he answered.

There was a crackle on the line and she could hear Noah's voice cutting in and out. He must be in the top field where there was often no phone signal.

As the sheep in front of her retched and threw up a filthy green froth, Jude knew she had to act fast. She pocketed the phone and ran out of the paddock, into the campsite where four vets were sleeping. It was early but she had little choice, she'd make it up to them later but for now she was focused on finding help for her sheep.

Which one was the farm vet? Jude thought. It was the one who'd arrived last, the one with the kind face and bouncy curls, Ellie.

She ran past the spent barbecue and was alarmed to see that the tent she'd set up for Khadija to sleep in was flattened onto its wooden platform – just a couple of bumps to indicate where the single bed and small cabinet were. Was that a huge tear in it too? That would have to wait.

By a process of elimination, Jude guessed that Ellie would be asleep in the bell tent closest to the hedge and Jude rattled the zip, calling her name gently at first and then a little louder.

The zipper was pulled up and a sleepy head poked out, her dark curls a tangled mop and her eyes blinking as they adjusted to the sunlight.

'I'm so sorry to bother you,' said Jude. 'But I've got four sick sheep and I'm not sure they'll last if I wait for our regular vet to come out here.'

Ellie was instantly alert. 'I'll get my bag.'

Less than two minutes later, Ellie was kneeling on the grass, still in her pyjamas, next to one of the sheep.

'They've been poisoned,' she said. 'Look how bloated this poor girl is and judging by the vomit, I'd say that it's almost certainly going to be something like rhododendron. It's very unusual for ruminants to vomit except for in cases of quite specific poisoning, you see, so that gives us a pretty clear indication.'

'Can you do anything?' Jude asked.

'We're lucky. I came straight from work so I have a well-stocked bag. I can give an initial dose of anti-inflammatory meds, painkillers and some charcoal. Strong tea might also help as it contains tannins and we must get some oral fluids into them, but Jude, I have to warn you that it doesn't look good for this one particularly.'

Jude felt a wash of anguish as she looked at the sheep so clearly in pain.

'I only got them yesterday,' she said. 'Could they have eaten something at the mart?'

Ellie shook her head. 'No, it'll have been in the past few hours.'

Jude looked around. There were no rhododendron plants in the paddock – she'd done a thorough check of the foliage before suggesting the sheep were put there, and she knew Noah would have done the same. Then she saw a tub of sheep lick next to the water trough. She hadn't put it there and she'd be very surprised if Noah had either – not when the grass in the paddock was so lush.

Feeling nauseous herself, Jude went over to investigate and found green leaves crushed into the caked molasses. Her head pounded and her mouth dried instantly as she realised the awful truth. Somebody had done this on purpose.

3

Ellie was fantastic with the sheep and Jude went into a sort of stunned autopilot as she followed the vet's instructions. Once they'd done all they could for the Kerries, Jude and Ellie sat back and waited. Jude's phone buzzed and she numbly picked it up.

'Jude?' It was Noah. 'Sorry, I couldn't hear you up in the field. One of the yearlings got herself stuck in the hedge and it took a bit of work to get her fleece and the hedge separated. Lord knows how she managed it. Everything okay?'

'The Kerries are sick,' Jude said. 'One of the vets from the campsite is here and Eden's coming but it looks like someone poisoned them.'

'What?'

Jude could hear his incredulity and it matched her own.

'There was a sheep lick with rhododendron leaves squashed into it.'

'Bloody hell, Jude. I'm on my way.'

* * *

Eden, the farm's regular vet, applauded Ellie's quick diagnosis and told Jude that it was her immediate care that had saved three of the four ewes.

The last one, though, had clearly ingested more of the poisonous leaves than the others and was far sicker.

'You'll need to keep a close eye on her, Jude,' he said. 'I've seen sheep this sick turn the corner but it's not a given by any means.'

'Thanks, Eden.' Jude hugged her arms around herself. She could feel the weight of the morning already descending on her and it wasn't even coffee break time yet.

'You need to report it to the police,' said Eden as he packed his things into the boot of his truck. 'It's clearly been done deliberately.' He turned back to her and shook his head. 'What the hell goes through some folks' minds?'

Jude had no answer.

'Thanks for your help,' she said. 'Hopefully, that's the last we'll see of whoever was responsible.'

'It's a shocking shame. Any idea who could have done it?'

Jude shook her head. There was one name that did immediately spring to mind but she had no proof. Still, she'd be taking a walk around to Mike Trout's house later to let him know what had happened and to make sure he knew that the police were involved.

'I'd better get down to the campsite,' she said. 'I noticed one of the tents was down.'

'No rest for you, hey, Jude?' Eden patted her on the shoulder and climbed into the cab of his truck. 'Keep an eye on them and keep them hydrated. My bet is those three'll be right as rain in a day or so,' he called through the window. 'Maybe even the fourth if she's got luck on her side.'

Jude nodded her thanks and watched him drive off before she wandered down to see the hen party. The smell of barbecued bacon wafted over to her through the open gateway and she could see some of the hens sitting out, enjoying the spring sunshine.

As she neared the shower block, Jude heard voices coming from behind the repurposed horsebox – the two women she recognised as Ellie and Khadija.

'You need to leave Seren alone,' said Ellie. 'You're far too hard on her and she's close to breaking.'

'Rubbish. I'm doing her a favour. She needs to toughen up or she'll always get walked over.' Khadija's voice was so arrogant it made Jude's top lip curl.

She knew this conversation had nothing to do with her but she found her interest irrepressibly piqued so she walked up to the shower block under the pretence of doing a quick check of the facilities. Opening the door silently, she stepped inside and eased it closed, finding that, if she stood between the showers and the changing space, she could hear perfectly through the thin wall.

'You've done enough. Just let her get on with her life now.' Jude had the feeling that Ellie wasn't asking but telling Khadija, something she suspected didn't happen all that often. 'She's a good vet. A brilliant one, actually, so let her do her job.'

'That pathetic waste of a veterinary qualification? You do remember what she did that ended up getting us both fired?'

'It was a slip,' said Ellie. 'A one-off. You know as well as I do that at uni she was the most diligent one of us all. I was surprised to hear that she was the one who'd made such a terrible mistake that day.'

'What exactly are you trying to say, Ellie?' Khadija's voice had a note of warning.

'I'm saying back off.' Ellie was clearly unfazed by Khadija's attempt at intimidation. 'I'm telling you that I've had enough of just letting you walk all over whoever you like just because you can.'

Jude inwardly cheered for Ellie as she took the bully on head-first, sticking up for Seren.

Then Khadija's voice dropped to a low mumble and Jude found that, even with her ear crushed against the wooden wall, she couldn't hear what was being said.

There was a frustratingly low exchange of words that were just out of Jude's reach but even with only the cadence of Khadija's mumbling to go by, and Ellie's hissed replies, she could tell the conversation had taken a turn for the nasty.

'You wouldn't!' Ellie suddenly exploded, making Jude jump.

'Why wouldn't I?' said Khadija. 'I'm sure that neither you nor Seren want to test me.'

Jude heard footsteps as one of the women walked away. A loud exhalation of annoyance followed by several expletives indicated that Ellie had been left stewing by Khadija's parting shot. Jude waited until she heard her following Khadija back to the camp before she let herself out of the horsebox and headed that way too.

When Ellie saw Jude, she stood up and came to meet her.

'How are the Kerries?' she asked.

'I'm just so grateful you spotted what the problem was quickly enough to save at least three of them,' Jude said. 'Possibly all four if we're lucky. Eden thinks there would have been certain fatalities if you hadn't treated them quickly. How did you know it was rhododendrons of all things?'

'I had a case on a farm when I was still at vet school. We'd had a harsh winter with some very late snow and the grazing animals were looking for something to eat.' She rubbed her eyes and Jude could see how tired she looked. Was that the drama of the early morning and the sick sheep, or the conversation Jude had just overheard?

'There were around twenty sheep who got into a neighbouring garden and took out half a rhododendron bush,' Ellie continued. 'The vet I was on placement with knew exactly what had happened because the vomit gave it away; that and the bloated stomachs, poor things, just like yours. I can't believe it was on purpose, that's horrific. Can you think who would have done it?'

'I have my suspicions,' said Jude, glancing down the field to the back of the Trouts' garden.

'I was just about to come and see you,' said Khadija, storming over with a look of thunder on her face. 'The tent you put me in collapsed in the night, whilst I was in it.'

The angry woman stood in front of Jude, fists on her hips and eyebrows drawn together in fury.

'Khadija, I'm so sorry,' Jude said. 'I can't think what happened. Are you okay?'

'I am now,' she said. 'But I wasn't at two o'clock this morning when I couldn't get the tent zip undone and the panic caused my asthma to go berserk. Luckily I managed to fumble around in the dark and find my toiletry bag so I could get my inhaler and a pair of scissors to cut myself out. Do you have any idea how it feels not being able to breathe?'

Jude had a very painful experience of just this feeling but the memory was not one she wanted to delve into, so she pushed it away and tried to pacify Khadija.

'I can only apologise and look into what went wrong. You will of course not be charged for that tent and I am more than happy to set you up in the other single tent if you'd like, also free for the remainder of your stay?'

'Actually, I think I'll take the larger tent,' Khadija said. 'And if you want any money from any of us then you need to make sure there are no more glitches. First there was the bonfire smoke, then I was gawped at when I left the shower and now my tent collapses in the middle of the night. You're lucky I can never be bothered to leave reviews anywhere.'

Jude forced a smile. This was clearly a woman used to getting her own way and Jude could not risk any negative attention so she had no choice but to agree. This would mean a new set of double sheets instead of reusing the single from the collapsed tent but that could end up being a small price to pay.

'I'll get that set up for you,' she said.

'Oh, and whilst we're at it, you can have a word with your idiot neighbour.'

'Mr Trout?' Jude's stomach dropped. What had he been up to now?

'I don't know what fish he's named after but he came storming round yesterday evening to tell us we weren't allowed to be out of the tents after ten as we were disturbing him and his wife. We had no music playing, we were by the firepit, miles away from his house and we were making hardly any noise. Just like it says in your mega list of camp rules.'

Jude was fuming but if she had any hope of winning the furious bridesmaid around then she had to be careful.

'I am so sorry,' she said. 'He had absolutely no right to do this. I'll have a word with him today and tell him to leave you alone. I think you've all got my phone number so please do call if you have any further issues with him and I'll be straight over.'

'Yeah, well, I've a good mind to turn up the music extra loud tonight, just to piss him off.' Khadija clearly liked to have the last say and had the habit of flouncing off as soon as she'd said her piece.

Whilst Jude couldn't actually blame Khadija, she really hoped that this was an empty threat as the hens still had two more nights booked and it was going to be a very long stay if Jude was having to play mediator between them and Mike. If this happened, there was bound to be only one real loser: her.

Before Jude went back to the farm to collect the new sheets, she decided to go and look at the collapsed tent in the hope of finding a clue as to what had happened. When she'd researched the different options for setting up permanent camping facilities, she'd looked at many different types of tents and had settled on the canvas ones for their style but also their robustness and durability. With the help of Noah and Spud, a man from the village who often helped out on the farm, they'd built strong platforms to raise the tents off the ground and away from any rain puddles. The tents had been erected with thick guy ropes to tether them to the platforms and protect them from the wind when it came. It baffled Jude, therefore, how one of them could have just collapsed so completely in the middle of the night.

As she approached the platform, it was very clear that the tent was irreparably damaged. A huge slash tore one side open.

Jude's already black mood turned even darker. These tents weren't cheap and there was no spare cash in the bank to replace it. She looked at the wooden pegs that were screwed securely into the platform. They were all still in place, but several of the ropes that should have been tied to them were lying loose like snakes. There was no way they could have come undone on their own, which meant only one thing: someone had deliberately untied them.

First the sheep and then the tent – this now felt personal. And the more she considered it, the more she was certain who was responsible. There was only one culprit who wanted to harm her business and potentially shut it down. Her insides burned as she thought of Mike Trout. There was no doubt in her mind that he was trying to sabotage her – the bonfire was proof of this – but he'd gone way too far now. She had four sick sheep on her hands, one of which might not survive, not to mention the danger he'd put one of her campers in.

Mike wouldn't have known about Khadija's life-threatening breathing difficulties but that was beside the point. It was a reckless, ill-thought-out act of trickery that had gone too far and if Khadija hadn't managed to cut her way free, he could now be looking at a murder charge.

Jude located the zip-pull which, even with the tent in such a crumpled state, pulled open easily. So why had Khadija struggled so much she'd had to take a pair of scissors to the canvas? It must have been down to panic but it had cost Jude dearly.

'Can I help?' Seren asked.

Jude looked up to see concern on the face of the quietest of the hens. She was twizzling her blonde hair between her fingers in a slightly awkward fashion.

'That's really kind of you, but I don't think this poor tent can be saved. I feel terrible about the whole thing. First the sheep and then this, it's been a bit of a bad start to the day.' Jude checked herself. 'Oh, gosh, I'm so sorry. This isn't your problem, you're here to enjoy yourselves.'

'Please don't worry about us,' Seren said, trying to reassure her. 'It's a gorgeous spot here and the weather looks like it's going to be on our side so I'm sure we're going to have a great time.'

'Thank you,' said Jude. The last thing she needed was to be worrying about her guests leaving early and demanding refunds. Although she suspected that not all of them were quite as understanding about things as Seren. At that moment, Khadija strutted over, confirming this very notion.

'I've been thinking. The tent you're in, Seren, is probably best for me as it's away from the barbecue area. You don't mind, do you? Jude can just swap the bedding over.'

'Actually...' Seren started to stand her ground but tailed off when she saw the warning in Khadija's stare.

'I mean, it's not as though you were technically invited,' Khadija said. 'You just happened to be standing there when Shaz asked me and Ellie. She's always been too kind to you and I think you sometimes take advantage of her good nature, if I'm honest.'

Seren blushed a bright rose and Jude itched with embarrassment for her.

'It's fine,' Jude cut in. 'I'm happy to change things around. Why don't I help you move your things, Seren?'

'Thank you.' Seren was unable to look directly at either Jude or Khadija. 'I'll go and pack.'

Khadija had obviously just expected things to go her way because she hadn't waited to hear the result of the exchange. She was already heading back to claim her brunch at the barbecue, her long hair swishing perfectly as she went.

As Jude returned to the farm to collect more bedding, every muscle in her body was tense with the injustice. The poor, sick sheep and the fact that it had been a deliberate act of malevolence, the collapsed tent which had clearly been tampered with, costing her not only the price of a replacement but also the time involved in setting up another tent and the potential for her first bad review.

Back at the campsite with a bag full of sheets, Jude decided on impulse to set the bed up for Seren in the biggest and most expensive of the remaining bell tents. It had a full king-sized bed inside with a futon that pulled out to create extra sleeping space for children.

Once Jude had finished making the bed with a plump sage-green duvet and folding the warm blanket made from the grey wool of Herdwick sheep carefully across the foot of the bed, she gave the dressing table and chest of drawers a quick dust, switched on the fairy lights and went to find Seren.

'Are you sure?' Seren asked when Jude took her to the large bell tent. 'I'd be quite happy in the single tent.'

'I feel so rotten about the whole situation that I definitely owe you something in the way of compensation,' she said.

'But then surely the tent should go to Khadija?'

'I believe she made it very clear which tent she wanted.' Jude winked at Seren, who smiled shyly back. 'Only perhaps don't let on which tent you're in until she's unpacked her things.'

When both tents were ready, Jude bundled the used sheets into a laundry bag to be sent off for cleaning, trying not to think of the extra money this would cost on top of everything else. She threw the bag into the quad bike's trailer but, instead of driving straight back to the farm, she went to the opposite end of the campsite and left the quad by the gate, next to Khadija's big black 4x4.

Jude knew there was a correct course of action and there were things that should be done in a certain order, but sod that. She was beyond furious and wanted to have it out directly with the man who'd thrown her morning into disarray so brutally, so she stormed out of the gate and walked the few yards to the entrance of Mike Trout's house. It felt good to let the gate slam into the hedge as she pushed through into his garden, noticing as she did the large rhododendron bush in full bloom at the side of the path. Jude hammered on the front door with one fist whilst ringing the doorbell with the finger of her other hand until Mike answered.

'What on earth are you doing?' His face distorted in familiar anger as he opened the door.

'I've come to tell you that your little escapades last night almost cost a life. Might still, in fact; we're waiting to hear. The police are on their way.'

Jude noticed a catch, just a brief moment of uncertainty before he spoke.

'What do you mean?'

'I mean your little pranks. I'm not sure how much you thought things through, but did you know that the woman in the tent you collapsed was asthmatic?'

It was perhaps a little unfair of her to make it seem as though her last two statements were linked, knowing that Mike would assume the life she'd mentioned hanging in the balance was human, but to hell with him. With a slightly different twist of fate, that was exactly what they could have been looking at and it wouldn't do him any harm to sweat for a heartbeat or two.

His face fell and his eyes opened satisfyingly wide in alarm.

'Someone's hurt?' he asked, and Jude had to put him out of his misery.

'Not a person, no. You're lucky she had a pair of scissors to hand and managed to cut herself out of the tent. My sheep, on the other hand, weren't so lucky. Your little games with the rhododendron in the sheep lick made them all ill, as you were no doubt hoping. One of them might not be saved and if she dies, you will have blood on your hands. When I prove it was you, and I *will* prove it, I'll make sure you pay me back for everything. For the sheep, the tent, the vet and lost earnings. Every single penny.'

Mike Trout stared at her, his doughy mouth opening and closing in the way his namesake fish might if someone had pulled it from the water.

'In the meantime, stay away from my farm. Stay away from my animals and for God's sake leave my campsite and guests alone.'

Jude didn't wait for his reply, there was nothing that he could say that would interest her and, with her insides boiling, she marched out of the garden and back to her quad. She was in no state to be in charge of a vehicle so she sat on the bike and waited for the anger to subside, her eyes shut and her hands clenched white around the handlebars.

'Everything okay?'

Jude opened her eyes and saw Shaznay and Neesh watching her in concern.

'Sorry,' she said. 'Yes, I'll get out of your hair. Hopefully, that's all the drama you'll see on your visit.'

'Been round to see your lovely neighbour?' Shaznay raised an eyebrow.

'He's a nightmare,' Jude replied. 'I just hope he doesn't cause any more issues this week.'

'Oh, don't worry about us. We've dealt with some pretty horrendous neighbours in our lives. When Neesh and I were kids, we lived in a semi-detached and our neighbour was the worst, wasn't he, Neesh?'

'Mr Derekson?' Neesh whooped at the memory. 'He was a right pain. Used to have this angle grinder in a shed at the bottom of the garden and he used it at all hours of the day and night. He didn't care about the noise or the fact my mum was a shift worker and needed her sleep. And his wife was just as bad, remember her?'

'Blimey, yes.' Shaznay hit her palm against her forehead. 'She had a thing for karaoke and thought she was the next Mariah Carey. It was like cats being slaughtered and it didn't matter how much we turned the telly up, we could still hear her.'

Jude grinned at the thought. At least living on a farm meant that the neighbours were far enough away to not be a constant source of noise pollution.

'Did you complain?'

'All the time!' Shaznay said. 'Only not directly to them. Our parents would groan about them to each other constantly but when they met them in the street it was always "Lovely morning, isn't it?" or "Nice to see your roses doing so well this year." Shaz and I weren't quite as subtle. We would stand in the back garden talking to each other loudly about the tossers who woke us up when we were trying hard to study for our exams.'

'Let me guess – they didn't take the hint.'

'Worse than that,' Shaznay giggled. 'They complained to our parents about the bad language!'

Jude snorted with laughter. She supposed it didn't matter where you lived, you were always going to find some people who thought the world revolved only for them.

'Like always, I got it worse than you did, though.' Neesh rubbed her hand along the short fuzz of hair on her head. 'Tanisha—' she slipped into an accent that Jude supposed mimicked her parents '—why are you leading your wonderfully clever and always well-behaved sister astray? Didn't you know she's going to vet school?'

'Give it a rest,' said Shaznay. 'You know that's not true.'

'It so is. And that was before I had a baby without even being married.'

'Would you stop looking for sympathy?' Shaznay poked her sister, who grinned. 'They love Reggie.'

'Everyone does.' Neesh looked at Jude. 'Your neighbour, though, I think he was out last night. I got up for a pee sometime around two in the morning and there was someone in the campsite.'

'What?' Jude was suddenly on high alert. 'Mike was there?'

'I couldn't say for certain, not 100 per cent anyway, but it looked very much like him. I thought he was snooping around to make sure we were sticking to the rules or something. Then we were all woken, I suppose, about half an hour later, by Khad hollering about her collapsed tent and now I wonder if he had anything to do with it.'

Jude bristled. She'd known he was involved; his reaction when she'd confronted him had all but proven this in her mind. And now here Neesh was confirming it. But would it be enough for the police to charge him with anything?

'Ellie said your sheep had been deliberately poisoned,' Shaznay grimaced. 'You don't think that was another of his tricks, do you?'

Jude didn't really want to get into this with her paying guests so she just shrugged, which Neesh obviously took to mean that this was exactly what she thought.

'Men that like him deserve to be hung out to dry,' Neesh said. 'Maybe next time he goes into your sheep field, you can have a massive bull or something waiting for him instead.'

She put her fist out for Shaznay to bump.

'Would you mind talking to the police?' Jude asked, keen to move on past this particular conversation. 'I need to call them about the sheep poisoning and I think they'd be interested to hear what you saw as well. Sorry, I know that's not exactly the ideal thing to be doing whilst you're on holiday.'

'No, it's fine,' said Neesh. 'There's not much I can tell them but I'm happy to say what I saw if it helps.'

'Thanks.' Jude shuffled on the quad's seat. It wasn't a good look for her business, asking the visiting bride's sister to give a witness statement to the police.

'I'm going to go and get myself ready,' said Shaznay. 'We're going to the spa this afternoon.'

'It's gorgeous there,' said Jude. 'Have fun.'

'I'll catch you up in a bit,' said Neesh. She waved as her sister set off to her hut.

'I just wanted to say that it's a proper shame it was Khad in the tent that collapsed. Of everyone here, she's the one who causes the most fuss about everything. I hope she doesn't milk it too much, she can be that sort of person when she wants to be.'

'I think she's saving it all up for Seren,' said Jude, instantly worrying that she'd overstepped the line. But Neesh didn't seem bothered.

'Seren and Ash,' she said. 'She treats them both equally badly if you ask me. Poor Ash. They'd been dating for years before Khadija was okay to come out of the closet and now imagine Khad deciding to break it off just like that. And on Shaz's hen do. What a catty thing to do, right?'

Jude nodded.

'Not that I think she ever properly saw her and Ash as a thing, or at least not in the way Ash does. It's all an attention thing with Khadija. This week's supposed to be for Shaz, but Khad doesn't like the spotlight moving off her so she decided to cause a fuss and Ash got caught up in it. I feel sorry for her, she's absolutely besotted.'

Jude wasn't quite sure what to say. Conversations like this always made her feel awkward but Neesh saved her by tapping the handlebars of the quad.

'Anyway, I just wanted to make sure you knew that the rest of us are having a ball on your farm. Thanks for looking after us.'

Jude was grateful for the gesture and gave Neesh a smile.

'Have a brilliant time at the spa,' she said.

'Oh, I fully intend to,' said Neesh. 'See you later, then.'

Jude pulled the quad out of the gate and turned onto the farm drive-way, feeling calmer but even more intent on holding Mike Trout to account for his actions.

* * *

Jude had to go into Great Malvern that morning to run some errands so she decided to see if Binnie was free for a quick catch-up in person rather than try to explain everything to her over the phone. Binnie had a rare window in her schedule and suggested they meet for a coffee in town, so Jude parked the Land Rover by the theatre and walked up through the grounds of the majestic Priory to Mac and Jac's café. She remembered coming here as a child when it was still a butchers but much preferred it now that there was coffee and cake on offer instead of the smell of raw meat. Binnie had already secured a table outside and had ordered two cappuccinos, which were delivered as Jude sat down.

'That was good timing,' Jude said. 'Thanks for this.'

'It's nice to get out of the station this morning,' Binnie admitted. 'The DCI is in a filthy mood for some reason. But I can't be too long so let's get to it. You said something about poisoned sheep?'

Jude told Binnie about everything from the sheep poisoning to the tent collapse and Neesh spotting Mike Trout lurking about just before it happened. Binnie sipped her coffee as she listened, only interrupting to clarify a point here or there.

'He's clearly trying to scupper the campsite.' Jude scooped the foam off her coffee. 'Nothing new there but this time he's gone too far.'

'He certainly has. *If* he really is behind both the poisoning and the tent collapse.'

'Of course it's him.' Jude tapped her teaspoon on the side of her cup in frustration. 'Who else would do it? Besides, one of the campers saw him.'

'For what it's worth, I'm sure you're right but you know that's not enough.'

'Is there nothing that can be done?' Jude asked.

Binnie drew in a deep sigh. 'I'll send someone round, but unless there's substantial proof Mr Trout had anything to do with it then it'll just be logged and that will be that. There's not the funding to carry out extensive investigations into cases like this, I'm afraid.'

'Then I suppose I'll have to find the proof, won't I?' said Jude.

4

Despite the fact there was no real evidence of Mike Trout's involvement in either the collapsed tent or the poisoned sheep, Binnie herself paid him a visit early that afternoon along with a uniformed officer.

'There's nothing much we can do with regards to last night's incidents,' she said when she popped in to update Jude and Lucy. 'But I'd say we did a proper job of putting him off any more attempts at sabotaging the farm by reminding him that the consequences of wilfully endangering life and causing deliberate harm to livestock are severe.'

'I'd have loved to have seen his face when you went round,' said Jude.

The door opened and Noah came in. He'd spent much of the morning down in the paddock tending to the sick Kerries so the smile on his face filled Jude with hope.

'Well?' she asked. 'How are they?'

'Three are pretty much right as rain,' he said as he tested the teapot to see if there was anything left in it. 'And the fourth I'd say is past the worst. She's still shaky on her legs but at least she's back on them again.'

Jude clasped her hands together in delight and relief. 'Oh, that's fantastic news.'

At that moment, Sebbie came running into the kitchen with an urgency that would have been useful if the house had been on fire.

'Aunty Judy, quick!' He grabbed Jude's hand and tried to pull her to her feet.

'Careful, Sebbie, I've got hot tea.'

'You have to come now.'

'What's wrong?' Lucy asked as she set the mug back onto the table.

'Alfie got in with Pancake and Gertie again.'

'I thought I'd patched up the last hole in that hedge.' Noah rolled his eyes. 'How in heaven's name is he still getting out?'

'He's a clever boy,' said Jude. 'He loves it in the orchard so much it seems he'll always manage to find a way.'

'There's no shortage of intelligence there,' Noah agreed. 'Just a lack of training.'

Jude sighed. She knew the puppy training hadn't been as rigid as she'd intended but there always seemed to be so many other things to do around the farm. Once Alfie had mastered the basics of sit, wait and heel, she'd not tried to take it any further.

He was safe around the animals and she knew she'd find him sniffing in the grass with Pancake and Gertie right there next to him, just as they were in the painting that Marco had gifted her before he left, which now hung over the kitchen table. Jude looked at the perfectly captured contentment of her animals in the painting. She was in no hurry to drag Alfie back to the house only to have to go and fetch him again later in the day.

'You could train him to run with the sheep,' suggested Noah. 'Like I said, he's smart enough.'

Jude looked at him suspiciously, trying to read any trickery behind his steady gaze. He'd mentioned to her on several occasions that he'd thought she'd make a good shepherdess, sentiments that she'd always pushed away.

'He'd be a good working dog and like I've said, you'd be a lot better than you think at training him if I show you the ropes.'

Ned was already proving to be a very capable member of the team, although he still had a way to go before he was fully trained, but Alfie had been bought as a pet.

Jude was aware of Noah's steady gaze on her and, not for the first time, she wondered if this had been his agenda all along. She had to admit that Alfie wasn't a total rogue and that most of his faults were down to her, not him.

'Haven't we left it too late anyway?' she asked. 'You've been training Ned for ages already.'

'Ned was ready early, one of those dogs born with an instinct for what to do,' Noah said. 'That's unusual. Eight to twelve months is the normal age I'd take a pup to the training field so we're spot on and trust me, I wouldn't let him near the sheep if I didn't think he was ready. I know I tease you but he listens to you. He knows all the commands so far and he's desperate for more. If you're keen, why don't we take him out with the Hebrideans and see how he does? They're used to my dogs already so Alfie won't bother them.'

Jude hesitated. There was so much going on in her life and she wasn't sure if she was ready to add another layer. Besides, what if she turned out to be a total dud when it came to training dogs?

'Go on, Judy,' Lucy encouraged, reading her mind perfectly. 'You'll never know unless you try.'

'It would be great to have another dog handler on the farm,' said Noah. 'If you and Alfie learn how to bring in the sheep, just think how much easier it will be when it comes to shearing and lambing. It'll be like it used to be when Adam was still here.'

The mention of Adam was what finally persuaded her.

'Okay,' she said. 'Promise to be gentle with me and Alfie and we'll give it a go.'

Something fizzed inside Jude as she made this decision out loud. An energy and excitement that cemented the idea of a new challenge as the right choice. She was a person who always needed to have something to focus her mind on and, now that the campsite was up and running, she decided that sheepdog training might just be the perfect project. It would help keep her mind off her awful neighbour too.

'No better time than now,' said Noah. 'Let's go and fetch that little chap of yours from the orchard and give him – and you – your first lesson.'

* * *

Whilst Noah went to fetch Floss from the pink cottage, Jude called Alfie from the orchard and took him up to the smallest of the fields, round the far side of the house, where a packet of eight black Hebridean sheep were grazing lazily.

Jude bent to rub Alfie between his ears, which had lost their puppy floppiness and stood proudly on his head like two furry lateen sails ready to catch the wind. Black, velvet soft and perfect for picking up the whistles and calls they would both be learning courtesy of Noah.

'I'll do you a deal,' she whispered. 'I'll try my hardest if you do too. Okay?'

Alfie looked at her quizzically, his warm brown eyes and dancing eyebrows melting her heart as always. When he'd first come to live with them at just two months old, he'd been frenetic and mischievous but he'd settled well and Jude knew that if she could learn to speak his language then he would almost certainly respond brilliantly.

When Noah and Floss arrived, they went straight into the paddock, where Noah gave her instructions. Then he called over the fence to Jude.

'We don't want to do much with him today and he'll be too excited to pay us much attention anyway but stick the long line on him and let's see how we get on.'

Jude clipped on the long, bright orange lead and joined Noah in the field. Alfie's ears were alert and his eyes were on the sheep, desperate to get in with them and show them who was boss.

'Don't look so worried,' said Noah. 'Let go of the line but be ready to stand on it if he needs bringing in.'

Jude wasn't sure but she trusted Noah so she let go and watched him dart forward towards the sheep, who started charging around. This only made things more exciting for Alfie, who began to chase, nipping at the heels of the sheep at the back.

'Alfie,' Jude called, wanting to bring him back under control so the sheep weren't hurt.

'He's okay,' said Noah. 'These sheep are used to it and a little nip now and then won't do them any harm. If you call him to you now, chances are he won't come and you're teaching him he doesn't need to.'

Jude realised he was right and, when she watched the sheep more closely, she could see that they really weren't all that bothered by Alfie, unlike the main flock, who would have been deeply traumatised.

'He's doing well,' said Noah. 'His natural instinct to herd is kicking in.'

Sure enough, Alfie was running rings around the sheep, keeping them together and his eye closely on them.

'Now give him a call but grab the end of his line so that he has no option.'

Jude called Alfie's name and jumped on the end of the line as he tore past.

Alfie slowed and looked at her and then back at the sheep, trying to work out which was the stronger pull, the sheep or his human. To Jude's delight, he made his decision to run towards her before the line went taut, his tongue dangling from the side of his mouth and his tail waving behind him like a streamer. Jude bent down to greet him and he launched himself at her, pushing her backwards so she ended up flattened.

'That'll do, Alf,' said Noah, hauling him off. 'Good boy. That'll do.'

At the end of the training session, Jude was delighted with the progress she and Alfie had made and as they headed back to the farm, she felt the smudgy residue of doubt disappear.

It was in good spirits that she arrived back in the yard at the same time as the hen party.

'How did you like the spa?' Jude asked as the six women got out of the taxi and Neesh paid the driver.

'It was amazing.' Ellie's dark curls were still slicked back from the massage oils and her smile was warm and catching. However, nobody seemed to have told the rest of the party as the faces of the other five ranged from furious (Ash) to haughty and aloof (Khadija), with Shaz and Neesh looking fed up and Seren as though she wished she could slink off to the sheep shed and not come out until it was time for the party to dissolve and everyone to go home.

'How are the Kerries?' Ellie asked.

'We've given them plenty of water and more tea and I think they'll be fine now. Even the sickest looks like she'll pull through, thanks to you.'

'That's great news,' said Ellie. 'Happy to help.'

'Really, I think you should be waiving the remainder of our bill,' said Khadija. 'First the tent and then using our services to look after your animals. Ellie was on holiday, you know, she shouldn't have to work whilst we're paying to stay here.'

Jude opened her mouth to try and pacify the bridesmaid but lovely Ellie stepped in before she had to say a word.

'Don't be daft, Khad. Jude has looked after us brilliantly. It's not her fault your tent fell down, and I certainly didn't mind going to help with the sheep.'

'You did do me an enormous favour,' said Jude, feeling beyond awkward. 'I hope you will invoice me your usual call-out fee.'

'Don't be ridiculous.' Ellie looked a little offended at the thought. 'I'd have been cross if you hadn't asked me, Jude. It would have been cruel to allow the sheep to suffer more than they did when you have a field full of vets who could have helped them.'

'Ellie's right, Khad,' said Neesh. 'We'll pay what we owe and I'm glad to do it. If any of us aren't having a good time then it isn't because of Jude or the campsite.'

Khadija spun on the wedged heel of her silver sandal to face her.

'Meaning?' she asked in a dangerously composed voice.

'I'm not talking in riddles. I mean exactly what I said. Jude hasn't been the problem here.'

'And I am?'

Neesh held her hands up in a pseudo-show of submission. 'I didn't say that.'

'Oh, cut the crap, you two,' Shaznay said. 'This is supposed to be my hen do. Can everyone please leave their bickering behind now so we can get on and enjoy the rest of our time here? Jude, of course you'll be paid what we owe you.'

Jude felt beyond awkward at the debate over whether she should be paid or not and she noticed how Khadija inwardly seethed as she was over-ridden by the rest of the party. She wondered what had happened at the spa to make the hens so tetchy. Whatever it was, Jude hoped they could find a way to move past their differences so Shaznay could enjoy the rest of her hen do.

'Well, I'd better get on and check the Kerries are okay,' she said. 'Let me know if there's anything else I can do for you.'

'Do you mind if I come with you?' Seren asked. 'I got a particular soft spot for sheep and I'd love to meet them.'

'That would be lovely,' said Jude.

'I'll come too,' said Ellie. 'I was going to jump in the shower to get these oils out of my hair, but it would be good to go and see how my patients are doing first.'

She bent down to tickle Alfie's head. 'Are you coming too, little guy? Where's your big sister?'

'Pip's in the house. This one's just had his first training session with the sheep so we thought it would be best to have as few distractions as possible.'

'Ooh, how exciting!' Ellie exclaimed. 'How did he get on?'

'Pretty well. Much better than I expected, if you don't take into account the fact he was so excited he knocked me flying when he came back at the end.'

'He came back to you, though, so that's a great start,' said Seren. 'Most dogs will be far too preoccupied by the sheep to take notice of a recall on their first go.'

'You clearly know your sheepdogs,' said Jude.

She was watching Seren as they walked through the gate into the paddock where the Kerries were happily munching on the spring grass, all signs of poisoning now gone. It was amazing how some people lit up when they spoke about the thing that most ignited their passion and Jude could see Seren's face take on an almost ethereal glow as she approached the sheep.

'I love them. Sheep farming is what I know.'

'Didn't you say you mainly deal with smaller pets?' Jude asked.

'Yes. For now, at least.'

Seren looked downcast as she wandered over to see the Kerry Hill sheep and something made Jude hang back a little with Ellie.

'She's clearly got a passion for it,' Jude said. 'She'd be brilliant in a farm-centred practice.'

'She was, for a very short time.' Ellie's voice dropped to a whisper. 'She and Khadija went for the same job at a big rural practice in Kent, straight from vet school, and they both ended up being offered a position. They were supposed to always go out with an experienced vet but there was a day when they were the only two available to attend a farm call-out so they went together. It was awful. A cow died on their watch, a prize heifer too so it cost the farmer a fair bit and he even tried to take them to court.'

Jude could imagine the impact of such a mistake and felt instantly sorry for Seren. 'Were they sacked?'

'I'm not 100 per cent sure what happened but they both left and took jobs in different smaller practices and that's where they are now. Khad said it was something to do with the mis-administration of a drug called Micotil.'

'I know it,' said Jude. 'Eden's used it on a couple of our lame sheep. It's lethal to humans, though, isn't it?'

'Very much so. Even a needle-stick injury can be fatal to us, nasty way to go too. But you're right, there's nothing else that works quite as well for a sheep with a bad case of foot rot, and it's also great for respiratory problems in cows. Thing is, it has to be administered as a subcutaneous injection but Khadija said that Seren gave it intravenously which is what killed the cow.'

'Big mistake to make.'

'It is,' Ellie agreed. 'I've never been exactly sure what to make of it, though. Seren is a stickler for detail, especially when it comes to animal safety, but then she's never given us an alternative explanation, so who knows?'

Jude didn't reply because Seren had left the sheep and was heading back over.

'They seem absolutely fine now,' Seren said when she reached them. 'You got yourself a lovely group of ladies there.'

Jude felt something akin to a protective impulse as she looked at the tiny woman who had so much anxiety and need for reassurance hiding –

not very successfully – behind her large glasses. She was exactly the sort of prey a strong, confident woman with a penchant for bullying would attack.

'I found this down by the feeding trough,' Seren said, holding up a single Yale key attached to a keyring in the shape of Blackpool Tower.

Jude took the key. It wasn't one she recognised but she'd keep hold of it in case someone came to claim it. Perhaps Eden had dropped it when he'd been to see the sheep, or maybe it had fallen from the pocket of the police officer who'd been to take a look around. And then Jude had another thought. What if it had been dropped by whoever had been in to poison the sheep?

* * *

That evening, Jude was stacking the dishwasher when there was a knock on the kitchen door. She glanced up at the clock and saw that it was nudging ten already, far too late for visitors, or at least for visitors that weren't bringing bad news of some sort.

Jude looked through the window, expecting to see someone from the village there to tell her one of the sheep had got out again, but instead found herself looking at Shaznay and Neesh. The bride was looking worried but if Jude had to assign an emotion to her sister, she'd have gone more for annoyance.

'Sorry to bother you so late,' said Shaznay. 'We just wondered if you'd seen Khadija?'

'No. I'm so sorry. Not since you all got back from the spa. Is everything okay?'

'She went for a walk just after that and we haven't seen her since,' said Shaznay. 'Missed dinner and everything.'

'What time was that?'

'I reckon it was about five,' said Neesh. 'If you ask me, she's just attention-seeking as usual. She'll have holed herself up in a pub somewhere chatting up the locals.'

'Don't be a cow, Neesh. I'm really worried,' said Shaznay before turning her attention back to Jude. 'I found her phone charging in her tent. She wouldn't go off without that, not if she wasn't intending on coming back soon anyway.'

'Don't panic just yet,' said Jude. 'Her car's still here so she can't have gone far. The only pub in walking distance really is The Lamb in the village so let's start by giving them a ring. If she's not there then there's Four Trees B&B and if there's still no luck, I'll call my friend at the police. She'll be able to help us with next steps.'

'It's dark out there.' Shaznay sniffed, her concern evident in the slump of her shoulders and the tears that had budded in the corners of her eyes. 'And I know she was wearing ridiculous heels for walking over farmland. What if...'

'If there's one thing I've learnt over the years,' Neesh said as she laid an arm around her sister's shoulders, 'it's that what ifs are completely useless baggage. The only thing we can do is to take the facts we know and go from there. We know Khad is missing and that she left her phone and that it's dark, yes. But we also know she is always stirring trouble and craving everyone's eyes on her. She argued with almost every one of us at the spa and didn't want to join us for food because we overruled her and chose to go for an Indian takeaway. She's hard work, Shaz, and you know it.'

Shaz did not have the chance to either agree or object as both sisters were distracted by the arrival of Ellie, who ran up waving an asthma inhaler.

'It's Khad's, I think,' she said. 'I found it stuck behind the compost toilet.'

Neesh took the inhaler from Ellie and turned it over in her hand.

'Oh, shit,' she said, starting to look concerned for the first time. 'That's not good, she uses this thing all the time.'

Jude could read the message on all three of their faces. If Khadija didn't have her inhaler with her, what would happen if she had an asthma attack? What might already have happened?

5

Jude beckoned for the three women to come inside. 'Will Khadija have another inhaler?' she asked.

'I hope so,' said Ellie. 'Have you phoned the police yet, Shaz?'

Shaznay shook her head. 'I didn't know if we should.'

Jude set the kettle on the Aga before pulling her phone from its charging cable. 'There's mugs and teabags in that cupboard and milk in the fridge,' she said. 'Let me make a few calls.'

Jude phoned Ted down at The Lamb and gave him a brief description of Khadija, which was shouted around the pub loud enough for Jude to have to move the phone away from her ear for a moment.

'Sorry, Jude, no sign of her here but everyone knows to keep their eyes open and let you know if they see anything.'

A quick call to Paddy at Four Trees B&B eliminated the theory that Khadija had booked in to stay there for the night, so Jude decided it was time to get the police involved. When she called 101, someone took Khadija's details and, although she was logged as a missing person with West Mercia Police, Jude was told it was considered a low-risk case and to call back in the morning if there was still no sign of her.

'We can't just go to bed and wait to see what happens,' said Shaznay.

'Ash's convinced she's done something stupid. She's going out of her mind.'

Jude could see the desperation in her eyes and, although she was still fairly sure Khadija was exactly the sort of person to disappear on purpose just to cause a stir – especially as she'd argued with so many of the hens that day – she felt sorry for Shaznay.

'I'll give my friend a ring,' she said. 'And then I'll help you look for her.'

Binnie sounded as though Jude had just pulled her from sleep when she answered her phone but was quickly alert, her voice becoming a reassuring mix of calmness and authority that never failed to make Jude feel a little better about whatever situation she found herself a part of. Binnie was exceptionally good at her job because to her, it meant more than just solving crime. For Binnie, it was about the victims first. She was driven to find answers and seek justice for the sake of those who had suffered and that humane approach often meant she went above and beyond what was expected of her.

For the thousandth time since they'd met, Jude was grateful to have Binnie in her corner and listened carefully as she gave her advice – advice which Jude then relayed to the hens assembled in the farm kitchen.

'Firstly, she said we shouldn't pre-empt anything and that these incidents are very often resolved when the person has cooled off and they come back of their own accord.'

'What about the phone and the inhaler?' asked Shaznay.

'We don't know for sure that the inhaler Ellie found was Khadija's,' Jude pointed out. 'It could have been dropped there by any of my guests. And if it was Khadija's then there's every chance she has a second with her. If I had asthma as bad as she does then I wouldn't trust bringing just one away with me. As for the phone, perhaps she just needed a complete break without anyone contacting her.'

'I just don't think she would.' Shaznay's eyes had taken on a slightly haunted look, the sort Jude saw in her sheep when they knew something bad was about to happen. 'Her phone has everything on it, including her bank card. Without it, she won't be able to pay for a taxi, hotel, nothing.'

'Perhaps she keeps a credit card or some cash in a different place, a purse maybe,' said Neesh. 'I know I do, just in case I lose my phone when I'm out.'

'Maybe,' said Shaznay, although she didn't look convinced.

'Binnie's trying local taxi companies, hospitals, hotels and guest houses,' said Jude. 'She'll call if she hears anything but, in the meantime, let's have a good look around the farm and see if there's any sign of her.'

'Seren and Ash are out at the moment with their torches,' Ellie said. 'It's hard to see anything in the dark, though, and I guess she could be anywhere. Where do we start?'

Jude thought about it. If Khadija didn't want to be found then they had almost zero chance of uncovering her hiding place. But what if she *did* want to be found? What if something had happened to her and she was hoping to hear the sound of rescuers? She'd been gone for five hours, which was not long in the eyes of the law, especially for an adult who left of her own accord, but it was definitely long enough for any number of things to have happened to her. She could have walked miles from the farm into the woods that stretched far beyond the sheep fields, and fallen, breaking a leg. There were hidden pools too, obscured by trees and foliage during the day, almost completely camouflaged by the shadowy cover of the evening. It really was going to be like searching for a lost earring in a haystack, and Jude never had recovered the ruby stud that Adam had dislodged during their first fumble in the hay barn all those years ago.

* * *

Sure enough, the search proved fruitless. Lucy stayed back at the farm with Sebbie but everyone else took to the fields and woods, wearing head torches or waving handheld ones that Noah and Jude had dished out. Much more effective than the built-in phone torches that Seren and Ash had been using to begin with. Not that it did any good. There was just too much land to cover, and that was if they stuck to known paths and rights of way, choosing to ignore the fact that Khadija herself might not have done the same.

By midnight, Jude knew that there was no real hope of finding Khadija under the cloak of the moonless night.

'We'd be better off getting some sleep now to recharge batteries and give us all the energy to start again fresh when the sun's up,' she said to Neesh and Seren, who were her search partners.

'I think that's a great idea.' Neesh rubbed her hand across her forehead and Jude could see that she looked as tired as Jude felt.

'Come on,' said Jude. 'Let's go back to the hut. I'll call the others and tell them what we're doing. If they're sensible they'll do the same.'

Noah was searching the woods that spanned out towards the incline of the hills. He'd already come to the same conclusion as Jude and was heading back towards the farm. When Jude called Ellie, who was with the other two hens combing the paths that skirted around the village itself, she heard Shaznay's quiet agreement, but Ash was far from okay with the situation. A debate ensued – Ash loud and headstrong, Shaznay tearful and Ellie diplomatic.

'You've always hated her, Shaz,' Ash shouted. 'You never really trusted her after you found out about her and Joe, did you?'

'That's not true,' sobbed Shaznay. 'It was before Joe and I got together so why would I have a problem?'

'Was it you who told her parents about us? Was it?'

'Come on now,' said Ellie, as though she was soothing a couple of aggrieved toddlers. 'Let's go back and we can try and get a bit of sleep. Jude's right, it'll be much easier after sunrise. Besides, you know Khad. She might already have sneaked back and be fast asleep herself.'

This seemed to pacify Ash enough to agree to the decision.

'We're heading back to the campsite,' Ellie informed Jude. 'See you there.'

But when they all returned to the campsite, there was still no sign of Khadija, and Binnie called to say that she'd had no better luck on the phone. Jude tried not to jump the gun and expect the worst. There were all sorts of reasons why Khadija might have taken herself off for the night and there was every chance she would have turned up before the morning broke and yet, as Jude hung her coat up in the porch, she couldn't help fearing the worst.

* * *

The next morning, as Jude was standing in the yard with her foot propped on the cider press so she could tie the lace of her trainer, Binnie arrived with Sami, a uniformed officer. It was not yet nine but Jude suspected the hens would all be up and about already, if they'd slept at all.

'Morning, Jude,' said Sami. 'Great barbecue the other day, sorry I had to rush off.'

'It was nice to have you on the farm without it being in an official capacity,' said Jude, who had taken to Binnie's cheeky protégé the first time they'd all been out for a drink together.

'Don't forget you're in uniform today, though, Police Officer Abadi,' Binnie said. 'Jude, what can you tell me?'

'Nothing much more than when I spoke to you yesterday.' Jude finished tying her laces and stood up. 'They spent the afternoon at the spa and when the taxi dropped them back here, Khadija looked as though she was about ready to throttle someone. The others all looked pretty miserable too. I'm not sure what happened but whatever it was, even the spa couldn't work its magic on them.'

'Do you think she's just taken herself off and will turn up when she's ready?' Binnie asked. 'Off the record, of course.'

'I honestly don't know. She's definitely got it in her to do something like that from what I've seen. There's a mean streak and she really does relish being the centre of the group. But why not take her phone with her?'

'Who knows? Perhaps to create exactly the effect she's having on her friends,' suggested Sami.

'Where's the phone now?' Binnie asked.

'Still in her tent,' said Jude. 'The hens decided to leave it there in case she came back. Maybe she already has. I was just going down to see them.' She reached into the pocket of her fleece and pulled out a band to scoop her hair up and out of the way. 'I don't mind admitting that I'll be glad when this lot go home. Thank goodness all of my guests aren't quite so exciting to host.'

Lucy came out into the yard, still in her pyjamas with an old sweat-shirt on top sporting a faded picture of a sheep. The cuffs were ratty and there was a small bleach mark on one sleeve. Jude marvelled at how her towny sister had shaken off the very last vestiges of her suburban upbringing and was blossoming in old second-hand clothes and puppy-chewed flip-flops.

'Morning,' Jude said. 'Is Sebbie still in bed?'

'He's having his breakfast, more's the miracle. Might even have him at nursery on time for a change and then I'll be heading off to work.'

'We're just heading down to see what's happened on the campsite overnight,' said Jude.

A shout from the kitchen demanding more milk had Lucy rolling her eyes.

'I'll have to catch up with you later.'

Lucy hurried back in to Sebbie whilst Jude, Binnie and Sami turned to walk across the yard. They made their way around the pond where Jude noticed a couple of Canadian Geese had set up home. Seeing the pond made her think of the stranger who'd been parked there the day before and Khadija's reaction to him. Jude had assumed at the time that she was angry because of his revolting, libidinous leer when he'd seen her. But had there been something more behind her behaviour? She remembered seeing real hatred in her eyes, she'd noticed it at the time and thought it a very strong reaction to a one-line comment and lusty stare. Anger would be a normal reaction – she'd been furious herself – but the deep hate she'd seen had seemed a more personal response somehow.

'I'm not sure if it's important,' Jude said as they passed the exact spot his car had been, 'but there was someone here yesterday. A man who said he wanted to book a tent for the night, which I'm pretty sure was a lie.'

'What makes you say that?' Binnie asked.

'His manner, for one thing. And the fact that he seemed more inter-ested in Khadija, who'd just come out of the shower, than the tents.' They'd passed the pond now and were heading to the top entrance of the camping field. 'He was revolting, a total perve.'

'I bet Khadija was furious.' Binnie stopped at the gate and paused with her hand on the catch.

'She was. But looking back I think it was more than that. It's difficult to explain but she seemed to really hate him and it's now making me wonder if perhaps she knew who he was.'

'Could you describe him?' Binnie nodded at Sami, who took out his pocketbook.

'He was a real weasel, you know the sort. All pointy features and mean eyes. A bit taller than me, pretty skinny but I reckon one of those that's stronger than they look. And he had long hair, muddy blond and tied in a ponytail.'

'Got that?' Binnie asked Sami, who nodded as he scribbled down the last of Jude's description. 'We'll see if this rings any bells down at the station. Let me know if he comes back.'

They were still by the gate and Binnie hadn't yet made a move to open it.

'Before we go and meet them, give me a heads up,' she said. 'What do you think of the hen party?'

'I like them. Well, most of them. Shaznay, the bride, seems nice.'

'Shame for her that her hen do isn't quite what she hoped for,' said Binnie. 'What about the others?'

'Shaznay has a sister, Tanisha – Neesh. I get the feeling she'd be a real laugh to go out with, and I can imagine her as the one who makes sure everyone is looked after and gets home at the end of the night. Her or Ellie, the one who saved the Kerries.'

'Where are the problem links in the group?'

'Other than Khadija herself?' Jude pushed her fringe out of her eyes. 'There's her girlfriend, Ash. I'm not sure what to make of her. I heard them arguing when they first arrived and then Khadija broke up with her. It's why they needed the extra tent.'

'Do you know what they were arguing about?'

'Khadija was cross because her parents had just discovered she was in a relationship with another woman and clearly didn't approve. It sounds like they've cut her off completely. Blocked her on their phones too.'

Sami winced. 'That's pretty harsh. No wonder she was mad.'

'So she split up with Ash because of them?' Binnie tapped her finger against her top lip.

'I don't think so. It sounded more like she thought Ash was the one who'd told them about the relationship.'

'How did Ash take it?' Binnie unlatched the gate but still didn't push it open.

'Not well from what I could hear.' She thought back to the argument and also the snatches she'd overheard when she'd been on the phone to Ellie during the search the night before. 'She thinks Shaznay might have been the one to tell Khadija's parents as some sort of payback because Khadija had a fling with Shaznay's fiancé.'

'Blimey, what a tangled web.' Sami grinned, seemingly enjoying the drama, but the grin fell with one quick stare from Binnie.

'So we've got Shaznay, Tanisha, Ellie and Ash,' Binnie counted them off on her fingers. 'Anyone else?'

'There's Seren. She's really shy and quiet, the perfect doormat for someone like Khadija. You should have seen them on the day they arrived. It was like Khadija thought Seren was her personal beck and call girl the way she ordered her around and Seren just went along with it.'

Binnie looked at her friend. 'You really don't like her, do you?'

'I don't like bullies,' said Jude. 'And Khadija is a bully. Although obviously, I hope that she turns up safely.'

'Obviously,' said Sami as Binnie pushed the gate open and they all trooped through.

The campsite appeared to be deserted as they made their way from tent to tent.

'Which one is Khadija's?' asked Binnie and, when Jude pointed it out, she sent Sami over to have a look. 'See if there's anything that might tell us where she is and pick up her phone whilst you're in there. Then look around the camp for anything useful.'

When they got to the two shepherd's huts at the bottom of the field, they could hear music coming from one of them. Jude knocked on the door which swung open almost instantly.

'Any news?' Neesh asked.

'We were coming to ask you the same thing,' said Binnie. 'I'm DI

Binita Khatri, heading the investigation into Khadija's disappearance. Are you the only one here?'

Neesh stepped out of the hut and down the metal step onto the dewy grass. Jude saw her wriggle her bare toes into the damp blades and recognised the simple pleasure as something she'd always loved doing when the early morning promised a warm day ahead.

'The others all got up as soon as it was light and went out looking for Khad. I stayed behind, in case she shows up here.'

'Sounds like a sensible idea,' Binnie said. 'There's still a good chance Khadija spent the night somewhere and is now on her way back.'

'I doubt that,' said Neesh. 'She never gets up before ten unless it's a workday.'

'Do you mind if I ask you about the events of yesterday that led to Khadija walking out of the party?' Binnie asked.

Whatever was going on, Jude was glad to have Binnie there, asking the questions that needed answering and injecting a level of gravitas that the hens needed to reassure them that someone was taking their concerns seriously.

'Sure,' said Neesh, leaning against the hut. 'What would you like to know?'

'How would you say Khadija was when she left?' Binnie asked. 'Was she her usual self?'

Neesh rolled her eyes. 'The thing about Khad is that her *usual self* is pre-programmed to be grumpy and self-centred, so the fact that she was both these things when she left wasn't really that earth-shattering, to be honest.'

'Did she have any particular reason to be grumpy yesterday?' Binnie asked.

Neesh crossed her arms and took a deep breath.

'I suppose she had a few reasons. None of us are keen on how she's been treating Ash recently and it all blew up at the spa. First, she refused to sit next to Ash at lunch and then she wouldn't stop making snarky comments about her being needy. I think Khad thought we'd all be on her side because she was our friend first but it was nasty to watch and in the end, Ash went off crying. To be honest, I don't know why she still wants to be with Khad when she's such a cow all the time.'

Binnie and Jude said nothing, although Jude was agreeing whole-heartedly inside.

'Ellie went off to find Ash, and Khad didn't like that so she started bitching about Ellie. That's when I had to say something. I mean, it's Ellie, right? She's such a total sweetheart.'

Again, Jude had to agree with her.

'Can you remember what you said?' Binnie asked.

'I didn't go anywhere near as far as I wanted to,' said Neesh. 'If it hadn't been my sister's hen do and we weren't in the middle of a very nice spa then I'd have told her exactly what I thought of her. In fact, if she does turn up here whilst they're all out then I might just do that.'

'But whatever you said was enough to put her in a bad mood?' Binnie clarified.

'Not so much what I said, more that everyone else agreed with me. I think we've all just had enough of being pushed around by her, you know? Except Seren. She didn't say anything and, after Ash, she's the one with the most right to get upset with Khadija. You must have noticed how she is with her. It's embarrassing.'

'Can you tell me what you mean by that?' Binnie asked.

'She bullies her badly. It's always *Seren, get me this* or *Seren, do that* or *Seren, why are you here?*' Jude thought Neesh's mimicry was spot on, right down to the hand on the hip and the curl of the top lip.

'And how does Seren respond?'

'I wish she'd bloody well punch her one.' Neesh balled her hand into a fist. 'I would if I was her. But she's not the sort. She just goes along with it all, that's why Khad keeps doing it to her.'

'What about Shaznay?' Jude asked. 'Did she have any reason to dislike Khadija?'

'What do you mean by that?' Neesh asked, looking wary.

'Sorry, it's just when I was talking to Ellie on the phone last night, I heard Shaznay arguing with Ash and I wondered if that might have had anything to do with Khadija leaving so suddenly.'

'I assume you're talking about the fact Khad used to go out with Shaz's fiancé, Joe?'

Jude nodded.

'No, that had nothing to do with the row yesterday. If I'm honest, I don't think Khadija has ever really forgiven Joe for dumping her or Shaz for going out with him. Not that she can moan at Shaz, really. I mean, she didn't even know that Khad and Joe had a thing, Khad made him keep it quiet, like she was embarrassed by him or something.'

'How did you all find out?' Jude asked.

'Truth has a habit of getting out, doesn't it? In this case, it was one of Joe's friends who saw them together and spilled the beans.'

'I bet that didn't go down too well with Khadija.'

'You could say that. She made out like it had just been a bit of fun and they'd never really been serious but one night Joe had a skinful and told us his side of the story. Apparently, he'd told her he didn't like the secrecy and he'd had enough of being ordered about so he was off. According to Joe, she pleaded for him to take her back but he'd already fallen for Shaz by then. Khadija still flirts like mad with Joe whenever they're together. I think she just does it to wind Shaz up. God, I wish he would just tell her where to go sometimes.'

'So, he doesn't hold a candle for Khadija now?' Binnie asked.

'God, no!' exclaimed Neesh. 'He's totally in love with Shaznay. And why wouldn't he be? She's completely gorgeous, really fun, and a lot less hard work than Khad's ever been.'

Jude wondered what the truth about Khadija and Joe's relationship was. If Khadija really had been dumped and replaced so quickly by one of her best friends then watching Shaznay and Joe prepare for their wedding couldn't be easy. Was it possible that she still held a little torch of something for Joe and that was the real reason that she was so awful to Ash? Or was she just the difficult, self-centred narcissist Jude had pegged her as from the start? Either way, this new revelation did add another layer to the suggestion that it had all got too much for Khadija and she'd done a runner.

The throaty sound of a car turning into the gate at the bottom of the campsite made all three women look round. A white Porsche pulled up next to Khadija's shiny Range Rover and two men got out and started to walk towards them.

The driver was wearing sunglasses, jeans and a white T-shirt that looked two sizes too small, in the hope, Jude thought, that women would notice his gym-fit body. The passenger was also wearing sunglasses but on him, it looked as though their sole purpose was to shade his eyes rather than as a fashion accessory. Fashion did not seem to be top of his priority list as he sported a Glastonbury Festival 2013 T-shirt and his jeans were old and worn.

'Oh, you have to be kidding me,' exclaimed Neesh.

'Do you know them?' Jude asked.

'That's Joe.' She pointed at the driver. 'And the other guy is my boyfriend, Dex.'

6

Sometimes, Jude mused, it was okay to judge a book by its cover and be proven absolutely right.

When he arrived on the farm, Joe oozed everything that Jude didn't like. Before he'd even opened his mouth, she'd made her opinion on the sort of person he was. His car, showy with personalised licence plates and a red stripe across the roof, was the sort that came with the message *Look! I have cash enough for a swanky car and that makes me something pretty special, don't you think?* But it was the swagger that set her judgement in stone and her teeth on edge. She'd seen the same entitled, overconfident strut in plenty of men in her time. Guys who thought that all men envied whatever it was that they thought they had in spades, and all women were lining up to fall at their feet.

And then he opened his mouth.

'Didn't I tell you, Dex? A bunch of women on a farm together with no men to keep an eye on them, well, that was never going to end well. All right, Neesh? You lot been cat fighting again, have you?'

There it was. Less than thirty seconds after he started speaking and Jude knew she'd been absolutely right.

Neesh was clearly bristling but said nothing to Joe, instead turning her attention to the second man, who was standing awkwardly behind, his hands in his pockets and his shoulders slightly hunched over.

'What are you doing here, Dex? Where's Reggie?'

'I left him with my parents. I wanted to come and see how you were doing.' He stepped forward and held his arms open for Neesh to step into. As she moved into his embrace, he kissed her head. 'Joe thought you might need some help looking for Khadija. Any news?'

'How did you know about Khad?' Neesh asked.

'Shaz tells me everything.' Joe took a vape from his pocket and took a long drag that filled the air with the sickly-sweet smell of strawberry bootlaces. 'You know there are no secrets between your sister and me. Poor girl was destroyed when I spoke to her so I promised to come and bail you all out as soon as I could.'

'Great,' said Jude, unable to stop herself. 'Bail away. Your fiancée and her friends have been searching pretty much through the night and haven't found any sign yet. We've checked hospitals, hotels, everywhere we can think of but they've all been dead ends, so it's super you're here now to shine some new light onto things.'

Joe lifted his sunglasses up and rested them on his head, something that always reminded Jude of the Alice bands she'd worn as a child to keep her growing-out fringe away from her eyes. She caught a waft of something close to amusement in his eyes, followed quickly by the kind of interest Jude had never enjoyed receiving from men.

'And you are?' Joe asked.

'I'm Jude Gray.' Jude forced herself to hold out a hand for him to shake. 'I own Malvern Farm.'

'A female farmer,' said Joe, replacing the sunglasses over his eyes and ignoring her hand. 'I should have known.'

'Known what?'

'Nothing. It's just when Shaz showed me pictures of the campsite and said it was on a farm, it didn't really add up. But now I get it.'

'Well, that's good,' said Jude. 'At least one of us does. Now you said you want to help?'

'It's what I came for.' He pulled his phone from his pocket. It was one of the fancy ones where the screen split in two to allow it to fold together. Not cheap, Jude imagined. 'What's the closest hospital? Malvern?'

'If you're looking for some physiotherapy or you need help with your family planning,' said Binnie. 'But if you're looking for Khadija then don't worry, I've already covered all bases locally.'

Joe's glasses were once more pushed onto the top of his head. 'Sorry, who are you?'

There was no longer any amusement in his eyes, just irritation and the disdain of someone who felt himself to be far superior to the person he was talking to.

Binnie took her badge from the pocket of her navy work suit and showed it to Joe, whose ego visibly shrank.

'DI Binita Khatri. I'm leading the investigation into the disappearance of Khadija Habib. Best thing you can do is get yourselves ready and we'll point you in the direction of the woods we've all been trawling.'

'Woods?' Joe asked. 'Are they muddy? I'm not sure I've got the best footwear for that.'

'Not too bad at this time of the year,' said Binnie. 'You're wearing trainers, so I'd say you'll be fine.'

'These are Ralph Lauren, not really the sort of thing for traipsing around the countryside in.' Joe took another drag on his vape.

'I'm sure Ralph wouldn't mind, given the circumstances,' said Binnie. 'Or, failing that, perhaps Jude has a spare pair of wellies you could borrow.'

Dex stifled a grin and Jude liked him all the more for it, but Joe's face took on the condescending look of someone who was not about to take instruction from anyone, including a detective.

'I think I'll drive around the area, knock on doors and ask if anyone has seen her,' he said. 'Dex, you coming?'

'Nah, you go, mate. I'll stick around here and see if there's anything useful I can do.'

For a moment, it looked as though Joe was going to say something but he seemed to change his mind. He pushed his sunglasses back down over his furiously dipped eyebrows, gave Dex one last meaningful scowl and then huffed back to the Porsche. Jude knew he'd rev the engine, which he did, and she had a feeling he'd wheel skid out of the field onto the road, which he also didn't disappoint her with.

'Who was that?' Sami asked as he joined them, having completed his search of Khadija's tent and the rest of the campsite.

'That'll be the groom,' said Binnie.

'That'll be the next reason my grumpy neighbour comes round with something new to complain about, I should think,' Jude said.

'I'm sorry about him,' said Dex and Jude saw how embarrassed he looked.

'Not your fault.' Neesh put her arm around his waist. 'Come on, I'll show you the hut.'

'Before you go,' Binnie cut in, 'there was a man here yesterday and Khadija seemed upset by his presence. Tall, skinny, long hair and sharp features. Does that ring any bells?'

Neesh wrinkled her brow. 'I'm afraid not. Dex?'

He shook his head. 'Do you think he's got something to do with Khadija going missing?'

'He's currently just a person of interest to us. If you do see someone matching that description, or think of anything else that could be helpful, then please get in touch.' She handed over a little bundle of contact cards. 'If you could pass these on to the others, I'd appreciate it.'

'Will do,' said Neesh and she went back into the hut and closed the door.

Binnie turned to Sami. 'Did you find anything interesting?'

'Not really,' he replied. 'In fact, I think you'll be more interested to hear about what I *didn't* find.'

'Sami, you know I don't like riddles.' Binnie sighed. 'Just spit it out.'

'Khadija's phone isn't in her tent.'

Jude thought about what this meant. 'The hens were adamant that nobody had taken it so either one of them sneaked in secretly for some reason...'

'...or Khadija herself came back to fetch it,' Binnie concluded.

* * *

By the time Lucy and Sebbie came home later that afternoon, the search had thrown up no new leads. Most of the hens had returned to the campsite for lunch, realising that it was a fruitless game, but Ash had refused to give up and stayed out. A police search unit had then arrived with dogs and, when the hens pointed them in the direction Khadija had headed, they started moving out to sweep the area. Ellie and Shaznay followed them but Seren decided to stay with Neesh.

'What have the police said?' Lucy asked. She put Sebbie's nursery bag on the kitchen chair and took a bottle of milk from the fridge.

'They sent a couple of officers round to take more details from the hens and me but they had nothing much to tell us. The weird thing is that Khadija's phone has gone missing from her tent and nobody seems to know where it is.'

'Did she come back and fetch it?' Lucy was listening intently as she rifled through Sebbie's backpack for his snack tub, which she threw into the sink.

'Maybe.' Jude rustled in the vegetable rack for an onion and a couple of carrots and started to peel them. 'Or one of the hens did and is now denying it for some reason.'

'Either way, it's all very weird.' Lucy fetched a pan from the cupboard and added a good slug of oil before setting it on the hot plate of the Aga.

'Oh, and Joe, the fiancé, turned up and has spent the day driving around in his Porsche knocking on doors,' said Jude as she threw the onions into the pan and watched them sizzle as they hit the hot oil.

'I bet Janet Timms and the other old busybodies enjoyed that.' Lucy laughed.

'I don't like him at all. He's the epitome of a self-inflated—' She checked herself before swearing in front of her young nephew. 'Arsehole,' she mouthed. 'And he clearly thought that all farmers have flat chests, hairy legs and Adam's apples.'

Lucy looked her sister up and down and pulled a face to imply that she thought Joe might have a point. Jude responded by throwing a tea towel at her.

'Don't throw things in the house, Aunty Judy,' said Sebbie, wagging a half-eaten custard cream at her.

'That's right, Sebbie,' said Lucy in delight. 'Aunty Judy is very naughty.'

'Sorry, Sebbie,' said Jude. 'Will you forgive me if I find the Tony's chocolate and give you a nibble?'

Jude had introduced her nephew to chocolate quite by accident and now it was a sure way of sneaking into his good books no matter what she'd done.

'Just one piece,' said Lucy. 'He's already had a biscuit and it's not long until supper.'

Jude broke off a small bit and handed it over to Sebbie before taking a slightly bigger chunk for herself. 'Want some?' she offered but Lucy declined and carried on stirring the onions.

'Anyway.' Jude picked up a knife and started chopping the carrots. 'They've taken DNA from Khadija's hairbrush and told us not to touch anything else. Binnie said they've circulated her details and photo to other forces too and there's a small team up in the woods now with sniffer dogs so maybe they'll turn something up.'

Jude stopped cubing the carrots and set the knife down on the board.

'I have to say it makes me nervous if I think too hard about it,' she said. 'In all probability, Khadija is sitting pretty somewhere at the moment, making her friends pay for not falling over themselves to pander to her. But what if she isn't? What if the police find her and it's too late?'

'Judy,' chastised Lucy. 'Don't even go there.'

'There was a man here yesterday, over by the campsite. A proper nasty sort and I got the feeling that Khadija might have known him.'

Lucy frowned. 'Did you tell Binnie?'

'Of course I did. She asked the hens if anyone recognised his description but none of them did.' Jude shook her head to clear her thoughts. 'I've probably become too sensitive about these things, always on the lookout for trouble.'

She put a handful of the chopped carrots into a bowl for Sebbie before tipping the rest into the pan. She thought about the hen party and Khadija, who was either to be pitied or loathed depending on the outcome of her mysterious disappearance. Whatever happened, Jude wouldn't wish the sort of stress Khadija's friends were currently experiencing on anyone.

'Pass me another onion,' she said. 'Let's pad this mince out and take some down to the campsite. I imagine the hens will be hungry when they finish for the day.'

Jude wished there was more she could do for her guests as they worried about their friend but for now, shepherd's pie would have to do.

Time spent with family was precious to Jude and she pushed everything to one side for a bit as she immersed herself in Sebbie's wonderful and constant stream of chatter as she and Lucy finished cooking the pies. She watched his earnest face, so full of empathy as he told her the awful story of his friend, poor Kai who'd come to nursery without his snack and had been given a squishy banana by the unquestionably lovely Mrs Wheeler.

'It had black bits on the skin and it smelled funny but Mrs Wheeler said he had to eat it all up. I said he could have some of my grapes but Mrs Wheeler said he couldn't so I told her that the banana smelled like sheep poo and then Kai cried but he still ate the banana because he was scared of Mrs Wheeler.'

Noah joined them in the kitchen and kissed Lucy tenderly before ruffling Sebbie's hair and sitting down next to him at the table to drink a mug of tea.

'You cooking for an army, are you?' He nodded at the mince that had been rehomed in the largest pan and was spitting tiny rust-coloured drips onto the tiles behind the Aga. On the other hot plate was a second enormous pan full of potatoes in furiously boiling water that was flicking starchy white flecks to add to the Jackson Pollock design.

'We thought it might be nice to take some food to the campsite,' said Jude. 'I can't imagine they've spent a moment thinking of what to eat today.'

'That's a kind thought. I was down there a moment ago sorting the compost toilets and it looks like they're all back. Two men there too. I s'pose it's them who brought that ridiculous car?'

'That would be the fiancé,' said Jude. 'He's a bit of a muck-twit but his friend seems okay.'

Noah grinned at the use of the family's favourite insult that had been adopted when Sebbie had overheard the fruitier version and decided to parrot it back in the most inopportune situations. They'd managed to persuade him that he'd misheard and the new, and rather satisfying, child-friendly alternative had been brought into the world.

'The potatoes are ready to mash,' said Lucy. She heaved the pan over to the sink and drained them whilst Noah abandoned his tea to get the masher from the drawer.

After he'd pounded the potatoes with butter, milk and cream cheese into the perfect lids for two shepherd's pies, all that was needed was a quick blast under the grill to crisp the tops and they were ready to go.

Jude put one in the bottom compartment of the Aga to keep warm before walking down to the campsite with the second pie, where she found the hens bunched around the firepit.

'I can light that for you if you like,' she offered.

'It's okay, love. We can manage if we want it.' Joe took a vape from his pocket. 'I didn't know this place was catered. Cool, just stick it on the table and we'll help ourselves.'

Jude glared at him and set the pie down.

Joe took a puff of the vape and puffed strawberry smoke all over Jude and the pie.

'Put that bloody thing away,' said Shaznay, flapping her hand in front of her nose. 'You told me you'd quit.'

'I have. Just need a puff or two now and again.' He caught the look Shaznay fired at him and put the vape down on the table next to the pie. 'Okay, okay. No more vaping. Seren, can you go and find cutlery and plates?'

'Don't worry, Seren,' said Jude forcefully. 'There are plates, knives and forks in all your tents and huts. Everyone can get their own.'

Joe cocked his head at Jude. 'Seren doesn't mind, do you?' He turned to the woman who was doing everything she could to avoid his gaze, staring at the ground and pulling her hair so that it shielded her face. 'She's just grateful to be here.'

Seren stood up without a word, focusing her attention towards the bottom of the campsite so that Joe might miss the fact she was blushing furiously. The sight of her made Jude want to push his nasty, sneering face into the shepherd's pie.

'That's enough, Joe,' said Shaznay. 'Seren, don't listen to him – I'm really glad you're here. We'll all fetch our own things. If anyone wasn't invited to my hen party then it's Joe, not you.'

'Babe, don't be like that.' Joe's voice was whiny and childlike. 'I came to check on my best girl and make sure she's okay.'

'Who? Me or Khadija?'

Joe looked somewhat affronted and started to object but Shaznay ignored him and turned her attention to Jude.

'I can't believe you brought us food, that's so kind of you.'

'It's no bother,' said Jude, flicking away the gratitude. 'I also came to see if there's any news?'

'Nothing,' said Neesh. 'It's like she just disappeared off the face of the planet.'

Ash stood up abruptly and faced the rest of the group.

'She has to be somewhere,' she said, her eyes darkening with passion and frustration. 'What are we all doing sitting around here? We should still be out there looking for her.'

'You heard the police,' said Ellie, gently taking Ash's arm. 'They said they're still hopeful she'll turn up when she's ready. There's no sign of a struggle, no sign of anything untoward.'

Ash shook her arm roughly to free it from Ellie's grasp.

'There's no sign of Khad,' she hissed. 'Nowhere. And that is *not* what I'd call a hopeful situation.'

'Calm down, Ash.' Joe was sitting with his feet together, knees spread wide and elbows hanging nonchalantly over the arms of the director's chair. 'You're not helping things here.'

Ash spun around and marched the few steps it took to reach him, so much anger in her eyes that Jude wouldn't have been all that surprised if steam started to pour from her ears. Joe clearly didn't like to be on a lower platform and he stood up to flex his advantage in height and power.

'I told you to calm down,' he said.

Ash shoved him so hard with the flats of both hands that he stumbled backwards, only just managing to stay on his feet, his arms windmilling in the air like a cartoon character. The surprise on Joe's face quickly morphed into anger as he steadied himself and took a step towards Ash, his fists balled in front of him.

Dex was quick to move between them.

'None of that,' he said, raising his hands in an effort to disperse the tension. 'Come on, it's been a rough day. Get some food in you and then we can all work out what's to be done next.'

'All right, mate,' said Joe, shoving Dex to one side. 'Ash's just a bit hormonal.'

'You arsehole,' said Ash, who clearly hadn't yet finished with him. 'I know what you did.'

Joe's cocky bravado froze for a second and Jude had a strong feeling that whatever Ash knew, Joe didn't want it to be made common knowledge. He managed to organise his face into some semblance of indifference.

'You're off your rocker,' he said.

'It was you who told Khad to break things off with me,' Ash fumed.

'Not me,' he said, the bumptiousness returning. 'If Khad finally saw sense then that's her business. She always said you were needy. Wouldn't be surprised if you're the reason she buggered off; I know I would if I thought I was stuck in a relationship with someone like you.'

'I saw your text.' Ash's elfin features were still puce with rage. 'She didn't know I was looking when you sent it yesterday, but I did. We were at the spa, celebrating your marriage to Shaznay and you were busy texting your ex-girlfriend to make sure she'd broken up with me.'

Shaznay looked at Joe in disbelief. 'Is this true?'

Neesh went over to stand next to her sister as though taking on the role of chief protector for whatever was coming next.

'So what?' Joe said petulantly. 'She's wrong for Khad. We all know it. I was just the only one brave enough to tell her.'

'Was that your only reason, Joe?' Shaznay asked.

'What's that supposed to mean?'

'It means did you have another motive for wanting Khadija to be single again?' Shaznay stared at her fiancé.

Jude didn't envy her. Whatever the outcome of this situation was, there was clearly no trust in this relationship and that was not a good indication of a happy marriage to come.

'Are you going to come clean, Joe?' Ash squared up to him, her tiny frame no match for his inflated muscles, and yet she was so full of burning hatred that if it became physical, Jude wouldn't write her off. 'You see, the text you sent yesterday wasn't the only one I've seen on Khad's phone lately.'

Joe tried to laugh the comment off as insecurity and another good reason why Khad wanted to leave, but Ash hadn't finished.

'Did you tell Shaznay that she was runner-up in the race for your heart and that you'd leave her if there was any chance Khad wanted you back? Or were those exact words only for Khadija?'

Before Joe had a chance to try and wriggle out of Ash's accusation, Neesh jumped forward and threw a punch at him, missing his face, but catching him hard on the shoulder. As he steadied himself, clutching the site of the impact, Neesh readied herself for another attack but Dex caught her swiftly before she could land a second punch.

'You are a snake,' Neesh snarled at Joe. 'You always have been and now everyone knows just what a bastard you are.'

'Careful, little sister.' Joe's eyes flashed dangerously. 'That's no way to treat a member of your own family, is it?'

'You'll never be a part of my family if I have any say in it.' Neesh was wriggling for Dex to let her go but Jude was glad to see that he was maintaining a strong hold.

'That really isn't your choice to make, though, is it?'

'Maybe not,' said Shaznay quietly. 'But it is mine and I'd like you to leave.'

'Shaz, don't listen to them.' Joe was all contrition and smooth talking as he turned to his fiancée. 'The whole thing is nonsense. You know I'm yours and nothing will change that. Ash's just pissed off because Khad couldn't face being with her any more and Neesh has always been jealous of us.'

Shaznay looked a little uncertain and Jude hoped she wasn't daft enough to be taken in by the obvious tosh he was spouting, but then she knew love could make the mind play dirty tricks.

'I can't deal with any of this right now,' Shaznay said. 'I'm going to bed.'

Joe tried to follow her back to her hut but she stopped him in his tracks. 'And I'm going alone.'

'I'll book you a room at the B&B in the village,' said Jude, glad that at least one problem would be removed from the campsite for that night at least.

7

The next day was Friday, the day that the hens were supposed to be packing up and leaving the farm. This put Jude in a very difficult position as she had three bookings for the weekend but she knew she couldn't allow them to visit whilst the hens were still there and the search for Khadija was still going on. She also knew that she couldn't ask the hens to leave until they were ready.

As she called the families who'd made the bookings, apologising deeply and offering a sizeable discount on a re-booking, she tried hard not to think about the lost income and possible bad reviews this was going to cost her. There was still a woman missing, not to mention the hearts that had been broken and the anxiety the whole sad situation had caused.

Lucy was on the early shift at the care home, which meant Jude was in charge of Sebbie's breakfast and getting him ready for nursery. This was always a brilliant distraction and Jude was glad to allow herself to slip into his world as he told her all about Kai's latest trip to hospital to get the Lego head out of his ear.

'Mrs Wheeler said Lego heads shouldn't go in anyone's ears, mouths or noses so Kai is a silly banana head,' said Sebbie as he loaded his spoon up with a big mound of porridge.

'I don't think we should be calling Kai names, Sebbie,' said Jude, although she had to agree that she'd always thought of Sebbie's best friend as a bit of a *banana head*, and that was when she was erring on the kinder side.

'I didn't say it. Mohan did. He said that putting Lego in your ear is what banana heads do.'

'Well, I don't want you to join in if he says that again, please.'

Sebbie nodded solemnly as though this sort of language would never have crossed his mind if he hadn't been led astray by Mohan.

'Good. Now hurry up and finish that porridge and we can go over the field on Maz if you like, for a treat.'

With the promise of a trip to nursery in the cab of his favourite tractor, Sebbie gulped down the rest of his breakfast in double quick time and ran upstairs to get himself dressed whilst Jude commenced a quick surface tidy of the kitchen. Five minutes later and Sebbie was back downstairs dressed in a turquoise mermaid tail that he'd become instantly obsessed with when he'd seen it in the charity shop. He'd teamed it with a T-shirt emblazoned with a variety of farm animals and the maxim *Farmer in Training*, and a yellow plastic hard hat with a picture of Bob the Builder on the front.

Jude knew that Lucy would have marched him back upstairs to put on something more appropriate for nursery but Jude was in charge that morning, so mer-farmer on his way to the building site it was!

It was a bit of a squash in the cab of the Massey-Ferguson 298 but Noah had created a small seat, complete with seatbelt, especially for Sebbie and he loved to sit in there when the old tractor was having a run out. Jude sat in the driving seat, with the black leatherette held together in places with duct tape. There was a nostalgically wonderful engine smell that accompanied the throaty chug as she turned the key in the ignition and brought the old girl to life. It wasn't long before they were bumping over the yard and up to the wide gate into the large pasture field at the back of the farm where Noah was waiting with Floss and Ned.

Jude stopped the tractor and Noah stepped up and opened the door to poke his head into the cab.

'Are you off to nursery, young Sebbie?'

'Yes. And I got Marmite for Mrs Wheeler.' Sebbie proudly held up a nearly empty jar and Noah looked at Jude quizzically.

'Sophie brought in some rhubarb jam that she made with her granny yesterday but Sebbie thinks Mrs Wheeler might be more of a Marmite sort of woman,' she explained.

'Then I'm sure she'll be very pleased.' Noah smiled. 'Have a good day, littl'un.'

He shut the cab door with a bang and stepped back down, then he opened the six-bar gate into the field to let Jude drive through and up amongst her flock. Sebbie had lived on the farm for almost two years and yet he still watched in fascination at the sheep and spring lambs running away across the pasture as the tractor approached them. And in turn, Jude never tired of watching her young nephew's reaction as he took in the beauty of the countryside he'd learnt to embrace so completely.

'One day I would like to drive Maz,' he said as they reached the top of the field and Jude stilled the tractor in preparation so she could jump down and open the next gate. She leant across and gave Sebbie the biggest hug that was possible in the cramped space.

'Of course you will,' she said. 'And you can learn to drive the quad and round up the sheep and bring in the hay and maybe Noah will even teach you to train the sheepdogs.'

Sebbie looked at Jude disparagingly. 'Aunty Judy, I can already train Alfie.'

* * *

With Maz parked in the last field before the village, Jude and Sebbie got out and walked the five minutes to nursery. The weather had been fair for a while so the sparkly tail made it to nursery without too much mud clinging to the sequins. Jude deposited Sebbie safely in Mrs Wheeler's tenderly efficient care and continued walking down the road to the village shop and post office.

The little bell tinkled its welcome as she pushed the door open and stepped inside, a welcome echoed by the friendly woman who ran the store.

'Hello, Jude,' said Mrs James with a smile that shrank her eyes into the wrinkles that surrounded them. 'I haven't seen you for a little while. How have things been at the farm?'

Jude didn't really want to talk about Khadija and the hens; however, she knew that word would have got around and, even if Mrs James hadn't been questioned by the police herself, which was exceptionally unlikely, many of her regular customers would have been and the village was no doubt buzzing with the story.

'There's still no news about the missing woman,' Jude said as she took a scrap of paper from her pocket with a hastily scribbled shopping list on it. 'It's all such a mystery.'

Mrs James tutted and shook her head. Jude wasn't one for standing around gossiping so she picked up a loaf of bread and set it down on the counter before moving over to the fridge to choose some yoghurts for Sebbie.

'Those poor women, they must be so anxious about their friend,' Mrs James continued.

There were some folk in the village who had a nasty habit of feigning concern for the sake of a juicy bit of tittle-tattle they could pass on to their friends but Jude knew that Mrs James was not one such lady. Whilst she very much liked to be kept in the know when it came to local news, she was truly a kind person and Jude knew that her sentiment was heartfelt.

'Everyone is hopeful that she'll turn up as right as rain very soon,' Jude said.

'And in the meantime, those girls are staying on at the farm?'

'For the time being, yes.'

The bell above the door rang, heralding another customer, and Jude turned to see Val Trout walk in with an empty tote bag hanging from her crooked elbow. Jude wasn't sure if Mike had mentioned anything to his wife about Jude's accusations and she concentrated hard on the different yoghurts to avoid looking directly at her.

'Good morning, Mrs James,' Val said. 'And Jude, it's nice to see you. How are the police getting on with the search?'

Jude took this to mean that Val was none the wiser.

'Still no news,' said Mrs James, cutting in before Jude had a chance to answer. Not that she minded. In fact, she was pleased to pass the role of town crier over to someone else whilst she carried on ticking things off her shopping list.

'Well, that is a worry,' said Val. 'I hope she turns up soon so that poor bride can get on with her wedding plans.'

Jude thought of Shaznay and the altercation she'd unwillingly borne witness to the evening before and thought that it was very unlikely that the wedding would go ahead after Ash's revelation. Who would want to marry someone knowing that they were second choice right from the beginning? She'd seen Shaznay's face and the way she'd looked at Joe with contempt and loathing, as though this had been the last straw.

'Janet Timms said that the missing woman's car is still parked at the campsite so she can't have taken herself off back home,' said Mrs James. 'Is that right, Jude? And that there's another car that's joined it? A fancy sporty thing?'

'Yes. That's all true. Gosh, you can't keep a sneeze secret round these parts.' She smiled to show that she wasn't really accusing the shopkeeper of gossiping.

'That's true enough,' said Mrs James, returning the smile with a knowing one of her own. 'Now then, Val, what can I do for you?'

'I was hoping I could put this note in your window. It's about our shed key.'

'Oh, yes?'

'Mike lost it somewhere a couple of days ago and I can't get the garden furniture and parasol out until we find it. I'm so cross as I've been asking him to get a second key cut for ages but like so many things, he just didn't get round to it.'

Instantly Jude's mind turned to the key Seren had found in the paddock. With all the drama over Khadija's disappearance she'd forgotten about it, but if it was Mike's key then surely that meant more questions needed to be asked.

'Of course you can,' said Mrs James. She took the notice and read it aloud. 'Lost Yale key with Blackpool Tower keyring. If found, please hand in at the post office.'

That was it! Proof that it was Mike Trout's key that had been found in her sheep paddock next to the poisoned sheep lick and the timing matched as well. Val had said it had been lost a couple of days ago so... Would he still be able to deny everything if she could pin him to the location and the time? It wouldn't be enough on its own, but it was something. She glanced at the notice. Val's garden furniture was going to have to wait as Jude wasn't about to give back a piece of evidence that might help prove Val's husband was responsible for both poisoning four sheep and collapsing the tent of a woman who had now gone missing. She paid for her shopping and then headed back to Maz's cab. As soon as she'd stowed her bags and settled into the driving seat, she called Binnie to tell her about the key.

'Interesting,' said Binnie, sounding distracted. Jude could hear chatter in the background and was that a sheep bleating? 'Look, Jude, I'm actually at the farm at the moment. We've got a team to search the campsite again, see if there's anything we've missed. I'll talk to you when you get here.'

Jude knew Binnie well enough to read the nuances in her voice and she could tell that all was not well. She pushed the accelerator hard onto the rubber mat beneath but Maz was steady and reliable rather than frisky and keen to play. The going was less than speedy as Maz's wheels steadily turned over the pasture and up the hill. Once she'd breached the top, gravity was able to lend a hand so on the other side, to return to the farmyard, they were slightly faster coming down through the fields.

There were no police cars waiting but Jude supposed they'd have parked in the campsite and that was exactly where she headed. She met Binnie by the gate at the top of the field.

'I was just coming to find you.' Binnie looked sombre and that made Jude's pulse instantly quicken in response.

'What is it? Have you found her?' The word *alive* was stuck on the back of her tongue.

'No. There's still no sign of Khadija but we found something else. There were some very small bits of green yarn next to the door of the collapsed tent and these seem to match fibres that were found caught in the teeth of the door zipper, and the zip head itself.'

Jude wasn't quite sure why this seemed to be such an important discovery. 'Surely that just means someone snagged their clothes on the zip as they went in or out of the tent. It could belong to anyone who's ever stayed in it.'

Binnie shook her head.

'The bits of yarn have been cut cleanly with a knife or scissors, not ripped by the zipper.'

Jude knew what Binnie was insinuating.

'You think someone used the yarn to tie the zipper shut so Khadija couldn't get out of the tent when it collapsed. Someone who knew she suffered from asthma and a shock like that would almost certainly bring on an attack.' The thought was too awful to consider and yet once voiced it seemed utterly plausible. 'What if they'd also taken her inhaler and hid it behind the toilet?'

'It's a possibility, yes,' said Binnie, looking bleak. 'But there's a lot of supposition there so we can't get ahead of ourselves. We need to do some more analysis on the tent and the yarn, and obviously it doesn't take us any closer to finding Khadija.'

'But you think someone tried to kill her and now we must wonder if they had another go?'

'There are a lot of questions we need answered before we jump to that conclusion.' Binnie was measured in her response but Jude could tell this was exactly what she was thinking.

'Did you find her phone?' she asked.

Binnie shook her head. 'No, but we have got hold of the phone records. It was last switched on for around half an hour at six this morning. They've managed to trace it to the area around the farm.'

'So either she's got it, or someone who knows her passcode has,' said Jude.

'Precisely.' Binnie was looking serious and this always made Jude anxious.

'What now?' she asked.

'We're bringing in more dogs and upping the search team in the local area. If she's still in the vicinity then we'll find her.'

It seemed more and more likely that if Khadija was still near the farm, then she wouldn't be found alive.

8

The discovery of the yarn linked with Neesh's eyewitness statement that she'd seen Mike Trout snooping around the campsite and the fact that his shed key was found near the poisoned sheep lick gave Binnie just cause to bring him in for questioning.

Jude was itchy for truths and longed to be able to go straight round to Mike Trout's and demand answers, but she knew that this time she had to leave it to the police.

'When I told him we had a positive identification that placed him in the campsite that night, he didn't try to deny it but he's adamant he left Khadija's tent in a stable position and has no idea what happened after-wards,' Binnie said when she called after lunch. 'He seemed to have no idea about the green yarn either.'

'Do you believe him?' Jude asked when Binnie had filled her in on all the details.

'I think he's telling the truth when it comes to the tent. He might be an irritation, but attempted murder is surely above his remit.'

Jude had to agree with her, but she was still convinced he wasn't quite so concerned for the lives of her animals.

'What about my poor sheep? Did he own up to that?'

'He says he had nothing to do with the rhododendron poisoning and, apart from the keyring, there's nothing much we can pin on him.' The skin around Binnie's eyes crinkled slightly as she pursed her lips in resignation. 'Anyway, the focus will be on finding Khadija, or the person responsible for her disappearance. Unless the sheep are linked in any way to that investigation then I think we have to draw a line under it.'

'You're right.'

Jude's heart was still sore from the needless pain and distress caused to her sheep but there were now bigger mysteries to be investigated and it was only right that Binnie and her colleagues focused on those. But there was nothing stopping her having another snoop around in the paddock to see if there was anything else she could find that might make it harder for Mike Trout to wriggle away from his guilt.

'Thanks for the update, Binnie.'

'Keep your eyes open and let me know if you see anything,' Binnie replied before ending the call.

Jude gave a single whistle and both dogs leapt from their beds next to the Aga and were at the door ready for her before she'd pulled the first of her wellies on.

Down in the paddock, she let herself through the gate and saw that there was already someone with the sheep. For a moment she assumed it was Noah but anger and worry soon clubbed together to flood her system with an adrenaline boost when she recognised Mike Trout.

'What the hell do you think you're doing?' Jude yelled as she marched down the paddock with Pip trotting beside her like a dressage pony and Alfie pulling at the lead. 'Get away from my sheep.'

Mike Trout sprang around, clearly surprised to have been caught out. 'I'm not doing any harm.' He raised his hands in the air as though Jude was pointing a shotgun at him. 'I just came to see how they were doing.'

'You expect me to believe that?' Jude's heart was racing and her hands were shaking.

Mike lowered his hands. 'Well, it's the truth. Have you ever stopped to think that I'm not the monster you clearly think I am?'

'How would you describe yourself, then?' Jude demanded. 'You tried to kill my sheep and then you collapsed a tent whilst someone was still inside it. Did you tie it shut as well so that she couldn't get out?'

Mike glowered at her as she approached him. 'You are deranged, Mrs Gray. I have done nothing wrong except perhaps taking an interest in my ovine neighbours.'

'You were seen, Mike,' said Jude. 'You were seen in the campsite just before the tent collapsed and your keyring was found by the poisoned sheep lick.'

'I don't know what you're trying to prove but you won't be able to pin this all on me. I won't let you.'

He stalked past her and she found herself wishing that the vein throbbing at his temple would burst.

'You're wrong, you know,' she shouted after him. 'I have a habit of getting to the truth in the end.'

Mike Trout didn't turn around but carried on to the top of the field and out through the gate. Jude was still shaking from the audacity of the man as she looped Alfie's lead through the metal hoop on the stable door. Pip had been around the sheep for years and could be trusted to leave them alone but Alfie was young and frisky still and the Kerries had been through enough trauma in the past few days.

Jude looked around her to see if Mike had left behind any obvious signs of what he'd been doing there but she found nothing. All four of the sheep were huddled together in a tight group beneath a large beech tree that stood next to the stable block. They stared at Jude suspiciously as she approached, backing away so she couldn't get close enough to check them over.

'You'll be fine now,' she said in her most soothing voice, pleased to see them all back on their feet and looking so much better.

Jude pulled the end of the hosepipe, which was coiled like a banana-yellow snake over a large hook on the outside of the tack room, and put it in the sheep's water trough. Then she turned on the tap and waited for the trough to fill up.

'There you go. I don't think you'll be needing anything other than Malvern's finest grass to fill you up. I definitely won't be giving you any molasses licks for a while yet.'

The grass in the paddock was the perfect, lustrous green that only came in the spring when the new growth was at its healthiest, before the summer months brought hot weather to scorch it to crispy blades. It was on the long side as Jude hadn't had any sheep grazing in it yet that year so it really did offer the four lucky Kerries a wonderful banquet.

The sheep looked out earnestly from beneath their tree at Jude but she knew that they'd scarper pretty quickly if she tried to touch them. If it was a petting farm she was after then she'd have to hope that by handling the first batch of Kerry lambs in the spring, they'd get used to humans and allow the campsite's guests to stroke them and perhaps even hand-feed them a few sheep nuts.

'Have it your own way,' she said, leaving them to it and turning her attention to the square patch of ground that was still flattened from the ruined sheep lick, now in the industrial bin, waiting to be collected with the rest of the farm's rubbish. Another £25 down the drain to add to everything else.

'It's a shame you aren't a trained sniffer dog, Pip,' she said, looking down at her collie. 'Perhaps then you'd be able to find a clue that would be impossible for that little weasel Trout to explain away.'

Jude knelt down and started to work through the grass, section by section. She didn't know what she hoped to find but if there was something there then she didn't want to miss it.

'At the very least, I want him to understand that he can't mess with me and my animals without getting caught, but if he could be made to pay out too then that would definitely be a bonus,' she muttered.

'Everything okay here?'

Jude looked up to see Noah watching her with an amused look on his face.

'Should I be concerned to find you on your hands and knees in the grass muttering away to yourself?' he teased.

'Mike Trout was here.' Jude knelt up so she could face him. 'And that keyring that Seren found by the feed trough – it belongs to him.'

'Jude, you've got to drop this.' Any trace of humour had left Noah's face and he looked at her in concern for a second before holding his hands out to help her up. 'Only trouble lies in getting too caught up in something you're never going to be able to prove.'

Refusing his help, Jude pushed herself angrily off the ground and dusted her hands together to get rid of the loose bits of grass.

'He almost killed one of my sheep,' she said, outraged that Noah wasn't on her side. 'And he was just here again, what if it was so he could have another go?'

Noah looked confused. 'What? He was here just now?'

Jude felt exasperated. 'That's what I was trying to tell you.'

'Did you ask him what he wanted?' said Noah.

'He said he'd just come to check on the Kerries.'

Noah rubbed his chin. 'Funny thing for an animal-phobe to do, isn't it?'

'Exactly. So now do you see why I was looking for something to show me what he was up to? Because he's definitely up to something but, without proof, what are we supposed to do?'

'We do what we always do,' said Noah, gently laying his hands on her shoulders. 'We take things one step at a time and we go by the facts we have. I don't have any idea what he was doing up here but I do think he's not daft enough to have another pop at the sheep now that the police are on to him. And I'm sorry to say it but there are bigger problems at the moment, like a missing camping guest.'

Jude knew he was right. Although there was still a chance Khadija would turn up unharmed, the reality was that the discovery of the green yarn had made this more unlikely, as did the more time that passed with no news.

Noah let go of her shoulders. 'It'll all come good,' he said. 'Now, aren't you going to ask me what I'm doing down here in the paddock?'

Jude gave a small smile at the sudden eagerness on his face. 'Go on, you're clearly popping to tell me.'

'It's Sebbie's birthday on Sunday, which is only a couple of days away.'

'Goodness, yes. It's crept up somewhat with everything that's been going on around here.' Jude took out her phone and set a reminder to write his card and wrap the England rugby shirt she'd bought him.

'And what did I say I'd get him?' Noah prompted.

For a moment, Jude wasn't sure what he was talking about but then, after a little bit of dreadful miming on Noah's part, she remembered the passing comment he'd made when she first brought the Kerry Hill ewes back to the farm. Despite it all, she felt a little buzz of excitement fizz inside her.

'You found some Runner ducks?'

'Found, bought and being delivered tomorrow.' Noah looked so proud of his ridiculously wonderful gift and Jude could tell that he was going to enjoy giving the ducks to Sebbie just as much as Sebbie was going to be ecstatic about the fact his birthday would be celebrated by an amazing new type of animal added to the farm's menagerie.

'You are officially fabulous.' Jude clapped her hands together. 'He'll love them.'

'That's the idea. I just need to prepare the paddock. Can't let them loose in here as it is, they'll be under the hedge and onto the road before they've been here a day.'

'Or worse, they'll get into Mike Trout's garden and end up in pancake rolls.'

'Heaven forbid.' Noah chuckled.

Despite the fooling around, Jude couldn't stop feeling anxious about having animals in the field so close to the house of the man responsible for poisoning her sheep already. But there was nothing for it. She had to trust Noah was right when he said that Mike wouldn't be daft enough to try anything else.

'Set me to task, what do you need to get this place duck ready?'

'Main thing is to make it secure and get one of the stables emptied out to put them in at night so a fox doesn't get to them.' Noah walked over to the stables and Jude followed, her heart sinking just a little as she thought of the jumble of junk inside that she'd have to work through.

'It's not as bad as it looks,' said Noah. 'A lot of that stuff is easy enough to lug out and we can load it all on the trailer and find a space for it at the back of the tractor barn for now.'

'What about water?' Jude asked, the excitement of the imminent arrival of the Runner ducks dampened slightly by the extra work they were already bringing. 'Won't they need a pond to swim in?'

'We'll need to dig one out before too long, but for now I'm sure I can find something big enough for them to drink from and dunk their heads under – as long as we put a ramp up so they can get in and out.'

'We'd better get cracking then if we're going to have everything ready in time. I'll make a start on the stable.' Jude pulled a band from her wrist and tugged her auburn hair up into a knot on top of her head, ready for action.

'Do you want me to take the dogs back to the house?' Noah asked. 'I'm going that way to fetch the chicken wire.'

Jude looked at Alfie, who had been lying patiently, resigned to the fact that his freedom had been curtailed. 'Might be a good idea. Just throw them in the garden.'

Whilst Noah went to find the chicken wire, Jude opened the first of the two stable doors. It was stuffed to the gunwales but Noah was right – whoever had packed the jumps in had done a very neat job and, at first glance at least, there was no extra junk that would need sorting. Jude decided to leave that stable for now as it would be easier to pull things out and put them straight into the trailer. The second stable was half as full but it was not nearly as well ordered. Jude almost decided to close the door and deal with it another day but she knew that was just delaying the inevitable as they'd need both stables soon enough. There was also an element of her well-used coping mechanism kicking in, the one that made her want to keep herself busy whenever her mind was swamped.

There were some boxes at the very front of the stable and, when she opened the first, she discovered it was full of wine glasses, all neatly separated with cardboard dividers. A quick count revealed that there must be thirty glasses and a peek into the second and third boxes showed her that there were also pint and half-pint glasses. Presumably Adam's family had used them for parties in the past and they would certainly be useful for larger gatherings in the future. For now, though, she took them out and put them to one side to be taken back to the house for storage in the attic.

By the time Noah returned, driving the Land Rover with the big trailer attached, Jude had made a dent in the contents of the second shed. There was quite a large pile that would go straight to the tip, things that Adam's parents must have had a use for at some point but were now just clutter that Jude didn't need. A second, smaller pile was for keeping and relocating either to the attic or the garden sheds.

'Told you it wasn't so bad,' Noah said, getting out of the car. He opened the back flap of the trailer and pulled out a roll of chicken wire which he set down by the side of the stable.

'There's still a way to go,' said Jude. 'It might be better to shift the jumps now that we can put them straight into the trailer. At least we'll be able to get that ready for the ducks, even if I run out of time with the stuff from the other stable.'

'Need a hand?' Noah asked.

'No, you carry on with the chicken wire, I've got the jumps.'

Whilst Noah carried the roll of wire across to the far hedge to begin patching the holes, Jude began dragging out the notched supports of the adjustable wooden jumps and hefting them up the ramp into the metal bed of the trailer. There were only six but they took up a fair amount of space and once she'd rolled the old oil drums in to rest on their ends, there wasn't much room left. She managed to slide in the red and white striped jump poles one by one and lie them next to each other and the trailer was full. There was plenty of room inside the Land Rover, though, so she began to stack the boxes of glasses onto the back seats.

She was so engrossed in what she was doing that she didn't hear Seren coming. When she called out to say hello, Jude stood up too quickly and knocked her head on the doorframe of the car.

'Oh, I'm so sorry,' blustered Seren, now the colour of a sun-ripened strawberry.

'No need to apologise, I was in my own little world.' Jude rubbed at the tender patch on the top of her head to dull the pain. 'How are things going? I'm sorry not to have been more present on the camp but I thought you might like your space to get on with whatever needs doing.'

'It's all a bit of a weird limbo at the moment. None of us really know what to do whilst we're waiting to find out what's happened to Khadija. Neesh is trying to persuade us all that she'll turn up when she's in a better mood and Joe is looking for someone to blame for her leaving the camp in the first place.'

'It sounds awful. Is there anything I can do to help?'

'No.' Seren looked at the dry skin on the side of her finger and started to pick at the corner of it. 'Thank you, but I think we just have to wait for the police to tell us what to do next. I'm hoping I can go home soon, especially as I'm on call on Sunday, but Joe says none of us can leave until she's found. We can't stay here forever, though, can we?'

Jude balked inwardly at the very thought of it. It could be days, weeks or months before the police found anything. Where did she stand with the ethics of evicting a hen party from the campsite in these circumstances? The harsh reality was that the longer this dragged on, the more bookings she'd have to cancel and the more money she'd lose, not to mention the dent in her reputation.

'You don't have to do everything Joe tells you, Seren. Or anyone else for that matter.'

'I know I must look like a complete doormat to you but it isn't that easy.' Seren continued to give the skin around her fingernail attention and Jude could see it beginning to pull away, leaving an open, red wound behind. It matched several others that ran down from the corners of her fingernails. 'When it comes to Joe and Khadija, I don't have much of a choice.'

It seemed as though there was more for Seren to say but Noah walked up at that moment to see how Jude was getting on and to take the first trailerful away.

'Sorry about that,' said Jude, when he'd driven off with the trailer bumping behind. 'You were saying about Joe and Khadija?'

'It doesn't matter.' Seren stopped picking at her fingers and looked towards the stable. 'It's nice to get away from the camp for a bit. If you don't mind a bit of help then I'm happy to be an extra pair of hands.'

There was no point in pushing so Jude gratefully accepted the offer and the two women set about pulling the remains of the stable's contents out into the paddock.

'What do you want me to do with these sacks of hen grit?' Seren asked. 'They look untouched.'

'I think they kept chickens in here for a while but now they're all in the henhouses in the orchard. Leave it to the side and I'll drop it off when Noah brings the trailer back.'

Jude marvelled as Seren, who'd always looked so breakable and help-less, picked up two of the heavy sacks, one in each hand, and lugged them over to the trailer pile. Her arms were well-defined and strong and Jude recognised them as the capable arms of someone who spent a lot of time doing heavy manual work.

'You look like you're used to hefting grit sacks around.'

Seren beamed at her as she picked up the last two. 'I spend as much time as I can back on my parents' farm. It's where I'm happiest.'

Jude found herself wondering again about the unfortunate incident with the heifer that had taken Seren away from the life of a farm vet when she was clearly so cut out for the job, but she knew better than to pry so she went back to the job at hand. It was gratifying to see that both stables were almost empty and it really hadn't taken long at all, especially with Seren's help.

There was an old sun lounger at the back of the stable, one of the last things to pull out. The springs had rusted and the cushion smelled of mould, perhaps in part due to the fact that a family of mice had clearly had fun with it at some point, nibbling away at the fabric and pulling the stuffing through the hole they'd made. Something bright yellow had been stuffed inside and Jude wrinkled her nose as she went to pick it up.

'This is definitely destined for the dump pile.'

'Here, let me take that for you.' Seren grabbed the lounger and pulled it out and towards the heap of junk ready to be loaded up and taken off to the tip.

There was a rumble from the corner of the paddock – Noah had returned. Jude went over to open the gate and let him, the Land Rover and trailer back in.

'You've been busy,' he said through the window, gesturing to the piles that stood like twin funeral pyres waiting to be lit. Seren had her back to them and was adjusting something in one of the piles.

'I've had help.' Jude opened the driver's door. 'Do you mind going back to fetch one of the quads with the small trailer? I'll take this down and start loading up the rubbish for the skip.'

'Right you are.' Noah jumped down to let Jude climb into the driving seat and, as he headed back to the farm for the quad, Jude drove the Land Rover down to Seren and the piles of stuff.

'Everything okay?' Jude asked as she climbed out of the car.

Seren looked flustered, like a child who'd just been caught rifling through their Christmas presents before the big day had arrived. Jude looked at her suspiciously but Seren was quick to look away. 'Yes, all good. What are we starting with?'

'All of this is to go into the trailer.' She pointed at the rubbish pile. 'But you don't have to help me, you've already done plenty and you're supposed to be a guest here.'

'It's no worry, really.' Seren picked up the dead sun lounger. 'Is this going straight to the tip?' she asked.

'I think it is sadly beyond repair,' said Jude. 'There was something tucked into it, though, can I just check what it was before it goes?'

Jude noticed Seren's already pink cheeks deepen as she gave a cursory peek into the folds of the lounger's cushion. 'Nothing there,' she said.

Jude was now incredibly suspicious. What on earth was she trying to hide?

'Let me have a look,' she said. 'There was definitely something bright yellow tucked inside when we took it out of the stable.'

Seren reluctantly stepped aside and Jude opened the rusted frame to reveal what looked like a bright yellow jumper that had been partly pushed into a hole in the decaying cushion. The jumper was damaged but not from mice or age.

Jude held it up for Seren to see. 'You don't know who this belongs to, do you?'

Seren put her hand out to take it but Jude wasn't ready to pass it over until she knew what it was and why Seren had been so keen to hide it.

'Yes,' Seren said quietly. 'It's Khadija's.'

Jude took a closer look at the jumper and realised that, although the main body was a rich buttercup yellow, there was a thin grass-green edge to the cuffs and the neckline. Around the bottom hem, there was also the remains of a band of green edging but it had come away and the loose end of yarn dangled freely. The implication of this was instantly clear and Jude was absolutely certain that if she were to pull at it then the next row of knitting would unravel easily, and the yarn that she'd end up with would exactly match the piece that had been used to tie Khadija's tent door shut.

9

There was a horrible moment as Jude stared at the jumper and then at Seren, whose pink cheeks had been replaced by a ghostly sheen. If this was the jumper that had given up its yarn in order to tie Khadija's tent shut then surely that meant Seren only had one possible reason for hiding it.

'Can I have that, please?' Seren asked, her hand still held out expectantly.

'You know I can't let you take it.' Jude's voice was gentle. She still couldn't shake the feeling that Seren somehow needed to be protected. Despite the enormous questions that hung over the jumper and the way in which Seren had so obviously tried to hide it, she still projected a vulnerability that Jude couldn't bring herself to exacerbate with accusations or angry demands. And yet the jumper was without question an important piece of evidence that she would have to pass on to Binnie.

'What are you going to do with it?' Seren's voice was quaking and her jaw trembled as she asked the question.

Jude decided not to answer. Seren had clearly already realised the inevitability of the jumper being handed over to the police. 'Why did you hide it?' she said instead.

Jude didn't think that Binnie had told the hens that it looked as though someone had used yarn to deliberately stop Khadija escaping when her tent collapsed. She'd told Jude that she hadn't wanted to alarm them until they were sure they knew what was going on. If she hadn't and Seren let slip that she already knew about it then there would certainly be a big question to ask.

Seren hung her head and started to pick at the red raw skin around her fingernails, making Jude want to grab her hands to stop her from hurting herself further.

'I—' she stammered but didn't go on.

'Seren, do you know where Khadija is?'

The vet's head snapped up and Jude could see almost an entire ring of white encircling each green iris. 'I don't know where she is. I don't know and the worst bit is that I don't think I even care. Everyone else is so worried but I would rather she never came back from wherever she's hiding.'

Seren caught herself and put the back of her thumb to her lips as though to stop herself from carrying on. Jude was surprised by the outburst and yet not at all by the sentiment. She'd seen exactly how badly Seren had been treated by Khadija and, if she was in Seren's position, Jude thought she'd also not be as upset as the rest of the hen party. But would Seren be so keen to see the back of Khadija that she might be tempted to do something to make sure it happened? It seemed inconceivable and yet it was exactly the question the police would be asking once they were involved.

'You think she's hiding somewhere?' Jude was desperate to find out exactly what was going on and she knew that Seren was bound to clam up as soon as Noah returned with the quad.

'Of course she is. It's exactly the sort of thing she'd do, create as much chaos as possible and then swan back in and lay the guilt on thickly. She's always been like that, Jude. She's a nasty piece of work and I hate that everyone just lets her get away with it. Whatever Khadija wants she gets. It's as though all the bad stuff that happens to the rest of us just slides off her because she refuses to let it stick.' Seren was scratching at the back of her hand in aggravation, causing the skin to become scarlet and angry. 'If it wasn't for her, I'd still have a job working as a farm vet. *She* made the mistake but she made sure I took the fall for it as well.'

Jude remembered what Ellie had told her about the mistaken administration of the Micotil that had killed the prize heifer.

'It was Khadija who gave the injection?'

'Yes. I told her it should be given subcut and never straight into a vein but she wouldn't listen.' Seren looked at her bitterly, making Jude realise that this was probably the first time she'd admitted this.

'Why didn't you say anything?'

'Because of who she is. It would have been her word against mine and nobody ever takes my side. It was either share the blame with her, say it was a joint decision, or she'd say that it was all me.'

It was clear how much Seren believed this and yet Jude couldn't help doubting her fears.

'Seren, I don't know either of you particularly well but I've seen enough to be fairly sure that I'd hold your word above that of Khadija's. Surely the vets you worked with would have come to the same conclusion if you'd both put your version of the truth across independently.'

Seren's face clouded with the closest thing Jude had seen to anger in her.

'You have no idea what she's capable of,' she said darkly. 'Khadija Habib is dangerous. If she wanted to bring me down then she could. She could do that to any one of us and she makes sure we all know it. It's why people don't often say no to her. It's why she was invited to come here in the first place. Shaz was too scared to leave her out.'

Jude could well believe this. She hadn't seen much warmth between Khadija and Shaz – or any of the hens, for that matter. She thought about the conversation she'd overheard between Ellie and Khadija. Ellie had stood up to her then, told her to leave Seren alone. But then something else had been said. Something that Jude hadn't been able to hear but that had caused a change in Ellie. Had she been threatening her too?

'For what it's worth, I think you have every right to be angry with Khadija and I hope to God that you're right and she is hiding out somewhere for whatever reason but I also think we have to face the facts. The police are investigating her disappearance as possibly something more and you have just tried to get rid of a piece of evidence that could be vital.'

Seren visibly blanched and Jude wondered if her starkness was perhaps a little too much, but it was the truth of the situation and she wasn't doing Seren any favours by hiding it under a whitewash of sympathy.

'The jumper was Khadija's favourite.' Seren could not hold eye contact, instead choosing to stare at her hand that had been scratched so much that tiny pricks of blood stood proud in neat lines where her nails had broken the skin. 'It cost her a fortune, made by some impressive designer that I'd never heard of but she kept going on about. When she sent me down to get her stuff out of the tent, I saw it lying on her bed and I couldn't help it. I took her nail scissors and snipped the thread in a few little places. Tiny holes that I knew would grow into massive ones really quickly. It did make me feel good whilst I was doing it and I imagined her putting it on and thinking that moths had got at it. But then I couldn't stop worrying. If she knew someone had ruined it on purpose then she'd guess it was me and she'd make sure I paid for it, both in money and – you know...'

Jude nodded. She could well imagine what would happen if Khadija found out what Seren had done to the jumper and she could see why she'd want to get rid of the evidence before it came to that. She took a closer look at the jumper and saw that, as well as the obvious damage to the bottom, there were small holes all over the place too.

'So that's why you hid it?'

Seren gave a small nod. 'That's why I hid it just then, but I didn't put it in the lounger in the first place. When I last saw it, it was still in Khadija's tent after I'd destroyed it.' She looked so earnest that Jude couldn't help believing her. 'But I was so worried about being found out that I sneaked back later on to get the jumper so that I could throw it away and she'd just think she'd lost it. But it had already gone.'

Jude's mind was whirring. She had no reason to believe Seren wasn't telling the truth. She'd already been caught hiding the jumper so why lie about being the one to put it there in the first place? Assuming that Binnie hadn't told the hens that yarn had been used to secure Khadija's tent door, it stood to reason that Seren was unaware that the significance of the discovery was far darker than the brutal murder of a jumper. And if she was telling the truth, then someone else had hidden the jumper. It had to be Mike. *That* was the reason he'd been back in the paddock – he'd come to collect it so that he could get rid of it properly.

'I do need to give this to the police,' Jude said, watching Seren flinch.

'Do you think they'll tell Khadija what happened to it?' The anxiety coursing through Seren was as real as her belief that Khadija was going to turn up alive, well and thoroughly pissed off about the fact her jumper was now totally unwearable. Jude's insides melted and she couldn't bring herself to add further worries to the woman's already loaded shoulders.

'Let me have a word with my friend who's a detective,' she said. 'She's brilliant at things like this and I can't see any reason why she would need to tell Khadija. As soon as she turns up, the case will be closed anyway so there'd be no need.'

'Thank you.' Seren looked relieved and Jude hoped that, whatever the outcome of the investigation into Khadija's whereabouts, Seren would find the courage to bulldoze the bully right out of her life.

'Now, I'm sorry to be brusque but I have to get all of this cleared out as we're expecting some new arrivals soon,' said Jude, very aware of the time marching on.

Seren was only too happy to stick around to help and they worked in silence to shift the pile of rubbish into the waiting trailer. As she worked, Jude thought more about Mike Trout. And the more she thought about it, the more she was sure that he was responsible not only for the poisoning of her beautiful Kerry Hills but also for the collapsing of Khadija's tent and the yarn tying the door together. It was an extreme and dangerous way of trying to close the campsite that could have ended up with the deaths of four sheep and one bridesmaid, and yet she felt sure that was what had happened. She stopped short of imagining him capable of murder and he wouldn't have known that Khadija had asthma; perhaps he'd meant to cut the thread after he'd thought she'd had a big enough scare. Perhaps he'd already cut it before she used her scissors to make an emergency escape exit.

'That's the last of it.' Seren broke into her thoughts as she loaded the last unwanted rusty oil can into the heaving trailer.

Despite the tempest in her mind, Jude looked at the stable block, now empty and ready for a quick scrub down before the ducks arrived in the morning, with immense satisfaction.

'That's brilliant,' she said. 'Thank you so much for all your hard work.'

'It was way nicer than being in the campsite,' Seren replied.

'Well, I was very glad to have you. It would have taken me twice as long on my own but now I can just give it a clean and then get rid of all this stuff.'

'I can hose it out if that's helpful?' Seren looked as though her offer of help was actually a request to be able to stay for a little longer, and Jude was only too happy to let her.

Whilst Seren took the hose into the stable to wash out the years of dust and grime, Jude set about sweeping the cobbles outside, checking for anything nasty that could do harm to webbed or cloven foot.

Once again, her mind turned to Mike and Khadija. He'd collapsed the tent, she was sure of it. But then what? Jude had seen the look on his face when she'd originally confronted him about the sheep. He'd been genuinely alarmed when she'd let him believe that he'd almost killed someone so he couldn't have anything to do with her disappearance.

Which meant that, even if she had solved the mystery of the poisoned sheep and the collapsed tent, it still hadn't got her any closer to finding out what had happened to Khadija. And, until she'd got to the bottom of that mystery, she was still a long way from getting the hens out of the campsite.

There was still the slim chance that Khadija would somehow still show up of her own accord, as noxious as ever and with no sign of an explanation or apology. But Jude had the increasing sense that someone had made sure that this wasn't going to happen. And if so, then who? There were plenty who might have wanted to teach Khadija a lesson; Seren wasn't alone in that. In the short time she'd been on the farm, Jude had heard her arguing with pretty much all of the hens at one point. But did any of them have a great enough reason to want her gone for good?

As Jude finished sweeping, she finally saw Noah, who'd been much longer than expected, driving the quad rather cautiously across the paddock towards her. As he drew up, Jude was surprised to see that the trailer wasn't empty. Around ten smooth heads, varying in colour from white, through shades of brown to almost black, were peering through the bars.

'Are you ready for the new inmates?' he asked as he climbed off and put the helmet in the dog box on the back.

'I thought you said they were coming tomorrow?' Jude was doubly grateful for Seren's help as the ducks' stable was almost ready.

'Change of plan. Barry, from the duck farm, was in the yard when I got up there. He mixed up the days; had them down for delivery on the 6th, same as me, but Barry thought that was today.'

Jude went over to the trailer and looked inside. The ducks were standing in crates and as every one of them looked up at her, her heart melted just a little. She'd always had a soft spot for the ducks in the Winter Gardens where her mum had taken her as a child. Nowadays you weren't allowed to feed them but back then they would take the unloved crusts of sliced bread and break them over the sides of the wooden bridge. The gentle noises of appreciation as the ducks waggled their tails at her and gobbled up the crusts had been food for her soul and the memory of those days made her ache just a little for her lost childhood and a mum who'd died too young.

'Five girls and four boys,' Noah told her. 'Who knows, maybe babies to come.'

'That would be amazing.' Jude was already starting to imagine a little cloud of yellow fluff filling the stable the following spring.

She caught sight of Seren, still hovering by the stable door, looking wrung out after her sudden expulsion of pent-up rage.

'Come and have a look,' Jude called over to her.

Seren walked over to the trailer and peered inside. 'Indian Runner ducks,' she said. 'They're beautiful.'

'They're Noah's birthday gift to my nephew. He's turning four on Sunday.'

'He's a lucky boy.' Although Seren was stroking the head of the duck closest to her, Jude saw that the joy she might have felt being in the company of such adorable creatures was dampened by the effect of her outburst and the discovery of the jumper. 'I'd better get back to the tents. In fact, do you know of a local taxi company that would come out to the farm?'

'Is there somewhere you need to get to?' Jude asked. 'I might be able to give you a lift depending on when you want to leave.'

'That's really kind of you but a taxi's fine. I been thinkin' about what you said and I'm going to go home. There's a train from Malvern Link at four thirty so I'll aim for that.'

Jude glanced at her watch. It was already almost three which meant Lucy and Sebbie would be home from work and nursery in a couple of hours and there was still so much to take care of. A trip to the station on the other side of the hills wasn't ideal but she felt she should offer as Seren had spent the best part of an hour and a half sorting out the stables with her.

'We'd best leave at four, then.'

'No, really, I'm fine with a taxi.'

Jude knew the look of someone who just wanted to be left alone so she didn't push it.

'Look up Nib's Cabs online,' suggested Noah. 'I went to school with the owner, Nick. He lives not too far away in Cradley and he's a good sort. If he's got a car spare, he can be with you in fifteen minutes.'

'Thanks,' said Seren. She turned back to Jude and for a moment Jude thought she was going to hug her but she obviously thought better of it. 'And thank you too, Jude. I'm sorry we've given you so many problems.'

'Not your fault at all. Perhaps you'll come back and visit another time. Maybe when the petting farm is all set up so you can meet the animals.'

Seren nodded and gave a small smile before walking across the paddock, back to face the hens and tell them her decision. Or perhaps the first Shaznay and the others would know of Seren's plan to leave might be when the taxi pulled up to take her away.

'She's a bit of an odd one,' Noah said when she was out of earshot.

'I think she's just had a really rough time of it. I feel sorry for her.'

There was a single quack from the trailer and Noah clucked to reassure the ducks inside that they hadn't been forgotten.

'Okay, you lot, let's get you into the stable for now until we've set up a pen for you.'

'I thought the chicken wire over the hedges meant you were thinking of letting them have the run of the paddock,' said Jude.

'No,' chuckled Noah. 'That's just in case we've got any Houdinis here. I'm sure we'll be able to teach the dogs to round them up at the end of each day soon enough, but until then, I don't fancy charging round this whole field trying to catch nine ducks.' He opened the door of the furthest stable. 'Don't look so worried, Jude. Spud's on his way and we'll have it set up in no time. They'll be happy as anything in the stable for now as long as we give them some water and something to eat. Barry said they'll enjoy any veg scraps from the kitchen but when they're outside they'll find what they need in the way of grass and slugs.'

Jude sighed. There was always something unexpected going on at the farm. It was what made her life so colourful but it also made things hard to get on top of sometimes.

Whilst Noah expertly reversed the quad, Jude helped guide the trailer so it lined up perfectly with the door to the stable. She unclipped the back of the trailer and allowed it to drop down onto the concrete floor, creating a ramp. There was a lot of flapping and quacking as the ducks were released from their crates and ran down into their new home. There was a nervous moment when Noah had to remove the trailer, and therefore the barrier between the ducks and their freedom, but thanks to some very fine flapping of her own, Jude ensured there weren't any escapees. With the exit clear, she stepped outside and was very happy to close the bottom half of the stable door, knowing that they were safe.

The bang of the bird scarer went off and Jude sighed when she checked her watch. 'That is definitely more than every three hours,' she said. 'The timer must be out again.'

'I'll check it when I've got a moment,' said Noah. 'But nothing else is happening today until I've sorted this run out.'

Noah set to work with the roll of chicken wire and Jude loaded the remainder of the stable's contents into the trailer, making sure the paddock was clear of debris before climbing onto the quad and picking up the helmet.

'You'd better give Lucy a ring,' she said. 'Make sure she keeps Sebbie away from the paddock until Sunday. You wouldn't want to ruin his birthday surprise.'

Noah saluted and Jude turned the quad round and headed for the top of the field. The bags of hen grit were at the front of the trailer so it made sense to head to the orchard first to drop them off in the hens' shed. Jude turned down the driveway and passed the red brick wall that separated the farm's severely neglected kitchen garden from the drive. It gave way to the hedge that ran alongside the main garden before she reached Noah's pink stone cottage which marked the point where, on the opposite side of the drive, the track began to lead down to the orchard.

Turning onto the rutted track that split the garden from the orchard, Jude drove carefully between the two ditches that flanked it on either side. The gate into the orchard was secured with a piece of baling twine as well as the latch in order to stop Gertie, the too-clever Golden Guernsey goat, from opening it and releasing not just herself and Pancake but all the free-range bantam hens who lived inside as well. Jude unhooked the twine and opened the gate, allowing herself just enough space to drive through before shutting it quickly behind her.

There was no sign of either Pancake or Gertie, though, which seemed unusual but Jude assumed they were munching grass on the other side of the orchard. She drove the quad very slowly across the grass, looking constantly at the ground around her to make sure she wasn't about to run over goat, sheep or chicken, until she reached the row of henhouses and parked by the storage shed at the end. Taking the key from the peg where it hung, she clicked the goat-proof padlock on the shed door open so she could get inside to dump the sacks. As she was shifting the last one into place, the air was suddenly and terrifyingly filled with a shrill shriek.

Jude abandoned her task and rushed out of the shed to find Seren standing by the tiny side gate that led straight onto the drive. The row of six wooden henhouses stood between Jude and the spot where Seren was staring down into the grass with a look of horror on her face. Her heart quickened and the sound of a low timpani drum in her ears made Jude freeze for a moment before she rushed over to find out just how awful the truth behind Seren's scream was.

As she got to the final henhouse and looked around the corner of the wooden hut, it became sickeningly clear that it was about as awful as it could be. Wishing it to be anything different was not going to change the fact that the thing in the grass that had caused a reaction of such magnitude in the usually quiet vet was a body. The thumping in Jude's ears increased until her entire head was consumed by it and, if Seren had spoken to her at that moment, Jude probably wouldn't have heard her. But she didn't need words to explain the horror in front of her.

Joe's body was lying awkwardly on the ground, his sky-blue Lacoste polo shirt decorated with the deathly stain of blood seeping from a single bullet hole that tunnelled deep down into the cavity of his chest. The skin on his face was loose and pale and his eyes stared at a perfectly cloudless sky above, which he would never see again.

10

Before Jude had a chance to pull out her phone and call the police, there was a shout from the gate. Jude turned to see a man pushing it open. Then he started to walk towards them.

'Everything okay? I heard a scream.'

Jude recognised him as Noah's friend Nick from Nib's Cabs. A friendly man she'd shared a table with at The Lamb a couple of times when she and Noah had been down for an evening drink.

'Holy shit!' he exclaimed as he reached them. 'Has he been shot?'

Jude nodded and stepped away from the body to make the dreadful, necessary phone call. As she waited for the call to connect, she listened to Seren's breathless monologue as Nick guided her over to a fallen tree trunk that had been carved into a bench beneath the fruit trees.

'I only came in here to say goodbye to Jude. I was waiting on the drive and I saw her over the hedge – oh my God – I saw him lying there and—'

Jude moved further away so she could concentrate on giving her own shaky account over the phone, which would trigger a response team to come haring up the drive to Malvern Farm, bringing with it yet more tumult and plenty of questions.

The ambulance arrived first, blue lights making the trees flash with the sign of catastrophe even before Jude picked out the sound of the tyres chewing at the crumbling old tarmac of the driveway. Nick was standing by the gate ready to direct the two paramedics to their patient. They ran in, carrying life-saving equipment that would not be used as it took just seconds for first one and then the other to agree that Joe's last breath had already been expelled.

'What the hell's going on?' Noah appeared from the other side of the orchard.

'It's the groom,' Jude explained, attempting to keep her voice level but aware of a not insignificant wobble to it, nonetheless. 'Looks like someone shot him in the chest.'

'Bloody hell fire,' said Noah. 'Is he dead?'

Jude gave a tiny nod. She swallowed and ran her tongue around her teeth, trying to defy the dryness that had taken hold of her mouth and throat.

The police arrived then, two cars that added further intensity to the blue illuminations that flashed out across the orchard. Jude breathed in a great sigh of relief as Binnie strode purposefully through the gate, dressed in a smart dark-grey trouser suit and mustard-yellow blouse. Four uniformed officers accompanied her, Sami being one of them, with a grim look and an air of determination.

They stopped when they reached Joe's body and Jude saw Binnie having a quick conversation with the paramedics. Jude imagined it would be a while before the body could be removed to the mortuary.

'Are you okay?' Jude asked an ashen Seren, who was seated rigidly on the fallen tree. Her arms were wrapped around her still-shaking chest and she was staring at the worn denim of her jeans. She didn't look up but gave a small nod and Jude lightly patted her shoulder before leaving her with Nick and walking over with Noah to talk to Binnie.

'I want someone to locate all members of the hen party,' Binnie said to her officers. 'Jude, can we use one of the barns as a base for initial questioning?'

'The lambing shed's empty, you can set up in there,' said Noah. 'I'll show you where it is and you can tell me what you need.'

'Perfect, thank you. Roland, you can go with Noah. Paula, go too and Noah can point you towards the camp where you should be able to find the hen party. Sami and Jez, scan the area but keep away from the body and touch as little as you can,' Binnie directed her officers. 'We don't want to disturb anything until forensics have been through with a fine-tooth comb.'

The four officers scattered to do their various duties and Noah gave Jude a darkly ominous look that smacked of foreboding as he led two officers towards the yard. Jude's own temper matched Noah's look and a sickening weight embedded itself like gravel at the base of her stomach.

'Jude, what can you tell me?' Binnie was straight to the point and Jude knew from her experience that she would leave nothing unchecked. There was nobody better equipped to solve Joe's murder and Jude would help in any way she could.

She glanced back at Seren, now sitting with Nick's puffer jacket over her shoulders but still ghostly white, her legs trembling so much that Jude could see them shudder even from a distance. Seren had been so desperate to leave the hen party behind and return to the job she loved but this would now have to wait. She'd discovered a body – not just that, but the body of someone to whom she was directly connected and had reason to dislike, perhaps even despise. There was no doubt that Binnie would not be willing to let her go anywhere for the time being, especially as Khadija was still missing and Joe's violent death had just made her disappearance all the more concerning.

'I was in there.' Jude pointed back towards the shed where she'd been stacking the hen grit when she'd heard Seren's scream. 'I came in through the other gate so the first thing I knew about the body was when Seren shrieked loud enough to wake the hills themselves.'

'It was Seren who found the body?'

Jude nodded. 'Poor thing. She was nervous enough as it was. It'll take a long time for her to get over this.'

'Nervous? What do you mean by that?'

'You met her.' Jude puffed out a great sigh as the enormity of the situation started to take over, after the initial adrenaline kick. 'She's anxiety personified, it's why she makes such an easy prey for the stronger characters in the group.'

'Like who?'

Binnie was as economical with her words as Jude knew she would be when questioning any witness. Short, direct, nothing leading, just what she needed to get an initial scope of the situation and the players involved.

'Khadija and Joe,' said Jude, hating herself as she did so but knowing she had no alternative. Binnie would deal with the information sensitively and with her usual level-headedness but that didn't stop Jude from feeling as though she was throwing poor, timid Seren under the combine harvester. With one member of the party already lying dead beside the henhouses, it seemed somehow inevitable now that a second body was out there, yet to reveal itself. 'Binnie, there's something else—'

'Joe!'

The pained cry stopped Jude in her tracks and she looked across to see Shaznay stumble on a tussock as she ran to where the body of her fiancé was lying stiff and cold on the grass. Neesh was a couple of steps behind and reached her in time to hold her back from the horrifying sight.

'Shaz, don't look.' Neesh grabbed her sister by the wrists and held strong as she tried to break free. 'Sweetie, look at me. I said, look at me.'

Shaznay stopped trying to wriggle out of Neesh's grasp and Neesh moved in front of her, wordlessly lifting her chin to gain her attention. Shaznay stared into her eyes as though somehow she could be healed by the power of her sister's love and protection. And then, after just a moment or two, Jude could see her body submit as she slumped forward into Neesh's arms.

'Is he really dead?' she sobbed.

'I'm here, my darling girl.' Neesh wisely chose to ignore the question as she stroked the long, shiny curls that hung down Shaznay's back.

Binnie pulled Jude to one side, out of earshot of the hens.

'What do I need to know?' she asked.

'I heard a shot being fired at around three twenty.' Jude lowered her voice to match Binnie's. 'I thought the bird scarer's timer was out, so I checked my watch but now it looks as though it wasn't the bird scarer at all.'

'The amount of times that bloody thing goes off, I'd say we can assume that anyone else hearing the gun would have thought the same as you. But that's good, we have a clear time.'

'Mike Trout was here a couple of hours earlier.' Jude forced herself to stay factual and not let her anger cloud her account. 'I found him in the paddock. He said he was there to check on the sheep but I don't buy it.'

Binnie looked almost comical in her incredulity. 'I'd be inclined to agree. Do you have any idea what he was actually doing?'

'I think he could have been there to retrieve Khadija's jumper.'

Jude briefly laid out the details of the jumper and how she'd found it. She had no choice but to include Seren's attempt at re-hiding it but she also added the gist of the following conversation they'd had and her reason for not wanting the jumper to be found.

'And you believe her?' Binnie asked as Jude took her over to the quad where the jumper was folded in the dog box behind her seat.

'I've no reason not to.'

As she took the jumper out and handed it to Binnie, Jude caught Seren's eye and the wild look of terror in it would stay with her all evening.

* * *

Back in the farmhouse, Jude filled the old metal kettle and set it on the Aga plate. She took the brown melamine tray, swirled with a pattern of yellow and green flowers, that had belonged to her mother and put it on the counter. Then she went through the same ritual she had done a thousand times before, so ingrained that it needed very little of her attention. She opened the cupboard and took out an assortment of mugs collected from visiting reps over the years, with slogans advertising everything from crop sprays to lambs' feed. These were put on the tray along with a bottle of milk, threequarters full with the thumb-dented foil lid perched on top. Jude added a handful of teaspoons and a jam jar of sugar before throwing three teabags each into the three biggest teapots. Then she leant back on the rail of the Aga to wait for the kettle to boil. Throughout the process, her mind raced as it pieced together everything she knew, everything she thought she knew, and everything that was still a complete mystery.

Binnie was currently sitting in the lambing shed talking to the hens one by one and soon enough it would be Jude's turn to be formally interviewed. But what could she say? What did she actually know about what had happened on her land? She had her opinions and suspicions about each of the women staying in the campsite but were any of them capable of murder? It seemed so unlikely and yet there was a body lying in the orchard with a bullet wound in his chest.

The kitchen door burst open and Jude's musings came to an abrupt end as Sebbie rushed inside and threw his little nursery backpack on the floor.

'Aunty Judy, there are police cars in the drive,' he said with great excitement. 'Mummy said I'm not allowed to go in one but can I? Please?'

'Sebbie, I already said no.' Lucy bent to pick up the abandoned backpack and passed it to Sebbie. 'Now go and put that away properly, please, and then you can take some strawberry milk and a biscuit into the playroom.'

'But I wanted to see the police cars.'

'I'm not going to ask you again. You do as you're told or you'll only get plain milk and no biscuit.'

For a second it looked as though Sebbie had another round of objections in him, but he decided against it and took the bag with a scowl. Jude was impressed; perhaps the toddler tantrums they'd been living with recently were on their way out. Sebbie hung his bag on the low hook that Noah had attached to the wall of the porch.

'How long has the kettle been whistling?' Lucy took it off the heat and closed the Aga lid. 'I assume this amount of tea is for more than just the two of us?' she said as she poured boiling water onto the waiting teabags.

'Where are the dogs?' Sebbie asked.

'Oh, bugger it!' Jude had let them out into the garden for a quick loo break and had completely forgotten to let them back in again. Alfie's current habit of escaping into the orchard could be catastrophic, bearing in mind what was currently going on in there. She ran over to the back door and pulled it open. To Jude's great relief, a single whistle brought two black and white bundles flying round the side of the house. They bounded over to greet Sebbie, who giggled as Alfie pushed his wet nose into the crook of his arm and Pip waited patiently, her tail wagging furiously, knowing that Sebbie would soon turn his attention to her.

'Why don't you take them into the playroom with you whilst I get your snack ready?' Lucy's question was more of an instruction and Sebbie was only too keen to oblige.

'Come here, PipanAlf,' he called, the words running together and becoming one name, which the dogs recognised and responded to instantly with much enthusiasm. Like the Pied Piper, Sebbie walked out of the kitchen with a dog at each heel, both looking up adoringly at the child who was only a foot or so taller than they were.

As soon as they were out of earshot, Lucy turned to face Jude.

'Spill,' she demanded. 'I want to know everything.'

Where should she begin? She could pussyfoot around and lead up slowly to the horror of the circumstances that required a police presence once more on Malvern Farm, but that wouldn't soften the blow.

'There's a dead body by the henhouses, and it isn't Khadija's.'

It didn't take very long for Jude to tell Lucy all that she knew as there was so little to tell. Lucy listened in silence, her face getting paler and her eyes larger as she propped herself against the rail of the Aga. When Jude had finished talking, the kitchen remained silent except for the hum of the ancient Smeg fridge and the distant sounds of Sebbie as he chatted to the dogs in the playroom. Jude knew that Lucy would be going through all the emotions that she herself had earlier that afternoon. And with an unsolved murder on their doorstep, there was also the terrifying knowledge that someone capable of such an awful deed was almost certainly not too far away.

* * *

Jude took the tray of tea mugs outside whilst Lucy pulled sausages from the freezer to defrost and tried to make things at the farmhouse as normal for Sebbie as possible.

Roland, one of the uniformed officers, was standing by the closed door of the lambing shed and Jude offered him a mug.

'Thanks. That's very kind of you.' He added two spoons of sugar and a splash of milk which he stirred into the tea. 'I'm afraid I can't let you in there at the moment.' He indicated towards the shed. 'Boss is interviewing.'

The loaded tray was heavy in Jude's hands so she set it on the back of the quad that Noah must have retrieved from the orchard.

'I've made plenty for the hen party. Do you know where they all are?'

'My colleague, Paula Norris, is with them down at the campsite. They're being interviewed one at a time, you see.'

Jude's heart went out to them all. She knew what it felt like to be interviewed in connection with the murder of someone close to you and felt a wash of empathy for them all. She supposed it was police protocol to keep them under surveillance of sorts until the initial interviews had taken place. The chilling fact was that there was a high probability that one of them had pulled the trigger and that person would now be desperate to do whatever they could to avoid detection. But Binnie was incredibly good at her job and would be pulling apart every aspect of each of their accounts of where they'd been, what they'd heard or seen, and all the time she'd be looking for the underlayer of what was being held back or hidden from her.

'I'll leave this one here for Binnie.' Jude stirred a generous glug of milk into one of the mugs, just as she knew her friend preferred her tea, and put it down with a second mug for Sami, who was assisting the interviews. She picked up the tray, now a little lighter. 'I assume it's okay for me to take these down to the campsite?'

'I'm sure they'd all appreciate it. I know Paula wouldn't say no to a mug.'

The mood around the deadened, burnt-out remains of the camp's firepit was understandably sombre. Neesh and Dex sat side by side, his arm around her shoulders and her head resting on his chest. Ash was pacing up and down with her arms, clad in an oversized woollen cardigan, clasped tightly around her. Ellie and Seren each had one of the director's chairs. Ellie sat rigidly staring into the firepit and Jude could see that Seren's legs were still shaking as she hunched over. Officer Paula Norris was overseeing the party but there was no sign of Shaznay. Jude assumed this meant that she was currently in the lambing shed with Binnie, taking her turn to deliver her initial statement.

Not a word was spoken, although they all looked her way as she approached with the tea tray. Jude set it down on the picnic table.

'I thought you might like a cuppa,' she said. 'Should still be just about hot.'

'Thanks,' said Paula. 'That's kind of you.'

Jude felt awkward as she turned to the assembled group of distressed and worried friends. She knew that they would not just be thinking about the awfulness of Joe's violent death but also what that meant for Khadija. Not only that but the nature of the situation meant that they would also be watching each other carefully with a sense of doubt and suspicion, wondering which of them had been responsible.

'I just wanted to say how sorry I am.' Jude knew the words sounded hollow but she had begun and so gave a small cough before she carried on. 'You're all free to stay here as long as you need and if there's anything we can do to help then please shout. You know where I am.'

'What can you do?' Ash exploded. 'Can you find Khad? Can you tell us she's okay and bring her back?'

Ellie stood up and tried to put her hand on the distraught woman's shoulder but Ash shrugged it off roughly.

'No,' she said through teeth clenched tightly together in anger and worry. 'Don't touch me. We're all here pretending to be upset about a man who quite frankly was nothing more than a tosser who enjoyed screwing people over when what we should really be doing is trying even harder to find Khadija. What if she's been... I mean, if someone... It's—' She stopped trying to formulate sentences, voicing what they must all be thinking, and instead let out an animalistic cry of pain.

Ellie tried to comfort her again and this time Ash let her. She clung on to the other woman and allowed herself to let go of her emotions, sobbing into Ellie's hair. Jude caught Ellie's eye and the look said everything it needed to. Every single one of them understood that the chances of Khadija being found alive were now almost non-existent.

11

Binnie left Jude until last to interview but it was decided that they should remain in the lambing shed where Noah had thrown a cloth over an old table to hide the filthiness from years of iodine staining, spilt colostrum feed, tea mug rings and general grime.

Binnie stood up when Jude walked in and ushered her into a chair on one side of the table. Jude recognised it as one of the carvers from Noah's own cottage and she could see that Binnie was settling herself back down into the other whilst Sami sat in one taken from the farmhouse dining room. It was all so hotch-potched and incredibly surreal but Jude knew that they all had their parts to play and, in that moment, Jude was no different.

'Thank you for being so accommodating, I know how difficult this must be for you and everyone else here at the farm,' said Binnie. 'I have the initial notes that I took after I saw you at the crime scene earlier today but I still have some questions and wanted to give you the chance to tell us anything else that you think might be important, is that okay?'

'Of course. Fire away.'

'We're at a dead end when it comes to finding Joe's phone,' Binnie began. 'Did you see it when you were in the orchard earlier?'

Jude shook her head. 'No. I remember seeing him using it before, though, it's one of those fancy ones with a split screen.'

'That's right,' said Sami. 'We've had the same description from several of the others. We still haven't found Khadija's either, so that's two phones to keep your eyes open for now.'

'I'll tell Noah and Lucy to look out for them as well.'

'Thank you.' Binnie took a bottle of water from her bag and drank deeply from it. 'Sorry, it's been a long day and I've spent most of the afternoon talking.'

'I know.' Jude slumped back in her chair. 'The whole thing is a nightmare. Do we have much to go by?'

'The picture we currently have is that Joe was a rather egotistical man who wasn't particularly well-liked. Even his friend, Dex, didn't seem to think much of him, or at least he disapproved of the way Joe treated people.' Binnie took another swig of her water and replaced the cap. 'Interestingly, he told us that earlier today Joe had been bragging about the fact he was leading this double life. Engaged to one and planning on running away with another. He told Dex that he and Khadija had been making plans to disappear together for a while.'

'Did Dex tell Neesh?' Jude could imagine Neesh's response if she found out what Joe had been saying about her sister.

'No, he hadn't plucked up the courage yet. But he seemed to think that Joe was adamant that Khadija is still alive and would be phoning him very soon.'

Sami coughed back a chuckle. 'Dex also said that Joe is well known for his bullshit and that he didn't believe a word of it.'

Binnie gave him a firm stare. 'The point, Police Officer Abadi, is that whether he was making up stories or telling the truth, Joseph Birch clearly was not invested in the woman he was actually supposed to be marrying. Ellie and Neesh both made it clear that they didn't think he was good enough for Shaznay. We didn't get much out of Seren but Ash had plenty to say.' Binnie stopped to pull the book towards her and flick through Sami's notes. 'She called him a Machiavellian, twisted narcissist.'

'No mincing her words there.' Jude wasn't surprised given the way

Ash had reacted to the texts she had seen from him on Khadija's phone. 'Did you ask her about Khadija's parents?'

Binnie sighed. 'She said the same as you. When they found out about her relationship with Ash, they cut Khadija off completely. We've been trying to get hold of them since she went missing but they're on a world cruise and not keen to answer the messages we've left for them. I think it's time to get a little more demanding now.'

Jude had half wondered if they might've been involved somehow in Joe's death and Khadija's disappearance but if they were halfway around the world on a cruise ship then they had the best alibi of all. Unless... Someone else sprang to mind.

'Could they have hired someone to do their dirty work whilst they made sure they were well out of the picture? Perhaps the man who had Khadija so revved up by the shower block the other day?'

Binnie put her hand to her chin and let her face collapse into it. 'I can see why they'd have a reason to kill Khadija or even Ash, but not Joe.' She indicated Sami's notebook. 'Definitely worth making a note, though, and getting an urgent call out to the ship they're on. We need to talk to them.'

Jude was working her way through the other hens in her mind.

'How was Shaznay? I'm not sure if it's relevant but I think she intended to call off the wedding.'

Binnie looked at her sharply. 'Not one of the hens thought to mention this. Go on.'

Jude recalled what she'd heard in the campsite when Ash confronted Joe about the texts.

'The look Shaznay gave Joe didn't leave much room for forgiveness and I don't blame her in the slightest,' said Jude. 'I mean, what sort of man becomes engaged to one woman as a sort of backup plan whilst still trying to hook up with his ex?'

Sami tapped his front teeth with the end of his pen. 'Is there a possibility that Shaznay's anger spilt over enough to want to shoot him in the heart?' he asked.

'It's a possibility,' said Binnie.

'What about the sister, Neesh?' Jude leant forward, feeling as though the official interview had definitely morphed more into a brainstorming session now. This suited her as she wanted answers just as much as Binnie and Sami did; perhaps more so as her own life and livelihood were intrinsically tangled up in everything that was happening. 'Neesh was furious at the way Shaznay had been treated. You should have seen how she went for Joe when Ash told them about his texts to Khadija. It was like she wanted to throttle him. Not that he didn't deserve it, I'm sure I'd have been the same if it was Lucy.'

Yet again, Jude felt like a teller of tales but she was just sticking with facts and if one of the hens had killed Joe then they needed to look at each one objectively and with suspicion. Neesh clearly idolised her big sister; was it enough to want to give her the gift of freedom from his toxicity?

'It's possible,' said Binnie. 'She says she was in the shower around the time Joe was shot, which isn't a great alibi as nobody can really vouch for her. Dex was in their hut and concurs that she left for a shower with her towel and sponge bag, but it's not enough to stand up on its own.'

'So that means Dex was in his hut alone during that time?' said Jude.

'None of them have decent alibis,' said Sami. 'Dexter was in his hut, Shaznay was in hers, Tanisha was in the shower, Ellie had gone for a walk, Ash was resting in her tent and Seren was packing her bags.'

Jude thought of poor Seren, so desperate to go home and get away from them all. 'I assume she didn't leave as planned?'

'We've asked them all to stay on for the time being, which I know is a complete pain for you. Sorry.' Binnie grimaced at Jude. 'They could all go and stay in a B&B if that's easier? As long as we know where they are and they remain local.'

'No, it's fine,' said Jude in resignation. 'I've already cancelled the bookings for the weekend, and next week is clear anyway. Let's just hope it doesn't drag on for too long.'

'We'll do our very best.' Sami looked serious and Jude didn't think she'd ever seen him more so.

'We haven't got much to go on at the moment but there's a team working in the orchard and we'll search the campsite too.' Binnie stood up and stretched her spine out before leaning on the back of the chair. 'We just need to get a couple of strong leads and then we can start to eliminate people and get to the bottom of this but, until then, nobody is off the suspect list. We need to think of possible motives. So far we've got Shaznay, the rejected bride, Tanisha, the protective sister, Seren, the bullied mouse and Ash, who clearly hated him and blamed him for the break-up of her relationship. And possibly Khadija's parents, perhaps with the help of the man you saw at the campsite.'

'I don't think we can discount the possibility that Khadija killed Joe either.' Sami looked to Binnie as though asking for her permission to continue.

'Go on,' she said.

'We still don't know where Khadija is. I think it's possible that she set this entire thing up. If she wanted to get away with murder then what better alibi than to just disappear?'

Binnie nodded. 'You're absolutely right. The search for her continues and, if she's found alive, then she's going to have a heap of questions to answer.'

Jude's mind turned to Khadija. Literally the missing link in this whole thing. Sami was right, she could be the brain behind everything, but Jude thought it far more likely that she was a second victim. If she'd been planning to kill and then disappear into the ether, Malvern End was a terrible place to choose. You couldn't have an attack of the hiccoughs without everyone knowing about it. So where was she?

'Did you talk to Mike Trout?' Jude asked.

'He wasn't at home but we will definitely be following up tomorrow.' Binnie laced her fingers together thoughtfully. 'Earlier you seemed so sure that he was tangled up in all of this, but I can't work out why.'

Jude looked away and stared at the pile of flattened lambing pens stacked in one corner, trying to catch the right words to explain what made her so wary of her neighbour.

'Initially, I thought he was playing games to try and close the campsite,' she said. 'But then the yarn was found and now Joe has been shot which has to come with a much bigger motive. If it *is* Mike who's behind everything then I can't think for the life of me why he'd do it, but I don't trust him.' Jude paused to align the facts in her head before saying them aloud.

'He's lying, that I do know, but I don't know to what extent. Going on facts alone, his shed key went missing on the day the sheep were poisoned and turned up in the paddock the following morning. Rhododendrons were used in the sheep lick and I know he has a bush in his front garden. On the same night, Khadija's tent was deliberately collapsed and we now know that someone tied yarn to the zip to stop her escaping. Neesh and Tanisha saw Mike in the campsite around half an hour before this happened, and I found him snooping around the paddock again today with no proper explanation an hour or two before Joe was shot.'

'And that's where you found the jumper.' Sami was staring at her intently.

'Yes,' said Jude. 'What did you make of the jumper? Could it be a match for the yarn?'

Binnie nodded. 'It's been sent off for testing but visually it's an exact match.' She rubbed her eyes and rolled her head to release the tension in her neck. 'There's a lot to think about and, right now, I've reached overload. You know where I am if you need me, Jude. But I think it's time we left you in peace for the night.'

'It's a tough one,' said Sami, picking up both mugs from the table. 'But I reckon we'll figure it all out, one way or another.'

Jude held her hand out to relieve him of the mugs. 'I've no doubt we will.'

* * *

Noah was in the kitchen with Lucy when Jude walked in and kicked her boots off by the front door.

'I've moved Pancake and Gertie over to the paddock for now as there's a tent up over the crime scene in the orchard and I knew they'd get in the way.'

'Thanks, Noah.' Jude ran the kitchen tap until it began to feel warm and then she washed her hands thoroughly with plenty of soap. Farming was always a mucky job but some days just felt dirtier than others. 'What about the bantams? We can't possibly move all of them.'

'I've put them in their coops for now. Binnie reckons they can come out in the next couple of days or so. It won't do them any harm.'

Jude dried her hands on the towel and went over to the table where she sat down with a slight thud and hung her head, which was starting to feel a little too heavy.

'What a mess,' she said as she propped her elbow on the table and rested her forehead in her hand.

Jude felt Lucy's fingers rub the knotted patch between her shoulder blades and she heard the clink of a tea mug being set before her. For a moment, she sat where she was and concentrated on her breathing as a way of harnessing some sort of control over what had been a truly horrendous day. It was hard to find anything to cling on to that served to ground her when so many thoughts and half-thoughts were jostling for her attention.

'Did they find the gun?' Lucy asked. The deep concern in her voice pulled Jude's mind back to the kitchen. 'Or is it still out there somewhere, waiting for Sebbie to discover in a bush?'

Jude turned to face her sister, who looked every bit as washed out as she felt but with an added layer of terror that Jude hadn't considered. Whilst she'd been worrying about the fact that there was a murderer currently staying on the farm, she hadn't allowed herself to harbour any lasting thoughts about her family's immediate safety. Whoever had killed Joe, and possibly Khadija, had no arguments with the inhabitants of Malvern Farm, after all. They'd just been caught up in somebody else's drama which would pass as soon as the murder was solved and those involved had been removed from the farm. But Lucy was looking at things through the eyes of a mother and seeing the greater dangers and threats.

'As far as I know, it hasn't been recovered yet.' Jude pulled her sister into the chair next to hers and wrapped her hands round Lucy's clenched fist. 'Do you want to take Sebbie away until this is all over?'

Lucy's eyes were shiny with tears that pooled inside her bottom lids but didn't quite spill over. 'I can't. I've nowhere to go, for starters.'

'What about staying in a hotel for a little while?'

Lucy shook her head and a tiny tear escaped from the corner of her eye before trickling lazily down the side of her nose. 'That would cost money we need for other things.'

'It's money well spent if it'll give you peace of mind.' Noah came to stand behind her and rested a hand on each shoulder. Lucy reached up and laced her fingers with his.

'He'd hate being away from the farm, especially as it's his birthday on Sunday. He's been talking about it for months. I can't take that away from him because of my neuroses. Besides, if I wasn't here, I'd just be spending my time worrying about both of you instead. No, we'll stick together and see this out. We'll all just have to keep an extra-watchful eye on him.'

Jude gave what she hoped was a reassuring smile and Noah bent down and dropped a kiss on the top of Lucy's head. There were going to be more rocky times ahead of them – Jude knew there was no way of dodging that – but they'd weathered tough times before and there was definitely strength in being together.

12

Lying in bed at four in the morning, wide awake, Jude felt lonely. Lucy and Sebbie were both fast asleep in their rooms and she knew Noah was only a stone's throw away in his cottage but she craved something more. Even though he'd been gone for three years, she missed Adam's steady presence in her life and the understanding that she was half of a partnership. If he'd been there, she could've snuggled up to his warmth knowing that they could weather the storm together. It was partly because of Adam's memory and her loyalty to it that Jude had turned Marco down, but at that moment she knew that her husband would not have wanted this for her. A cold bed and a mind full of lonely worries. She knew he'd want her to get on with living and finding the support and happiness that she deserved.

Sleep was about as far away as it ever could be so she went downstairs and put the kettle on to boil. Nursing a cup of tea, she put the telly on low and whistled gently for Pip and Alfie to join her on the sofa. Wanting something easy to watch, she flicked through the different channels until she stumbled upon an old black and white film that was easy to follow and just about entertaining enough to keep her mind busy until the cloak of night began to lift and she could head out to tend the animals.

First stop was the paddock to check on the growing menagerie housed there. Pancake and Gertie had set up a home for two in the second stable where someone, Jude assumed either Noah or Spud, had laid out a carpet of straw. They were hunkered down tightly together whilst the four Kerry Hills stood at a respectful distance, chewing the first grass of the morning.

Jude went into the stable, exciting the sheep and goat just enough to raise their heads up and bleat a little in welcome, but not enough to give up their cosy huddle. If there was a bucket of food involved then Jude knew it would be a different story but she relished the peace and quiet as she crouched down and felt the warmth of the two animals' combined body heat.

'How did you find your first night in your new home?' she asked them.

Jude hadn't expected their move but it seemed to suit them and she wondered if it might become a more permanent arrangement. They'd both be a super addition to the petting farm, especially as they'd grown up surrounded by the love and attention of a small boy so were used to being handled – or manhandled – by little, enthusiastic hands.

There was a fair amount of chatter from the ducks as Jude let them out of their stable into the area that Noah and Spud had fenced off. Somebody had had the brilliant idea of bringing the old three-person canoe into the paddock to fill with water. It had been doing nothing but growing a thick layer of algae for the past fifteen years or so and it was great to see it repurposed as a handsome duck pond. The little troop of ducks looked most distinguished as they waddled out to take their morning dip in the old canoe. They formed a pretty orderly queue to clamber up the ramp which had been secured for them and followed one another into the water with a series of happy plops and much appreciative flapping.

'How are we going to keep you guys off Sebbie's radar until tomorrow?'

Jude had wondered about the logistics anyway but now that Pancake and Gertie had moved in next door, it was going to be that much harder.

Being a Saturday there was no nursery to keep him out of mischief's way so they'd just have to find other distractions.

Leaving the paddock animals happy, Jude made her way back to the top gate, led by Pip who stepped back to let Jude through, as she always did, but made sure she was just ahead of Alfie as they crossed the threshold. Everyone in their correct place, just as Pip liked it.

Jude knew that the hens needed tending to, even more so than usual as she wouldn't be able to let them out of the coops until the orchard was no longer an active crime scene. She didn't relish the thought of seeing the white tent up, a dreadful reminder of what had happened on the spot it covered. She assumed the body had been taken away as soon as the forensic team had finished their work, but it would take a while for Joe's blood to be reclaimed by the land below the tent.

Luckily for her, she met Noah outside his pink cottage.

'If you're heading in to sort them hens then you don't need to worry.' He pointed to a neat stack of egg boxes that were piled up by his porch. 'I've been in and given them their breakfast. Seems murder on their patch hasn't done anything to stop their laying. There are plenty of eggs for Roy's shop, Mrs James and a fair amount left over for the honesty box.'

Jude was very relieved to hear she had no need to go into the orchard.

'Hopefully, it won't be too long though before they can go out,' she said. 'It feels like they've only just been let out after that last bout of bloody bird flu.'

The birds loved being outside during the day where they could scratch at the ground and stretch their wings. It had been awful watching them pine when the restrictions had come in and all farm birds had to be kept inside to hinder the spread of the avian influenza that had torn many farms apart. The restrictions had only been lifted for a little over a month and now her poor birds were back inside again. Hopefully, though, it would only be for a few days this time.

'What are your plans today then, Jude?' Noah asked.

'I'll spray the oilseed rape this afternoon but I think I need to get away from the farm for a couple of hours, give myself a change of scene after everything that's happened around here.'

'Sounds like a good idea. Do you have anywhere in mind?'

Jude hadn't thought about it until that moment but the answer was yes – she did have somewhere in mind.

'I think I'll head over and see Granny Margot. I might even give Lucy a break and take Sebbie with me. Granny Margot always loves to see him and it'll keep him away from the paddock.'

'I was wondering how we'd keep that little tyke out of the way today,' said Noah.

'I'll only be gone for a couple of hours or so, though. You and Lucy will have to take shifts this afternoon.'

'That's a deal,' said Noah with a smile.

* * *

Jude stopped by the honesty box at the end of the drive and Sebbie helped to carefully stack the boxes of small but notoriously delicious bantam eggs in the custom-built shelter.

'Here, you take these empty boxes that people have left us and put them in this.' Jude passed him a shopping bag and Sebbie did his job with an earnest sense of doing it well. 'Perfect. Now look at this, there are plenty of pennies in here for us today.' Jude shook the money box, the heavy sound of coins clanging against each other and the sides of the metal container ringing out. 'I'd say there may be enough in there for some chocolate if you're a good boy with Granny Margot.'

The deal was set and, true to his solemn – chocolate-inspired – promise, Sebbie ran into the Perrins House Care Home as though he was bringing with him the sun, the stars and a rainbow for good measure.

'Hello, Gwen,' he said as Gerwain came out of the day room to meet them. Sebbie had never quite mastered the pronunciation of the carer's name, managing to change his gender in the process, but Gerwain didn't seem to mind in the slightest.

'Well, hello to you, Sebbie. Is that chocolate you've brought for me? How very kind.'

'No. It isn't for you.' Sebbie looked horrified. 'One's for me and one's for Granny Margot.'

'Oh, well, that is a shame. If you're going to be full of chocolate you probably won't want any cake that Jacinta has just been icing in the kitchen.'

Sebbie looked at the two bars of Tony's chocolate in his hands and then up at Gerwain, weighing up his options.

'If I give you a little bit of chocolate then can I have cake?'

Gerwain rubbed his chin thoughtfully. 'I think that sounds like a good deal. Or maybe there's a way of keeping all your chocolate and still having cake?'

Sebbie looked up at Jude, clearly a little uncertain about the rights and wrongs of this.

'As Sebbie's agent, you'd better run your scheme past me first,' Jude said, joining in with the serious discussion.

'I'm about to start a game of bingo and I need someone to pick out the number balls. Perhaps I can employ Sebbie for the wage of one slice of Victoria sponge cake.'

Sebbie's head was tick-tocking from one face to the other as the grown-ups decided the details of his contract.

'If you throw in a glass of squash for Sebbie and a cup of tea for me then we have a deal.'

Gerwain held his hand out and Jude gave it a formal shake.

'Now, you must shake Gerwain's hand too, Sebbie, just to show that you promise to be sensible and do what he says.'

'And I get cake?'

'You certainly do.' Gerwain's eyes sparkled with amusement but his mouth stayed in a serious line.

'And keep my chocolate?'

'Yes, but perhaps save it for a little bit later on so you don't feel sick.' Jude opened her bag up. 'Pop it in there for safekeeping.'

Sebbie dropped one of the chocolate bars into Jude's bag and held his hand out for Gerwain to shake.

'It's a pleasure doing business with you, young man,' said Gerwain. 'Now, let's go and find Margot because I'm sure she'll be very pleased to have a chat before we start the bingo.'

Granny Margot always lit up whenever Jude went to see her, but that was nothing to the joy that fizzed from her when she saw Sebbie. Although he wasn't a blood relation, Jude knew that the bond between them was every bit as strong as if they had been cut from the same cloth. They shared a lust for adventure and an inability to accept what was in front of them just because others did. It was wonderful to see them together and, as Sebbie climbed onto the bright red corduroy trousers that covered Granny Margot's legs, Jude felt a tingle of warmth in her chest.

'I got you chocolate,' Sebbie said, holding out the bar of Tony's Chocolonely as though it was the most precious gift in the world.

'Ooh, how lovely. Thank you, my darling. I think we should open it right now, don't you?' Granny Margot started to open the wrapper but Sebbie caught hold of her hand to stop her.

'No, Granny Margot. If you do that, we won't get cake.'

Granny Margot looked at Jude quizzically.

'He's right,' Jude concurred. 'He made a deal with Gerwain. Some of Jacinta's Victoria sponge with our elevenses but only if we save the chocolate for later on.'

Sebbie's head twisted round so he could look at Granny Margot. 'And I got to help Gwen do the numbers.'

'Do you mean the bingo numbers?' She rubbed his back as she talked to him. 'Well now, that's a very important job so I'm glad he's got you to lend a hand. And what about you?' Granny Margot looked at Jude. 'You look like you've got the weight of the world on your shoulders.'

'Nothing that a slice of cake and a good natter won't fix.'

Jude wondered if the news of the shooting in her orchard had made it through to the residents of Perrins House yet. It hadn't even been twenty-four hours but somehow, between the OAPs living in the care home, there was a pretty substantial network of grapevines that meant it wasn't unthinkable that news had reached Granny Margot before she had.

'Here we are. Jacinta with the tea trolley,' said Granny Margot with a quick glance at the old station clock that hung on the wall. 'Ten thirty, always bang on time.'

Sebbie was straight out of Granny Margot's lap, eager to check that

Jacinta had been told about the extra-big slice that was meant to be coming his way. Whilst he was out of earshot, Granny Margot leant across to Jude, who'd pulled up one of the brown plastic visitors' chairs to sit by her. She took both of Jude's hands in hers and Jude looked into her wise, kind face – more papery and pale than it had been when they'd first met but she still reminded Jude of a fairy godmother, full of sparkle and fun.

'Something's wrong,' Granny Margot said, still as bright and as sharp as a pin. 'Is it that woman? Have they found her?'

'Worse than that,' said Jude, before giving a very quick, potted account of what had been happening on the farm.

'Good heavens. Well, no wonder you've a look of the damned about you.'

Granny Margot let go of Jude's hands and reached around the side of her chair for the wheeled frame that was waiting for her. 'I think perhaps we'll leave our two favourite bingo callers to it and have our tea in the snug room.'

Jude looked towards the front of the room where Gerwain was showing Sebbie how the ball spinner worked, whilst the little boy sat on the floor next to him, his legs stuck straight out in front and an enormous piece of cake in his hands. Gerwain saw Jude and gave a double thumbs up to show that he would be fine with his young charge, whilst Jude took Granny Margot off for a chat.

The snug room was indeed very snug and cosy – it was also thankfully empty. A small fireplace still stood at one end, although Jude imagined it had been many years since a fire had danced on the hearth. The chairs in this room were similar to those in the day room, high enough to get out of easily and covered in a dark blue and pale green patterned fabric that looked tough enough to survive even the harshest of scrubbings.

'Right then,' said Granny Margot as she lowered herself into one of the chairs. 'I hope Jacinta saw us come in here. We'll need our tea and cake more than anyone if we're going to solve this murder.'

'I'll keep an ear open.' Jude smiled at her priorities and sat down in the chair next to her.

'So, what have we got? A man shot in the orchard. A woman missing, possibly also dead, and five people staying on your campsite who are linked to them both if I remember correctly from the stories Lucy has been telling me.'

'Six,' Jude corrected. 'The five other hens and Dex.'

'Of course, I forgot the feller. He came with the groom, didn't he? Married to the bride's sister?'

'Not married, no. But they have a little boy together and are in what looks like a very happy relationship. He's staying in Neesh's hut.'

'Neesh is the sister of Shaznay, who's the bride.' Granny Margot listed off the rest of the group, including the relationships between various members, with an impressive lack of further mistakes. 'Is there anyone else we need to be keeping our eye on?'

'There was a man snooping around the day before Khadija went missing.' Jude could picture his face clearly, revolting as it was. 'A really nasty sort and, looking back, I wonder if Khadija knew him.'

'An odd acquaintance.' Granny Margot tapped her fingers across her lips. 'He so foul and she so fair by all accounts.'

'Both pretty odious when it came to personality, though,' Jude pointed out. 'And then there's Mike Trout.'

'That old devil.' Granny Margot scowled. 'Lucy told me he's been playing tricks, but you think he might be linked to the murder?'

'I'm not sure. But he has got himself well and truly tangled up in everything and has more evidence stacked against him than anyone else. He was there when Khadija's tent collapsed, he was there just before Joe was shot and he was there when my sheep were poisoned.'

'Oh, those poor animals,' Granny cut in, her face crinkled in concern. 'How are they?'

'Completely well now. Thanks to one of the hens who was on hand with her well-stocked vet bag and experience with the symptoms of rhododendron poisoning.'

'Thank goodness for her. Now you were telling me about our Mr Trout.'

Jude laid out everything she knew and Granny Margot nodded along as the facts were lined up.

'All the evidence, as you say,' she said when Jude had finished. 'But no real motive for murder.'

'No,' said Jude. 'Although plenty of motive for the sheep and the tent.'

'Perhaps we should stop assuming that all things are linked. It is highly likely that Mike poisoned the sheep and I wouldn't put it past him to have collapsed the tent either. That all makes sense. But murder? That I'm not so sure about.'

Jude patted a rhythm with her hands against the thick fabric of the armchair and thought back to Binnie's discovery of the green yarn and realised that, although it felt like ages ago, it had only been the previous day. 'Yesterday the police found fibres of yarn caught up in the tent zip. It was used to tie the door closed.'

Granny Margot's eyebrows shot upwards into the wrinkles of her forehead. 'Well, that changes everything as I suppose we must make the sensible supposition that someone trapping an asthmatic under a thick canvas sheet and blocking their only means of escape would suggest they wanted Khadija dead.'

Jude nodded in agreement. There was nothing new coming to light but it was helpful to set the facts out in this way to create a bedrock of clarity to build on.

Granny Margot laced her fingers together and clutched her hands to her chest. 'It sounds like she would have been too, if she hadn't managed to find those scissors. I wonder why she didn't wake up sooner. Surely if someone was outside her tent pulling at the ropes and tying up her door then she'd have been screaming the place down for help, but it appears as though this woman needed the entire thing to collapse on her head before she woke up.'

Jude mulled this over. It was true, of course it was. And then she remembered something that Khadija had said when she'd been ordering Seren to go and collect her things from Ash's tent on the first night.

'She'd taken a sleeping tablet,' Jude said. 'They were prescription too, so strong. She made a big thing about needing them if she was going to have a chance of sleeping in a tent.'

'Who else would have known that?'

'All of the hens.' Jude could picture them around the barbecue on that first sunny evening, blissfully unaware of the chaos that was heading their way.

'That's very interesting,' said Granny Margot. 'Good thing she had her inhaler with her.'

'But an inhaler was found behind one of the compost toilets,' Jude said. 'I thought it might have been dropped there but it's possible that someone stole and hid what they considered to be her life-saving support without realising she kept a spare.'

Granny Margot nodded sagely. 'I think we must assume that someone wants her dead and that her extended absence is a horrible indication that they may have succeeded. That way if she turns up it's a wonderful surprise but we aren't losing any time waiting for it to happen.'

Jude breathed out a deep sigh of resignation, knowing that, bleak as it was, Granny Margot's hypothesis was the most obvious one. They sat in quiet contemplation for a little while, which was how Jacinta found them when she came in with two cups of too-milky tea and two slices of springy sponge cake oozing with jam and buttercream.

'I thought you wanted to chat,' she said as she set the tray down on the little table between the stony-faced friends.

'Sometimes the best chatting comes after we've all had time to think,' said Granny Margot. 'And cake is definitely good thinking food. Thank you, my dear.'

Jude added her thanks and Jacinta left them to it.

'It seems to me that Mike Trout was almost certainly there that night, wanting to create havoc on the farm,' Granny Margot said as she leant forward to drop a sugar lump into one of the cups. 'But I think we both agree that there's very little chance he's our murderer as there seems to be absolutely no motive for that.'

'Gah!' Jude exhaled loudly. 'It feels like we're going around in circles.'

'Not at all.' Granny Margot sipped her tea nonchalantly. 'We have figured out something quite important.'

Jude looked at her quizzically. 'What do you mean?'

'We've worked out that Mike Trout was up to no good in the campsite that night but the most logical theory is that he was not the only one. My guess is that he's denying everything because he knows that if he can be

categorically placed at the scene of the crime then he will automatically
be suspected of everything that happened that night. The things he did,
and the things he didn't.'

Jude felt a little fizz of something begin to form in her mind. If
Granny Margot was right and there had been two people out that night,
then that raised two questions.

Who was it? And what did Mike Trout see?

13

Jude dropped Sebbie back at the farm in time for his lunch but he was so tired after his morning escapades and so full after his cake and chocolate that he objected greatly when Lucy tried to get him to sit down for a sandwich.

'Come on, then.' Lucy recognised the signs and scooped him up so that his head rested on her shoulder as she carried him towards the back of the house. 'Nap time for you.'

'I'm not tired.' Sebbie's protestation was less than half-hearted and Jude thought he might actually fall asleep before Lucy managed to get him upstairs for an afternoon snooze.

As well as Sebbie's crustless cheese and cucumber sandwiches, there were two plates of heartier ones filled with salad and, when Jude opened the lid of one, she saw ham and brie as well. She moved them both over to the table and filled two glasses with water before sitting down to enjoy her lunch. Lucy joined her before she'd taken the first bite.

'That was quick,' said Jude. 'Is he asleep?'

'Before I even got to the top of the stairs.' Lucy pulled out the other chair and sat down. 'What on earth did you do to him?'

Jude grinned through a mouthful of sandwich. 'That would be Granny Margot, Gerwain and maybe a large slab of Jacinta's sponge cake.'

'That would do it.' Lucy shrugged and picked up her own sandwich. 'I assume you and Margot talked about what's been going on here. Did you come up with anything new?'

'Not really,' said Jude. 'Other than the fact that Mike Trout is probably not our killer and that someone else must have been out the night he poisoned the sheep.'

'We don't know that was definitely him,' Lucy pointed out, to which Jude raised an eyebrow. 'Fair enough. So who else was out there that night? One of the hens?'

'I've been going over it all again and again and yes, possibly one of the hens. We know they all had good reason to want to harm Khadija. Or perhaps it was that man I saw skulking about the campsite. Whoever it was, though, I reckon there's a good chance it's the same person who killed Joe, and maybe Khadija too.'

'I can't stop thinking about the gun,' Lucy said. 'Where did it come from?'

This was something that Jude had been asking herself a lot too. And, perhaps more worryingly for a place full of animals and a child, where was it now?

As was so often the case at Malvern Farm, Jude's contemplations were broken into by a knock at the door.

'Can we have a word?' asked Neesh, who was standing there, hand in hand with Dex.

'Of course.' Jude forced some civility into her voice, even though all she wanted to do was tell them to go away and come back later when she'd had the chance to finish her lunch and chat with her sister. 'Would you like to come inside?'

'No, you're okay.' Dex, looking a little uncomfortable, glanced over Jude's shoulder to where Lucy was still sitting. 'Actually, it might be better out here?'

Jude looked back towards Lucy and rolled her eyes before stepping out into the yard and closing the door. 'How can I help?'

'We just wondered if you had a number for that police friend of yours,' said Dex. 'She gave us her card but we can't find it anywhere and we didn't like to ask any of the others because... Well, you know.'

Neesh appeared to be jittery and she nudged Dex gently with the back of the hand that was still holding hers.

'Go on, Dex,' she said. 'Tell Jude what you told me.'

Dex looked awkward. 'I really think it might be better to wait for the police.'

Jude was very interested to know what this new piece of information was that Neesh was so keen to share, even though Dex was obviously reluctant.

'I don't think Binnie's on duty today so she probably won't answer her work phone but I can give her a ring on her personal one.' Jude pulled her phone from her pocket. 'I'm sure you understand that I can't pass on that number to you but I can ask her to give you a ring back.'

'Thank you, that would be really helpful.' Dex sat on the edge of the old stone cider press that stemmed back from the days when the farm's apples would have been thrown into the circular trough.

As Jude clicked on Binnie's number and waited for her to answer, she let herself imagine a carthorse dragging the huge stone wheel – currently sitting proudly in the centre of the press – around in circles across the apples, pressing the juice out ready to be turned into cider.

The dialling tone gave way to a robotic voice inviting the caller to leave a message.

'Hi, Binnie. It's Jude.' She shrugged an apology towards Dex. 'Can you please give me a ring when you have a moment, I've got Neesh and Dex here and they think they might have something of interest for you. Bye, then.'

'Thanks anyway for trying,' said Dex. 'Do you want to take my number to give her when she calls back?'

'Don't be an idiot,' said Neesh, whose jitters were clearly not keen to be contained, judging by the way she was unable to stand still. 'If you won't tell Jude then I will. On the day he was killed, Joe told Dex he thought Khadija was still alive and that she'd been wanting to make a break for a while.'

'Neesh!' Dex didn't appear to be pleased that his girlfriend was sharing things that he thought should be for the ears of the police first, and Jude wasn't going to let on that she already knew this particular piece of information because Binnie had told her when they'd been in the lambing shed discussing Joe's murder.

'What? I think Jude should know. This is her farm, isn't it? She's as wrapped up in all of this as any of us.'

'Fine,' Dex conceded. 'It's like Neesh said. Joe told me that he was hoping he could find her before she'd gone too far as he thought he would be the one to persuade her to come back.'

Jude was a little disappointed at this, having hoped for something more substantial. This was nothing more than an overinflated boast by a man who had a tendency to put himself on a pedestal and who was no longer around to confirm what he'd said and what it meant.

'To start with, Dex thought it was Joe's usual bullshit,' said Neesh. A sentiment that Jude could well understand. 'But then I just found this and it changes everything.' She held out a scrunched-up piece of paper which Jude took and smoothed out to read. Some of the words had been scribbled out, as though the writer had been drafting something and trying to perfect it, but Jude could read most of it.

I know what you've got yourself messed up in and I don't care. What you're doing doesn't change anything. I mean it Khad. I love you and I want you to know I'd still love you whatever you did. I even hired a private investigator to keep an eye on you

That line had been particularly harshly crossed out and Jude could see why. It was surely never a good idea to tell someone that you had hired a spy to keep an eye on them, even if it was in the name of love.

Jude stopped reading and looked up. 'Joe wrote this?'

'Yes,' Dex said. 'It's exactly the sort of thing he'd do, too. For all his bravado he was constantly worried about what people thought of him, like he had a fear of making a fool of himself. Whenever he knew he had to have an important conversation, he'd write it down beforehand so he could decide on the wording and practise the delivery. I saw him do it loads of times with his boss, his parents, even Shaz.'

This surprised Jude as the man she'd met had not come across as anything other than stupendously cocksure of himself. She carried on reading.

> *Shaz told me that you've been ~~desperate~~ trying to get some money together and I'm pretty sure I can guess why. You're going to leave, aren't you? You're worried that what you're doing is going to catch up with you and you want to get away. That's why you've been acting ~~like a mad woman~~ so ~~weird~~ oddly and why you've started to push me away. You still love me, I know you do.*
>
> *I've got a suggestion. Let me come with you. I've got ~~enough money~~ loads of money so we can go wherever you want. Scotland, Spain, South America. .*
>
> *I haven't been to the police ~~yet~~ and so you must see that shows that I'm the good guy here. You know you can trust me.*
>
> *I know you've got —— others involved.*

The name here had been so well scrubbed out that Jude couldn't decipher it, no matter how long she stared at it.

> *If you think anyone's going to be a problem then let me know and I can deal with them. ~~Or maybe we can   death and then nobody will ever   you~~. Whatever happens, you'll be safe with me and I reckon we could have ~~a pretty good life an amazing life~~ the best life together. What do you think?*

'Bloody hell,' said Jude when she'd finished reading.

'He's an arsehole, right?' Neesh was looking at her expectantly.

'Do you know what he's talking about? What was she involved in?' Jude asked. 'It must have been something pretty awful if he thought the police would be interested in it.'

'I've got no idea,' said Dex. He looked at Neesh but she shook her head as well.

'No, but you're right – it must be bad,' Neesh said. 'And look what he wrote here.'

She pointed to a line that had been scribbled over so that it was barely legible.

'Or maybe we can... something... death and then nobody will ever... something... for you?' Jude read it aloud and looked at Neesh. 'I can't read it.'

'I can.' Neesh put the torch of her phone on and held her hand out for Jude to give her back the paper. 'Look carefully.'

Jude watched as Neesh held the torch under the paper and the light shone through. Slowly the missing letters started to make themselves more visible as Jude's eyes adjusted to what she was looking at.

Or maybe we can fake your death and then nobody will ever come looking for you.

14

'Where did you find this?' Jude asked.

'It was in the bin in the loo block,' said Neesh. 'I haven't shown it to Shaznay yet and I'm kinda hoping she never has to know. She's been through enough.'

Jude could understand that but it wasn't her decision to make. What happened to the note and its content next would be down to the police.

'I can't make out the name that's been crossed out,' she said. 'Even with the torch underneath. Could you read it?'

'No,' said Neesh. 'I wish I could, though. I keep thinking about who else could have been involved in whatever she was up to. Don't you, Dex?'

Dex, who'd hardly said a word since handing the note over, shrugged. 'It could be anyone. Might not even be someone you know, Neesh.'

'But what if it is? What if it's someone else here? Cos it's making me wonder. If Joe knew something big that could get someone in trouble, then maybe that someone would want to keep him quiet.'

Jude had been thinking along the same lines. Was it even possible that Khadija herself had been willing to kill to stop the truth coming out? And then what? Disappear into the ether and set up a life elsewhere to try and outrun her sins just as Joe himself had suggested in the note he'd written?

'I think we should talk to all of them. I bet I could tell a mile off if any of them are lying.' Neesh had become very animated and Jude could almost feel the energy bouncing off her.

'This is all wrong.' Dex stood up and rubbed his hands across the back of his jeans to brush off the little bits of grit and lichen that the denim had picked up from the stone press. 'We either call the police and give them the note, which is what I said we should have done in the first place, or we wait for the detective to call Jude back.'

'You can do what you like.' Neesh was waving her finger in front of Dex's face. 'I'm not waiting, though. Something big has gone down between Khadija and Joe and someone here knows more than they're letting on. My sister is left bawling her eyes out in a hut because her fiancé wanted to run off with her bridesmaid and now Joe is dead and Khadija has disappeared off the face of the earth.' Jude saw tears begin to fall as Neesh's frustration overspilled. 'So excuse me if I want to find some answers so Shaz, and all of us actually, can move on with our lives. I just want to go home and see Reggie. I know it's only been a couple of days but it feels like weeks and I hate not being with my little boy.'

The speech was impassioned and Jude could see the ache Neesh was shouldering, recognising it as the same that she felt when big things happened in Lucy's life, causing her pain that Jude was unable to protect her from.

At that moment, Jude's phone rang.

'It's Binnie,' she said as she swiped to answer.

'Jude? What have you got?'

This was no-nonsense-work-mode Binnie and Jude was grateful for it.

'There's been a bit of a development. I know it's your weekend off but can you come to the farm?'

'Jude, you know there's no such thing as a proper weekend off for either of us. I'll be with you in fifteen minutes.'

Whilst Binnie drove from her home on the Worcestershire side of the hills to Malvern Farm on the Herefordshire side, Jude and Dex sat on the cider press to wait for her. Neesh was like a tightly wound-up clockwork toy, unable to sit still, and was pacing up and down across the gravel. Jude wondered about inviting them inside to wait for Binnie in the kitchen but decided that she wanted Sebbie as removed as possible from what was happening.

Dex remained silent the entire time, just staring at his hands or down at the ground. Neesh however hardly stopped talking, although it seemed to be mainly to herself as a way of processing what was happening. Jude took the opportunity to try and clarify the new facts in her own mind:

1. Khadija had got herself mixed up in something almost certainly bad enough to get her into trouble with the law.
2. Joe definitely knew about it.
3. At least one other person was also involved, possibly one of the hens.
4. Joe had either offered to run away with Khadija or was intending to do so. There was no way of knowing whether he'd found the opportunity to deliver the drafted monologue he'd prepared or not. Either way, she assumed that, as the suggestion to fake her own death had been crossed out enthusiastically, he had decided to leave this part out.
5. They now had a motive for Khadija to both kill Joe and want to disappear.

As soon as Binnie's car pulled into the yard, before Binnie had even switched off the engine, Neesh was beside her car pulling at the handle to try and get it open. There was a click as Binnie unlocked the door and then she stepped out into a torrent of information, supposition, theory and demands from Neesh.

'Woah!' Binnie held her hands up to stop the verbal tidal wave. 'One thing at a time. Let's strip this back to facts. There's some sort of note, I gather?'

Dex held out the crumpled piece of paper and there was silence, even from Neesh, as Binnie read and digested its contents.

Jude pointed to the final paragraph and the scribbled-out message it held. 'We've worked out that this part is suggesting they fake Khadija's death so that she can disappear.'

Binnie looked up with only the faintest hint of the interest that Jude knew this revelation would have caused.

'Do you have any other examples of Joe's handwriting?' she asked. 'It would be helpful to verify that this has definitely been written by him.'

'Who else would have written it?' Dex challenged.

'We just have to cover all angles. But for now, let's assume that these are Joe's words. Have you shown it to anyone else?'

'No,' said Dex. 'As soon as I read it, I showed Neesh and she said to come up and find Jude so we could call you.'

'Good.' Binnie took out a plastic evidence bag from her pocket and dropped the note inside. 'Do either of you know whose name might have been blanked out here?'

'No idea, I'm afraid,' said Dex. 'It really could be anyone.'

'And you don't know what Joe was talking about when he said he thought Khadija had got herself into a mess?'

Dex shook his head.

'I reckon you need to talk to Ash,' said Neesh. 'These past few years nobody was closer to Khadija than her. If she was up to something dodgy then I reckon there's a good chance Ash would have had an idea.'

'I've got an officer coming up,' said Binnie. 'As soon as they get here, we'll go and talk to everyone again. In the meantime, though, what can you tell me about the private investigator Joe says he hired? Did he share any details of this with you, Dexter?'

Jude had already wondered if this could be the explanation for the skinny man she'd seen in the campsite and she wondered if Binnie had made this connection too.

'I can't believe he actually did that.' Dex looked appalled at the thought. 'If he'd said anything to me about it, I'd have told him he was being a tosser.' His shoulders slumped and he sat back down on the cider press. 'I'm beginning to realise that I didn't know him at all, really.' He reached back and scratched his neck just below his hairline before glancing across at Neesh. 'I know she's hurting now but Shaz really is so much better off without him.'

Neesh wrapped her arms around herself and her face crumpled again.

'I just want to get out of here now and take Shaz with me. When do you think we can go home?' She looked at Binnie with eyes like a distraught bush baby. 'I need to go and see my boy.'

'You're under no obligation to stay,' said Binnie. 'However, it would be a huge help to keep everyone together for another couple of days if you can, just whilst we're still in the early, critical part of the enquiry, and we will need to know if you do decide to leave.'

'We'll stay on for a bit,' said Dex. 'Reggie's fine with my mum and Shaz needs you more than ever.'

Neesh looked deflated but nodded her agreement. 'Just another night or two. Then we're going, Shaz too. It's not good for her to be around here and I don't think she should be going back to her house with all those ghosts of Joe everywhere either.'

'I'll leave you to decide,' said Binnie. 'But as I say, keep me in the loop.'

Jude's phone rang again and she glanced at the screen, where she saw Val Trout's name illuminated. She stepped away from the others and put the heel of her hand against her free ear so she could concentrate on the phone call.

'Ah, Jude, hello,' said Val. 'I'm sorry to call as I know how much you have on your plate at the moment but I thought you should know there's a pretty insalubrious character sniffing around at the bottom of your camping field.'

Jude was instantly alert and indicated to Binnie to follow her as she set off across the yard. 'Is he there now?'

'I'm afraid so. He's parked his car across our drive, which will make Mike furious when he gets back from town, but I'm not sure I fancy the thought of asking him to move whilst I'm on my own. I wondered if there was someone at the farm who could come and give me a bit of moral support?'

'I'm on my way and I've got DI Khatri with me too. Why don't you stay inside and I'll give you a call back when he's gone.'

Jude and Binnie, along with Dex and Neesh, were walking fast and were already halfway across to the top end of the campsite.

'Thanks, Jude.' The relief in Val's voice was evident.

Jude ended the call and pushed her phone into the back pocket of her jeans.

'That was Val Trout.' Jude sped up to a jog as they approached the gate. 'She's seen a man snooping around at the bottom of the campsite.'

'Shaz!' Neesh puffed, clearly not quite as fit as the rest of them. 'She's still in her hut.'

'Where are the others?' Binnie asked as Jude unlatched the gate to let everyone through.

'I don't know,' said Neesh.

The camp was pretty quiet as they headed past the tents, straight towards the bottom end where Val had seen the trespasser.

'I need to check on Shaz,' Neesh panted as they approached the huts. 'Dex, stay with them, in case you're needed.'

Neesh ran over to her sister's hut and knocked on the door whilst the rest of the group stopped and looked around them for any sign of the man. Jude saw Shaz open the door of the hut and hug her sister before they both went inside but there was no sign of the stranger.

The sudden shock of a loud yelp from beyond the cars parked at the very bottom of the field made Jude's heart quicken. It was the sound of a human in danger and had the effect of igniting speed in those close enough to hear it. Jude started to run, aware that Binnie and Dex were doing the same. She couldn't see anyone there at first, and then suddenly, the ponytailed head of a man appeared from behind Khadija's 4x4.

'It's him,' said Jude, recognising him instantly. 'The guy who was snooping round before.'

He turned and saw them, his face every bit as rough and nasty as Jude remembered, and then he started to run.

'Stop!' Binnie shouted. 'I'm a police detective and you are required by law to stop.'

It wasn't a surprise to anyone that the man chose to ignore Binnie's instruction. He sprinted on spindly legs out of the gate and disappeared round the corner a fair way ahead of his pursuers. Jude heard a car door slam and then an engine roared into life but by the time they'd reached the lane, the car had sped away and the tall hedgerow blocked any view they might have had of it.

'Bugger it,' said Binnie.

Jude, though, had already turned back around to see who'd made the yelp and saw Ellie sitting next to the 4x4, gingerly pressing her fingers against the skin around her left eye.

Jude rushed over, reaching her at the same time as Dex.

'What happened?' she asked Ellie, whose eye socket was beginning to puff up, already the colour of a Valentine's rose.

'He just went for me.' Ellie's voice was as shaky as her hands.

'Dex, there should be ice in the little freezer part of the fridges in the huts,' said Jude. 'Could you go and wrap some in a tea towel or something for Ellie?'

'Sure.' Dex got up and ran over to the hut where Neesh and Shaznay were.

Jude was aware of Binnie standing by her shoulder, her phone pressed to her ear.

'It's DI Khatri. Get cars out in the Malvern End area immediately. We need to locate a vehicle speeding from the village towards the Hereford–Worcester road. Difficult to get good eyes on the vehicle but it's a dark blue or black hatchback, licence plate beginning RC. Possible ambulance also needed...' She looked at Ellie, who shook her head. 'Forget that. No ambulance required.'

When the call had ended, Binnie crouched down next to Jude and Ellie, who was making no sign of wanting to stand up just yet.

'Do you know who that man was?' Binnie asked.

'No. He was asking questions about Joe and Khadija, so I thought maybe a journalist?' Ellie winced as she tried to close her swollen eye. 'I told him he shouldn't be here but he just started swearing at me. I tried to stand my ground... I mean, having someone like that around is the last thing any of us need... and then he clouted me. I think he was going to have another go too if you hadn't arrived when you did.'

At that moment, the door of the shepherd's hut burst open and Dex, Neesh and Shaznay rushed out. They ran over and Shaznay, brandishing something that Jude realised was a tea towel filled with ice, dropped to her knees.

'Oh my God, Ellie!' Shaznay held out the ice pack for Ellie to take. 'What the hell happened?'

Jude stood up to give the friends some space and felt the buzz of her phone in the back pocket of her jeans. She took it out and saw that a message had arrived from Val Trout. Opening it, Jude could see that it contained no text, just a single photo that was frustratingly refusing to download, just a shadowy image with a swirl over the top, so she put it back in her pocket.

'I have to say that I don't fancy sleeping in a tent tonight after that.' Ellie leant on one hand so she could push herself up off the grass, supported on one side by Shaznay with Neesh on the other.

'I don't blame you,' said Jude as they walked steadily towards the cluster of chairs outside the closest hut. 'Would you like me to get you all booked into Four Trees? It's a B&B in the village.'

'Thanks,' said Ellie. 'You don't get all that much protection from a tent if someone comes snooping around.'

'Dex and I are fine in our hut,' said Neesh as she helped Ellie into a chair, 'so don't worry about us.'

'I'll be okay too,' Shaznay added. 'But you're right about the tents, Ellie. I for one would feel happier if Seren and Ash went with you.'

Jude tried hard not to let the little selfish streak that had hoped all the hens would go so that she could start claiming her campsite back take over.

'I'll get that sorted for you,' she said.

The sound of a car pulling off the lane into the car park made them all turn to see a marked police car arriving. Sami got out and raised a hand in greeting as he started to make his way over to them.

'Do you know where Seren and Ashleigh are?' Binnie asked the other hens. 'We'll need to talk to all of you about what's just happened.'

'I'm not sure.' Ellie looked at Shaznay and Neesh, who both shrugged. 'I assume they're in their tents.'

'Afternoon.' Sami met everyone with a cheery smile. 'Blimey, that's a corker.' He pointed at Ellie's eye as she took the ice pack away for a moment.

'Police Officer Abadi,' Binnie cut in with a warning tone, 'if you could please fetch Seren and Ashleigh from their tents and ask them to join us?'

'Right you are.' Sami looked around the campsite and Jude pointed him towards Ash's tent. 'Thanks, Jude.'

Whilst Sami wandered off to find the missing hens, Jude phoned Paddy at Four Trees B&B to book rooms for the hens.

'All sorted.' She turned to Ellie when the booking had been made. 'She's got three rooms for you and is expecting you whenever you're ready.'

'Thanks,' said Ellie. 'I'm so sorry for all the trouble we're causing you.'

'Goodness, don't worry about me,' said Jude.

Sami came back to the group then, shaking his head. 'No sign of either of them in the tents. Can you think of where else they might be?'

The sound of the metal gate slamming shut pulled everyone's attention to the top of the field, where Ash and Seren had just come in and were walking down to the rest of the group.

When Ash saw Binnie and Sami, she broke away from Seren and ran across the grass.

'Have you got any news on Khad?' The worry etched on her face was palpable and Jude's heart went out to her.

'I'm afraid not,' said Binnie.

Ash turned to look at her friends and caught sight of Ellie's still-swelling eye.

'Ellie, what the hell?'

Ellie reached her hand up to test the swollen flesh around her eye. 'Some creep came round trying to get the lowdown on Khad and Joe.'

Ash's eyes flashed in anger. 'What did you tell them?'

'Nothing. God, Ash. Calm down. Of course I wouldn't give some journo the time of day.' She pointed at her eye. 'That's why he got so mad.'

'Sorry,' said Ash. 'I'm not thinking straight at the moment, I just want to find her and it feels like she's getting further and further away.'

'That's what we want too,' said Binnie, calmly. 'Which is why I have a few more questions for all of you, if you'd care to take a seat.'

Whilst the hens sat down, Jude turned to Binnie. 'I'll head back to the house if that's okay?'

'Thanks, Jude.' Binnie put her hand on Jude's arm. 'I'll pop in before I head off.'

As she walked away from the little group about to be questioned by Binnie, Jude wondered what Binnie might uncover. She knew that Binnie would let her know if there was anything worth noting but she'd still have liked to have stayed and listened for herself.

She took her phone out and checked the message Val Trout had sent to see if the photo had downloaded properly yet.

It had, and Jude gave a little fist pump when she saw it.

'Val, you star,' she said aloud as she turned round and went back to show Binnie the clear photo Val had captured of a dark blue hatchback with the entire number plate clearly visible.

15

Back in the farmhouse kitchen, Jude found a note on the table.

We gave up waiting for you – gone into town to play on the swings.
Love you. L & S xxx

'Looks like it's just the three of us, then,' she said to Pip and Alfie, who had got out of their beds to offer her an enthusiastic welcome home.

Jude crouched down to give them the attention they deserved in return for such a show of affection. There was nothing quite like the unconditional love of a dog and Jude felt her shoulders lose some of their tension as she wrapped an arm around each of the black and white bundles with their tail-ends wagging frantically and their head-ends burying themselves in the crooks of her elbows.

After a moment or two, she stood up and gave them one last tickle behind the ears. It was nice to have a little respite from the chaotic day and Jude put the kettle on to boil. Her stomach gave a loud grumble so she fetched the battered old biscuit tin and took out three chocolate Hobnobs, one of which she took a huge bite of before putting the rest down on the table. With her mouth full of chocolate and oats, she took the milk bottle from the fridge and nudged the door shut with her shoulder before turning her attention to the kettle whistling on the Aga.

Carrying a big mug of tea, Jude went back to the table where she found both dogs, ears pricked and eyes trained on the Hobnobs.

'These are definitely not for you.' She chuckled as she sat down. 'Into your beds.'

The dog beds were in the warmest corner of the kitchen between the Aga and the utility room and, although Pip and Alfie went over and climbed in obediently, Jude could feel their close scrutiny with every bite of biscuit she took. It wasn't until Jude's plate was in the dishwasher that Pip and Alfie settled down. With the sneakiness of a ninja, Alfie crept across the side of his bed and into Pip's where he snuggled up to her and settled down for an afternoon nap. Pip opened her eyes but made no objection and Jude's heart filled up at the sight of them joined together like two halves of a yin-yang symbol.

Jude checked the kitchen clock. It was already nudging four in the afternoon – most of the day had disappeared and tomorrow was Sebbie's birthday. Somehow they'd have to try and forget the awfulness of the current situation and celebrate little Sebbie who, in Jude's eyes at least, deserved the very best of everything they could offer. A birthday party had been planned and – thanks to the chaos on the farm – cancelled. Instead, Lucy had arranged a special birthday tea with his family, including Noah and Binnie.

Jude pulled out the birthday card she'd hidden in the kitchen dresser and unpeeled the price label. On the front was a huge number four made from hay bales surrounded by a menagerie of farm animals. The first pen she picked up left nothing but an indent on the card. She scribbled on the back of an envelope but it didn't help release the ink, so she tried another.

Once the card was written, she turned her attention to wrapping his present. He'd become obsessed with rugby after watching the Six Nations that spring so she'd bought him his own England shirt with his name and the number four printed on the back.

'Bugger,' she said when she went to fetch some wrapping paper and found only a roll of Christmas paper covered in snowmen, and an empty brown tube. Oh, well. Sebbie loved snowmen and he wouldn't give a jot what his present was wrapped in, so she took the roll back to the table where the rugby shirt was waiting.

She'd just wrapped it and was squirrelling it away out of sight in the utility room when Binnie arrived.

Jude let her in and put the kettle on to refresh the teapot.

'Are you finished down at the campsite?'

'For now,' said Binnie. 'Sami's gone back to the station to write it all up but I thought I'd call in for a catch-up before I go home. Thanks for forwarding that photo to me.'

Jude fetched her own mug from the table and put it next to the clean one she'd got out for Binnie. 'That should give us a good lead, right?'

Binnie screwed up her nose. 'I ran the licence plate through the system but it isn't registered, or at least not any longer. It belonged to a beige Volvo estate that was taken off the road a year ago.'

'What?' Jude couldn't hide the frustration in her voice. 'How can that happen?'

'It's a trick people use when they want to drive around undetected. He'll have a bank of plates taken from a junkyard somewhere. If he hasn't swapped the one in the photo for another by now then I reckon he will have by the end of the day, which makes him pretty much untraceable.'

'Damn it.' Jude scratched at the back of her neck. 'Do you think he's the private investigator Joe hired?'

'I'm not sure.' Binnie took the mug Jude offered her and they both went to sit at the table. 'If he is, then what's he doing back here now that Joe's dead and Khadija's missing?'

'He's been here at least twice now so, whoever he is, he's obviously after something.' Jude felt a chill run through her despite the warm mug she was gripping. 'Which means, if he hasn't already got it, he might come back to have another go.'

'If he does then you don't need me to tell you to call it through as an urgent 999. We need to speak to him immediately and not just about the assault on Ellie. He's clearly wrapped up in all of this somehow.'

Jude couldn't have agreed more. Violent strangers didn't just arrive on the doorstep at the same time as people were murdered without the two being connected. She turned her attention back to the original reason for Binnie's latest visit to the farm.

'What did the hens have to say when you asked them about Joe's note? Did any of them know what he was talking about?'

'No. Ashleigh thinks Joe is delusional. She was adamant that if Khadija was mixed up in anything that might have given Joe cause to involve the police, she'd have known about it.'

'I'd say Joe was definitely delusional and unreliable about many things,' said Jude, 'but I still think there has to be something in his accusations. He clearly thought she had reason to be afraid of the police, enough of a reason to suggest running away from everything.'

'My thoughts exactly, which means either Ashleigh really doesn't know Khadija as well as she thinks she does...'

'Or she is lying to protect her,' Jude finished. 'She's still the only person who seems to believe that Khadija is still alive somewhere. I assumed it was a case of denial but suppose she has a valid reason to think she could have run away.'

'Maybe.' Binnie blew across her tea and took a sip. 'There's something else you might find interesting. I did a DNA test on the inhaler that was found behind the toilet and it's a match with the hair sample we took from Khadija's brush.'

'We know it was definitely hers, then,' said Jude. 'What we don't know is whether it was dropped by her or hidden there by someone else.'

'And did she have a backup or was she without her medication when she went missing?'

Jude mulled over Binnie's words and their implication for a moment. One of her closest friends at university, Helen, had been asthmatic and Jude had witnessed the way she guarded her inhaler, knowing that it might be the difference between her getting oxygen into her system or not in the event of a bad attack. Khadija had been the same and Jude felt sure that she'd have taken better care of her inhalers, and certainly gone nowhere without one.

And then another thought occurred to Jude.

'She didn't like using the compost loos anyway,' she said to Binnie. 'I heard her complaining and Shaznay saying she could use the one in her hut instead.'

'That doesn't mean she was never in the compost toilets,' Binnie reasoned. 'She may have been caught short when Shaznay was out or using the bathroom herself.'

Jude knew this was true but it all seemed like snatches of could-bes and maybes. The idea that Khadija may have killed Joe and made herself disappear suddenly seemed as unlikely now as it had felt plausible just a few minutes before. There was no doubt that someone wished her harm, collapsing her tent and possibly taking her life-saving medication. Unless...

'What if Khadija was never in any harm?'

'Go on?' said Binnie but before Jude had a chance to expand, the door crashed open and an excited bundle of an almost-four-year-old hurtled inside, bringing with him a whirlwind of excitement that caught up both dogs and sent all three of them skittering around the flagstones on the kitchen floor.

'It's my birthday tomorrow,' Sebbie shouted as he flew around the kitchen with his arms stretched out like the wings of one of the hang-gliders that took off from the crest of the hills in good weather.

'It is indeed.' Lucy joined them with her arms full of bags. 'But if you want any of these special treats you've chosen for your birthday lunch then you need to settle down now and go and have a wee before we get supper ready.'

'Okay, okay, okay.' Making a sound that was far more tractor than hang-glider, Sebbie whizzed out of the kitchen towards the downstairs loo.

'Someone's excited,' said Binnie with a smile.

'We just popped to the supermarket to pick up some bits and I may have gone a bit overboard.' Lucy dumped the bags on the kitchen table and Jude could see a colourful assortment of wrappers poking out from the top.

'You do know it's just the five of us, don't you? And I'm not sure how many party rings Noah will get through.'

'I know.' Lucy's voice was resigned and Jude imagined her traipsing around the aisles with a trolley, succumbing to every demand from her young son. 'I just feel really bad for him. Last year he hadn't started nursery and his birthday was just us so I know he was really looking forward to a party with his friends this time. I suppose I figured that by getting all of this junk it would make up for it somehow.'

'We'll make sure he has an amazing day, whatever else happens.' Jude squeezed her sister into a hug. 'I'm done for the day so I can help get everything ready and make it really special.'

Lucy looked a little appeased. 'And you'll be here tomorrow too?' she asked Binnie.

'Wouldn't miss it for the world,' said Binnie.

'Mum, help me!' Sebbie yelled from the loo and Lucy rolled her eyes before going to see what the problem was.

Binnie picked up her empty mug and loaded it into the dishwasher. 'What were you going to say?' she asked. 'Just before the whirling dervish arrived.'

Jude put the milk back in the fridge and felt her overloaded mind go blank.

'You suggested that perhaps Khadija was never in any harm,' Binnie prompted.

'Oh, yes. It was only that I wondered if Khadija might have planted the inhaler herself knowing that it would eventually be found. It might be another way of making it look as though someone wanted to hurt her.' Jude rubbed her aching eyes. 'It seems as though we answer one question only to throw ourselves another few. There's so much to work out and we seem a long way off untangling any of it.'

'We'll get there.' Binnie sounded so sure that Jude believed her completely. They *would* get to the bottom of it, that seemed highly probable, but would they get there before anyone else was harmed?

Binnie's phone beeped and she looked at the screen. Jude watched as her eyes grew round with interest and then she looked up.

'We've had a ballistics report back on the bullet that was used to kill Joe,' she said. 'It's from a .32 single-shot revolver.'

'You make that sound interesting.' Jude couldn't understand what it was she was supposed to be taking from this piece of information.

'It's the kind of gun used in veterinary practice for euthanising large animals such as bulls or horses.'

'Holy cow,' said Jude.

'Exactly,' said Binnie. 'Do you happen to know if any of the vets brought such a gun with them?'

Jude looked at her friend reproachfully. 'Seriously, Binnie – do you not think I'd have mentioned to you if I'd seen anything like that?'

'I had to ask.'

'No. I haven't seen any of them with a gun. Ellie came straight from work so she had her vet's bag with her, but I assume she can't just have a gun thrown in with the bandages and anti-inflammatories. Aren't these things heavily regulated?'

'There are laws about the correct storage of guns and ammunition, yes, but in theory, any one of the vets could have got hold of a euthanasia revolver and brought it with them. That would of course suggest pre-meditation and yet, from what I can tell, Joe's arrival on the farm was a bit of a surprise to everyone.'

Jude digested this information, another signpost to one of the vets being up to their eyeballs in trouble. 'So, we're looking predominantly at Seren, Ellie and Shaznay?'

'Perhaps, but I'm not discounting Ashleigh, Tanisha and Dexter as well. Just because they aren't vets doesn't mean they aren't involved. They have connections with enough vets to remain in the frame.'

Jude knew that this was true. When it came to murder, nobody should be kept below the radar.

16

Jude was awakened by the sound of scrabbling by her bedroom door.

She sat up, immediately alert. There was silence and then a tapping sound, followed by the door inching open slowly. Her initial instinct was to wonder if one of the dogs was paying her a visit.

'Aunty Judy?'

So not the dogs, then. Jude looked at the winking red numbers of her alarm clock.

'Sebbie, it's very early, my darling.' That was an understatement even on the scale of her farming body clock. Three in the morning was no time to be awake. 'Are you okay?'

The door opened fully and Sebbie wandered in, clad in his favourite pyjamas, covered in little pictures of border collies, and clutching his beloved teddy by the arm. The whites of his eyes stood out in the dim light and Jude could see that his hair was still tousled from sleep.

'It's my birthday, Aunty Judy,' he said in earnest, as though this gave him a free pass to wander around at whatever time of night he felt like.

Jude's heart melted and she called him in.

'It's not your birth-*day* just yet so you must wait to wake Mummy up for your presents, but we could call it your birth-*night* instead.'

Sebbie looked as though he might be able to get on board with this idea as he climbed under the covers of Jude's bed.

'What happens on my birth-night?' he asked.

'You get to snuggle down with Teddy in my lovely squishy bed and I will tell you a story.'

'Do I have to go back to bed when you finish the story?'

'Let's see, shall we?' Jude fully intended on relaxing him to the point of sleep so that he would be malleable enough to scoop up and pop back into bed as quickly as possible. She needed a little more sleep herself in preparation for the day ahead.

'What would you like in your story?'

'Can it be about Pip and Alfie?'

'Of course it can.'

'And Pancake and Gertie and all the sheep and chickens too?'

Jude thought for a moment. 'How about I tell you about the day they all went for a ride in an aeroplane?'

As Jude spun a tale about the animals of Malvern Farm flying over to join the bears, bison and squirrels of Yellowstone National Park, she felt her own eyes get heavy and then close. She woke up a moment or so later still voicing whatever absolute nonsense her subconscious had conjured up. Sebbie was fast asleep next to her and she smiled as she slid down so that her head was back on the pillow, then she closed her eyes and didn't wake again until she could feel Sebbie bouncing on her bed.

'It's daytime now.' He clapped when he saw that she was awake. 'It's my birthday-day-day and I am four.'

It was still only just past five but as the sun was up and Sebbie had gifted her with another couple of hours' sleep, Jude didn't feel like she could argue with him this time. She caught him up in a big bear hug and bundled him onto the duvet in a giggling heap.

'Happy birthday, you lovely thing. Now run on in to see Mummy. She'll want to say happy birthday to you and then we can see if there are any presents.'

Sebbie rolled across the mattress and dangled his legs over the side of the bed until they touched the floor. Then he was off and Jude could hear his feet slapping the floorboards as he ran into Lucy's bedroom.

Jude was a little slower to get up and she pulled her dressing gown on before retrieving the present and the card from the wardrobe where she'd hidden them the night before. A hearty but slightly out-of-tune rendition of 'Happy Birthday' met her as she went into Lucy's room and found her sitting up in bed with Sebbie next to her. Jude soaked the scene in as a reminder that there was so much in her life that made it all worthwhile.

'Morning, Lou Lou,' she said, dropping a kiss on her sister's head. 'I have a present for you.' She winked at Lucy as she passed her the parcel wrapped in Christmas paper. Sebbie intercepted it quickly but Lucy was faster and held it up over her head.

'No, it's *my* birthday, not yours.' Sebbie sat back indignantly.

'In that case, this must be for you.' Lucy passed him the parcel covered in snowmen. 'And if you look under my bed you might find one or two from me there as well.'

Sebbie dropped Jude's present on the duvet and slid off the bed to investigate what was underneath. The rugby ball Lucy had bought him went down a storm until he threw it across the room and it knocked over a lamp that was standing in the corner.

'I think we'll wait until we can take that one outside, don't you?' Jude suggested. 'See what else you've got.'

Lucy had bought a mini electronic keyboard which was perfect for his little fingers but not quite as perfect for the ears of the grown-ups in his life, especially at that time of the morning.

'Here,' said Jude, passing over her gift to distract Sebbie from the keyboard long enough for Lucy to find the *off* button. Sebbie ripped off the paper and squealed with pleasure as he shook out the England rugby shirt.

Never mind that it had been bought in the end-of-season sale and would already be out of date by the next time his team played, or that white wasn't the best colour for romping around on the farm; that was what the washing machine was for. Sebbie clearly loved it and was busy jamming it on over his pyjamas before anyone could cut the labels out.

* * *

Noah joined them for breakfast and, when Sebbie had polished off the last of the pancakes, the bowls and plates had all been loaded into the dishwasher and everyone was in some state of dress at least semi-appropriate to be seen in – for Sebbie that meant a quick swap of pyjama bottoms for his jeans whilst retaining the rugby shirt over pyjama top look – they all set off towards the paddock.

'Can Pancake and Gertie come to the house for my birthday party?' Sebbie was holding Noah's hand, not wanting to let go as he ran forward a couple of steps and then back again. Jude smiled at the way Noah's strong arm was being pulled and twisted by Sebbie, who was so full of energy and birthday excitement that walking steadily in a straight line was not an option.

'Not in the house,' said Noah. 'That's why we're going to see them now, so they can wish you a happy birthday.'

'How do they know it's my birthday?'

'Haven't you told them a million times already?' Lucy took hold of Sebbie's free hand and bent to give it a quick kiss. 'How about some birthday swings?'

'Make them really high,' Sebbie said with gusto.

'Okay, then. You asked for it,' Noah said as he and Lucy both pulled their arms back with Sebbie between them.

Jude felt a bubble of tangled emotions as she watched from a few steps behind. Sebbie crouched low like a coiled spring and then, on Lucy's count of three, he sprang forward and Lucy and Noah swung him high into the air amid squeals of pure delight. It was wonderful to see the three of them bonding so well as a family unit – everything that Jude could have wished for her sister and certainly everything she deserved. But deep down there was an unwelcome hint of sadness that had started to make itself known whenever Jude felt herself becoming peripheral to these family scenes.

If Lucy and Noah stayed together, and Jude very much hoped that they did, then things were bound to change. At some point, Lucy would want to move in with him and there was no space down at the pink cottage for all three of them. Then what? Would they find a house down in the village to rent and all leave in one go? Could she persuade them to live together in the farmhouse with her? Would she even want that or would she end up constantly feeling like the spare wheel in her own home?

Jude found her thoughts turning to Marco again. She hadn't heard anything from him since she'd turned down his offer to visit him in Cornwall. That ship had clearly well and truly sailed now.

'Aunty Judy, you're not answering me.' The indignant voice of her nephew cut into her thoughts as Noah unfastened the gate and they all walked into the paddock.

'Sorry, my love. I was a million miles away. What was it you were saying?'

'I said can you help me—' But whatever he needed help with was instantly forgotten when the sound of nine Runner ducks quacking and rasping caught his attention.

'Do we have ducks?' Sebbie looked up at Jude.

'You do,' she replied. 'These are your own ducks. Noah got them for your birthday.'

'Well, really they're from Pancake and Gertie,' Noah said, never one to seek the gratitude of another. 'They told me they wanted to get you something special and they thought Runner ducks would be the very thing.'

Sebbie wrapped his arms around Noah's thighs and the total adoration on his scrunched-up face made every one of Jude's worries turn to vapour. Sebbie was what mattered most to her, Sebbie and Lucy, who was looking on with such contentment that Jude felt every maternal fibre trigger. Things were bound to change – this was an inevitability that nobody could fight – but if change meant more of this adoration and contentment for her family then Jude would find a way to make everything else work.

'Come on, then,' said Noah, peeling Sebbie off him. 'You've got nine names to come up with.'

As Sebbie, with Noah hot on his heels, ran down to where the ducks were fenced off, Jude felt Lucy slip her arm into hers.

'Everything okay?' she asked.

'You mean apart from the dead body in the orchard, the missing person and a campsite full of expensive, empty tents that I can't rent out until the police have stopped their investigations?'

'Yes. I mean, apart from all of that. I mean you. How are you?'

'I'm tired,' Jude said honestly. 'And I'm frustrated that the answers we need to make all of this go away are just out of reach. But otherwise, I'm fine.'

'You know we all love you and that you'll always be more important to Sebbie and me than anyone else.'

Jude's breath caught a little at the uncanny way her sister sometimes knew exactly what was bothering her.

'Don't be daft.' Jude attempted a light-hearted response and an immediate change of tack in order to stop her emotions from bubbling out of control. 'I love you too but be under no illusion, if Daniel Craig comes knocking on the door of Malvern Farm then you and Sebbie will be out on your ear.'

Lucy squeezed her arm and grinned. They both looked at Sebbie, who was squatting down with his hands resting on the edge of the old canoe, where two of the ducks were taking a morning dip. Noah was pointing something out to him. 'I think he's having a good birthday,' said Lucy.

'Of course he is,' Jude reassured her. 'He's got everyone he loves around him, a field full of animals, he's had chocolate for breakfast and he's got the most enormous cake for lunch.'

Lucy dropped Jude's arm and looked at her aghast. 'Oh, bugger!'

'What?' Jude asked in alarm.

'Candles.' Lucy huffed out the word as though it contained all the woes of the world. 'I forgot to get candles for the cake.'

'Is that all?' Jude said in relief. 'I'm sure Sebbie won't mind.'

'He can't have a birthday cake without candles.' Lucy looked at her watch. 'I haven't got time to drive into town and back. Do you think Binnie's already left? Maybe I can ask her to pick some up.'

'Look, why don't I walk over to Mrs James? I'm sure she'll have some and I can pick up the *Gazette* and the Sunday papers whilst I'm there.'

Lucy looked uncertain. 'Are you sure?'

'Of course. To be honest, I could do with a bit of a walk out and so could the dogs.'

'Thanks, Jude.'

Jude waved Lucy's gratitude away and left the three of them to enjoy the ducks, walking back to the house to pick the dogs up and then setting out across the fields to the track that took her down to the village. When she got to Mrs James's shop, she tied Alfie and Pip to the railing and went inside.

'Good morning, Jude.' Val Trout put down one of the two jars of jam that she was choosing between. 'How's everything at the farm? Any news on that awful man who was at the campsite yesterday?'

'Thanks for the photo,' Jude said. 'They haven't caught him yet, though.'

'We've all been very worried about you up there with a killer on the loose.' Mrs James joined the conversation.

'We're trying to forget about it all today actually as we're celebrating Sebbie's birthday and trying to make it as memorable for him as we can, in all the right ways.'

'Of course, how lovely,' said Val. 'Would he be four now?'

'Yes, which means we are all obviously at his beck and call completely for the day. In fact, that's really why I'm here, Mrs James. Do you have any birthday cake candles?'

'I do indeed, Jude. If you take a look at that shelf along the back wall you should find a couple of different types to choose from.'

Jude went off to investigate and sure enough, on a shelf sandwiched between the vanilla extract and baking powder, there were packs of tiny candles. Jude chose a set in various bold colours and took them back to the desk where Mrs James and Val Trout were now deep in conversation.

'Sometimes I forget why I ever married him in the first place,' said Val. 'He's a nightmare to live with these days. If he isn't complaining about the way I fold his washing, he's giving me grief about the state of the kitchen or telling me off for something or other. Do you know, I can't remember the last time he gave me a compliment or said something that made me laugh.'

'Marriage can be a mixed bag,' said Mrs James. 'I can't deny that there were times when I'd have gladly throttled my Arthur but generally, we rubbed along together pretty well.'

'He was a lovely man,' Val agreed. 'You were one of the lucky ones.

Mike was fine when he was teaching but since he retired, he's been impossible to live with. And I think he's gambling again.'

'Oh, Val.' Mrs James was the picture of sympathy as she rang up her shopping. 'Surely not.'

Jude felt uncomfortable listening to Val and she tried to assume an air of distance from the conversation as she picked up copies of the Sunday paper and *Malvern Gazette* from the display by the till.

'Well, he's up to something. He used to be so thrifty and now he's splashing the cash around like he's won the lottery. He's even swapped our online grocery shop to Ocado.'

'Wow,' said Mrs James, 'that *is* extravagant. But it doesn't mean he's gambling. Perhaps he's just treating you with his teachers' pension.'

'No,' Val said sadly. 'I found a bank statement for an account I didn't even know he had. It's quite full too.'

Jude pretended to be scanning the headlines on the front page of the *Gazette* but in reality, she was now completely invested in what Val was saying. Why did Mike have a secret account? And if his own wife thought he was up to no good then surely something was going on.

'Did you ask him about it?' Mrs James helped Val load her shopping into a string bag.

Val sighed as she tapped her card on the credit card machine. 'I haven't. I know I should but it's bound to make him cross so I just need to pick the right moment.'

'What about looking on his phone? Or does he have a complicated code to keep you locked out?'

'Complicated?' Val chuckled. 'He's about as uncomplicated as they come with things like this. It's stupid, really, he uses my birthday for all his codes.'

'There you go, then. If he's doing something dodgy, I bet you'd find it on there.'

Val shook her head. 'He's so jittery at the moment with the police asking him all sorts of questions. I know he can be a difficult sod a lot of the time these days, but the idea that he would want to poison sheep and deliberately pull down someone's tent is ridiculous.'

Jude kept her head down and her eyes trained on the newspaper in her hand, not wanting to be drawn into this particular conversation. If Mike Trout was as innocent as his wife seemed to think he was, then there would be no need for him to feel jittery around the police, would there?

'If he caught me going through his phone then he'd think I didn't believe him either,' Val continued. 'I'll find a way to talk to him properly.'

'Very sensible,' said Mrs James. 'I'm sure he'll have his reasons. Maybe he's saving up for something like that, hey, Jude?'

Jude looked up at the sound of her name and saw that Mrs James was pointing to the newspaper she was holding.

'Ex-RAF pilot organises flyover for his wife to mark their golden wedding anniversary,' Mrs James read aloud. 'Now that's something, isn't it?'

Val snorted. 'Chance would be a fine thing.'

'Here, let me ring those through for you.' Mrs James held her hand out and Jude passed her the pack of candles before setting the newspapers down on the counter.

Whilst Jude paid, Mrs James reached across to where bags of sweets hung from a display stand. 'Here you are.' She pulled off a bag of giant chocolate buttons and laid them on top of the newspapers. 'These are from me to wish Sebbie a happy birthday.'

Jude thanked the shopkeeper and put the chocolate into her backpack along with the newspapers and candles. She said her goodbyes before leaving to unclip the dogs and start the short walk back to the farm, her mind full of Mike Trout and what he was doing to be able to fill up a secret bank account.

As she turned into the track that led up to the top of her field, Jude bumped into Ellie, Ash and Seren heading the same way. Jude winced at the sight of the nasty red and purple bruise on Ellie's face, which was covering almost the entirety of her eye now.

'Oh, Ellie, that does look sore,' said Jude. 'He certainly did a proper job on you.'

Ellie put her hand to her eye. 'It is pretty painful but it might have been worse if you hadn't shown up when you did. I don't suppose there's any news on finding him?'

'Not as far as I know.' Jude wished she could say otherwise but she suspected the man would be virtually impossible to trace if he didn't come back to the farm again.

Jude let the dogs off their leads as they all started to walk up the track together. 'How did you all sleep at the B&B?' she asked.

'Not bad at all,' said Ellie. 'I must have been much more tired than I thought, and I have to say it was nice to be able to lock the door behind me.'

Ash and Seren were very quiet, giving the bare minimum in the way of responses to Jude, who wondered if either of them had managed to get any rest at all. They both looked dreadful, with matching bloodshot eyes and slightly grey skin that only came from sickness or total exhaustion.

'Were the others okay in the huts?' Jude asked.

'Yes.' Ellie unzipped her hoodie a little as the day started to warm up. 'I didn't like Shaz being on her own so I offered to share but she said she wanted her own space. At least she had Neesh and Dex with her.'

'How is Shaznay?'

'Not doing too well.' Ellie glanced towards the other two but as neither offered anything she carried on. 'I can't imagine what it's like for her to lose so much all at once. I mean, what happened to Joe is bad enough but to come off the back of the enormous fallout they had when she found out about Khadija. It's so much for her to take on board.'

'He was an arsehole.' Ash joined the conversation for the first time. Her face was a picture of disgust at the mention of Joe's name and hatred dripped from her words like blood from a dagger. 'She should be celebrating now he's gone, not moping about the fact that someone had the balls to do what most of us probably wished we had the guts for.'

'Ash.' Seren's voice was little more than a whisper as she laid a hand on her friend's arm.

'What?' Ash shrugged her off. 'It's the truth. Shaz, Khad, all of us are better off without him toxifying our lives. Men like him deserve what they get, in my opinion, and I won't pretend I think otherwise.'

Seren threw a worried glance over at Jude, who couldn't condone Ash's sentiment but then neither could she completely disagree with her.

She noticed with interest that Ash was still using Khadija's name in the present tense, as though certain she was still alive somewhere.

'Thank goodness not all men are beastly,' Ellie said, obviously trying to move the conversation away from the awkward dead end it had been driven down. 'What about you, Jude? Anyone special in your life?'

Whilst Jude was glad of the diversion, she wasn't all that keen on where the new road was taking them.

'Not at the moment,' she said.

'It must be nice to have your sister with you,' said Seren. 'I always wished I had a sibling.'

'Lucy's fantastic, I'm lucky to have her and Sebbie.' She whistled for the dogs who'd wandered a little too far away and they both pelted back and waited for the nod before carrying on. 'Neesh and Shaznay seem close too.'

'Those two have always been more like twins than just regular siblings,' said Ellie. 'I think their parents are pretty hard work, which may be part of the reason. From the stories they tell, it sounds as though it was the two of them against their mum and dad.'

Jude thought about her own father and the fact that his uselessness and cruelty had often united her and Lucy in the same way.

'Are they really strict?' Jude asked.

'Not strict so much as pushy and demanding. I don't know who it's worse for – Neesh for thinking she let them down by failing her A levels and getting pregnant out of wedlock or Shaz for having the pressure piled on to achieve so much that she's frightened of failure.'

By this time, they'd reached the top of the track and were just about to turn into the gate for the top field when there was a yap from the hedge. Jude looked to see Alfie's skinny rear end sticking out of the undergrowth whilst his head was so far in that his collar had caught on a briar.

'You silly dog,' she said, going to his rescue. Jude carefully snapped the end of the briar off and cushioned his head with her hands as she helped him to reverse out without causing himself any damage. 'What were you doing in there?'

'Was there a rabbit?' Seren asked, tousling the white ruff around the back of his neck.

'No.' Jude could see something shining in the hedge. 'It looks like someone has been chucking litter in there. It makes me so cross as, apart from anything else, it can play havoc with the sheep if they eat it.'

Jude moved the branches of the hedge aside and realised that what she had discovered was not rubbish at all but a mobile phone. She pulled it out and held it out for the hens to see.

'That's Khad's.' Ash snatched it from Jude and cradled it as though it was somehow a part of Khadija herself.

'Can you switch it on?' Seren asked.

Ash looked at the screen as though frightened of the secrets it might be holding. Then she pressed the tiny button on the side of the phone and Jude felt everyone pause as they waited for the screen to decide whether or not it still contained any life. For a moment, it looked as though nothing was going to happen but, when Ash pushed her thumb for longer against the side button, a rainbow-coloured Google logo appeared in the middle of the black screen. Nobody said a word as the logo was replaced by a single G with a moving line underneath to show that it was doing whatever it needed to do in order to restart.

'I think we should wait until the police have seen it,' Jude said, as keen as anyone to see if they could find any clue as to where Khadija was, but also knowing the protocol.

Ash was visibly shaking as the blackness was replaced by Ash's lock screen. Beneath the cracked glass, the date and a clock sat over a photo of Khadija standing behind an older couple who were seated on stools. All three of them were dressed in beautifully smart clothes and they looked formally posed with ramrod-straight backs, and positioned just so to make the best of everyone's better sides.

Ash stared at the photo as tears streamed down her cheeks. Ellie stepped forward to try and comfort her but she was pushed aside roughly.

'Her bloody parents.' Ash stared at the phone, jabbing her finger at it so that the sleeping black screen once more revealed the photo. 'I hate you. I hate you both so much. You archaic, prejudiced, small-minded tyrants. You broke her and you broke me too and I will never, ever forgive you for that.'

17

Jude eased the phone out of Ash's fingers and was surprised that there was no resistance from the desolate woman. It was as though seeing the photo on the screen had zapped her of all her fight. She allowed herself to be guided into the field by Seren and Ellie, who continued to mutter gentle encouragement until they'd made it all the way back to the farm-yard where they found Neesh, Shaz and Dex.

'We were coming to find you,' said Neesh. 'Thought we could do with some fresh air.'

She stopped as she caught sight of Ash.

'What's happened? Have you heard something? Is it Khad, have you found her?'

Ellie shook her head. 'Ash's just had a shock.'

'You'd better all come in,' said Jude. *So much for my day off and Sebbie's relaxing birthday party*, she thought to herself as she went through the porch to open the door into the kitchen where Binnie, who'd clearly arrived early for Sebbie's party, was helping Lucy with a tray of sausage rolls.

If Lucy and Binnie were surprised to see the little party of hens follow her inside then they didn't show it. Lucy took one look at Ash and filled the kettle for a brew whilst Binnie ushered her to the kitchen table to sit down with Ellie on one side and Seren on the other. Neesh and Shaz took two of the other chairs but Dex chose to stand behind Neesh, his hands on her shoulders.

'Sebbie and Noah are still in the paddock,' said Lucy. 'They should be coming back in a few minutes but should I give Noah a ring and ask him to stay out for another half hour?'

'Might be wise.' Jude took the phone from her pocket and passed it to Binnie. 'We found this thrown right inside the hedge at the top of the field. It's Khadija's.'

'I need to tell you something,' said Ash, so quietly that Jude wasn't sure if she'd heard properly.

'Okay,' said Binnie, pulling up the chair opposite Ash and sitting in it.

Ash looked as though she was in two minds about whether or not to continue but Binnie gave her an encouraging nod. 'If you have any information about what might have happened to Khadija then you need to tell us,' she said.

'I should have told you right at the start but I thought she was alive and I didn't want to get her in trouble. But now this—' she pointed to the broken phone that Binnie had put on the table '—and what happened to Ellie yesterday, and Joe's note. I'm so sorry.'

Her face crumpled and she let Ellie comfort her.

'Let's not worry about what you should have done,' said Binnie kindly. 'Let's go from here. What is it that you know?'

Ash looked up. 'Khadija wanted to run away; get away from them and the hold they had over her.' She jabbed her finger towards the phone again.

'Them?' Binnie asked, gently.

'Her sodding parents. If evil ever walked on the earth then it would look like them. They treated her like a little child. No, worse than that, they treated her like a piece of clay that they could push around and mould into whatever they wanted. They never gave her any love or positivity in her life. It was always *do better, work harder, do this, don't be that*. They thought that if they threw enough money at her then they owned her. Have they even noticed she's missing yet?' She looked defiantly at Binnie.

'We're still trying to speak to them.'

'Well, when you do, tell them from me that the reason she's missing is all down to them and their incessant threats and need for perfection.' Ash's lip curled upwards in a snarl. 'She wanted to travel the world and write about it but they wouldn't let her. Instead, they gave her a list of suitable careers that she wasn't allowed to deviate from. They wanted her to get married and have children but she wanted me.'

Ash was crying now, not noisy sobs but silent tears that coursed down her face. 'I said we should just forget about them and do our own thing but Khad was always trying to pacify them; it's why she had them as her background instead of us. And then one day, about a year ago, she came up with the plan of just disappearing. We were going to do it together. Change our names, come up with new identities and just leave.' The tears started to fall thicker now. 'I thought that's what she'd done. I really thought she'd made the break and just left without me.' She pushed the tears away with the back of her hand. 'Honestly, I kept hoping she'd call me at some point and tell me where to meet her but now...'

She put her face in her hands and allowed the sobs to finally come.

Jude fetched a box of tissues and set them down on the table whilst everyone waited for Ash to collect herself. 'Do you think I could have a glass of water?' she asked when she finally looked up.

'The kettle's boiled if you'd rather have tea?' Lucy said.

'Water's fine,' said Ash, pulling a tissue from the box and blowing her nose. 'Sorry, it's just this is really hard.'

'It's okay,' said Binnie. 'Take your time.'

Ash drank half of the glass that Lucy put down for her and then laced her hands behind her head, which dropped forward.

'She became obsessed with trying to make money quickly, enough of it so that we could literally leave without a trace.' Ash's hands were shaking and Jude could see the surface of the water shiver in the glass she was holding. 'She did it quickly, too. I have no idea what she was up to, but she was earning thousands and putting it all into a separate building society account, one that her parents had no idea she had.'

Jude's head snapped up when she heard this. Two people in the same day had talked about secret accounts and large deposits. Was there a possibility that the two were linked? Had Mike Trout known Khadija before the hens made the visit to the farm? Had he even been the one to suggest Malvern Farm to Khadija, whose name was on the booking? But if this was the case, what were they both mixed up in?

'Did you ask her how she was getting hold of so much money?' Binnie asked.

'Of course I did, but she just said she'd been doing extra hours at a livery and that the racehorse owners paid really well. I didn't question it. The quicker the money came in, the sooner we could be off. She'd even gone as far as changing her name through deed poll so that she could apply for a new passport so her parents couldn't trace her. We were so close but then Joe stuck his nose in – egocentric prick, thinking that he could just take my place.'

'That bastard,' Neesh spat as she took her sister's hand. 'I'm sorry, Shaz. I know you're hurting but I will not shed a tear for that man.'

Shaznay said nothing but Jude saw her grip Neesh's hand tightly.

Jude thought about the note that Joe had written. The private investigator he'd hired and what he'd potentially uncovered. She also remembered the row she'd heard on the hens' first day at the campsite. Khadija furious as she thought that Ash had told her parents about their relationship. There was something still that didn't quite add up.

'Khadija was really angry when she found out someone had told her parents about you,' she said. 'But I can't understand why she'd be upset they'd cut her off when it sounds like she was desperate for a clean break from them anyway.'

Ash looked at her steadily. 'She didn't want them in her life but it had to be on her terms. She was frightened of them.'

'Can you tell me what you mean by this?' Binnie asked.

'I mean that she needed to completely disappear, become untraceable. It's why she was taking such care to set things up properly so that they couldn't find her.' Ash's voice had become steely hard. 'But then Joe told them and we were no longer in control. Khadija didn't know what they would do and I thought that was why she left. I thought she'd set everything up so everyone would think she'd been taken or murdered –

just like we'd planned.' Her head dropped forward again and she rubbed the back of her neck so hard that she left red marks.

Jude watched her. There was so much to take in and she could see why Ash had kept all of this quiet up until now as she clearly thought Khadija had done what she said she was going to. Perhaps she still had. Perhaps she'd set everything up and even killed Joe to make her disappearance look more sinister. But why come back for her phone and then hide it in the bush? And there was still the mystery of the man who'd attacked Ellie. If he was the PI hired by Joe then there was no reason for him to still be snooping around. Had he been sent by Khadija's parents? That would explain why she recognised him. It would also explain why she'd chosen to run away so soon afterwards. Or had he got something to do with the money-making scheme Khadija had got mixed up in?

And how did bloody Mike Trout fit into all of this?

'Thank you for your honesty.' Binnie picked up the phone and asked Jude for a clean food bag to drop it into. 'It's a bit like locking the door after the horse has bolted but let's not get any more prints on it if we can help it.'

'Mine will be on it,' said Ellie. 'I was using it a couple of days ago to look up treatments at the spa.'

'Mine too,' said Neesh. 'I was in charge of music in the car on the way here.'

'We've probably all used it at some point,' said Seren.

'Never mind. I suspect that what's inside the phone will be of more interest than whose prints are on the outside anyway.'

The oven timer buzzed and Lucy apologised as she opened the Aga to pull out a tray of piping hot sausage rolls followed by another of crinkle-cut oven chips.

'It looks like you've got plans,' said Ellie, standing up.

'It's Sebbie's birthday today,' said Jude. 'Hence the beige food.'

'We must get out of your way, then,' said Neesh.

The rest of the hens stood up, Ash red-eyed and broken, and the others sombre and quiet. Jude opened the door for them. 'Please let me know if you need anything,' she said, although she knew that what they all really needed was for the mystery of Khadija's whereabouts to be solved.

'What do you make of that?' Lucy asked when it was just the three of them left.

'I think Khadija was living one very messy life and I think there are still loads of things we don't yet know about her,' said Jude. 'If we could only find out what she was messed up in. That could be the key to getting to the bottom of this whole thing.'

'We might have news on that,' said Binnie. 'That car with the dodgy plates belonging to the guy who walloped Ellie was involved in a police chase this morning.'

Jude felt a little prickle of excitement at this. 'Did they catch the driver?'

'He escaped but there were a lot of drugs found on board.' Binnie rested her elbows on the table and made a cradle with her laced fingers on which she rested her chin. 'Not any old drugs, either – these were all animal drugs only available on prescription from a vet.'

Jude felt her brain go into overdrive once again. The man hadn't been a private investigator, he'd been a drug dealer and that turned everything on its head again. 'And you think that's what Khadija was involved in?'

'I can't believe that everything that's happening at the moment is by coincidence,' said Binnie.

'Nor can I.' Jude remembered the look of anger she'd seen Khadija give this man when he'd caught her coming out of the shower. She'd thought she had recognised him and now there was an explanation as to why that might have been.

'We'll have to talk about this later,' said Lucy. 'That sounds like Sebbie and Noah back from the ducks.'

They both came in, flushed from being outside for most of the morning and sporting huge smiles.

'I have new ducks,' Sebbie was quick to tell Binnie. 'Pancake and Gertie gave them to me and they live in a boat. The boys are called Captain, because he's the boss, Bob, because he bobs in the water, Brown Head, because he's got a brown head and Charlie like Charlie and Lola.'

Sebbie paused just long enough for Binnie to say, 'Very cool,' before he began on the list of girls.

'Lola is called Lola because Charlie and Lola, Whitey is the white one and Noisy is the noisiest one of all; she does not stop quacking. Sweetie Duck is really sweet and has a curly tail and the last one is Apple.'

'Why is she called Apple?' Binnie asked.

'I don't know,' said Sebbie. 'But did you know that only girl ducks can quack?'

'I did not,' said Binnie, trying hard to remain serious as the little boy in front of her imparted his duck-based knowledge. 'It sounds like you've had a brilliant birthday so far. Is that a new shirt I see as well?'

Sebbie looked down at the now not-quite-so-white rugby shirt and then he spun around to show Binnie the back.

'Look, Binnie. It says four because I am four years.'

'All grown up. And now you look just like one of the team too,' Binnie said. 'Who's your favourite player?'

'Abby Dow. She has the same shirt as me but it has a different number on the back, doesn't it, Aunty Jude?'

Before Jude could confirm this, Sebbie had returned to Binnie, who patiently listened as he ran through the names of some of his other favourite players from both the men's and women's teams.

'Come on now, birthday boy.' Lucy clapped her hands to get his attention. 'There are sausage rolls and crinkle chips going cold, so quickly go and wash those grubby little mitts of yours before I eat all the party food myself.'

* * *

That afternoon, once the sausage rolls, carrot sticks and crinkle-cut chips had been eaten, the birthday cake candles blown out and everyone had listened to countless stories of ducks and rugby players from an excited four-year-old, Binnie went home to enjoy the rest of her day off.

Lucy had promised that they'd all pop over to see Granny Margot so that she could wish Sebbie a happy birthday too. As they drove past the police station, it was no surprise to Jude that Binnie's car was parked outside.

Over an hour later, after a visit that had involved more cake and Sebbie entertaining the residents of the care home with his impressions of each different duck, they saw that Binnie's car was still there.

'Does she ever switch off?' Lucy asked.

'I don't think so,' Jude replied. 'She'll want to chase up whatever was on Khadija's phone and probably try and get in touch with her parents again too. Sometimes I think she doesn't know how to take a day off.'

'Look who's talking,' said Noah, who was sitting in the back of Jude's Land Rover with Sebbie.

Jude grunted. She was off duty now, wasn't she? Although her mind wasn't. No, that was fired up and trying to digest the latest twists to the story of the hen party. Since Binnie's bombshell about the drug dealer, Jude had not been able to stop thinking about the wider ripples of what this could mean. Drugs meant money, large sums of it too, that often went into hidden bank accounts and that gave her even more reason to suspect Mike Trout's involvement. As she drove past his house, she resolved to go and do a little digging up of evidence of her own as soon as she could.

By the time they got back to the farm, Sebbie was asleep in his car seat and Lucy had to wake him when they pulled up outside the house.

'It's nearly supper time,' she said when he grumbled his objections.

'Can I go and say goodnight to the ducks?' he asked sleepily.

'Sebbie, you're too tired,' said Lucy. 'They'll still be there in the morning.'

'But it won't be my birthday in the morning.'

'The boy has a point,' said Noah. 'Wait here, I'll only be a minute.'

True to his word, Noah was gone for less time than it took for Jude to open the front door to let the dogs out, and he was pushing a wheelbarrow with a big grin on his face. There were some hessian feed sacks in the bottom of the barrow and Noah lifted Sebbie from his seat and plonked him on top of them.

'Your birthday chariot.' He bowed and then saluted the delighted wheelbarrow passenger.

'You're crazy,' said Lucy, giving first Noah and then Sebbie a kiss. 'Hang on whilst I get him a coat. It's starting to get a bit nippy out.'

Bundled up and as happy as Larry, Sebbie gripped on to the sides of the barrow as Noah picked up the handles and set off with him across the yard to say goodnight to his little family of animals.

Supper was a speedy affair for Sebbie, who was starting to get grouchy as Lucy plated up his tomato pasta. Noah, Lucy and Jude sat down at the kitchen table with relief when their exhausted birthday boy was safely tucked up in bed, still wearing the rugby shirt and clutching both his new rugby ball and the toy police car that Binnie had given him.

'Cider, anyone?' Lucy pulled a bottle of Westons Rose towards her and flicked the cap off with the bottle opener.

The uptake was unanimous so she split the bottle between three tumblers which they chinked together in solidarity at a day well executed, despite everything that had been put in the way to scupper it.

Jude drank hers slowly as she thought about Mike Trout and how she was going to find the proof she needed that he was not as innocent as he was still pretending to be. It was still early enough for her to make a house call, but how would she play it if she managed to blag her way inside?

'Anyone hungry?' Lucy asked. 'There's pasta in the pan.'

'Or looks like you bought enough party rings to keep us going until the apocalypse,' teased Noah.

A *ping* from the table alerted them all to the fact that Jude's phone had just received a text message. It was an update from Binnie:

> We've identified the driver of the car. It was covered in prints of someone already on the system, Gareth Johnson. I've ordered a raid on his house so hopefully we'll have him in custody in the morning.

> Thanks again for today. B x

'What car's this?' Noah asked.

'Sorry, we've been so busy today I haven't updated you,' said Lucy.

'That guy who gave Ellie a black eye. They found his car and it was full of vet prescription drugs.'

'He was a drug dealer?' Noah said. 'Do you think he was sniffing about hoping to find some supplies lying around?'

'No, I don't.' Jude was very sure of why that man had been on her farm. 'I think Khadija has been supplying him. Maybe one of the other hens too. They brought an organised crime organisation to our doorstep and it's time we got to the bottom of this so that we can finally get rid of them.'

What Jude didn't say was that she thought there was someone else, much closer to home, who could also be involved. She didn't have any solid evidence but she would do all she could to change that. Mike Trout was in this up to his eyeballs and Jude was going to prove it.

18

Half an hour later, Jude was standing on the Trouts' doorstep with only the loosest of plans beyond getting inside and having a look around. She'd toyed with the idea of talking to Binnie first but what could she do with nothing solid to go on? Binnie would have to follow the correct procedure and this would be a tepid response at best. There would be no raid, no deep questioning, no delving into banking or phone records; for that to happen, they would have to have something more than the flaky concerns of an aggrieved neighbour who'd overheard Mike's wife talking about a large sum of money he seemed to have suddenly got hold of.

Jude needed something concrete she could use to nail him and she was going to do her best to find it.

It was Val who answered the door, looking exhausted in a pair of jeans and a sweatshirt that was so old Jude thought it would probably now be classed as *vintage* or *retro cool*.

'Jude, dear. It's nice to see you. How are things up at the farm?'

'Not the best, but the police are working hard so hopefully we'll have some answers soon.' She held out the bunch of lavender and a jar of Noah's fig chutney that she'd brought round as her cover. 'I know all of this must be causing you and Mike a lot of bother so I brought these to say sorry, and thank you for bearing with us.'

'Oh, Jude.' Val looked close to tears. She stepped outside and pulled the door to behind her. 'Thank you. It is taking a toll on us, actually. Mike particularly.' She was virtually whispering now. 'I'm really worried about him. Since he was questioned about that missing woman's tent collapsing and your poor sheep being poisoned, he's been acting very oddly. One minute he's just staring into his cup of tea and the next he's storming around the house like an angry bull.'

Behaviour, Jude thought, very much in keeping with a guilty man.

'I'm so sorry to hear that,' she said. 'Hopefully, all of this will be cleared up soon and then we can all move on with our lives.'

'The police seemed to think he was responsible for what happened to your sheep.' Val was absent-mindedly crushing one of the lavender flowers between her fingers and Jude could smell the distinctive aroma it was creating. 'He's deeply worried that you think it was him as well. You don't, though, do you?'

She looked so worried that Jude hadn't the heart to say that that was exactly what she thought. 'I can't imagine anyone wanting to deliberately hurt my animals,' she said.

'Despite his gruffness, he's a bit of a softy, especially when it comes to animals.' Val glanced over her shoulder. 'You wouldn't come in and have a chat with him, would you? Set his mind at rest?'

It wasn't exactly how she'd imagined getting into Mike Trout's house and yet it saved her from trying to blag her way in so she took it.

'If you think it might help,' she said.

Val smiled gratefully at her. 'Oh, thank you, Jude. He'll be so pleased to see you.'

Despite the fact they'd been neighbours for what must now be seven or even eight years, Jude hadn't stepped inside the house since the Trouts had moved in. It wasn't as old as Malvern Farm but it had still been standing at the end of the drive for over two centuries and had probably originally been built to house farm workers. The front door opened into a cosy sitting room with three pale green walls and the fourth, where the fireplace stood, a striking shade of warm mustard yellow.

Jude followed Val through the sitting room, past the stairs and into the dining room at the back of the house where Mike was sitting at the table with a bowl of soup in front of him.

'Sorry.' Jude pointed to the bowl of soup. 'I don't want to disturb you.'

Mike Trout pushed the soup away and looked at Jude, who noticed straight away that the glare of angry defiance which was usually a default setting was missing. As Val had suggested, he looked a very much troubled man. 'I'm not all that hungry. What do you want?'

'Jude's come round for a cup of tea and a chat.' Val waved the lavender and chutney at him. 'She's brought us presents too. You like a homemade chutney, don't you, Mike?'

Jude glanced subtly around the room, hoping to see something that might be useful and, unsurprisingly, finding nothing. What was she actually looking for? A huge file labelled *Michael Trout's suspicious paperwork – do not touch*? Jude started to feel a bit daft. Perhaps she would have been better to leave this to the police. Still, she was here now.

'You have a chat whilst I go and make some tea.' Val bustled out of the room, leaving behind an air of coldness that Jude was keen to stay in for as short a time as possible.

There was no invitation to sit so Jude remained standing. It suited her anyway as she had no intention of outstaying her welcome. She wanted to scream at the silent man in front of her and shake the truth out of him but she knew she needed to remain passive and calm if she was going to get anywhere.

'I'm sorry for the chaos around here at the moment,' she said.

'It's not pleasant being accused of things that I haven't done,' Mike said with a stare that told her he wasn't talking about the police's line of questioning. Jude decided to play his games in order to get him on side and perhaps make him slip up somehow.

'I'm sorry about the other day when you came to check on the sheep. I was surprised to see you there and I suppose I'm being oversensitive about people being where I don't expect them to be at the moment.'

Mike grunted. 'I know you think I'm some kind of sheep-poisoning monster but you've got me all wrong.'

'I don't think that. But your shed key was found in the paddock and I jumped to conclusions.' Conclusions that she still believed but wasn't going to let him know that. 'And then I found a yellow jumper.' She was fully aware that she shouldn't be saying this and yet she wanted to see his response. He looked at her blankly, a faint, disinterested incomprehension flashing across his brow for a second but nothing to show any sign of worry. 'Anyway, things were where they shouldn't have been and, like I say, I was on edge and jumped to conclusions. I'm sorry.'

The word felt poisonous in her mouth but she needed to keep up the pretence if she was going to make him reveal a card or two from his hand.

Val came in then with a tray of tea and, when Jude turned to look at her, she saw a phone lying on the sideboard by the door. If that was Mike's phone then it was possible that it would hold some of the answers she wanted. Perhaps bank details or email threads that would link him to the drug dealer. Maybe even messages between Mike and Khadija, although Khadija's phone might also throw those up if they existed. Jude remembered hearing Val in the village shop that morning telling Mrs James that Mike was uncomplicated when it came to phone safety. All Jude needed to know was Val's date of birth and she'd be able to unlock whatever secrets the phone held.

'Do you have sugar in your tea, Jude?' Val put the tray on the table and sat down.

'No, thanks, just a splash of milk.' Jude didn't really want tea at all but she needed time to work out how she was going to leave the Trouts' house with Mike's phone in her pocket and him none the wiser.

'Did little Sebbie enjoy his birthday?' Val poured far too much milk into Jude's mug of tea and pushed it towards her.

'Thank you,' said Jude. 'Yes, he's had us running around after him all day but he's had a super time, I think.'

'That's nice,' Val said. 'And you've got new ducks too? I think I've heard them quacking away in the paddock.'

Oh, great, something else for Mike to complain about, Jude thought. But he'd gone back to staring into his bowl of soup and seemed completely disinterested by the conversation.

'They're Indian Runner ducks and really very sweet.'

'I've a soft spot for ducks, always have. See?' Val pointed to a painting of a well-stocked duck pond on the wall of the dining room.

'You're very welcome to come and meet them all whenever you like,' said Jude. 'Sebbie can show you round, he's given them all names.'

'Of course he has,' Val smiled.

This was all well and good but Jude wasn't actually in the mood for chit-chat about her ducks. She wanted to get what she'd come for and go back home to figure out what to do with it next.

'Mike, go and get that duck doorstop from the bathroom,' said Val.

'What?' Mike looked up at his wife as though he just wanted both her and Jude to leave him to wallow in peace.

'You know the one. I bet Sebbie would like it for his bedroom. Go on, go and get it for him.'

Mike pushed the bowl of soup away and stood up with his cup of tea. 'Do what you like. I'm taking this into my study and I don't want to be disturbed.'

He walked out of the dining room and Jude was relieved to see that he'd left his phone where it was. All she needed to do now was make sure she left the dining room behind Val and she could swipe it on the way out.

'I'm sorry about him. He's really taking all of this very badly.' Val looked wrung out and Jude was full of empathy and compassion for her but her main focus right then was to get to the truth. Whatever Mike had done, Val was better off knowing about it and dealing with the reality rather than dancing around over the hot coals of uncertainty and confusion.

'I should be getting back.' Jude stood up, aware that she hadn't touched her tea. 'I've left Lucy clearing up all the party things.'

'Wait a moment.' Val stood too and headed towards the door. 'Let me at least go and get the duck for Sebbie.'

She bustled out and Jude took her chance. Mike's phone was still on the sideboard and she went over, picked it up and was just sliding it into the pocket of her fleece when Mike stepped out of a door under the stairs. The sound of the loo cistern filling told her that it was the downstairs toilet, and the look on his face told her that she'd been rumbled.

'What are you doing?' Mike demanded, striding towards her.

Jude tried to bluster her way out of the situation but her pulse was racing. 'I was just waiting for Val. She's gone to fetch something for Sebbie.'

'Did you just put my phone in your pocket?' There was that old angry forehead worm of Mike's again, pulsing away as his face darkened.

'What?' Jude could feel her own cheeks reddening. 'No, of course not.'

Mike pushed past her and looked at the sideboard where his phone had been up until a few seconds ago.

'What are you playing at?' He grabbed Jude's arm and tried to wrench her hand out of her pocket where it was gripping his phone, about to be undeniably uncovered.

'Michael!' Val ran down the stairs and over to her husband. 'What on earth are you doing?'

'She stole my phone.' He was properly angry now and Jude couldn't think of a single way in which she could wriggle out of this particular predicament.

Val looked at Jude's blushing face in surprise. 'Jude? Is this true?'

Jude was furious with herself. Not only had she buggered up her sole opportunity to get her hands on some evidence of what Mike was up to, in taking the phone she'd also let him know she was investigating him and had thus buggered up the element of a sneak attack. For a split second, she contemplated making a run for it with the phone still in her pocket but she knew this was a daft idea so she took it out and threw it back on the sideboard. She was never going to be let into this house again so her only chance of getting anything from Mike Trout now was to throw the weight of her accusations at him and see if he snapped.

'What are you up to?' she challenged. 'Despite what you told the police, I know you were on the campsite the night Khadija's tent collapsed. You were in the paddock when my sheep were poisoned and you were there again right before I found the jumper made from the yarn that was used to tie the tent door shut. That was also the day that Joe was shot.' Jude was in full flow but she stopped short of mentioning the secret bank account. That was one surprise card she'd keep up her sleeve for now. 'You are up to your eyeballs in all of this and I want to know exactly what you've done.'

Mike had gone a deathly shade of pale. To Jude's immense surprise, his shoulders collapsed forward and his usually poker-straight back lost several inches as his spine slumped into itself. His face contorted almost as though he was experiencing physical pain and his arms hung loosely by his sides.

'It's all such a bloody mess,' he said. 'It was just supposed to be a prank, a silly trick to try and get those women to raise a complaint against you.'

'A prank?' Jude's voice was harsh and she folded her arms in front of her. Finally, the truth was beginning to come out. 'What kind of person sneaks around in the middle of the night and deliberately collapses a heavy tent whilst there's someone sleeping inside it? I mean, we're not talking a flimsy Duke of Edinburgh tent here. Those things are built to last; the canvas on its own weighs a ton.'

'Mike?' Val was looking even more ashen than her husband, and Jude wondered what on earth must be going through her mind.

'I only untied some of the guy ropes.' He looked at his wife in desperation. 'That's all. I just wanted the tent to flap around a bit. I had no idea the whole thing would collapse.'

'But it did collapse, Mike,' Jude said. 'And you stood there and watched instead of helping Khadija get out. Or did you just run away, not caring whether she got out alive or not?'

'No.' Mike's anger was starting to return but Jude could more than match it with her own. 'What do you take me for? The tent was still standing when I left. I told you, I only untied a couple of the ropes to make the canvas flap. I didn't collapse it.'

'But you were there,' said Val quietly. 'And you *were* the reason it collapsed.'

'You tied the door shut too.' Jude's blood was boiling now. 'Just to make sure that she couldn't get out. And then what? You went up to try and kill my sheep too? Really teach me a lesson?'

Mike shook his head vehemently. 'No, you've got it all wrong. I would never have gone that far – why would I?'

'Same reason you messed with the tent: to make my campsite fail,' Jude hissed. 'To bring me down with it. It's what you've been trying to do since the day you moved in.' She stopped short of telling him of her suspicions that he also had a hand in the drug dealing that had brought that unsavoury man to her farm, and possibly led to at least one death. Without the phone, she had no proof whatsoever. She was out of her depth and it was time to let the police take over.

For the first time since Jude had known him, Mike looked contrite. 'You think I'd go to these lengths?'

'You were in the paddock that night; your key proves it. My poor girls were poisoned with rhododendron leaves, the same as the ones growing in your front garden. You've just admitted to untying the guy ropes that made the tent collapse, and you are the only person I can think of who would want to deliberately harm my livestock and my business.'

Any last remnants of bravado had left Mike and he looked at her with something close to defeat.

'I know what it looks like,' said Mike. 'But I swear I didn't harm your sheep. I didn't tie the tent door shut and I didn't want to hurt that woman. I was just in the wrong place at the wrong time and now I'm paying the price.'

Jude couldn't believe it. *He* was paying the price? *Him?* Mike Trout was so full of nonsense and Jude didn't want to hear any more of it.

'I need to go.' Jude pushed past Mike and Val and headed to the front door.

'Are you going to tell the police about me undoing the guy ropes?' Mike sounded so pathetic that Jude couldn't answer him. As it turned out, she didn't need to.

'Of course she is, you absolute fool,' said Val. 'It's what you should have done from the very beginning. I don't know what you're mixed up in but it's time to start coming clean and I've got a few questions of my own.'

The Trouts didn't notice as Jude opened their front door and let herself out. She walked past their garden shed and the rhododendron bush and went out onto the lane.

She needed to think so she sat down on the milk churn at the end of Malvern Farm's drive and looked towards the western side of the hills, which were bathed in the very last of the evening sun.

Had her visit to the Trouts made any progress or had she actually just made things worse by bowling in and confronting Mike? If only he hadn't seen her taking the phone and she'd managed to escape without the big showdown – but it had happened and that was that. She had at least managed to get him to confess to tampering with the tent, even though he was still adamant it was standing when he'd left and he had nothing to do with the door being tied shut. And he was still denying that he had anything to do with the poisoned sheep licks too, even though his shed key had been found right there at the scene of the crime.

The shed key. Something else that had been bothering Jude. Why had he taken it with him that night? It was possible that it had just been in his pocket for no reason other than he'd put it there the last time he'd used it. But wasn't it far more likely that he'd needed to get into his shed that night? Rhododendrons have thick, tough leaves; not at all the soft type that sheep would easily eat. When Jude had seen the leaves in the sheep lick, something had been used to grind them in so that the leaves had given up their juices readily into the molasses.

Whatever had been used would very likely be the sort of tool that might be stored in a garden shed. As, for that matter, would the tool that had been used to cut the leaves in the first place. If Jude could get her hands on these and find traces of both rhododendron leaf and molasses then surely not even Mike Trout would be able to wriggle out of having to own up to poisoning her sheep.

The sun had almost sunk completely into the Herefordshire countryside – if she walked back up the farm track now, she would get home before it disappeared altogether. Darkness was just around the corner and it was the friend she needed if she was going to come back and search the Trouts' shed.

* * *

Once she'd armed herself with a head torch, a pair of rubber gloves and bolt cutters for the padlock – living on a farm meant she was equipped with almost any tool she could possibly need in life – Jude decided to take the quad down as far as the bottom of the drive and leave it tucked there ready for a speedy return if necessary. Lucy had been relaxing in the bath when she'd sneaked into the house to change into all black clothes so she'd managed to get away without any awkward questioning on that front.

As she crept down the lane towards her neighbours' house, she felt like she was a character in some very bad spy film. If she hadn't been on such a serious mission then she might have found it comical, but Jude was focused on the task ahead.

She paused at the gate into the Trouts' garden and listened but all was quiet. There were no lights on in the front rooms of the house and she imagined that they were in the dining room at the back, maybe discussing her earlier visit or Mike's confession of tampering with the tent. When she was as certain as she could be that she wouldn't be heard, Jude opened the gate silently and walked into the garden. The rhododendron bush cast a large shadow in the moonlight that covered the side where the shed stood.

Jude had the rubber gloves on and the bolt cutters ready in her hand but when she got to the shed, she realised she didn't need them as there was no lock on the door. In fact, the entire bolt had been unscrewed, which Jude assumed had been done by Mike as a way in when he couldn't find his shed key.

The door creaked slightly as she opened it but there was still no sound from the house so she ducked in and closed it behind her.

It was pitch black inside and she had no choice but to switch on the head torch. There was a window on the side facing the house and, if anyone looked out, they would see her torchlight instantly. She glanced around for something to put across the window but, without hammering something in place or stacking things on top of each other, it was impossible, so she'd just have to do her best to keep away from the window and point the torch in the opposite direction as much as possible whilst keeping her fingers crossed that Mike Trout wouldn't look out at his front garden for however long it took her to search the shed.

Right at the back of the shed, and mercifully far from the window, there was a neat row of tools hanging up. Jude stepped over some bags of compost and wood chippings and picked up a pair of hedge trimmers. There were snags of something green where the two blades met but she decided to leave them behind. Even if it was rhododendron, it would mean nothing in a police investigation as Mike could have been cutting his own bushes at any point. There were various other tools hanging up – a fork, hoe, long branch loppers and a rake – but none of them were the sort that could have been used to crush up the leaves. For that he'd have needed something smaller and with some sort of grinding head.

She turned her attention to a set of shelves next to the tools where there was an assortment of cans and jars of oils, weed killers and plant food. Nothing of interest on that shelf, but when she moved to the one below, things began to look a little more promising. Here were the smaller tools that Mike and Val would use in the garden and around the house. A pair of secateurs, a cone-shaped dibber for planting spring bulbs, a hand fork, a mallet and a couple of trowels.

Jude picked up the fork first. It had muddy prongs but nothing of much interest. She had high hopes for the mallet, thinking that it would have been the perfect tool for grinding up the rhododendrons, but again it had nothing to offer.

A sudden clatter outside made Jude freeze and her heart pound. She was crouched on the floor to investigate the tools, and her torch, which she'd set to the palest beam, was pointing into the bottom corner of the shed so she just had to sit tight and hope that she wouldn't get caught. Jude heard the sound of someone knocking on the Trouts' door, followed shortly by Val's voice.

'Janet, hello.'

'Sorry to disturb you, Val,' came the voice of Malvern End's biggest gossip. 'I was just driving past and I thought I'd see if you'd finished with that copy of *Homes and Gardens* I lent you last week? It's just that there's something in it that I wanted to show Paddy. I was talking to her about the colour scheme of the lounge area at Four Trees. It's a bit dated, don't you think?'

'I can't say I've ever really thought about it, to be honest.' Jude could tell, even from her current position on the floor of the shed, that Val sounded tired. It made Jude feel a little guilty that she was currently in the process of trying to find evidence to get her husband into trouble. But then she reasoned that she was only looking for evidence and that it was

Mike who'd potentially got himself mixed up in the trouble in the first place.

'I'll just go and fetch it for you,' said Val. 'I'm sorry not to ask you in but it's not a good time.'

'Don't you worry,' Janet replied. 'We can have a natter another time.'

There was a pause as Val presumably went to fetch the magazine and then Janet spoke again. 'That's it, thank you. Here, let me show you the picture of the room decorated in what I think would be the perfect colours for Paddy's lounge.'

'Actually, Janet, do you mind if we save it for another time?' Val really did sound utterly exhausted. 'I am very busy at the moment.'

'Of course, Val. I'll see you tomorrow.'

'Thank you, Janet.'

Jude heard the front door bang shut and she held her breath as she listened to Janet's footsteps retreating back down the garden path. There was another clatter as she pushed through the gate and then all went quiet. She waited until she was certain the garden was empty again and then she went back to looking through the tools. When she picked up the bulb dibber and shone her torch at it, Jude could see that the round end that dug into the ground to create the holes for planting bulbs was smeared with something brown which, when she lifted it to her nose, she could tell instantly was sheep lick with its distinct sweet and sickly smell.

Bingo! she thought to herself as she realised that there were also specks of green mulched into the sticky molasses.

Now she just needed something to put it in and then she could head back to the quad and get home to phone Binnie and tell her what she'd discovered. Looking around, she found a pile of plastic bags stuffed into a tub next to a workbench. She went over to pick one out and discovered that it was an enormous bag that had once been used for compost. It would be filthy inside and Jude didn't want anything that was going to contaminate the evidence currently stuck to the dibber, so she decided to go for the Aldi bag beneath. When she picked it up, however, she realised that it already had something inside.

She looked in, thinking that she could probably take out whatever it was and leave it behind in the tub of plastic bags. But when she saw what was lying at the bottom of the bag, Jude's eyes opened so wide, they almost fell out to join it.

There, nestled into the plastic folds of the carrier bag, with the light from her headtorch bouncing off the black metal shaft, was a revolver.

Jude stared at it for a moment, her mind racing to keep up with the rate of her heartbeat. Should she take it?

No, she needed to put it back exactly where it was and she needed to make sure it was the police who officially found it. Grateful that she'd thought to wear gloves, Jude carefully put everything back exactly as it had been, including the bulb dibber. Picking up her bolt cutters and careful not to make a sound, she left the shed and made her way back down the garden path and out onto the lane. Her heart continued to pound as she expected Mike Trout to start chasing at any moment and she didn't feel safe until she was sitting on the quad at the bottom of Malvern Farm's drive.

With shaking hands, she pulled out her phone and called Binnie.

'Why the hell didn't you tell me you were going to start snooping around Mike's place?' Binnie said when Jude had finished giving her the short version of everything that had happened that evening.

'Because I had nothing to go on,' said Jude. 'What would you have been able to do with a suspicion about a full bank account and a gut feeling about a man who's been a constant pain in my arse for the past seven years?'

'We'll talk about this another time,' said Binnie crossly. 'Right now, I need to explain to my boss why I need a search warrant for a shed, based on the say-so of a wannabe amateur sleuth.'

Jude knew she should have told Binnie what she'd been planning on doing but she didn't feel much in the way of remorse that she'd gone behind her back this particular time. She had provided them with the murder weapon and leverage to fire Mike to the top of the suspect list.

'Will you be able to check his bank records and things now?' Jude said. 'I'm sure he must be mixed up with the drug dealer who was around here.'

'To do a deep search into his records, I'd need something pretty undeniable that pins the gun firmly on him,' Binnie said. 'You know that.'

'But it was found in his shed.' Jude was beginning to feel her resolve drip away. 'And the dibber too, it shows he was the one who poisoned the sheep.'

'Oh, don't be so naïve, Jude,' Binnie snapped. It was perhaps the first time Jude had heard the frustration in her voice aimed towards her. 'Without prints on the gun or residue on Mike's clothes, something solid to say that he was the one who shot it, we won't have much of a leg to stand on. You said yourself that the shed door hadn't been locked. Anyone could have gone in there to hide it.'

Jude felt utterly foolish as Binnie pointed out what should have been so obvious to her.

'Go home, Jude. I'll speak to you tomorrow.'

Binnie ended the call and Jude was left sitting on the quad feeling dejected. She had gone to the Trouts' to look for evidence to show Mike was mixed up in the chaos of the past week and so, when she'd discovered the gun in his shed, she'd seen that as unequivocal proof. But of course this was far from the case. Anyone could have hidden it there. One of the hens, perhaps to get it away from the campsite. Even Khadija herself could have shot Joe and hidden the weapon before disappearing for good.

She was tired and frustrated and was making mistakes. And yet she had found the murder weapon and it could still help them track down the murderer. Also, Jude would be able to reassure Lucy that at least the gun, if not the person who'd shot it, had been safely removed from harm's way.

19

It didn't matter what was happening in Jude's life; the farm would not wait for her to catch up. Some things could be put on hold but there were other things that could cost her dearly if she didn't deal with them, her flock being top of the list and the crops being a close second.

May was peak growing season and, once the dismally wet start to the year was behind them, the weather was shaping up to be pretty fair. The oilseed rape was in full bloom and the fields that sat on the opposite side of the lane to Malvern Farm were awash with bright yellow flowers. Jude had planted more acres of OSR than in previous years, hoping that the harvest when it came would bring in a decent amount. But in order for there to be a good harvest, the crop needed tending and if she didn't want to risk the whole lot succumbing to the destructive sclerotinia fungus then she needed to get out in the fields sooner rather than later to spray them.

The morning after Jude had discovered the gun in Mike Trout's shed, armed with a flask of coffee prepared to see her through the spraying of around eighty acres, Jude zipped herself into an old puffer jacket of Adam's, pulled her long hair into a rough bun and put on her work boots.

Noah was already in the yard with Floss and Ned, getting the quad ready for the first trip of the day up to the top fields to make sure the sheep grazing them were well, and Jude walked over to meet him.

Noah gave a single command to his dogs, 'Bike,' and both jumped instantly into the dog box on the back of the quad and sat there, eagerly waiting for their morning's work to begin.

'Morning, Jude,' Noah said. 'Lucy said you had a bit of an adventure after I left last night.'

'You could say that.' Jude scratched Ned between the ears, marvelling as she always did at the beauty of the heterochromia that made one of his eyes a pale blue and the other deep brown.

'I'm not sure I like you snooping around in the dark when there's a murderer out there somewhere.' Noah wasn't being judgemental, Jude knew that. Since Adam had died, he'd always seen it as his duty to take care of her, and Jude could see how her little adventure the night before might have worried him. 'So, was Mike arrested then?'

'They've got him in for questioning, but I don't know any more than that. I'm hoping Binnie might call with an update today, once she forgives me for going behind her back.'

Noah smiled at her. 'Knowing Binnie, I can't imagine that'll take too long. Especially as, however sneakily you did it, you did manage to find the murder weapon.'

Jude hoped he was right but she was still keen to talk to Binnie and make sure.

'Have you been into the paddock this morning?' she asked.

'Not yet. Just heading off to do the field rounds first and then I'll go down.'

'Don't worry, I'll do it whilst I wait for the sprayer to fill up,' said Jude, making sure she gave just as much attention to Floss, the oldest, most reliable dog in the Malvern Farm pack, too.

'Are you doing the OSR fields this morning?' Noah asked.

'Yes. I was going to do it a few days ago but with one thing or another it never quite happened.'

'That was my thinking when I woke up this morning,' Noah said. 'If you're happy to do that then I'll sort the hens when I get back from checking the sheep and then I wouldn't mind cracking on with training this'un.' He stroked Ned's ears. 'We'll get you and Alfie back out soon too. Don't want to leave it too long.'

Jude realised that she was as keen as Noah was to get on with Alfie's training and vowed to carve out some time to make it happen. First things first, though.

'Do you fancy helping with the sprayer before you head off?' Jude found hooking it up to the back of the tractor much easier with two people and Noah was happy to be the second pair of hands.

Pulling the keys to the John Deere from the pocket of Adam's puffer jacket, Jude led the way to the tractor shed and climbed up into the cab. It was a while since she'd been behind the wheel of the bigger of her two tractors, or did it just seem longer as time often played tricks when there was a lot of life to deal with? As she started the engine, she counted back the days since the barbecue they'd had to celebrate Binnie's promotion, the day the hens checked into the campsite. Was it really only five days ago? She counted again, sure that it had to be longer but no, only five days had passed and yet so much had happened.

With Noah's guidance, Jude expertly manoeuvred the tractor out of the shed and reversed it into place so Noah could hook it up, lock it in position and attach all the power cables it would need to function correctly out in the field.

'All set,' he called and Jude waved her thanks before driving out of the shed and parking up next to the hose.

Noah met her there with a large plastic bottle of fungicide. 'Here you go. Liquid gold, the amount this stuff costs these days.'

Jude didn't need to be told as she was the one who had to deal with the farm's accounts but she knew it would pay itself off many times over if it led to a healthy and profitable yield come July. She took the bottle from Noah and thanked him for his help before he left her to it and went off to begin his own list of jobs. Jude poured the fungicide carefully into the sprayer's tank and then pushed the end of the hose in, clipping it to the rim to stop it falling out mid-fill. She turned the tap on and then, once it was filling nicely, headed down to check on the animals in the paddock.

She knew the Runner ducks would be happy to be let out of the stable so they could enjoy the freedom of their pen and she was keen to see if Pancake and Gertie had made friends with the Kerry Hills yet or if they were still in two separate gangs occupying different sections of their territory. Jude crossed the yard and, as she skirted the pond, her eye was drawn to a discarded single-use vape casually thrown into the weeds that led down to the water.

'Bloody things,' she muttered as she stooped to pick it up between her finger and thumb. She didn't want it anywhere near her animals as the lithium battery could do all sorts of damage if it was accidentally ingested. When she got to the paddock gate, she set the vape down on the post. She'd dispose of it properly when she'd finished with the animals.

As she let herself in through the gate, she could see that the ducks were already in their pen and this worried her as Noah hadn't yet been down to see them. Jude felt the panic rising. What if he hadn't secured the stable door properly when he and Sebbie had gone down to put them to bed? What would she tell Sebbie if a fox had got in? But then, as she power walked across the grass, she noticed that there was someone else with them, sitting on an upturned oil drum with her back towards Jude.

It was Seren, with Pancake standing next to her enjoying the back rub she was getting, and she turned when she heard Jude approaching.

'All right then, Mam,' she said into the phone that was clasped to her ear. It was well-worn and old, clad in a case that was covered with cartoon pictures of sheep. 'Yes, I know and I will do. I gotta go now but I'll call you again later. Love you too.'

'Sorry, Jude.' Seren stood up. 'I hope you don't mind me coming here. I needed to get out of the B&B and away from the others for a bit.'

'Of course not. You're welcome any time and I'd say Pancake would agree with me too.'

One of the Kerries bleated and Seren looked over towards the little flock. Jude's attention, though, had been drawn to something on the ground next to the oil drum where Seren had just been sitting. It was a phone and a much smarter one than the old thing Seren had just put back in her pocket. With a jolt of surprise, Jude realised that it looked exactly the same as the fancy split-screen one she'd seen Joe using.

'They seem happier now,' Seren said, pointing over at the Kerries, who'd been joined by Pancake and Gertie and were all nibbling away at the grass together.

'They're settling in well enough now,' Jude replied, keeping her voice level so as not to reveal that her mind was spinning.

What was Seren doing with Joe's phone? She'd been the one to discover his body by the henhouse; had she taken it then? Whatever reason could she have had for doing so? Surely she couldn't have been the one to kill him? She looked at the quiet, passive woman currently watching the sheep with a gentle look of devotion on her face. It seemed beyond the realms of any possibility that she could be capable of killing in cold blood.

And yet Jude knew very well that everybody had a point to which they could be pushed before they snapped. Had Joe made Seren snap? She remembered the note Joe had written to tell Khadija he knew what she'd been involved in; quite possibly, as they now knew, the illegal dealing of veterinary drugs. He'd hinted that there was someone else involved too; was it possible that person was Seren?

Whatever her reasons for having Joe's phone, Seren clearly had no idea she'd dropped it and Jude wanted to keep it that way until she'd had a chance to retrieve it herself.

'Thanks for letting the ducks out,' Jude said. 'I bet they were pleased to see you.'

'They're real characters, aren't they?'

'Sebbie thinks so. He met them yesterday and by the time Noah brought him back to the farm he'd named all nine of them.'

Seren walked towards the pen and Jude saw her opportunity. She bent down quickly whilst the other woman was looking the other way and slipped the phone into her pocket.

'Listen, I'd better get on as I have eighty acres of oilseed rape to spray today and the tank will be overflowing if I don't get back to turn the tap off soon, but feel free to stay here as long as you like.'

'Thanks,' Seren replied without turning round. 'I like it here, it's peaceful.'

Jude had her doubts about the quiet woman who'd seemed so vulnerable when they'd first met but had now given Jude reason to cast her net of suspicion over her. There was no denying her love for the animals, however, so Jude felt no qualms about leaving her in the paddock.

The tank was almost full by the time Jude returned and she waited just another few minutes before turning the tap off. In the sanctuary of the tractor cab, she took her own phone from her pocket, feeling the weight of the one she'd just purloined from under Seren's nose lying heavy against her hip.

It was still early so Jude sent Binnie a text to ask her to call when she was awake. Binnie called back within twenty seconds.

'Hi, Binnie. Sorry if I woke you.'

'You think you're the only one who gets up with the larks?' Binnie said. 'Your message sounded important. Everything okay?'

'I found a phone and I'm pretty sure it's Joe's.' Sitting in the tractor cab, Jude relayed her encounter with Seren.

'And you didn't ask her about it?' Binnie said when Jude had finished.

'She doesn't even know I saw it.'

'Good. Where is it now?'

Jude tapped the pocket of the puffer jacker reflexively. 'It's with me. Zipped into my pocket.'

'Okay. I've got a few things to tie up here but I'll come round at some point this morning to pick it up.'

'Give me a ring when you do,' Jude said. 'I'm out in the fields today.'

'Will do.'

'Oh, and Binnie. I am sorry about last night,' said Jude. 'I should have told you I was going round to Mike Trout's.'

Binnie sighed. 'I should be furious with you, of course, but you gave us a bit of a lead, actually.'

'Really?' Jude was relieved to hear this. 'You managed to tie Mike to the drug dealer?'

'No. He's saying that he knows nothing about it and we have nothing solid to warrant a search into his personal affairs. We're releasing him this morning.'

Jude's heart sank. 'What about the gun?' That fact that Binnie had just said they were going to let him go made Jude sure she already knew the answer to this one. 'Or the dibber?'

'I'm sorry to be blunt, Jude, but with one dead body and a missing person to deal with, I'm afraid the dibber won't be high priority for testing so we'll have to wait on that. The gun, on the other hand, now *that* had a secret to reveal.'

'Fingerprints?' Jude asked.

'No. Both the gun and the bag it was in were clean but we used the serial number to find out who it's registered to. Do you want to guess?'

'Who?' The vets' names spun through Jude's mind like an old-fashioned Rolodex whilst she waited for Binnie, who was stringing it out like they were watching the final of *The Great British Bake Off*. 'Just tell me.'

'Khadija Habib.'

20

Jude turned the key and listened to the throaty roar of the tractor's powerful engine. Sometimes there was no better place to be than the cab of a tractor when trying to sort out her thoughts, and this was one of those times.

She pushed her Bluetooth buds into her ears and decided to lose herself in the music of Edward Elgar, who'd lived in the area and famously wrote many of his most popular pieces with the hills as his backdrop and motivation. Jude let the power of 'Nimrod' wash over her for a moment, but even Elgar couldn't iron out the huge brain wrinkles that had been caused by finding Seren with Joe's phone and then discovering he'd been shot with a gun registered to Khadija.

Jude put the tractor in gear and set off down the drive whilst going through all the possible explanations that these two things had thrown up, as well as all the new questions. Why had Seren wanted Joe's phone? Obviously, there was something on it that she had wanted to find, or make sure nobody else did – but what? Why had Khadija brought her gun with her on a hen do? Had she been intending on using it all along; to kill Joe? Or had she thought she might need it as protection? If her parents were prepared to disown her and cut her off, were they also willing to hire someone to kill her? And by sticking his nose in, had Joe put himself in the path of danger too? If that was the case then surely that would mean Ash was in danger as well.

Or was it more likely that Khadija was frightened of the people at the head of the drug dealing ring? There was still a chance that Mike was involved in this too.

Jude drove out into the lane and, as she passed the Trouts' house, she stared up towards the front door, wondering what was happening inside. Was Mike home from the police station yet? And what about Val? How was she coping with all of this?

At the first of the OSR fields, Jude turned in and, once the tractor was fully off the lane, she took it out of gear and jumped down to check the state of the crop.

The smell of overcooked cabbages hit her – one of the downsides of growing the stuff – but the plants were looking healthy and the flowers were a gloriously rich colour. Jude pinched one between her fingers – really they could have done with being sprayed a week or so ago as they were already showing the first signs of dropping, but better late than never.

Jude returned to the cab and dropped the spraying arms. She started to drive steadily up the first line, gazing out over the sea of yellow and still battling with the indecipherable puzzle consisting of Mike Trout, Khadija's gun, the hens, the drug dealer, her poisoned sheep and how it all tied together with Joe's death and Khadija's disappearance. The events of the morning so far had served to remind her that nobody was beyond suspicion.

When she reached the edge of the field, she stopped the spraying nozzles and contracted the booms so she could turn to begin the next row.

She'd only gone halfway back along the second line when a call cut the music in her earbuds and she clicked the answer button on her phone.

'Hi, Binnie.'

'Thought you should know we've had an update about Gareth Johnson,' Binnie came straight to the point.

'The drug dealer who gave Ellie her black eye?'

'That's the one. They did a dawn raid on his house in Gloucester this morning and nicked him. Interesting thing, though, is that they found a load more drugs and a bunch of paperwork that all pointed to a specific vets somewhere near London.'

'That's great news,' said Jude. 'So this is where the dealers have been getting their supplies?'

'It certainly looks this way and there's something else. We've got a list of the vets who work there and you're going to recognise one of the names, and it's not who you'd expect.'

'Go on,' said Jude.

'It's Eleana Shaw.'

'Ellie?' Jude gasped. Binnie was absolutely right. Ellie was the last person Jude had expected to be mixed up in drug dealing.

'We have no proof as yet that she's directly involved but the practice she works at is acting as a gateway for criminals wanting to get hold of animal drugs with a high street value. Ketamine, fentanyl, steroids, sedatives; there's a big market out there and they've been doing this for years.'

'How have they got away with it for so long?' Jude asked.

'They got creative. From the paperwork we found, it looks like senior vets have been signing off prescription drugs that aren't needed, prescribing drugs for fake accounts or animals that have already died. They've also been buying in huge amounts of unlicensed drugs from abroad. The set-up is enormous.'

Jude thought about Ellie, the woman who seemed to have so much integrity and had helped save the Kerries when they'd been poisoned. She couldn't imagine her being responsible for the misuse of drugs. Jude had read an article in the *Farmers Weekly* only the other month about the amount of illegal drugs being brought in from India, Thailand, South Africa, even as far as Australia. Farmers and pet owners alike bought them online as a cheaper alternative to going through a vet, and Jude could almost understand that; the amount she had to spend each year on animal medicines was extortionate, and rising. But these drugs were often not regulated and dangerous. How could Ellie be involved in distributing potentially harmful drugs to animals? Not to mention the humans that were taking them too for recreation or as body enhancers.

'And you think Ellie's involved?'

'We'll find out soon enough,' said Binnie. 'She's being brought in for questioning as we speak.'

Jude was nearing the bottom of the field and, from her elevated position in the tractor cab, she could see a line of crops that had been totally flattened and ruined.

'Gah, those bloody doggy Instagrammers,' she grumbled into the phone.

'Pardon?' Binnie sounded confused at the sudden change of tack.

'Sorry. It's the new thing. Dog owners let their pets loose in a farmer's field where they bounce around all over it for the sake of a social media post. They even have a name for it, *land dolphins*. It looks cute but they leave behind a trail of ruined crops that we've spent time and money growing.'

As the tractor reached the largest patch of flattened plants, Jude could see that there was something there that didn't belong and it had nothing to do with out-of-control dogs or land dolphins.

'Binnie?' she said as she stopped the tractor and switched off the sprayer. 'Are you still there?'

'Only just but I'm going to have to fly as I've got things that need doing before I come to the farm.'

Jude opened the door of the cab and was climbing out, a very uneasy feeling in the pit of her stomach.

'Could you just hang on a moment?' she asked, unsure of what she was about to find amongst her oilseed rape crop.

'Everything okay?' Binnie had picked up on the quaver in Jude's voice but Jude could only reply with a sharp intake of breath as she parted the rape and saw what it was that had caused the flattening of her crops. There, lying face down on a bed of crushed yellow flowers and green-leafed stems, Jude finally found Khadija Habib.

21

Khadija was stone cold when Jude checked her for any sign of life and, judging by the dried-out and withered state of the flowers beneath her, she'd been lying there for a couple of days at least.

'She's dead,' Jude whispered into the phone and then cleared her throat to speak with more clarity. 'It's Khadija. I just found her in the rapeseed field across the lane from the farm.'

'Stay where you are.' Jude could hear Binnie crashing through a door and could imagine her grabbing her car key as she spoke. 'I'm on my way.'

* * *

When Binnie arrived with a team of officers, she took in the scene, crouching down to observe Khadija whilst being careful not to disturb anything.

'Have you touched the body?' she asked Jude.

'Only to check for a pulse.' Jude indicated the area of her own neck where the carotid artery was busy pumping blood around her body with an increased determination.

'And you've moved nothing else?'

'Nothing,' Jude confirmed. She suddenly remembered the phone in her pocket and quickly retrieved it so she could hand it over.

'Evidence bag?' At Binnie's request, Sami held a plastic bag out for Jude to drop the phone into. 'Found this morning in the paddock of Malvern Farm by Judith Gray,' Binnie said as Sami filled in the form to identify the phone. 'Possibly belonged to Joseph Birch.'

Binnie gave out her instructions to each of the attending officers and then turned her attention to Jude.

'Well, that answers one question, I suppose,' she said with a solemn glance towards the body. 'At least we can stop looking for Khadija and we can offer those close to her some closure.'

'But we're no closer to finding out who killed either her or Joe,' said Jude with a heavy heart.

'I'm no expert but I'd say she's been dead for a few days, although we'll have to wait for pathology to give us a more accurate idea of exactly when she died.' Binnie's conclusion matched Jude's thoughts, after seeing the crushed plants around the body.

'I wonder why the police search didn't pick her up,' Jude said.

'It's as though she was swallowed up by the rapeseed, leaving no sign of her entry. This stuff stinks too, I imagine it would have overpowered the dogs' noses.'

'The perfect hiding place,' Jude said, hugging her arms around herself.

'Exactly. Now we just have to find out how she ended up here. I need to head over to the campsite to have a word with the hens. I'm afraid the tractor is going to have to stay put for the moment, until we've cleared the scene. Do you want to jump in the car and I'll give you a lift back to the farm?'

'Thanks,' said Jude, trying hard not to think about the wasted crop and the impact it would have on the farm's income. If she couldn't spray it, she might lose more to a bout of sclerotinia fungus. It seemed harsh to be thinking of the harvest when there was a dead body lying in her field and yet, over the years, she'd been conditioned to measure the impact of every little anomaly on the performance of the farm.

'Sami,' Binnie called, 'I'm going to need you to come with me to carry out further enquiries with the hen party.'

'Right you are, boss,' the chirpy officer replied as he joined them and he gave Jude a smile laced with empathy.

Binnie drove the squad car, thankfully a sturdy four-wheel-drive vehicle, across the already mangled remnants of the crop and Jude knew that when the ambulance and pathology team arrived it was only going to get worse.

'Sorry about the mess,' Binnie said, as though Jude's internal monologue was being piped through the car's speakers.

'Oh, don't worry about that. There are bigger things to worry about than a bit of flattened oilseed rape.'

'Talk to me,' said Binnie as they bumped slowly along the rutted field towards the lane. 'What do I need to know about Seren? What was she doing with Joe's phone?'

'I don't know what to make of her but she's definitely hiding something. Hiding the jumper was one thing but the phone is something else. She seems so gentle and submissive.'

Sami leant through from the back seat. 'It's always the quiet ones you need to watch out for, isn't that right, boss?'

'Sami, if you call me boss one more time I will have to ditch you and go back to get Jez instead. Binnie in private, DI Khatri in public or just plain "detective" works too.'

'Gotcha,' said Sami.

'It's not just Seren I want to have a word with,' Binnie continued. 'Ellie's at the station already but I want to talk to the others too. I want to find out who knew Khadija had brought a gun on holiday with her for a start. It might have been registered in her name but any one of the hens could have used it, if they'd known where it was. We need to ask ourselves what motives would each one have for killing Joe and Khadija.'

This was something that Jude had already been over a thousand times before in her head.

'Obviously, we need to look into Ellie and the drugs,' Binnie began. 'That note Joe wrote would have us believe he knew Khadija and someone else were into something dodgy. Assuming that he was in fact talking about the drug dealing, and assuming we can prove Ellie herself was up to her eyeballs in it, I'd say she has a pretty good reason to want them dead. But what about the others?'

'Shaznay was cheated on by them both, we know that.' Jude leant her forehead against the cool glass of the car's window to help focus her mind. 'And a woman scorned can be the most dangerous of all the earth's creatures.'

'And what about the sister, Tanisha?' Binnie said. 'She clearly idolises her big sister. Do you reckon she'd try and protect her by getting the two people who were causing her harm out of the way?'

Jude thought again of the theory that everyone is capable of murder if they're pushed far enough; she'd always wondered if her breaking point would be if Sebbie or Lucy were in danger. Could Neesh have felt the same way?

'Maybe,' said Jude. 'And there's Ash, of course. She clearly hated Joe and with good reason. She blamed him for her break-up with Khadija and also for her disappearance.' Jude had seen for herself the intensity of Ash's feelings and it wasn't unusual for passion that strong to boil over and become destructive. Is this what had happened here? 'But I think she really believed Khadija was still alive until we found her phone yesterday so I can't imagine that she's involved in her death.'

As she said it, Jude realised that Binnie was about to do what must be the hardest part of her job – informing someone that the person they loved most in the world had died in terrible circumstances.

'Seren still has it, in my opinion,' said Sami, once more leaning across to make sure his voice was heard. 'I think she's mixed up in the whole drug thing and wanted out of it.'

Jude had initially kept Seren's name a little distant as she was such an unlikely candidate for the role of murderer but she pushed that to one side in order to face facts. She had been found in possession of Joe's phone and also hiding the yellow jumper. But what reason did she have? They'd both bullied her, but was that enough for her to become a murderer?

'I take it you've not had any luck tracking down the private investigator Joe hired?' Jude asked.

'No, and now I know he was diving into the workings of a drug ring I have to say I'm not surprised he's proving tricky to trace.'

Binnie looked up and down the lane before turning out and driving the short distance to the entrance of the campsite where they pulled up next to Khadija's 4x4.

'I know the car has already been searched but it would be good to get eyes on it again, just in case we've missed something,' said Binnie. She sat with her hands on the steering wheel and Jude knew that she was steeling herself for the next difficult step of the investigation.

'Come on.' Binnie's words were accompanied by a heavy sigh. 'Let's get on with it.'

'Do you want me to come too?' Jude was half hoping that it would be against some sort of protocol and she would be free to go back to the farmhouse but Binnie had other ideas.

'If you don't mind, Jude. You can't be involved in any formal interviews but it would be helpful if you could be there, especially when I introduce the idea of the gun – see if you notice anything in their reactions. This sort of news is bound to make whoever pulled the trigger skittish and if Sami and I then take them off individually for statements, you can stay back with the others and be my spy.' She looked into the back of the car to Sami. 'Unofficially, of course, Police Officer Abadi, and not to be repeated.'

'Of course not, boss,' said Sami, either completely ignoring Binnie's request not to use this term or, more likely, using it deliberately to get a reaction from her. Either way it came with a broad grin not suitable for the gravity of the situation.

Neesh, Shaznay and Dex had taken all the folding director's chairs from their huts and set them out in a semicircle where they sat with Ash. At the sight of Binnie and Sami, Ash jumped up with such force that her chair fell backwards.

'What's happened?' she demanded. 'Does Ellie know what happened to Khad? Is that why you took her in?'

Sami, now the ultimate professional, righted the chair and guided Ash back into it. 'Is Seren with you?' he asked.

'No,' said Neesh, 'she wasn't coping well and said she needed to go for a walk on her own. Is she okay?'

'As far as we know, she's fine,' said Binnie. 'It's just I had hoped to find you all together.'

'You have news, don't you?' Ash was once more out of her chair but this time it remained upright.

'I'm afraid we do,' said Binnie. 'I'm so sorry to have to tell you that we've found Khadija.'

The sound that came from Ash before she crumpled to the ground, clutching at her chest as though her heart was breaking beneath her ribs, was bone-chilling. Neesh was the first to get to her and catch her up in an embrace that she was almost certainly too numb to feel.

'I'm so sorry,' said Jude, the helpless watcher-on. 'If there's anything I can do...'

She took the chance to look around the group sitting in front of her, wondering if she could spot any unusual reaction to the news that might help point her in the direction of a murderer, but she found none. Shaznay stood up and went over to join her sister in supporting Ash whilst Dex looked on, his face a picture of horror and shock.

'How did she die?' he asked quietly.

Ash's head snapped up. 'Was it Ellie? Is that why you arrested her?'

'No,' said Binnie. 'Ellie hasn't been arrested, she's helping us with a different line of enquiry.'

'So what happened to Khadija?' Ash demanded.

'We don't know at the moment,' said Binnie. 'She was found in the middle of a field of rapeseed.'

'Here on the farm?'

'Yes,' Binnie confirmed. 'Just on the other side of the lane.'

'It was one of you,' Ash shouted, scrambling to her feet and pointing her finger at each of the others in turn. 'Who did it? Who killed her?'

'We don't know for certain that it was murder,' said Binnie, to Jude's surprise. 'We won't know anything more until an autopsy has been done.'

'I want to see her,' said Ash, who'd already started to make her way to the bottom of the camping field.

Sami put out a hand to stop her. 'I'm afraid you can't. Not yet.'

'Of course I can,' Ash said, trying to push past. 'She was everything to me.'

'I'll make sure you get to see her as soon as possible but right now the area is being treated as a crime scene so I have to ask you all to keep away.'

Ash relented and sank into the chair that Dex put down next to her. She fell forward and her shoulders started to shake as a fresh wave of grief took over.

'I'm so sorry to have to do this but I'm afraid PC Abadi and I must ask you all a few more questions.' Binnie nodded to Sami, who took out his pocketbook, poised to record anything of importance. 'We've had some new information regarding the death of Joseph Birch, specifically the weapon used in his murder. It's been identified as the sort of revolver that those of you who are vets might be familiar with if you've ever had the unenviable task of euthanising a larger animal.'

Again, Jude tried to read the faces around her. She could have assigned the label *shifty* to virtually everyone there, as they glanced around or deliberately avoided eye contact. It was a natural reaction, she supposed, to discovering another signpost that one of them might be the killer.

'It was registered to Khadija and I wondered if any of you might know why she brought it with her?'

Jude noticed that Ash had gone particularly quiet at this and there was a general muttering of surprised denial from the others. Binnie dropped this line of enquiry, for the moment at least.

'Okay, well, if you want to speak to me in confidence then you can do so as part of your statement. I'm sure you all want the same thing as I do – to find out who is responsible for this tragedy.'

'Of course.' It was Shaznay who broke the silence. 'Thank you.'

'Perhaps we can use the tent at the top of the field to conduct the interviews?' Binnie asked and Jude nodded. It was the furthest away, which would mean those left behind wouldn't be able to hear what was being said inside. 'And I wonder if someone could call Seren. We'll need to speak to her as well.'

Shaznay was the first to go into the big bell tent with Binnie and Sami and, whilst she was gone, Neesh tried unsuccessfully to contact Seren. Jude knew how much Seren liked to be on her own so it was perhaps unsurprising, and yet her absence bothered Jude. There was a chance that Seren herself was in danger. Maybe she'd uncovered something she shouldn't have, perhaps something she'd stumbled across on Joe's phone that was incriminating against one of the others. Or maybe she was the guilty one in all of this and she'd decided to do a runner, feeling the walls starting to close in.

Jude tried to rein in her imagination, tuning back into those sitting in their sorry little group.

Ash hadn't looked up since she'd collapsed into the chair. Her arms were hugged tightly around her body as though trying to stop the pain in her heart and she was rocking very gently from side to side as tears coursed down her face.

Neesh was standing, her head clasped by both her hands as though she was mimicking Edvard Munch's *The Scream*. 'This is all too much,' she said to Dex, who was standing in front of her. 'I need to go home now. I need to see Reggie.'

'It won't be long.' Dex was soft and gentle, reminding Jude of Adam, who'd always been her voice of calm when things got on top of her. 'Just another day or so and then we'll go home.'

Neesh looked up, hopefully. 'Tomorrow? Do you think they'll let us leave?'

'I don't see why not. We've already been told that we're here out of choice to help them with their enquiries. Well, let's help as much as we can today and then, if they need anything else, they'll know where to find us.'

Neesh laid her head against Dex's chest and shut her eyes.

'Do you think Shaz will come back with us too?' she asked.

'I reckon so. You wait and see, this will all be over really soon.' But Dex's certainty was belied by the look of worry that Jude could see etched in every line of his face.

Shaznay and Sami returned to the group then and Neesh swapped places with her sister, going back to the tent with Sami to give her statement. The group remained quiet as they watched each other troop one by one up to the top of the field to answer Binnie's questions. She kept it brief and in less than half an hour, the entire group had been seen and Binnie had returned to join them.

'That's all for now,' she said. 'Thank you for your patience and help. I'll let you know as soon as we have any updates but, in the meantime, I would urge you to contact me if you think of anything that might be useful. And I do need to talk to Seren so please tell her to get in touch as soon as she turns up.'

Jude followed Binnie and Sami down to the squad car.

'Did you pick anything up I might be interested in?' Binnie asked as she opened the driver's door.

'Not much, they were all pretty quiet. You?'

'Nothing. Sami and I are going to head back to the crime scene to find out what's going on there and then we'll go to the B&B to see if there's any sign of Seren.' Binnie held her finger up as her phone started to ring. 'Hang on.'

'DI Khatri... Yep... That's good. When are they coming back? ...Seriously? I see, well, at least contact has been made. Thanks for letting me know.'

She switched off the phone and looked across the roof of the car to Sami, who had the passenger door open ready to get in. 'They've spoken to Khadija's parents. Apparently, they're halfway across the Pacific and they've no intention of coming back to the UK until they've finished their holiday.'

'You have to be joking?' said Jude, incredulous at the thought of people being so callous about the death of their daughter.

'Nope,' Binnie said. 'It seems Ash wasn't exaggerating about them. Or the father at least, who told the DS that Khadija had made her choices when she decided to turn her back on her family and start a forbidden relationship with a woman.'

'Does he know that she's dead?'

Binnie sighed and nodded.

'Poor Khadija.' Jude shrugged her shoulders to try and relieve some of the building tension in her neck. Was there really no limit to the depths of some people's true awfulness? 'No wonder she was the way she was.'

'Yeah,' Sami agreed. 'It's such a shame that she and Ash didn't manage to get away together whilst they had the chance.'

There was a moment of silence as the sadness of the situation washed over them and then Binnie broke it by climbing into the car. 'We've got work to do, Sami.'

There was no cheery quip from the police officer this time as he sombrely took his place in the passenger seat. Jude watched the car drive off and then she turned to walk back through the campsite.

Ash was still in exactly the same position as she had been when they'd left and Neesh and Dex were sitting next to her. There was no sign of Shaznay but the sound of cups clinking in her hut indicated that someone was making tea.

Jude didn't know what to say as she passed them but as nobody looked her way, she continued on up towards the top of the field.

* * *

It wasn't even half eleven and yet it seemed like at least an entire day, or even two, had passed since Jude had filled the sprayer that morning in the hope of getting all eighty acres finished before lunch. Now it looked as though it might not get done at all before the petals started to significantly drop, signalling that the window to protect the crop had closed.

As she walked back over the yard to the house, a weighty blanket of exhaustion settled over her. It had been a week of horror, disruption and turmoil and there was no sign of an end any time soon. Even if the hens were allowed to go home, as Neesh hoped they would, she would be left with the police investigation happening around her and another black cloud hanging over the farm's already dark reputation.

Jude craved a little stability and escapism, something that would help her forget what was going on just for a little while. What she needed was to go for a long walk with her dogs, out into the woodland at the edge of her land beyond the top fields that headed north along the bottom of the hills.

She stopped off at the farmhouse to collect Pip and Alfie and decided to take the opportunity to grab a quick bite to eat at the same time. Breakfast had been a long time ago and the way her day was shaping up, who knew when she'd next have the chance? The soft fur of the dogs as she stroked their backs, waiting for the bread to toast on the Aga plate, helped calm her mind.

'What would I do without you pair, hey?' she said as she stood up to rescue the toast before it burnt.

A good slather of local butter, some of Noah's piccalilli and some cold shredded chicken and she had a lunch fit for a farmer. She bent the whole thing in half and wrapped it in a sheet of kitchen paper.

'Come on, I need to get out of here,' she said to the dogs. 'I'll eat on the hoof.'

She stopped in the porch on the way out to collect a lead for Alfie but the peg where his usual green halter rope hung was empty so she picked up a long lead instead. It was annoying as it was a good lead and she'd only just splashed out on a new one. She must remember to ask Noah if he'd seen it.

The sandwich tasted delicious and helped to recharge her batteries as she crossed the yard. Making their way up the side of the first field, Jude gave Alfie a longer line and watched his reaction as he saw the sheep. He was certainly interested in them, lying low in the grass and watching them carefully, creeping forward bit by bit. Any time he started to run towards them, Jude flicked the end of the line and called him back to attention and he responded by halting and watching. His gaze never left the sheep, and Jude felt that if she let him off the lead then he'd not be able to resist the urge to chase them, but for now this was a good enough sign that he was learning and that was something to lift her spirits.

At the top of the field, she walked out into the woods and found it to be just the tonic she needed. The dogs ran between the trees, their tails high and their noses low to the ground, sniffing out the scents of rabbits, squirrels and foxes, with a feeling that was almost peaceful.

The sensation of peace was marred, though, by the incessant questions that refused to leave her alone.

Jude wondered what was happening at the police station. Had Ellie admitted to playing a part in the illegal drug distribution? Had they found Seren and, if so, had they discovered what she was doing with Joe's phone? Had either Khadija or Joe's phones thrown any new evidence into the mix?

And then there was Khadija herself, who'd died knowing that her parents had not only rejected her life choices but also her position in their family. Binnie had hinted at the fact that they weren't necessarily looking at murder but what did that mean? Had Khadija been so worn down by her life that she'd been responsible for her own death?

As Jude progressed further into the woods, she found that the questions and the frustration of feeling so far from any answers were gaining momentum and that her walk was becoming less and less relaxing. She called the dogs to her and turned round to head back to the farm. She wanted to talk everything through with Lucy or Binnie but they were both busy at work so she was going to have to be patient. Noah should be around somewhere, though, and he was an excellent listener as well as conjugator of facts. Jude remembered him saying that he was planning to do some training with Ned so she decided to take a detour via the paddock of Hebridean Blackies, in case he was still there.

Somewhere a cuckoo called, his voice standing out over the many other birds that chirruped and sang from the ancient hedgerow that marked both the edge of the paddock and the edge of her land. The hawthorn was full of frothy white May blossom and Jude could see the wild dog roses already budding, ready for their display of delicate pink blooms that would be bursting from their green shells in a few weeks.

The handsome Hebridean sheep with their striking horns and dark fleeces were all peacefully chewing on the grass of their paddock with no sign of a shepherd or a sheepdog other than her own in sight. A couple of them raised their heads in interest as Jude approached but they weren't in the least bit concerned by the presence of the dogs, even though Alfie was pulling on the end of the lead, clearly over-excited as he remembered the fun he'd had last time he'd been here.

'Maybe he's back at the pink cottage,' Jude wondered aloud. 'Let's go and have a look, shall we?'

She glanced down at the dogs but they were distracted by something and were both looking towards the hedge at the edge of the paddock. Jude followed their gaze and saw a small cloud of white smoke swirling into the air from behind a gorse bush that had grown into a large clump beside the tangle of ancient hedgerow.

'Walk here,' Jude instructed and the dogs followed her as she went into the paddock.

'Hello?' she called as she approached the vaguely biblical-looking smoking bush. There was no answer but when she looked around the edge of the gorse, she found Seren sitting on the grass on the other side, her knees hunched up to her chest and a vape in her hand. She didn't look as Jude sat down next to her.

'There is no other breed with more magnificent horns,' Seren said, staring ahead at the sheep grazing peacefully in front of her. 'Yours are all beautifully curled but have you ever seen a multi-horned ram where the pair on the top of his head are straight? Imagine the damage he could do if he wanted to.'

'Indeed,' Jude said. 'It's part of the reason we've not got any here. I wouldn't fancy ending up with a skewered collie.'

Seren still didn't take her eyes off the sheep and Jude realised that she didn't even appear to be blinking.

'I didn't have you down as a smoker,' she said.

Seren's almost trance-like state finally broke as she looked down at the vape in her hand.

'I'm not, really. Not now, at least, although I did get quite addicted in my finals year at vet school. It was the stress of the exams and the fear of failure.'

She turned her attention back to the sheep and put the vape to her lips again, drawing in a deep breath that triggered the filthy stick to release a thick cloud of strawberry-scented vapour into the air. She winced as the gas went down her throat.

'In those days I smoked proper cigarettes, though. I have to say this thing is horrid. It's the first time I tried one and I don't think I'll bother again, it's like it's burning my throat.' She looked at it again in disgust. 'And they're terrible for the environment too.'

'Then do you mind me asking why you've got it?' Jude asked.

'I found it on the gatepost by your paddock. It must be one of Joe's. He always had one with him, didn't care whose face he puffed it into. I saw it on my way out after you found me there this morning and I picked it up. I suppose the old addiction kicked in and I thought this would be better than nothing.'

She took another drag and again her face crumpled as she swallowed before turning to face Jude.

'I know you found Joe's phone in the paddock this morning and I'm pretty sure you know it was me who dropped it there.'

As she spoke, Seren's hand went to her throat and she swallowed again, wincing as she did so.

'Are you okay?' Jude asked, realising that Seren was clearly in some pain. 'Here, perhaps you should give that to me.'

Seren handed over the vape and Jude put it into her pocket.

'Jude, I need to tell you something.' Seren's hand was still on her throat, and she twisted her neck as if to find some relief from the pain.

'You really don't look well,' said Jude. 'Let's get you back to the farm and find you something to drink.'

'No, Jude. Listen, please, it's important.'

But, to Jude's horror, before she could say what was causing her so much distress, her eyes closed in pain and she fell backwards onto the grass.

'Seren,' Jude gasped as she knelt down next to Seren, but there was no response.

Fuelled by adrenaline, Jude's first aid training kicked in and she quickly checked for signs of life. Seeing that she was still breathing, Jude put her into the recovery position and phoned for an ambulance. Whilst she waited with Seren, Jude called Noah for backup and then she sat next to the unconscious woman, stroking her thin blonde hair and talking to her in a constant stream of what she hoped were soothing reassurances.

After what felt like ages, she heard the sound of an ambulance crossing the field to get to them, with Noah leading the way on the quad. When it stopped, two paramedics got out and rushed through the gate that Noah was holding open.

'Hello there. My name's Sue and this is my colleague, Raff. Who have we got here?' one of the paramedics asked whilst the other bent over to do an initial assessment.

'Her name's Seren.' Jude pulled the vape from her pocket and handed it over to them. 'I found her smoking this. She was clearly in quite a lot of pain when she breathed in and then she just collapsed.'

Sue looked at the vape. 'Nasty things,' she said, 'but it's extremely unlikely to have caused this reaction.' She passed it back to Jude, who zipped it into the pocket of her jacket.

'Do you know if she has any allergies?' Raff asked as he clipped an oxygen sats monitor to Seren's ghostly white finger.

'I have no idea,' said Jude. 'She's been staying on our campsite as a guest. You'd be better off talking to one of her friends but I'm afraid that might be a bit awkward.'

'Not to worry,' said Sue. 'Although it might be nice if she had someone she knows at the hospital with her.'

Jude looked at Noah, who nodded. 'I'll go down and see if I can find one of the hens.'

Sue raised an eyebrow. 'Hens?'

'She's here as part of a hen party,' Jude explained as Noah pulled his helmet on and got back onto the quad bike.

'I see. Would you have any idea if the hens were using any kind of recreational drugs?'

As Sue put it out there, Jude realised that it wasn't a totally ludicrous idea. At least one of the hens was involved in the illegal distribution of drugs. Seren was certainly not using anything to help the party spirit but had she taken something to take the edge off her evident anxiety?

'I couldn't say. But I suppose it isn't out of the question.'

At that moment there was a retching sound from Seren and a stream of vomit spewed from her mouth across the grass.

Pip and Alfie started to edge towards her to get a better sniff.

'Leave,' Jude bellowed and they backed off and lay down to observe from a safe distance.

'That's it,' said Raff, stroking Seren's back. 'You're okay there.'

Seren opened her eyes for a moment and stared at Jude in confusion. It looked as though she was trying to say something but another wave of retching took over, although this time it was dry.

'Right then, let's get her on the stretcher and take her in for a proper once-over at the infirmary.' Sue stood up and headed back to the ambulance.

Jude followed to help her fetch the stretcher so that Raff could stay with Seren.

'We'll have her right as rain before you know it,' Sue reassured her as she pulled the stretcher from her ambulance and the wheels dropped into place. 'You did a great job of looking after her.'

Jude knew that this was meant to make her feel better but it didn't. This was the second ambulance to attend the farm that day and it felt as though things were starting to unravel fast. It was becoming more and more difficult to cling on to the threads of evidence they had. Seren had wanted to tell her something and it sounded like it was something important. Was it linked to the two deaths of her friends? Except they weren't her friends, were they? She'd hated them both and with very good reason too.

'I'll go with you,' Jude said as Raff and Sue expertly lifted Seren onto the lowered stretcher.

'I'm sure she would appreciate that,' said Raff as he tucked a blanket over her.

Jude watched the two paramedics belt Seren into the stretcher securely and remove the various monitors that had been attached to her. Then they pushed her slowly over the bumpy grass to the ambulance, where she was lifted in through the back door. Once inside, Seren was reattached to monitors that blinked and flashed, giving readings that Jude knew to be her pulse, blood pressure, oxygen sats, and so on, although deciphering them was beyond what she'd been able to pick up from the evenings she and Lucy spent watching *Casualty*.

As she was about to climb into the back of the ambulance, the sound of the quad approaching made her turn around.

Noah stopped just short of them and his passenger jumped off the back and took off her helmet.

'Oh my God, Seren,' said Shaznay, clambering up into the ambulance and looking from the unconscious form of her friend to the paramedic who was tending her. 'Is she going to be okay?'

'We'll certainly do all we can to make sure she is,' Raff said. 'Are you a friend of hers?'

'Yes. Can I come with her to the hospital?'

Raff looked back at Jude. 'Only one of you can come, I'm afraid.'

'It should be Shaznay,' said Jude instantly. 'I was only stepping in so Seren wouldn't be alone but Shaznay's her friend. I'm sure Seren would be really grateful to see her when she wakes up.'

'Right, then.' Sue closed the back door. 'We'll be off.'

'Thank you,' said Jude, hoping Seren would make a fast recovery.

Noah and Jude watched the ambulance drive slowly over the field, Sue obviously trying her best to make the ride as smooth as possible for the patient inside.

'Well, then,' Noah said, putting an arm around Jude's shoulder and drawing her towards him. 'Do you think that's enough drama for one day?'

'I hope so.' Jude sighed. 'But you can never tell around here.'

22

Thankfully it turned out that the rest of the day was relatively quiet. Khadija's body was taken from the field and Jude was given permission to continue spraying the OSR, although she was asked to leave the immediate area around the crime scene alone. The place where the body had been discovered was marked with a cordon of black and yellow tape and the ground leading up to it had been completely destroyed by the various emergency vehicles that had needed to cross the field.

'It's only a hectare or so,' she said to Noah as he dropped her back down in the field where the tractor was still waiting for her. 'Nothing in the grand scheme of things, I suppose.'

'True enough,' Noah agreed. 'You'll be okay, will you?'

'Unless there are any more bodies lurking somewhere in there then I'll be fine.'

There was a curious absence of people by the crime scene itself but Jude assumed they'd investigated all they needed to and had packed up.

'I'll get back then but call if you need anything,' Noah said.

He turned his ancient Land Rover in a big loop and Jude climbed back up into the cab of the tractor. It took a bit of careful manoeuvring to back out of the way of the cordoned-off area and turn the tractor to retrace its last path to the top of the field. From there, Jude lowered the booms again and continued on her path up and down the field, staying well clear of the black and yellow tape.

There was something very therapeutic about the repetitive job of driving up and down the fields, keeping to the tramlines between the yellow flowers, only stopping when the spray tank needed re-filling. She listened to a couple of podcasts from Fed By Farmers and found the banter of hosts Cammy and Iona enough of a distraction to keep her absorbed and entertained until, at the end of the day, with a mixture of relief and satisfaction, she drove back up the drive and parked the tractor in the yard. She'd done a pretty accurate job of working out the right amount of spray needed and there was just a small amount of fungicide still slopping around in the bottom of the tank but she'd leave cleaning that and the sprayer nozzles for another day.

She left her boots in the porch, hung Adam's jacket on a peg and opened the door into the kitchen where she found Lucy and Sebbie sitting together with a jigsaw between them.

'Aunty Judy, come and help us,' said Sebbie, his little face lighting up at the sight of her.

Jude was dog-tired, a phrase she hadn't understood since first Pip and then Alfie had bowled into her life with their seemingly endless supplies of energy, and yet she couldn't say no to the offer of joining her two favourite people.

'Let me just wash my hands and make a cup of tea and then I'll come and see what you're up to,' she said.

'I spoke to Noah,' said Lucy as Jude turned the tap on in the kitchen sink. 'He told me what's been going on here today.'

'What has happened here today?' Sebbie asked, only half interested as he tried to force a puzzle piece into a space it wasn't supposed to fit in.

'Boring stuff,' said Lucy, taking the piece from his hand and swapping it for another. 'Stuff about tidying up and cleaning.'

Jude silently congratulated her sister for choosing probably the only two things that would mean Sebbie was switched off completely from the conversation.

'It was definitely a mess here today, that's for sure.' Jude dried her hands and put her hands under the knitted tea-cosy to check the warmth of the pot beneath.

'It's fresh,' said Lucy so Jude took a mug from the cupboard and filled it with tea and the smallest dash of milk. 'Do you think it's been cleaned up now?' Lucy asked. 'The big mess, I mean.'

'Binnie has been very helpful with the tidying but there are still lots of mucky spots that will need a much deeper clean. Lots of them I don't even know if there are sprays powerful enough to sort them out.'

'We'll get there,' said Lucy. 'We always do.'

'Mummy, that bit doesn't go there,' said Sebbie indignantly, taking a jigsaw piece from Lucy's hand. 'You're trying to put the piggy's tail on the cow's nose. Look.'

Lucy concentrated on what she was doing. 'My goodness, you're absolutely right. They're both pink and I got muddled up.'

'Silly Mummy.' Sebbie took the piece and put it into the correct place.

Jude picked up the box and looked at the stereotypical picture of a farm on the front. Chickens, pigs, a horse and a couple of cows all loose in the yard where two rosy-cheeked children in very clean welly boots were laughing together. A woman wearing dungarees with her hair caught up in a headscarf was scattering generic food out of a bucket whilst a man, presumably her husband, sat on a tractor that looked as though it belonged in a museum of rural life.

As a farmer, and a woman, she found so much to fault about the picture and yet there was something inherently reassuring about the smiling faces and general carefree nature of this perfect family.

'You've done so much of it already,' she said. 'Well done.'

'Kai gave it to him at nursery today and Sebbie wanted to crack it open as soon as we got home.'

'It's for my birthday.' Sebbie bent his strawberry-blond head over the jigsaw and picked up another piece. 'This is a sheep so it must go on the hill.'

Lucy and Jude exchanged a look over the top of his head.

'You okay?' Lucy mouthed and Jude replied with a nod.

'I had a message from Binnie,' she replied. 'Do you mind if I go over there this evening? Just for an hour or two. It definitely won't be a late one. You could come too if Noah's happy to look after Sebbie.'

'Yes, please.' Sebbie looked round at the sound of his name. 'I do like Noah looking after me and I can show him my new jigsaw.'

'We'll see,' Lucy replied.

When Noah called round less than ten minutes later, Sebbie didn't have any qualms about jumping straight in with his request.

'Of course I can look after you,' Noah said. 'It would do your mum and Aunty Jude good to get out for a bit.'

'That's settled then,' said Jude with a smile.

* * *

Binnie lived in Malvern Link on the other side of the hills and it took around fifteen minutes for Lucy to drive them there in her little car. Jude had offered to take the Land Rover but was secretly relieved when Lucy insisted as it meant she could indulge in a glass of wine or two.

When they arrived, Binnie opened the door dressed in tracksuit bottoms and thick knit jumper, her hair still slightly damp from the shower.

'Come in.' She stepped aside to let Jude and Lucy through the door where they were met by the smell of pizza cooking.

'This is for you.' Jude passed her the cold bottle of white wine, a layer of condensation frosting the glass. 'Actually, it's for me too. I thought we could use a glass or two after the day we've had.'

'Already a glass ahead of you,' Binnie laughed, pointing at the open kitchen door where a large glass sat at the kitchen table. 'Lucy, will you join us?'

'I'm the taxi service this evening so just a very small one for me.'

'Get down, Babur.' Binnie picked up a handsome cat with striking tiger markings from the kitchen worktop and plonked him on the floor, where he immediately wound himself around Jude's legs.

'Here you go.' Binnie passed Jude a fairly sizeable and extremely welcome glass of wine and a Lucy a more driver-friendly measure. 'Pizzas won't be long but there are nibbles on the table to keep us going. I don't know about you both but I'm famished.'

Jude was more than happy to take a seat at the clutter-free kitchen table, bearing only a beautifully embroidered jade-green runner and two plates of delicious-looking nibbles.

'No party rings and sausage rolls?' Lucy teased as she sat down next to Jude and helped herself to a deep-fried king prawn.

'I'm sure the corner shop is still open if you want to run out and get some,' said Binnie, joining them at the table with a bowl of some sort of pastry puffs.

'Thanks for this,' Jude said as she helped herself to a puff. 'This is exactly what I needed. Food, wine, a clean kitchen and two of my favourite women to share it all with. A bit of space from the insanity that's currently unravelling on the farm.' She bit into the puff and it burst with delicious spices.

'Sorry to pop the bubble but there are some updates that I think you'll be interested in,' Binnie said, helping herself to a pastry puff.

'Go on,' said Jude, who hadn't been naïve enough to think that she could have a night off from the hens. She was also keen to gain any information that might help solve the mystery and send them on their way.

'Firstly, the ballistics report is in and it proves that the bullet that shot Joe was definitely fired from the gun registered to Khadija.'

'No surprise there,' said Lucy.

'Maybe not but I had a call earlier this evening regarding Khadija that is perhaps far more surprising.' Binnie blew on her puff to cool it down. 'Initial investigations would suggest that she died from natural causes.'

'What?' This was the last thing Jude had expected.

'It seems she suffered a cardiac arrest almost certainly brought on by the prolonged respiratory exhaustion of an asthma attack.'

'She wasn't murdered?' Lucy was obviously as surprised by this as Jude was.

'I'm certainly not ruling it out yet and, under the circumstances, I've requested a deeper post-mortem.' Babur jumped onto Binnie's lap and settled down as she stroked his back. 'But preliminary tests show that her lungs were highly inflamed and in a pretty poor state. It's possible that the attack was triggered by exposure to the oilseed rape and she collapsed, never to regain consciousness.'

Jude mulled this new piece of information over. 'Could she have killed Joe and then run away to the field with no care for her own welfare as a direct reaction to her guilt?'

'We need to wait for further information but it's definitely plausible,' said Binnie.

Plausible. That word represented every mental line of enquiry that Jude was wrestling with. So many options involving so many possible murderers and each one of them plausible, but which one would lead them to the truth?

The oven timer rang out and Jude stood up. 'You stay there,' she said to Binnie. 'I don't want to get you in trouble with Babur.'

She went over to the cooker where a virtually immaculate, unblackened pair of oven gloves hung from the oven door. Silencing the timer, she opened the oven and pulled out the first pizza, which she rested on the top of the hob before reaching in to get the other.

A thought occurred to Jude and her brow furrowed as she tried to iron it out.

'What if someone was clever enough to stage Khadija's death to make it look accidental?' She put the pizzas onto big plates and started cutting them into slices.

'Always possible,' said Binnie. 'You look like you have another theory.'

'I'm just thinking about the inhaler that was found tucked behind the toilet.' Jude took the pizzas over to the table and put them down next to the bowls of nibbles. 'Everyone in the hen party knew the extent of Khadija's asthma and therefore would have known the danger she'd have been in if she was caught somewhere that was likely to trigger an attack. Especially if she didn't have her inhaler with her. Could they have taken it and somehow made her go into the field that was in full flower?'

'It's an interesting thought.' Binnie took another sip from her wine glass. 'The thing is, she did have an inhaler with her. It was found by the forensic team very close to her hand, which would lead us to conclude that she had either been trying to take her medication when she had the cardiac arrest, or she didn't manage to get enough in her before she fell unconscious.'

'How horrible.' Lucy grimaced at the thought.

'I'm still keeping an open mind about what happened in the rapeseed field but for now I think we're best focusing our efforts on trying to find out who killed Joe,' said Binnie. 'At least until we've had the results back from the deeper autopsy.'

Jude took a piece of chargrilled vegetable and chicken pizza and bit into it. She couldn't ally herself with the belief that Khadija's death had been nothing more than a tragic accident. It involved too many coincidences and Jude had learnt a long time ago not to overlook coincidences.

'What did you get from Ellie?' Lucy asked.

'Plenty,' said Binnie. 'She knew all about the drugs and, once we started questioning her, she didn't hold anything back. It was as though she was glad to finally come clean about everything.'

'Was she involved herself?' Jude was still struggling to align the thought of a ruthless drug dealer with the kind vet who'd saved four of her sheep.

Binnie took a sip of her wine. 'She was seduced by one of the senior partners quite soon into her career. According to Ellie, he promised her a role as a junior partner if she would do a few favours for him in return.'

Jude felt her stomach turn. 'Let me guess. What started out as something small escalated until she was in too deep to find a way out?'

'That's pretty much the shape of it. She said she feared that, if she went to the police, the men at the very top of the triangle would find a way to make her pay with far more than just money.'

'Poor Ellie,' said Lucy. 'Will she go down for it?'

'I can't say for sure what will happen but at the very least she'll be struck off for her part in it all.'

'It must have seemed like a golden opportunity to a young vet.' Jude could imagine it. Poor, naïve Ellie indeed, embarking on a career to save animals and getting so tangled up in the corruptness of her bosses that she couldn't see a way out. 'A dream job that ended up being a complete nightmare.'

'We've arrested the senior partners and I can imagine, with the weight of the evidence against them, they'll be put away for a very, very long time.'

'That's some good news,' said Lucy.

'And there's the other thing. Guess who got her the job in the first place?'

Jude raised her eyebrows and looked at Binnie. 'Khadija?'

'You got it in one,' said Binnie.

'So she *was* involved.' Lucy pushed her hair out of her eyes and shook her head slowly in disgust.

'Not just involved, but Ellie reckons pretty high up the ladder.'

'That's where all the money to run away was coming from,' said Jude. 'Do you think Ash knew the truth or did she really believe the bullshit about the racehorses?'

'I really don't know,' said Binnie. 'But Joe's private investigator certainly found out.'

'Did you manage to track him down?' Lucy picked a piece of chicken from her pizza and put it in her mouth.

'We're still working on it. We found an email thread on Joe's phone to someone he just calls G, who was following Khadija, but there are no other details on who G is. We have his email address, a generic Gmail account so no link to a company name or anything.' Binnie picked up the bottle of wine and topped Jude's glass up before adding a splash into her own. 'It's possible that the investigator used a different email address for each client, which will make him tricky to find. We do know from Ellie that Joe confronted her about the drugs and tried to blackmail her into giving him a cut to keep quiet.'

'Do you think she killed him to keep him quiet?' Lucy asked.

'It's possible,' said Binnie. 'But I can't help thinking that if she had killed Joe then she'd have been far more reluctant to tell us as much as she did. Ellie wasn't frightened of the police finding out about what she was involved in, I think she was relieved to have it all out in the open so I don't think she would have killed to stop the truth coming out.'

'You think the only reason she didn't come clean sooner was because she was afraid of what the people at the top would do to her,' suggested Jude.

'That's exactly what I think.'

'Is she safe from them now?' Lucy asked.

'We'll make sure of it.'

Jude thought of her in a prison cell. Ellie had been stupid and naïve but she wasn't a bad person. Far from it, and yet her life was ruined now in so many ways, even if the police could keep her safe. She would surely be facing a prison sentence for what she'd done and there was no chance she'd work as a vet again after this. All that hard work and dedication down the drain, not to mention the passion with which she looked after the animals in her care; Jude had seen that with the Kerry Hills.

Thinking about her sheep made her mind turn to Seren.

'Any news from the hospital?' Jude asked. 'Should we be looking at Seren as a possible third target?'

'It's impossible to say at this point. She's regained consciousness but any questioning will have to wait until tomorrow.'

'Do they know what happened to her?' Lucy asked, reaching forward to take another slice of pizza.

'No sign of any recreational drugs in her system but they're going to be carrying out more tests tomorrow.' Binnie picked up her wine glass and took a deep swig. 'I'm going in to talk to her as soon as she's up to it.'

'When I found her, she was trying to tell me something and it seemed really important to her.' Jude had been so preoccupied with everything else that this had only just come to her mind. 'But she was unconscious before she managed to get the words out.'

'Do you have any idea what it might have been about?' Binnie asked.

'She knew I'd found Joe's phone and that she'd taken it. I can't help wondering if there's anything on there that might be linked to whatever it was she wanted to tell me.'

Binnie picked Babur off her knee and put him on the floor. Then she went over to a stylish cabinet in the corner of the room, took out a bundle of papers and brought them over to set down between Jude and Lucy.

'I copied these at work. They're print-outs of some of the text threads we found on Joe's phone and they make for pretty nasty reading, I'm afraid.'

Jude picked up the first sheet and held it so that Lucy could read it as well. It was a string of messages between Joe and Shaznay.

JOE

> I am so lucky to have you in my life. I can't believe you actually said yes.

SHAZNAY

> Can't wait to be Mrs Birch.

JOE

> Let's not leave it too long. How are you fixed for the end of May?

SHAZNAY

> May? That's only a couple of months. My parents will have a fit.

JOE

> Your parents love me.

Joe was back to his usual overconfident self.

'All sounds pretty romantic to me,' said Jude.

'Not when you put it together with this thread that he sent to Khadija whilst he was already dating Shaznay.' Binnie passed her another sheet.

Jude glanced at it and read out a couple of messages that really stood out.

JOE

> What the hell is going on with you and this Ash woman? Shaz told me you think you're in a relationship. You're just going with a woman to mess with my head. I know it.

'I don't know why she doesn't just block him at this point,' said Lucy. 'Listen to this: "Let me know when your little game is over. You win, you've got my attention so let's just put this nonsense behind us and get back together."'

Jude read some of Khadija's replies.

KHADIJA

> You're going to have to get over it, Joe. I'm with Ash now and it isn't fake. I love her.

'Keep going,' said Binnie.

Jude cast her eyes down the page and it soon became very apparent that Joe was obsessed with Khadija and her new relationship, clearly thinking that it was all some kind of elaborate show for his benefit.

'Ash told us she and Khadija had been together for several years before they were open about it,' Jude reasoned, 'so it would seem that if anything was fake in Khadija's life, then it was any sort of relationship she'd had with Joe.'

'Well, he was clearly hedging his bets.' Lucy had flicked to the last page and was pointing at a group of messages near the bottom. Jude read the words with a growing feeling of disgust – words of love, commitment and loyalty, but not to the woman he had just asked to marry him.

JOE

> I know you still love me as much as I love you. We belong together and as soon as you admit that I will break things off with Shaz.

'I think we can assume that Khadija wasn't as forceful in her rejection of him as she perhaps should have been for a couple of reasons,' said Binnie. 'She certainly comes across as the sort of person to see the benefit of having someone so completely besotted with her. If you go back a few pages, she asks him for money and there are also other requests scattered through. Lifts here and there, a place to stay when she's had an argument with Ash, all sorts of things, and he, of course, was always only too happy to oblige.'

'They were both playing games,' said Lucy. 'It's Ash and Shaznay I feel sorry for. I wonder how much of this they knew was happening.'

Jude thought about the complex web of lies and abuse of trust that had been rife in the lives of the two people who were now resting in refrigerated drawers at the morgue.

'Not very nice characters,' said Jude, setting the clutch of paper down on the table.

'I shouldn't say this as an upstanding member of His Majesty's police force, but I can't feel any scrap of sadness over Joe's death. He really was one of those particularly nasty pieces of work and I wonder what loss he actually is to the world.'

Jude had never heard Binnie speak with such venom, and she'd dealt with some pretty horrendous characters in the time they'd known each other.

'I'm afraid I've saved the worst for last and it does not make for pleasant dinner-time reading.' She passed a final printed sheet over to Jude and Lucy. 'It isn't long but it seems to sum up everything that's despicable about the man.'

The sheet of paper contained just three messages. All of them to Seren and none of them with a reply.

JOE

> Hello Seren, it's Joe here. You must be excited to be getting a message from a man who isn't your dad. Haha! Just wanted to say that you looked hot tonight at the pub but you might find it easier to get laid if you smile a bit more and actually say something when a man talks to you. Free advice from someone who knows. You're welcome.

'What an arsehole,' said Lucy but Jude was already reading on. She could feel the pizza she'd just eaten start to congeal in her stomach.

JOE

> Glad you saw sense and unblocked me. I told you I had something important that you needed to hear and I am a man who always keeps a promise. I know your little secret – you're not as innocent as you appear, are you my little Welsh bird? Tell you what, why don't you come to my house at 7 this evening and see if you can persuade me not to tell anyone. Oh and wear some make-up – if you've got any.

According to the timestamps on the messages, the next one was sent at 7.11 that same evening.

JOE

> Oh my God, that is so funny. You stupid slapper, I can't believe you thought I'd actually want a piece of you!!! It's both pathetic and hilarious. Sorry I didn't open the door when you came round but unlike you, I'm not that desperate. Don't worry, your secret is safe. For now at least but you might want to make sure you don't block me again. More free advice. PS have fun at the hen do and try being nice to Khad, you might learn a thing or two from her.

Jude could come up with no words to voice her complete disgust. She thought of poor, shy Seren who loved animals and craved peace and quiet. How must she have felt reading these toxic, repugnant words? Worried enough to do exactly what Joe told her, but why? Was she also involved with the drugs scam? Perhaps this was what she wanted to tell Jude. If so, then what did that mean? Had she been the next intended victim? Or had she been the one to use a vet's revolver to take out the man who'd been blackmailing her?

23

Early the following morning, Jude went into the orchard to release the bantam hens for the first time since Joe's body had been discovered on the grass outside. She was slightly apprehensive about stepping into what had been the scene of such a horrific murder, but the white tent had been removed and someone must have been in with a hose to clean the area where the expansive blood stain had been.

The hens clucked and flapped their wings with gusto as they escaped the confines of the henhouse and scratched around on the grass, glad to be outside in the open air again after their short confinement.

'Have you been busy for me?' Jude picked up a basket from the shed and went to fill it with the small but perfect eggs, some still warm to the touch.

With the eggs safely deposited in the kitchen, Jude called for Pip to accompany her on the field rounds.

'Not you, Alfie,' she said to the ever-eager pup, who ran up hopefully. 'I need to know I can trust you properly with the sheep before you come and do the rounds with me.'

Out in the shed, Jude climbed onto the quad bike and Pip took her place in the dog box on the back. She sat tall with her tongue hanging out, anticipation of the fun she knew she was about to have making her alert and ready for the off.

Jude relished the drive up through the fields as much as Pip did and felt the early-morning sun warm her both inside and out as she toured each of the fields with her eyes flicking from sheep to sheep, checking for any sign of a problem. The lambs born that spring were three months old and growing well, now big and strong enough to be a little less of a worry than when they'd been tiny, vulnerable, newborn bundles. It was still a relief to shut the gate on each field having found all the inhabitants safe and well.

As she finished the tour of the furthest field and was about to head back down to the farm, Jude saw a figure walking in from the top path. It looked like Ash, a fact that was confirmed as she drove up to meet her.

'You're up early,' Jude said.

'I've been awake most of the night.' The wan pallor of the woman's face served to prove this and Jude felt a huge wave of empathy for her.

'I can imagine,' she said gently. 'I'm just about to head back to the farm for breakfast. Can I make you a bacon butty?'

Ash's already worried face knotted into further anguish. 'I couldn't eat a thing, but I was hoping to find you to see if you'd heard anything else from your friend about Khadija. Do they know how she died yet?'

Jude knew she wasn't at liberty to discuss the matter until it had been officially disclosed to the hens by Binnie, despite the strong desire to provide answers that might help this grieving woman begin to process what had happened.

'I'm so sorry, Ash,' she said. 'I'm sure Binnie will be around later to talk to you and give you any update that she has.'

'Neesh and Shaz think it's her asthma. They think she stropped off after things didn't go her way at the spa and wandered into the field in a huff.'

'But you don't buy it?' Jude asked, reading the doubt on Ash's face.

'I don't know what to buy.' Ash pushed both hands through her choppy elfin crop and shook her head. 'Dex wondered if there's some sort of nasty bug going round that knocked Seren out and did the same to Khad, except there was nobody there to call an ambulance for her.'

She started crying then and Jude put an arm around her in an instinctive way to try and buffer a little of her pain. She thought about Dex's suggestion and wondered if there could be some truth in it. Was there a link between Seren's collapse and Khadija's death? Had something attacked their bodies in the same way but Khadija's lungs hadn't been strong enough to withstand it? She doubted very much that it was a bug though, so what could it mean instead? Jude thought of the vape that Seren had been smoking. Sue, the paramedic, hadn't thought Seren's symptoms could have been triggered by the vape but what if there had been something else inside that little plastic stick that shouldn't have been there? Not that that would explain Khadija's death.

'Sorry.' Ash pulled away and took a tissue from her pocket to blow her nose on.

'Don't apologise,' said Jude. 'I only wish I could do something to help.'

Ash looked up slowly and found Jude's eyes. 'I just want answers.'

* * *

Jude got back to the farmhouse just as Sebbie dropped a bombshell on Lucy.

'Mummy, it's rainbow day at nursery so I need to wear my rainbowiest clothes and can you paint rainbows on my cheeks as well?'

Lucy's face as she put Sebbie's bowl of cereal down in front of him told Jude that she'd completely forgotten. 'Jude, you wouldn't get that face paint set out that Gerwain gave him, would you? I need to be out of the door in twenty minutes and I'm not even in my uniform yet.' She turned back to Sebbie. 'How about your red trousers, yellow T-shirt with the dinosaurs on it and your trainers are blue so I'd call that a rainbow.'

'I need green,' said Sebbie through a mouthful of banana and cornflakes.

'You can use your green hoody.' Jude shooed Lucy out of the kitchen. 'Now hurry up and eat that breakfast of yours so we can get you cleaned up ready for me to draw all over your face.'

At last, Sebbie was ready, although he'd already managed to smudge one of the rainbows Jude had painted so that it looked more like a psychedelic melting pot of colour sliding down his face.

'Are you coming to see Margot this morning?' Lucy asked Jude as she bundled him into his car seat.

'I said I'd pop in to take her to feed the ducks at the Winter Gardens.' Jude looked up at the sky where the warmth of the early sun had been replaced by a thick covering of cloud and a sense of approaching rain. 'If it's not pouring down, that is.'

'See you in a bit, then,' said Lucy, jumping into the car.

After she'd waved her little family off, Jude went back inside to grab her bag and keys and put Adam's puffer coat on in case the clouds didn't thin again. As she slid her arms into the sleeves, she felt the shape of the vape still in the pocket where she'd put it after taking it from Seren the day before. She would drop it in at the police station on her way to Perrins House, just in case there was something in her theory that it may have been contaminated.

Jude had just locked the front door of the house when the phone rang; a number she didn't recognise.

She accepted the call, ready to ditch it again at the first hint it was a salesperson on the other end.

'Hello, Jude?' The voice was small and husky and yet there was a little hint of something familiar about it.

'Speaking,' she said, not able to place it.

'It's Seren King here,' the voice rasped, making Jude stop in her tracks as she got to the Land Rover.

'Oh, my goodness, Seren,' she said. 'How are you?'

'Still sore but I do feel a bit better this morning. Thank you for looking after me yesterday.'

'Gosh, don't worry at all. Do they know what happened?'

'The tests they've done show inflammation in my chest. It looks like I had a nasty chest infection or something brewing and the vape must have brought it on.'

'But you're on the mend?'

Seren couldn't speak for a moment as she was racked with a terrible-sounding cough. Whilst she waited for it to pass, Jude opened the car and got in.

'Sorry about that,' gasped Seren.

'It sounds like you should be taking it easy,' said Jude.

'I need to tell you something, Jude.' Through the rasping, Jude could hear the same urgency now in Seren's voice that she'd heard the day before, right before Seren collapsed.

'That day, when I came to say goodbye to you in the orchard and I found Joe's body, I saw his phone lying by the side of him and I didn't stop to think. I knew he would have things on there that I didn't want anyone to see and so I just took it.'

Jude thought about the revolting texts Joe had sent Seren and her skin bristled all over again.

'Have the police opened his phone?' Seren asked. 'I couldn't figure out the code.'

'I don't know,' Jude fibbed.

'He'll ruin my career,' Seren whispered. 'If they find out what I did, I'll be struck off.'

Jude knew then that this was not about the text messages Joe had sent. They had pointed to the fact that Joe was holding something big over Seren, big enough to make her do whatever he asked her to do. She decided to hedge her bets. 'Is this about the drugs?'

'You know about that?' Seren sounded frightened and Jude knew that she was right. Ellie and Khadija clearly weren't the only vets to have been trapped in this particular venomous web. 'Do the police know?'

'They can help you,' said Jude. 'Talk to Binnie.'

'I can't lose my job.'

'Seren, these are dangerous people.' Jude wound the car window down a little as the air inside started to become a little too stuffy. 'You need to tell the police.'

Jude could hear Seren sobbing down the phone. 'I didn't even know that I'd done anything wrong. It was years ago when I was still working with Khadija. She got me to sign some prescriptions for her. I know I should have questioned it right from the start but I was stupid. I only did it twice and then realised something wasn't right so I told her I wouldn't do it again.'

Seren erupted into another round of hacking and Jude could picture her sitting up in a hospital bed in an NHS gown with her pale face contorted by the violent fit of coughing. Jude took the vape from her pocket and looked at it before putting it on the dashboard. Revolting as it was, it couldn't be responsible for such a terrible reaction on its own – even if Seren had been harbouring a chest infection as the doctors had suggested. And surely a chest infection of that magnitude would have made its presence known in some way beforehand? No, the more she thought about it, the more she felt sure that someone had spiked the vape.

Seren managed to get her breathing back under control and continued with her story. 'Khadija told me that she'd used the prescriptions I'd signed for use on the black market and that if I didn't carry on helping her, she would make sure I'd never work as a vet again.' Seren had stopped coughing but her voice sounded even hoarser as she spoke. 'That's when she injected the heifer. I don't know for sure but I think she killed her on purpose, as a warning.'

Jude couldn't believe what she was hearing. 'Surely she had as much to lose as you did.'

'Khadija always had a way of keeping herself out of trouble whilst she landed everyone else in it,' said Seren. 'Besides, she didn't care about being a vet. I love my job but she only went into veterinary practice because it was the one she hated least from her parents' list of acceptable careers.'

'So you carried on writing out bogus prescriptions for her?' Jude asked.

'I did a couple more but then I stopped, I just couldn't do it even if it did land me in trouble. She was mad for a while and I almost just went to the police then. I wish I had, even though it would have meant losing my job too, but at least it would have put a stop to her.' Seren paused and Jude could hear raspy breathing as she tried to take in more oxygen.

'Take your time,' Jude said.

'I'm okay,' croaked Seren. 'Anyway, then she moved to a different prac-

tice and I was too small for her to bother about. But she never let me
forget that I was under her thumb and she must have told Joe as well
because then he started too.'

Seren started to cough again then and Jude could hear her trying to
catch hard-fought breaths in between.

'Hey now, Seren,' came a friendly voice over the phone. 'You shouldn't
be out of bed. Let's get you back in, shall we? Then I'll have a look at your
sats and blood pressure to see how you're doing.'

The phone went dead and Jude stared at the black screen for a little
while as a thread of thoughts and snatched recollections lined up in
perfect order for once.

Ash had suggested that Khadija and Seren's symptoms were similar
and she was right. Both had inflamed lungs that had resulted in
breathing difficulties that had been fatal in Khadija and nearly so in
Seren. Dex had thought it was a horrendous bug but that was too easy.
Jude looked at the vape that she had set on the dashboard. Something in
that had to be the cause of Seren's collapse but Khadija would never have
touched a vape; it would have been stupid considering the extent of her
asthma.

Her asthma – of course!

'It was in her inhaler.' Jude punched the steering wheel as the realisation hit her.

The phone was still in her hand and she called Binnie straight away.

'I've just had a phone call from Seren,' said Jude when Binnie
answered.

'I'm in the car at the moment to go and see her in Worcester hospital,'
Binnie replied. 'I've got Sami with me.'

'Hi, Jude, how's it going?' Sami's voice was as jolly as always.

'Morning, Sami,' said Jude.

'Enough of the chatter,' said Binnie. 'What did Seren want?'

'She wanted to tell me that she knew about Khadija and the drugs.
She'd been involved herself on a very small scale.' Jude gave Binnie as
many details as she could remember of the phone conversation they'd
just had. 'There's something else too. I might be wrong but it sounds as
though she's experiencing a lot of the same symptoms that caused Khadi-

ja's death. So now I'm wondering if Khadija's asthma *was* the death of her but not in the way the killer wants us to think.'

'What do you mean?'

'Didn't you say her inhaler was found right next to her body?'

'That's right,' said Binnie.

'I think someone spiked it with something deadly. And I think they did the same to Joe's vape, except that Joe didn't use the vape. He told Shaznay that he was giving up.'

'And Seren smoked it instead.' Binnie sounded triumphant. 'Jude, I think you're on to something.'

'And when the vape didn't work on Joe, they had to resort to using a gun,' said Sami.

'Exactly,' said Jude. 'I took the vape away from Seren when she collapsed and I'm just heading into town to see Granny Margot. Shall I drop it off on the way?'

'Thanks. We're only just heading through Powick now so we'll be gone most of the morning. I'll call the station and let them know you're coming. We need to get the tests started on it asap.'

'Will do.' Jude cut the call and put her phone back in her bag. She took a clean tissue from the box in the glove compartment and wrapped the vape up in it before tucking it safely into the little empty pocket on the side of the bag.

As she fired the Land Rover up and set off down the drive, she wondered if she'd just worked out the *how* of Khadija's death. But even if she had, did it get them any closer to figuring out the *who did it*?

The sun had come out and was pushing the clouds ever further away as
Jude tucked a crocheted blanket around Granny Margot's legs.

24

The sun had come out and was pushing the clouds ever further away as
Jude tucked a crocheted blanket around Granny Margot's legs.

'We made this in our stitch and bitch group.' She was sitting in a
wheelchair at the entrance to Perrins House sporting a bright purple
bucket hat with little daisies printed over it, and a fuchsia-pink cagoule in
case it rained.

'Who came up with that name?' Jude asked as she pushed her down
the ramp and through the front garden.

'It was Flo. She's hopeless with needlework but a born gossip.' Granny
Margot stuck out her right arm like an indicator as Jude turned onto the
pavement. 'Now, how are you getting on back at the farm with the
remaining hens?'

The *remaining* hens; that word said so much. Six hens had come to
the farm a week ago, followed by Joe and Dex a couple of days later. Now,
out of the eight of them, two were dead, one was in hospital and another
was in a police cell being questioned about her involvement in an illegal
drug supply.

'They just keep throwing more and more at us,' she said. 'And I just
keep going around in circles.'

'Let's get ice cream when we get to the park.'

'Pardon?' Jude was surprised by the complete change in direction.

'Ice cream,' Granny Margot repeated. 'Food for the brain. Then we can sit down properly and run through all the different scenarios we could be looking at and see what jumps out at us.'

They turned out of Victoria Road onto the main street into Great Malvern and a bus clattered past. 'It's quieter there too,' said Granny Margot.

Jude pushed the chair up to the crossroads which, due to the gradient, was challenging. From there it was easier and they reached the theatre building at the top of the old Winter Gardens where they stopped to choose ice creams before carrying on down into the park itself.

'Do you want to go and see the ducks or sit by the bandstand?' Jude asked.

'These ice cream tubs are going to melt into milkshake soon. Let's just pull up here by this bench and then we've got a view of everything to keep us happy whilst we talk dirty deeds.'

Jude wheeled the chair to an angle next to the bench and put the brakes on before retrieving her ice cream and sitting down by Granny Margot.

'That's better.' Granny Margot popped the lid off her chocolate ice cream and found the little wooden spoon hidden underneath. 'Now, who's still on the suspect list? Tell me everything.'

'Where to begin?' said Jude, throwing both her lid and Granny Margot's in the bin by the bench. 'It's all very knotty.'

'Then let's try and untie some of those tangles, shall we? We have the bride, her sister and the sister's boyfriend in the frame, tell me about them.'

'Khadija and Joe treated Shaznay, that's the bride, really badly. She was furious, but not as angry as Neesh.'

'That's the sister?'

'Right.' Jude looked down towards the bandstand and tried to imagine either of them killing Joe and Khadija in a fit of rage. 'She's particularly feisty and has already said she'd do anything to protect her family.'

'Even kill?' Granny Margot asked.

'I really don't know.'

'If we're talking affairs of the heart then we still have the dead woman's girlfriend to consider, do we not?'

'We do.' Jude dug into the top of her buttery yellow caramel ice cream. 'She's every bit as feisty as Neesh and I can imagine her killing Joe but not Khadija.'

'Two murderers, then?' Granny Margot suggested.

'I don't think so,' said Jude. 'If I'm right then whoever killed Khadija with her inhaler tried to kill Joe in a similar way.' She elaborated on her latest theory.

'We can't completely rule out a second killer, though. If you're right and the vape and inhaler were tampered with, we still need someone to have pulled the trigger on the gun. I know that would mean two people had tried to kill Joe, but by the sound of it, he had enough enemies.'

Jude chewed the end of her wooden spoon thoughtfully. 'You're right.'

'Perhaps even Khadija herself?' Granny Margot continued.

'As far as I know, they haven't yet managed to pin an accurate time of death on her.' Jude's brain was spinning again. 'So it could be possible that she hid somewhere overnight, knowing that Joe would almost certainly come looking for her, which he did the next day. Then, she could have sneaked out of hiding and shot him before running into the OSR field to hide.'

'Without thinking about the pollen that would trigger her asthma and cause her to need her inhaler.' When Granny Margot said this, Jude thought it seemed unlikely. Someone with asthma as serious as Khadija's would know that a field of rapeseed was the last place she should go. Unless she'd panicked and just run. Who knew what went through anyone's mind in the minutes after they'd committed murder?

'There's also the matter of the lovely vet who saved my sheep, now locked up for dealing in illegal drugs.'

'There are drugs involved.' Granny Margot tutted sadly. 'The things people choose to get themselves into these days.'

'I don't think she had much of a choice,' said Jude.

'Everyone always has a choice.' Granny Margot licked her spoon. 'It's just some choices are harder than others.'

In between mouthfuls of ice cream, Jude went on to tell Granny

Margot everything she knew about the drugs and how Khadija, Ellie and even Seren had been mixed up with it. 'And Joe knew about all of it. He hired a private investigator and then used what he'd found out to blackmail them all. Well, all except Khadija. When it came to her, he wanted to use it as leverage to make her run away with him.'

'Ah, yes, manipulation. The heart of every healthy relationship.' Granny Margot put her spoon into the now empty tub and passed it to Jude to throw away. 'Shall we have a wander now?'

Jude released the brakes on Granny Margot's chair.

'So we have a motive for all of those involved in this drugs business to want both Khadija and Joe dead,' said Granny Margot as Jude pushed her down the tarmac path towards the bandstand.

'Yes, and I still think Mike Trout might be involved too. The gun was found in his shed and it would explain where his new cash injection has come from.'

'Jude, let's not jump the gun about that,' said Granny Margot. 'Pun completely intended, of course. I know he can be a tricky bugger, but it's a stretch to imagine that he is wrapped up in a world of murder and drugs.'

They reached the wooden bridge across the duckpond and Jude pushed hard to get the wheelchair over the dip as the tarmac met the first rickety slat.

'But he was there the night the tent collapsed. He admitted to untying the guy ropes, and his key was found next to the poisoned sheep.'

The bridge's slats clattered beneath the wheels as Jude pushed Granny Margot up to the brow of the bridge where they stopped to look down at the ducks in the pond below.

'Have you considered someone might be trying to frame him to take the spotlight away from them?' Granny Margot asked.

Jude sighed deeply. It was a thought that had crossed her mind but who would do that? And Mike himself had admitted to untying the tent.

'No,' she said. 'I can't see how anyone would have been able to make him sneak in and tamper with the tent. It wouldn't make any sense.'

As Jude pushed Granny Margot down the other side of the bridge and out towards the bottom exit of the park, her phone started to ring.

'Mrs Gray?' the voice on the other asked when she answered it.

'Speaking.'

'It's Jim from British Wool here.'

Bugger, Jude thought. She'd completely forgotten they were coming and she knew Noah was on his dad's farm for the day to help with the dipping so there was nobody at Malvern Farm. 'Just came to make your delivery but I couldn't see anyone so I'm just calling to say I left everything in your barn, okay?'

'I don't need to sign anything?'

'No, you're all set. Bye, then.'

'Something important?' Granny Margot asked as Jude put her phone away.

'We've got the shearer coming in next week. That was the delivery guy letting me know the sacks have arrived.' They were out of the park now and heading back to Perrins House.

'Well, let's hope this is all cleared up by then,' said Granny Margot, who'd helped out with many a shearing season in her younger years, known for making the tightest fleece bales. 'It does feel as though we're starting to close in on the truth.'

'Does it?' Jude's head was still a tangle of half facts and jumbled evidence.

'I have complete faith in you, my girl.' Granny Margot stretched behind her to pat Jude's hand on the handle of the wheelchair. 'You know more than you think. And I've no doubt that you'll work out how it all fits soon enough.'

As she deposited Granny Margot back at the care home and got in the car to head back to Malvern Farm, Jude wished she could share the old woman's optimism.

25

Jude grabbed a quick sandwich before heading into the lambing shed to find the delivery from British Wool, where all the fleeces would be sent for grading once they'd been taken off the sheep. Both this shed and the bigger one attached to it needed to be prepared for the shearer's arrival and Jude was the woman for the job.

They were having a shuffle around this year to get the sheep into the sheds and off pasture for longer so that they fasted for as long as possible before the shearing, both to make it more comfortable for the sheep and easier for the shearer.

She'd ordered new panels of green grid flooring for them to stand on whilst they waited so that any pee and poo would fall through the holes and not make the fleeces dirty.

These were piled high on pallets in the larger of the two sheds and this was where Jude decided to start. There was a large space to cover and she was glad to see that Noah had already got as far as emptying the shed, making her job that day much easier.

She flicked on the radio for company and reached into her pocket for her trusty penknife. Using the razor-sharp edge of the blade to easily slice through the packing tapes, she released the first batch of flooring panels. Each one was cumbersome but manageable and Jude found it really satisfying to see how quickly she'd finished the first pallet and had a pretty large area already covered.

As she was busy slicing the tape from the second pallet, she heard footsteps as someone joined her in the shed. Looking up, she saw it was Ash, so she laid the penknife down on top of the pile of panels and went to switch off the radio.

'Hi, Jude,' said Ash, whose name was now also a perfect description of her pallor. 'I just wanted to come and say goodbye.'

'You're going home?' Jude wondered if all the others would be following her now that Khadija had been found. The investigation would still continue regardless and it might take months to get to the truth. Nobody could expect them to stick around for that long, and she felt dreadful for feeling the relief of knowing that this would also move them further from her life.

'I think it's time. Khadija's gone and there's nothing I can do to bring her back.'

'I am so sorry.' It always seemed like such a pointless thing to say.

'At least she's free from it all now and I suppose I have Ellie to thank for that.'

'What do you mean?' Jude leant against one of the stacks of flooring panels.

Ash did the same to the pallet load next to her. 'I knew about the drugs, that Ellie was involved in them. Khad told me, she said that Ellie was making loads of money from it and that she wanted to get in on the action. I said not to touch them, that there were other ways of getting the money we needed to escape. I thought she'd listened to me.'

Jude kicked a stray piece of baling twine on the floor with her toe, wondering how many other lies Khadija had told Ash. 'And now?'

'Now I can see how blinkered I was. She told me the money was coming from the extra work she was doing at the racehorse livery and I suppose I wanted to believe her so I just didn't question it.' She rubbed the side of her face with her hand. 'I wanted to get away as much as she did and it was easier not to ask.'

'So why should you be thanking Ellie?' Jude asked. 'I don't quite understand.'

'I think she killed Joe because he knew about the drugs, that's pretty much what he wrote in that stupid note Neesh found. Dex said it was the sort of note that he made if he was about to have an important conversation.' Ash took a tissue from the sleeve of her jumper and wiped at the tears that had started to fall. 'I think he told Khadija that he knew and when she didn't jump to his tune and agree to run off with him, I think she panicked and bolted. She could be tempestuous and had a tendency to act without thinking. I can well imagine her running into the field before she stopped to think of her asthma if it all got too much for her. And everything had definitely got too much for her then. First finding out that her parents knew about us and then that Joe knew she was dealing drugs.'

Ash's shoulders dropped as she thought of the woman she loved and Khadija's last days of torment. Jude hadn't liked Khadija, she still didn't, but the grief of the woman in front of her made her heart bleed.

Before she could say anything else, two more voices could be heard walking across the yard. It was Neesh and Dex and it sounded as though they were in the middle of an argument.

'I'm trying to tell you that I don't mind,' said Dex. 'Whatever happened, I know you and I love you.'

'And what exactly are you saying has happened, Dex?' Neesh yelled. 'Because it sounds like I'm being accused of all sorts.'

'Keep your voice down, Neesh. Look, come in here with me where it's more private.'

Jude and Ash exchanged a glance as they heard Dex and Neesh open the door of the lambing shed next door and step inside. Although the outside walls of the shed were made of concrete blocks, the inside division that split the barn in two only stretched up six feet or so. Jude and Ash were hidden on the other side but they could hear everything that was going on.

'Neesh, you don't have to pretend. I know Reggie isn't mine.'

'I can't believe you're throwing this nonsense at me.' Neesh sounded furious.

'Khadija knew. She told Joe the day before we came here. He was coming to tell you that he was going to go for custody.'

'What?' Had the fury turned to worry?

Jude looked round at Ash, who was staring at the partition wall in surprise.

'They've got her phone, Neesh, Joe's too. If they find anything on there then it'll all come out soon enough anyway.'

Jude turned back to focus her attention on the concrete blocks in front of her and what was happening on the other side.

'It doesn't matter. I don't care. I know what he was like and I hate him for it but you... you are the most precious thing in my world. You and Reggie. I'd do anything for you, Neesh. Anything.'

'I'm sorry, Dex.' Neesh's voice was pleading and contrite. 'I don't know why I did it. I'd had a row with Shaz, she'd been going off on one about me again and I was so sick of always feeling like I wasn't as good as her. You know how she can be. Anyway, then Joe came along and before I knew it, I was just...' She tailed off.

'Come here,' said Dex and Jude could imagine him bringing her in for a hug. 'Don't say anything else. I know and it's okay. He was a terrible person. He treated you, Shaz, everyone so badly. Khadija was no better. I know she was blackmailing you to keep quiet about Reggie but I wish you'd told me yourself sooner rather than me finding out from Joe like that.'

'I know. And I'm sorry.' Neesh was crying now and the rest of what she said was incomprehensible.

'Shhhh, I won't let that happen,' said Dex. 'I told you. I'd do anything for you and Reggie and I meant it. Haven't I already shown you that? And I'll keep doing it – whatever it takes to keep harm away from you. The world is better off without the pair of them, and you just have to remember that.'

Jude glanced across at Ash, whose face had gone from grey to red.

'Thank you,' Neesh said. 'Thank you for making me feel safe again.'

'Come on, let's go and pack our things,' said Dex. 'It's time to go home and find our boy.'

Jude waited until their footsteps had gone before speaking. 'Ash, I'm...'

Ash stood up abruptly. 'Don't,' she said. 'I know that's what they all think of her. But Dex is right about one thing. It's time to go home now.'

She walked out of the shed and Jude let her go. Once more in this twisted tale she had to re-question everything that she'd thought. Neesh's precious son Reggie was Joe's baby. Not only did that give a brand-new layer to the mystery but it also threw up new motives for murder and, if Jude wasn't very much mistaken, she'd just heard what almost sounded like an admission of guilt.

You had to reach in and hunt for it, perhaps, but Dex had definitely known about the true parentage of his baby and he hadn't cared. Or at least he hadn't cared as far as Neesh went, although he hated Joe for the part he'd played and Khadija too for holding her gossip over Neesh's head and using it to blackmail her.

More than just forgiving her, he'd told her that he would do anything to look after her. *Haven't I already shown you that?* he'd said. *I'll keep doing it – whatever it takes to keep harm away from you. The world is better off without the pair of them, and you just have to remember that.*

Had he been telling her that it was him who'd done it? Him who'd shot Joe and laced Khadija's inhaler? And what form had Khadija's blackmail taken? Had Neesh been paying her to keep quiet? No wonder she always went for the budget supermarket crisps if this was the case.

Jude wanted to go straight down to the campsite and confront them but this time she knew she had to wait for Binnie. She called and frustratingly was sent directly to voicemail. She put the phone down and tried Sami, hoping that they might still be together.

'Judy, Judy, Judy,' he sang to her when he answered. 'How's my favourite farmer?'

'Not now, Sami. Is Binnie with you?'

'She's in an interview with Ellie, I think, at the moment. Everything okay?'

'Can you tell her to call me?' said Jude. 'I think I might have figured out who killed Joe but I haven't got any proof.'

'Joe *and* Khadija then,' said Sami. 'The tests came back from the inhaler and the vape and you were right. They both contained something called Micotil. Have you heard of it?'

Jude knew exactly what Micotil was. It was the saviour of many a lame sheep. It was the drug that was given incorrectly to the heifer in Khadija and Seren's care whose death was the reason why Seren hadn't been able to get a job as a farm vet. It was deadly to humans. And she'd been right; it was the thing that tied the two bodies together.

'Must have been used at different times, though, as we've had a more accurate time of death for Khadija and it looks like she was killed two days before Joe.'

As Sami was talking, Jude looked at the stack of flooring panels that Ash had been propped up against just a few minutes ago. It was the one that Jude had been opening before Ash had arrived and Jude was sure she'd put her penknife down on top of it when she'd gone to switch off the radio, but it wasn't there.

'Jude? What's going on?' Sami sounded worried.

'Just get Binnie here as soon as you can.' Jude's heart was pounding as she checked the top of the other stacks for the knife. 'Come to the campsite. It's urgent.'

Jude stuffed her phone into her pocket and searched the floor around the pallets just in case, but she was already sure that it wouldn't be there. She knew she'd promised Binnie that she wouldn't go bowling in on her own investigations without her but this was different. Ash had heard everything that Jude had and could just have easily come to the same conclusion.

Jude had seen how angry Ash could get, she'd seen it when she'd spoken about Khadija's parents with such venom. And she knew that this anger had the capacity to spill into violence because she'd seen her physically attack Joe in the campsite when she'd confronted him about the text messages he'd sent to Khadija.

She knew she had to be fast. Ash had her knife and Jude knew for certain where she was heading with it.

26

Jude wished that Frank had chosen any other day to dip his sheep so that Noah was on Malvern Farm instead of helping his father out. Still, at least Sami knew she needed help. With any luck, he and Binnie would be on hand soon enough if things escalated between Ash and Dex.

As she strode across the yard, once more heading to the campsite, Jude thought again about what she and Ash had just heard and if it really meant what it seemed to.

Although it felt as though she was close, something still wasn't adding up. Sami had said that Khadija had died two days before Joe. She tried to think how everything fitted together on the timeline of this disaster. Joe had only been at the B&B for one night so had been shot on the day after he and Dex had arrived on the farm. If Khadija had died two days earlier then that meant neither Joe nor Dex had been there when she'd been poisoned.

Either she'd completely misinterpreted Dex's meaning in the shed or he was only admitting to one of the murders, leaving the other still unsolved because he could not be responsible for Khadija's death. Whichever it was, though, Ash didn't know this and she was still armed and potentially dangerous.

As Jude hurried on towards the campsite, something else was bothering her. There was something about the words Dex had said. *I'd do anything for you and Reggie.* He'd proven this to Neesh in some way and told her that she had to remember the world was better off without Joe and Khadija in it. She'd taken this to mean that he had killed them both but what if he'd meant something else entirely?

Neesh had thanked him for making her safe. From what? From Joe and Khadija, as Jude had originally thought? Or was she thanking him for something else?

Jude could feel her pulse throbbing in her wrists and neck as she opened the gate to the field and the pieces of the puzzle finally started to slot together. Dex wasn't the only person to have sworn he would do anything to keep their family safe; Neesh had said pretty much those exact words when she'd been talking about Reggie. And Neesh had perhaps the biggest motive of all to kill. Self-preservation.

Neesh had no alibi when Joe had been shot, but nobody did. Except Neesh had been coming back from the shower. Was that to get rid of any gunshot residue?

Like a sickening waterfall of realisation, Jude knew exactly who'd killed both Joe and Khadija. Granny Margot had suggested that someone had been framing Mike Trout and she'd been right. Neesh herself had been the one to suggest that he should get hung up for what he'd done to her. And it was Neesh who'd seen him in the campsite untying the ropes to Khadija's tent. Had she taken her opportunity and gone out after he'd left to finish the job, hoping that it would look like a prank that had gone wrong?

And her beautiful sheep, was that Neesh's way of pointing the finger even further in Mike's direction? Collateral damage that would surely make everyone think he'd been out to cause trouble that night. If she'd somehow got hold of the key to his shed then it would have been easy for her to get in and take the tools she needed to cut some rhododendron leaves and grind them into the sheep lick, before dropping the key at the scene of the crime.

More and more things fell into place as Jude power-walked past the shower blocks.

Neesh had been the one to discover the note from Joe, the one she'd been so desperate for Jude to read and that suggested Khadija had been up to something dodgy. Was she covering her back here too? Jude could now see that by directing them towards the criminal life Khadija had become embroiled in, Neesh was taking the suspicion away from herself.

As she started to run, passing the tents including the one that Khadija had spent her last night in, Jude wondered if perhaps Neesh had sneaked in there when Khadija was missing and taken the gun, thinking that it might be useful. Jude felt even more certain of this when she thought of the bag it had been hidden in. An Aldi supermarket bag, not something that had seemed particularly important at the time but now it seemed a vital clue. In the village shop, Val had told Mrs James that these days Mike's shopping came from Ocado. Shaznay also shopped at the high-end supermarkets. She'd teased Neesh for getting cheap own-brand crisps.

An angry scream from near the shepherd's huts made Jude pick up her speed and, as she went past the largest of the bell tents, she saw Ash standing at the bottom of the field. She was shouting at Dex and Neesh and, as she got closer, Jude could see her penknife in Ash's hand, still folded into its red sheath.

'Let's all calm down.' As she reached them, Jude raised her hands to try and defuse the situation. Instead, her presence seemed to elevate things to the next level and Ash flew forward, grabbing Dex by the front of his T-shirt and flicking the knife open at the same time.

'Move away from him or I will use it,' Ash shouted and Neesh instantly stepped back a couple of paces.

'And again,' Ash yelled. 'You too, Jude.'

She pushed the blade into his chest and Jude knew that it was sharp. She kept it so to enable her to cut her sheep free from any bushes they tangled themselves in or slice off any infected chunks of a cloven hoof. She'd sharpened it only a week or so ago and knew that the point of the blade would pierce through skin and muscle with ease. If Ash were to get it in between Dex's ribs then there would be nothing to stop it reaching his heart.

This time Neesh didn't move and seconds later Dex cried out in pain as a small red bloom began to spread across his white T-shirt where the point of the knife was pressing in.

'Okay, okay,' said Neesh, taking another couple of steps backwards so that she was just an arm's distance from where Jude had retreated.

'You don't want to do this,' Jude said. 'It won't bring her back, Ash, but your own life will be ruined.'

'It's already ruined,' Ash screamed. 'He ruined it the moment he killed Khadija.'

'What are you talking about?' Neesh shouted, the fury in her voice matched in intensity to the panic in her eyes.

'Cut the crap, Neesh,' Ash spat. 'We heard you talking in the shed. He as good as admitted it too.'

Dex turned his head to look at Neesh, and Jude could see the message in his eyes clearly. The tiniest shake of the head that went with it to tell her to be quiet. Was he urging her not to give herself away? Jude remembered those words again: *I'd do anything for you and Reggie.* Did that mean taking the flack for what Neesh had done so that she could stay safe and be left alone to bring her child up?

'You've got it wrong,' said Jude. 'I don't think Dex killed anyone.'

At that moment, there was a noise as Shaznay appeared through the bottom entrance, carrying a bunch of wildflowers.

For a moment, she didn't read the situation but just saw her friends standing around together. 'I picked these from the verge,' she said. 'I thought we could put them by the entrance to the field Khad was found in before we go home.'

'Go and stand by your sister,' Ash barked.

Shaznay looked at her in surprise and then her eyes widened in shock as she noticed the blade in Ash's hand and the red mark that was seeping further across Dex's T-shirt.

'Ash? What's going on?'

'I said stand next to Tanisha.'

Ash twisted the blade just a fraction but it was enough to make Dex cry out in pain.

'Shaz!' Neesh screamed. 'Just come over here. She's gone mad.'

Still holding the bouquet of red campion, cow parsley and buttercups, Shaznay hurried over to her sister and put her free hand out for Neesh to take.

'How touching,' Ash said. 'I take it you haven't told her yet, then?'

Neesh looked at Ash and shook her head. Jude could see a new wave of fear cross her face as she silently pleaded with Ash not to tell Shaznay what she'd learnt. In that moment, Jude believed that if Ash gave Neesh the choice between saving her boyfriend's life or keeping Neesh's secret safe then she'd let Ash push the penknife into Dex's heart without thinking twice.

Neesh had so much to lose if the truth about Reggie came out. It had been enough to kill twice already to keep the secret safe and Jude had no doubt that she'd see more die to look after the family ties that she held most dear.

She craved the love and recognition of her parents and she idolised Shaznay. Family was clearly the core of everything she lived for and Joe and Khadija had found the key to destroy it all. And now Ash too could spoil everything.

'Told me what?' Shaznay asked.

'Don't listen to her,' said Dex. He let out a roar as Ash twisted the knife again.

Jude had to do something more than just wait for the police to arrive and hope that they did so before Ash did any serious damage to Dex. She took a step forward, her hands still raised to her chest in submission.

'Stay where you are, Jude,' Ash bellowed.

Jude side-stepped to put herself between Ash and Neesh. The last thing she wanted was for Ash to pull the knife from Dex only to thrust it into Neesh instead.

'You're wrong,' said Jude. 'I know what we heard and I made the same assumption to begin with but you're wrong. Dex didn't kill Khadija. He wasn't even here when it happened.'

Ash's face creased in confusion. 'What do you mean?'

'They've confirmed the time of death. Khadija died the day before Dex and Joe arrived.'

At that moment, a car skidded into the car park at the bottom of the field and Jude felt relief wash through her exhausted self. It was short-lived though as, out of the corner of her eye, she saw Neesh bend down to pick something off the floor. It was Alfie's lost green dog lead and before she knew what was happening, Neesh had looped it around Jude's neck and pulled it tight.

27

Jude's fingers clawed at the rope around her neck, desperate to pull it free but the more she fought, the tighter it became.

'Neesh, what are you doing?' Shaznay yelled.

'Stay back,' Neesh shouted. 'Just let me think.'

Jude tried to kick out backwards but the angle was all wrong and when she flung her arms behind her to try and reach her attacker, she found nothing but empty air.

'I don't want to hurt you, Jude,' Neesh hissed in her ear. 'Please, just stay still.'

Jude did as she was told and felt the rope loosen, only a fraction but enough to remove the immediate threat of asphyxia.

'Let go of them.' Binnie's voice, accompanied by the crackle of Sami's police walkie-talkie, was music to Jude's ears. Neesh, however, clearly didn't feel the same as there was a slight but noticeable increase in the pressure around Jude's neck.

'They killed Khadija,' Ash bellowed, showing no sign of releasing Dex.

'No,' Neesh shouted. 'You have it all wrong. It was Ellie. She was part of this massive illegal drugs thing and Joe and Khadija knew about it. You know they did, Joe's note said so.'

Jude could feel Neesh's heightened emotions as they vibrated through the rope that was around her neck.

'It was her. Look in the sharps box in her vet bag and I bet you'll find the empty vials of Micotil she used, and the needles too. Test them. I'm sure they'll tell you everything you need to know.'

Jude knew then that she had been right. The results of the Micotil poisoning had only just come through so, apart from those on the investigative team, the only person who would know about it was the killer.

Khadija had threatened to tell Joe that Reggie was his, so she had to die, but Neesh was too late and Joe had already found out. He wanted custody and Neesh couldn't let that happen. She didn't want to share her precious boy, especially not with a man as toxic as Joe Birch, and she couldn't let him tell Shaznay or her parents either. He had to die too. And now here Jude was with a noose around her neck. She'd discovered the truth; did that mean she had to die as well?

'Thank you for this lead. I'll definitely send someone round to check it out.' Binnie's voice was placatory, giving nothing away. 'But you need to let Jude go and then we can talk everything through and find out what you know about Ellie.'

'Don't say anything,' Dex shouted. 'You need to look after Reggie now. I admit it. It was all me. I killed Khadija and I shot Joe.'

Jude knew Dex had realised Neesh's mistake in mentioning the Micotil and she could hear the desperation in his voice as he tried to offer the woman he loved a lifeline. But it wouldn't work. Unless he could explain how he'd managed to kill Khadija when he'd been a two-hour drive away, at home looking after his son.

Ash growled and must have moved the knife as Dex yelped.

'Ashleigh, this isn't the way to deal with this,' Binnie said. 'Drop the knife and let us take it from here.'

'Not until I have the truth.' Ash spoke with force and looked towards Neesh as she did.

'It is the truth,' said Dex frantically. 'I hated Joe and I didn't want him to have anything to do with Reggie. He might have got the biology bit but I'm Reggie's real dad.'

'Of course you are,' Neesh said, pacifying him. 'He was nothing to either of us.'

'Reggie is Joe's child?' Shaznay stepped in front of Jude so that she could look Neesh in the eye and Jude could see the hurt and confusion on her face. 'Is this true?'

The lead around Jude's neck tightened again and she clutched at it to try and pull it free, but Neesh held firm.

'I'm sorry,' Neesh wailed. 'I should have told you but I didn't want you to hate me.'

'You slept with my fiancé.'

Jude felt the rope of the lead cutting into her and she focused hard on her breathing, trying to remain calm.

'It was just one night,' Neesh sobbed. 'One stupid night and I regretted it before it had even really started. I don't know why I didn't just stop things and walk away. I should have, I know that. I'm sorry.'

The space between them thickened with a connection that only came from so much shared DNA mixed with such a cocktail of hurt and Jude was stuck in the middle, fighting against the throbbing in her head as the blood struggled to reach it.

'Tanisha, you have to let Jude go now,' said Binnie, but Neesh wasn't listening.

'I'd do anything for you, Shaz. Anything and you don't see that. You only ever see me as the charity case who'll never amount to even half of what you do. That evening, I crumpled and I let my guard down – Joe offered a little bit of revenge and I took it. And I've been living with that ever since.' Neesh's voice softened and the repentant tears began. 'I love you, Shaz. Until Dex and Reggie, you were the only person who looked after me and saw me for who I am. In lots of ways, you still are. I can't lose you too.'

All the time the lead remained around Jude's neck and she knew that if it was pulled any tighter, it wouldn't take long before the lack of blood to her brain became fatal.

'You'd do anything for me?' Shaz asked.

'Of course I would.' Neesh sounded desperate.

'Even kill?'

Neesh said nothing and her silence said more than any confession could have.

Shaznay nodded. 'Darling one, don't make it worse. If you don't let go of Jude you're going to kill her too and she doesn't deserve this.'

To Jude's enormous relief, there was an instant drop in pressure as the rope loosened but Neesh wasn't yet ready to let her go completely.

'I just need time to think,' Neesh said. 'I'm not a bad person, it just all got out of hand so quickly. I knew I was in for a tough time when Khadija found out that Joe was Reggie's real dad. If she told my secret to everyone, she'd destroy my life but she'd also destroy Dex, Reggie's and yours too. She had that power and she used it again and again, making me do all sorts of things.' Neesh was speaking through gritted teeth. 'My family is everything to me, she knew that, just like she knew I'd lose you all if they found out.'

'So you killed her?' said Shaznay gently.

'I tried to get rid of her in other ways first,' said Neesh as though that made her less culpable. 'When she told us how worried she was about her parents and what they might do to her if they found out about her and Ash, I told them. I thought they might move her away or at least divert her attention away from me and Reggie.'

'That was you?' Ash thundered.

Jude looked up and saw Ash let go of Dex, who stumbled to the ground, clutching the wound on his chest. Sami went over to help him whilst Ash strode over to where Neesh still held Jude, the bloodied tip of the penknife in Ash's hand pointing towards them.

In Neesh's panic, she tightened the noose once more around Jude's neck.

'You have ruined my life,' Ash yelled. 'You took away the only person I have ever loved and I hope you rot in hell for it.'

'She wanted to ruin my life,' Neesh shouted back. 'She was going to take everything from me and so I killed her and I'm glad I did. If she was here, I'd do it again.'

As Neesh's temper took over, the lead tightened even more and Jude clawed at the rope, desperate to release it but unable to slip her fingers underneath as her breath rasped from her.

What happened next was all a bit of a blur to Jude. She heard a deep, guttural scream of fury as Ash lunged for Neesh and then the lead around her neck was dropped and she rolled across the grass out of the way. She was aware of an almighty kerfuffle as Ash and Neesh fought and then there was the sound of sirens as backup arrived.

Jude managed to sit up but her head was spinning so she couldn't get any further.

Binnie had pulled Ash away and was cuffing her whilst Shaznay and Neesh knelt on the ground together, their arms tightly wrapped around each other. Jude could see that the penknife had somehow been lost in the fracas and had come to land next to her. She reached over and took it, folding the blade out of harm's way, and slid it beneath her so that it could do no more damage.

Jude could hear Neesh's whispers as she repeated the same line, *I'm sorry*, over and over as though it might somehow rewind time and change what? The past half hour? The past day, week? What was she really sorry for and what would she do all over again if she could do it without getting caught?

More officers arrived on the scene and someone took Ash away whilst Binnie turned her attention to Neesh.

'Tanisha Nolan, I am arresting you on suspicion of the murders of Khadija Habib and Joseph Birch.'

Neesh pulled away from Shaznay but still clung on to her sister's hand as Binnie finished cautioning her. And then, when Binnie knelt down to handcuff her, Neesh buckled and let out a howl that would have put the frighteners on every sheep on the farm, right up to the ones at the very top of the furthest field.

'Reggie! Will they let me see my baby?'

'I can't promise anything but your life will definitely be easier if you make it easier for us,' said Binnie.

Sami came over to help lift Neesh into a standing position and escort her to the waiting police van.

'Take care of my boy,' she shouted over her shoulder back to where

Dex was sitting, clutching his chest, and Shaznay was frozen into position, still kneeling on the ground.

Whilst they waited for the ambulances to come for Dex and Jude, Binnie sat on the ground next to her friend.

'Is it over this time?' Jude asked.

'I bloody well hope so,' Binnie replied.

28

The following evening, when Jude was home from hospital, bruised and sore but otherwise okay, Binnie came round and the four friends sat on the saggy sofas with bowls of crisps, dips and nuts spread out on the table in front of them.

'Another glass, Jude?' Noah asked, picking up the Westons cider and offering it around. 'Or there's wine in the fridge if you'd rather.'

'With all the painkillers they've given me, I think I'll stop at just this one,' said Jude.

'Water?' said Lucy, who was sitting next to Noah with her arm draped affectionately over his knee.

Jude tapped the side of her cider glass. 'I'll stick with this, thanks.' Swallowing was still sore and she was taking it easy.

'I still can't believe Neesh set the whole thing up,' said Jude. 'She seemed so nice.'

'She was an opportunist,' said Binnie. 'And a sneaky one too, always looking out for ways to point the finger elsewhere.'

Jude picked up a piece of bread and tore out the soft part from the middle. 'Ah, yes, poor Mike Trout. I was absolutely convinced he was caught up in it all.' She dunked the bread in hummus and as she chewed it slowly, she made a mental note to go around the next day to apologise.

'He wasn't entirely faultless,' Lucy pointed out. 'He did undo the guy ropes.'

Jude cringed as she thought of the day she'd gone round to dig for information and ended up accusing him of trying to commit murder. This would not do their fragile neighbourly relationship any good at all. 'But he had all that money in his account.'

'Honestly come by,' said Binnie. 'He was playing the stock markets but wanted to keep it from Val as he didn't think she'd approve.'

'Pah,' snorted Lucy. 'More like he wanted to keep it from her because he likes holding the purse strings.'

'Either way, it wasn't the drug money I thought it was so I definitely owe him an apology.'

That was not a conversation she would be looking forward to.

'The thing I can't believe is that Dex was willing to take the rap for Neesh,' Lucy said as she put a peanut in her mouth. 'That's insane. You wouldn't do that for me, would you, Noah?'

Noah kissed her cheek. 'Let's hope you never have to put me to the test on that one.'

'So many lives ruined.' Jude felt utterly exhausted as she thought about everything that had happened. 'But at least the truth came out in the end. Now I suppose everyone will have to deal with the consequences, whatever that looks like for them.'

'It's hard to imagine,' said Lucy. Jude saw her glance towards the stairs and knew she was thinking about Sebbie sleeping peacefully in his bed. Somewhere there was a little boy, only a bit younger than he was, with a mother who loved him every bit as fiercely as Lucy loved Sebbie, but whose love had made her do things so awful she would be in prison through his entire childhood.

* * *

It was around a month or so later when Jude felt able to open the bookings up once more for Malvern Farm's campsite. She hadn't been keen to do so and she was worried that when details of the tragic hen party made headline news, it might give Mike Trout exactly what he'd been hoping for when he'd first tried to collapse Khadija's tent. But either people weren't that interested in the headlines or they hadn't made the connections because the diary soon started to book up with visitors wanting to come and stay over the summer months.

On the morning the first guests were due to arrive, Jude was glad to see that the sun was warm and the forecast was good. Noah came round at breakfast time to deliver the milk.

'Either my watch is wrong or yours is,' he teased as he set the three glass bottles on the counter. 'I thought you'd have been down in those huts as soon as the larks were up to make sure all the cushions were plumped and everything.'

'I did all that yesterday, I'll have you know.' Jude opened the fridge and Noah handed her one bottle at a time to stow inside. 'I've also been out to collect the eggs and feed the chickens so I'm ahead of the game. I was actually just about to put the kettle on if you've got time for a cuppa?'

'I might just have something better than a cup of tea waiting for you.' Noah was smiling and Jude cocked her head at him in question. 'You don't get any more than that, I'm afraid. Get some shoes on and come with me.'

'Where are we going?' Jude asked as she slipped her feet into her trainers.

'I'm not telling you that until we get there,' Noah said. 'But the dogs can come too.'

Since the hen party had left the campsite, Jude had thrown herself into training Alfie and he had come on such a lot, proving himself to be more than up to the challenge of learning how to herd sheep.

'Come on, then,' Jude called and both her dogs were right at her heel as she walked with Noah across the yard. 'Are you taking me to the campsite?' she asked. 'Oh, I know, you finally pulled the Fergie out of the shed and it's ready for painting?'

'No, still haven't got round to getting the rust off that old tractor yet, I'm afraid, but hopefully you'll think this is even better.'

It was soon apparent that the surprise Noah was guiding her towards wasn't in the campsite but the paddock next door.

'Have we got a new member of the family?' Jude's excitement levels rose as she thought of who Noah might have got to join Pancake, Gertie, the Kerry Hills and the Runner ducks.

'Maybe,' said Noah as he opened the gate.

Jude called the dogs to heel again and followed Noah down towards the stables. She could hear the ducks chattering to each other as they took a dip in the canoe and she could see the Kerries grazing happily as Pancake broke free from the flock they'd formed and charged up the grass to greet them, Gertie as usual just a step or two behind.

'Hello, you two,' Jude greeted them. 'I hear you may have a new friend or two, so where are you hiding them?'

'There you go, Jude.' Noah pointed back to the stable where two black faces surrounded by fluffy white fleeces were peeping out.

'Valais Blacknoses?' Jude knew how much these animals cost so she assumed Noah was looking after them for some reason. 'Who do they belong to?'

'You, you daft thing,' Noah chuckled. 'Why else do you think they're in your paddock?'

Jude stared at him. 'They're ours?' she said. 'But there's no way we can afford these.'

'Get your nose out of the accounts book,' Noah said. 'You don't need to worry. There was this fancy London lawyer, married to another fancy London lawyer, who moved down here and decided to try their hand at keeping animals.'

'That hardly ever goes well,' said Jude. 'Let me guess, he went for Valais because they look more like teddy bears than sheep and then realised they need looking after every day and you can't go away without finding someone to come in and feed them?'

'Something like that,' Noah said. 'Anyway, they needed a home and I thought they might fit right into our mad zoo here. Picked them up first thing this morning, didn't think you'd mind too much.'

Jude slapped him playfully on the arm. 'Mind? I'm absolutely delighted.'

'Come on then, let's go and meet them. Don't worry about Alfie, you've got him well enough trained now and, even if he does get a bit bouncy, this pair are used to it. You should have seen the two daft poodle things they had bouncing all over them in their last house, not a scrap of training between them.'

Unlike the Kerry Hills, who were still too nervous to come near a human, the Valais ewes were more than happy for Jude to go and make friends. They were just as soft as Jude had imagined them to be and she loved the way their fleeces sprang into curls beneath her fingers.

'Are you going to give them names, or leave that to Sebbie?' Noah asked.

'If I do then we'll be looking at Horny and Curly going by his track record, so I think I'll choose this time. How about Marlie and Maud?'

'Marlie and Maud it is,' said Noah.

* * *

That afternoon, Jude was sitting in the garden with Binnie and Lucy, enjoying an impromptu picnic cobbled together after Binnie arrived to meet Marlie and Maud. Sebbie was happily trundling around the garden on his pedal-powered tractor with Alfie running rings around him whilst Pip chose to lie next to Jude in the sun and have a kip.

'I had an email from Seren yesterday,' Jude told them. 'She's been given community service for her part in the drug scandal and she's still on suspension from work whilst all of this is being looked into but she's decided that she doesn't want to go back into practice.'

'Did she say what she's going to do next?' Binnie asked.

'She's back at the family farm, working with the sheep, and it sounds like she's really happy there. I wouldn't be surprised if she takes over completely when her dad retires.'

'Did she mention any of the others?' Lucy asked. 'I mean, I know that Neesh will be in prison for a fair while and Ellie's still awaiting trial for what she did but what about Shaznay and Ash?'

Jude knew that Dex hadn't wanted to press charges against Ash, saying that she'd already suffered enough. His wound had been pretty minor, the pain caused mainly by the knife being twisted rather than thrust in deeply, and so she'd been free to go.

'It sounds like Shaznay is helping Dex out a lot with Reggie. It's bound to be tough on all of them but I'm sure they'll find a way to make it work. And Ash has gone off travelling. Last Seren heard from her she was heading across the Indian Ocean.'

It was strange to think of the group that had been such an intrinsic part of Malvern Farm's history for that short but impactful time now far spread and leading such different lives.

Noah joined them in the garden. 'Taxi for a Mr Sebastian Berban,' he said.

'That's me.' Sebbie's little legs pumped hard to get the toy tractor to cross the grass as quickly as possible.

'Come on then, tinker,' said Lucy. 'Noah's here to take you to the dentist so you'd better get a wriggle on or the dentist will think aliens have taken you.'

'Don't be silly, Mummy, he won't think that.'

'He might do.' Lucy stood up. 'Come on, let's get those teeth extra sparkly before you go.'

'And if the dentist says you've been a good boy cleaning your teeth nicely then maybe we'll stop at the bookshop to get you a treat.'

Jude and Binnie watched the three of them walk away, chatting animatedly.

'Last time Lucy took him, he screamed the place down and refused to open his mouth,' Jude explained. 'So Noah's taking him instead. He usually saves his worst for Lucy.'

'Who? Sebbie or Noah?'

Jude grinned at her friend.

'There'll be wedding bells there before long,' Binnie said.

'Maybe.' Jude stretched her legs out in front of her and wriggled her toes in the sunshine, knowing that she'd be the one giving the biggest cheer of all if that happened.

The two women sat for a moment in companiable silence, enjoying the peace of the garden and the warmth of the sun. They heard Noah's Land Rover drive past on the way to the dentist and, soon after, Lucy rejoined them.

'All okay?' Jude asked.

'He'll behave for Noah,' Lucy said. 'He usually does.'

Jude caught her eye and smiled. It was wonderful to see her so happy.

'Mike was just in the yard,' Lucy said as she sat down next to her sister. 'He wanted to know if it was okay for him to see the sheep again.'

Jude rolled her eyes. 'I've told him he doesn't need to ask. He can let himself into the paddock whenever he likes.'

'I hear Mike's a bit of regular on the farm these days,' said Binnie.

'It was Val's suggestion,' said Jude. 'She knew retirement didn't suit him and she realised it was because he was bored. She sent him round to help roll fleeces when I was still too grotty to be much use during shearing and now he can't keep away.'

Lucy stroked Alfie, who'd given up chasing his ball around the garden and had come to flop down next to her. 'Turns out he really wasn't kidding when he said he'd never do anything to hurt your sheep.'

'Yes, and he really had just come around to check on them that day when Joe was shot,' added Jude. 'It turns out it's just people he has a problem with.'

'But he loves the animals,' Lucy finished.

'Don't we all?' Jude lay back on the blanket and closed her eyes. Summer was here, the crops were all doing well, the sheep had been shorn and were enjoying the early summer grass and her little family was happy. What more could she possibly want?

She heard the click of the gate at the side of the garden and opened one eye lazily to see who was coming in.

'Hello, Jude,' said a man wearing a loose-fitting pair of jeans and a faded red T-shirt. He pushed his unruly fringe out of his eyes and looked at her with an anxious expression of hope. 'I'm not interrupting, am I?'

'Marco!' Jude felt her heart start to race. 'It's really lovely to see you.'

ACKNOWLEDGEMENTS

Over the years I have learnt that some books toe the line from the beginning whilst others are a little trickier to pin down. This has been one of the trickier ones and so my best thanks go to my ever-patient editor and agent, Emily and Amanda, for bearing with me and helping me to shape the story into something we can be proud of.

Thank you to the Boldwood team for being so wonderful, utterly professional and yet still the kindest group of people I could hope to work with.

As always I'd like to send my enormous thanks to the farming community. Without farming there would be no food and no future. We should all be far more grateful for the incredible job they do in keeping the nation fed. Next time you're held up by a tractor, try giving them a cheery wave instead of an angry honk!

Minette Batters, whose NFU presidency ended this year and who spent her six years in the role championing farmers and fighting for their voices to be heard – thank you. You are truly an inspiration and one of our great farming heroes.

Tim Badger, one day I'll have sheep of my own but until then thank you for letting me into the world of yours; I always learn so much.

To my writing friends, what would I do without you and your constant support? It's been a year of debut launches and I am so proud to be there cheering you all on. Class of 2024: Tania, Jess, Jennie, Cara, Teri, Kristen, Sam – you and your books are all stars!

Nicola Baker, fellow farm storyteller, thank you for the support you have given me. It's been so lovely getting to know you and your brilliant book, and I'm looking forward to reading more from Whistledown Farm soon.

To all the readers, reviewers and bloggers who have embraced Jude and Malvern Farm, thank you. You are what drives the series and why I write the books and I am grateful to every single one of you.

And of course to my family, thank you for being the best team and biggest cheerleaders.

ABOUT THE AUTHOR

Kate Wells is the author of a number of well-reviewed books for children, and is now writing cosy crime set in the Malvern hills, inspired by the farm where she grew up.

Sign up to Kate Wells' mailing list for news, competitions and updates on future books.

Visit Kate's website: www.katepoels.co.uk

Follow Kate on social media:

X x.com/KatePoels
facebook.com/KatePoelsWest
instagram.com/KatePoelsWrites
youtube.com/Katepoels2508

ALSO BY KATE WELLS

Murder on the Farm

Stranger in the Village

A Body by the Henhouse

Poison
& Pens

POISON & PENS IS THE HOME OF
COZY MYSTERIES SO POUR YOURSELF
A CUP OF TEA & GET SLEUTHING!

DISCOVER PAGE-TURNING NOVELS FROM
YOUR FAVOURITE AUTHORS &
MEET NEW FRIENDS

JOIN OUR
FACEBOOK GROUP

BIT.LYPOISONANDPENSFB

SIGN UP TO OUR
NEWSLETTER

BIT.LY/POISONANDPENSNEWS

Boldwood

Boldwood Books is an award-winning fiction publishing company seeking out the best stories from around the world.

Find out more at www.boldwoodbooks.com

Join our reader community for brilliant books, competitions and offers!

Follow us
@BoldwoodBooks
@TheBoldBookClub

Sign up to our weekly deals newsletter

https://bit.ly/BoldwoodBNewsletter

9 781785 134388